HUNTED
WHEN NIGHTMARES REIGN (BOOK ONE)

MISU LOY

MISU LOY

Copyright © 2023 by Misu Loy

Book Cover by Emilie Snaith

Map by Melissa Nash

First edition 2024

ISBN ebook: 979-8-9894019-1-8

ISBN paperback: 979-8-9894019-0-1

CONTENTS

DEDICATION

For anyone who has pursued a dream with their whole heart

DEDICATION

For anyone who has pursued a dream with their whole heart

Dragon Fangs
Pashun
Historic Dragon Lands
Rokeshin
Chambrin Keep
Hollyhock Forest
Drakkus River
Sinopel
The Hellhole
The Fangwilds
Joltar
Oxlip
Tagetes
Allium
Vesper
Obanth
VALDENIA
N
E
S
W

CHAPTER ONE

Giggles carried on the late summer breeze, prickling Raine's concentration like floating thorns. Steel flashed against sunlight as he wiped his brow with his sword arm. Turning, he encountered a trio of fresh-faced laundresses.

They lined the front row of bleachers and faced the training yard. Chins cradled in water-pruned palms. Pink mouths tremulous with restrained laughter. Eyes, bright with heat and mischief as they trailed avidly down Raine's exposed chest.

Suppressing a sigh, he tipped his sword to the ground and relaxed his stance. Resting one hand on his hip, he let the women look their fill. He knew from experience their tittering spectatorship wouldn't abate without a thorough perusal of the goods. Many of the younger female servants—and a discomfiting amount of matrons—found reason to cross this expanse of courtyard when he exercised, shirtless or not.

The laundress seated center leaned forward, exposing her freckled bosom as she crooked a finger. Her companions squirmed with embarrassed glee at the daring gesture, waiting bug-eyed for Raine's reaction. He stiffened, then deliberately pushed his agitation aside. The women were a distraction, yes, but they meant no harm.

Even so, he ignored the wench's brash summons.

If the continuation of mankind relied upon Raine procreating, the world would be doomed. Flirtation, courtship, sex? It was all as appealing as a toothache. His father swore he would feel differently someday. That day was not today.

A swish of gray skirts drew his attention. Rounding the bailey was Moranda, the head housekeeper. Neck bent forward and shoulders swaying, she resembled a boarhound on the hunt. Her ruddy features darkened beneath her cowl as she marched for her laundresses. Winking and waving, Raine's impromptu audience remained none-the-wiser as their dour mistress stalked their backs.

Moranda's glower flicked to Raine, deepening to scorn. Scorn and fear. Only for an instant, but it was enough.

Clenching the sweat-slicked hilt of his dull practice sword, Raine angled his frame away from the servants' drama. Moranda was not the only superstitious person at Chambrin Keep. He ought to be accustomed to such attitudes.

But it was a damnable thing, illogical hate. Its nonsensical nature kept it fresh and new. And dreadful.

At nineteen, he was a grown man. Yet Raine's stomach still knotted at each stranger he encountered—never certain if they would loathe or fear him on sight for his unnaturally pale hair and eyes.

A chorus of shrill apologies erupted from behind as the head housekeeper confronted her idle laundresses. Coarse oaths interwove Moranda's barking commands as she dogged them back to work. Raine picked absently at a patch of white clover with his sword tip until they were gone.

Propping his blade against the newly vacant bleachers, he began to stretch his aching muscles. Nose to knee, he moaned as pure fire raced up his leg in a calf stretch. Even absent a sparring partner, he had exerted his entire body.

Raine switched legs, dragging his other booted heel upon the weather-beaten bench as the sun guttered like a wind-buffeted candle. Overhead, dragons flew with swift, fluid grace. Outward, the grassy field mirrored their motions. A play of sun and shadow which transformed the training yard into a verdant riverbed glimmering beneath rushing water.

After two centuries of rigorous breeding, Chambrin Keep boasted twenty-three war dragons. They smattered the sky like whizzing gems. Emeralds, rubies, amethysts, sapphires. Each dragon possessed its own uniquely radiant hue.

Ruby's lithe, serpentine figure was in the lead. She dodged the dragons flanking her left, then tucked into a tight barrel roll. Red scales gleamed more brilliantly than her namesake as she corkscrewed through pure azure sky.

A rider on her back clung to his makeshift saddle for dear life. Raine squinted until he identified the imbecile. *Thatcher.* As he suspected. The dragon handler had bragged of this very plan over his morning porridge in the dining hall. It had taken all Raine's willpower not to flip the man's sodden oats over his head.

A reluctant grin split Raine's face as a faint, high-pitched scream reached his ears. He craned his neck, savoring the scene. It served Thatcher right to be petrified.

Ruby pivoted, executing a series of graceful swoops and rolls while the other war dragons made a game of tagging her. Their game dragged on unduly long. Raine cocked his head, bemused.

He was accustomed to the dragons' ferocity; a hailstorm of glittering behemoths cracking and colliding like battle blows. Presently, the dragons treated Ruby with excessive delicacy, as if she possessed the frailty of blown glass.

Fern and Mayhem, a green female and red male respectively, boxed Ruby on either side. Raine almost looked away, figuring their game was finished. One or both would tag Ruby out.

Only, they didn't. Fern and Mayhem kept a wary distance from Ruby's flanks, neither so much as grazing her wingtips. Why were they so reluctant to tag her?

Ruby suddenly shot up, then down, as if riding invisible waves. Thatcher's screams renewed at a crystal-shattering treble, warbling in tandem with Ruby's shifting elevation. Fern and Mayhem abruptly fell away and circled low.

Raine's neck snapped straight as understanding dawned. The dragons weren't tagging Ruby because of her human passenger. They were probably leery of accidentally knocking Thatcher off her back.

A shame. Raine rather wished they would.

Thatcher was a fool, trying to craft some sort of aerial cavalry unit. One where soldiers would mount the backs of dragons and fly them into combat.

Dragons were as proud as they were stunning, as loyal as they were fierce. They deserved better from the humans they served and protected. Valdenia already possessed a lethally trained dragon battalion.

It was more than sufficient. Nobody needed to *ride* them. It was wrong, somehow.

His unease grew the longer Thatcher cleaved to Ruby, appearing as small as a tick at their soaring height. Raine's fingers itched to pluck the man off her back and squash him like the parasite he was.

Thatcher and Bulloch, the most senior dragon handlers, were as bold as they were craven. Waiting to implement their scheme in Arastus Chambrin's absence. Raine's father had left before daybreak, conducting his annual visits to the keep's surrounding farms and hamlets. He would return after dark, bearing a list of repairs and items needed to ensure his tenants' comfort and productivity for another year.

Father will put this plot to heel. Like Raine, his father—General Arastus Chambrin—regarded the dragons as fellow warriors. In many ways, as equals. He was going to tear strips from the handlers once he found out. *Perhaps he will saddle them and see how they fancy it.*

"Like what you see, snowballs?"

Raine stifled a groan as Olan's burly tone sounded over his shoulder. One of Raine's casual childhood tormentors, Olan was greener than the low-lying hills that Raine was the son of the illustrious Arastus Chambrin. Meanwhile, Olan was nothing more than a measly distant nephew, pawned off on Chambrin Keep by a family with too many mouths and not enough space.

Privately, Raine was certain Olan's family detested his foul, lazy attitude and got rid of him like a bad smell at their earliest opportunity. An unburdening that was directly at Raine's suffering, regrettably.

Another shrill scream. Thatcher's legs kicked frantically through the air, his saddle dangerously askew. Somebody hadn't fastened their girth straps properly.

Raine's grin returned despite present company. "Indeed, I do, Olan. Thanks for caring."

His words were a dismissal. He did not bother looking away from the sky as he spoke. Olan, whose thickness rivaled the walls of the keep, did not heed his dismissal.

"Nobody is getting handed a dragon rider's commission, not even precious little sons of generals. Soon, I'll be up there, and you'll be down here. So, keep watching, blanch. Maybe I'll give you a wave."

Smile easing from his lips, Raine slowly turned to face his cousin. Of course, odious Olan wanted to ride the dragons, too. Without an ounce of respect in his poorly groomed body, how could Olan respect the majestic creatures that called this castle their home?

"Good talk, Olan," he said pointedly. "I'll look forward to that wave. You have a nice day now." He bestowed his cousin with a beatific smile, pairing it with a jaunty wave of his own for good measure.

Olan's fuzzy upper lip curled, revealing equally fuzzy teeth. "You're a waste of fucking space. I bet you don't care how much of an embarrassment you are to Uncle Arastus. People question his leadership for keeping you here. They doubt his judgment. You should have been drowned at birth. Everyone thinks it. I'm just the only one brave enough to say it to your face."

Brave was not a word Raine used to describe Olan. His cousin's crass insults typically washed over Raine harmlessly. But this time, something stuck. Olan saw it in his expression, too. His mean, dark eyes brightened with petty malice.

"Blanches are bad luck, freak. Everyone knows it. Chambrin Keep is the most vital militant stronghold in the country, and for Uncle Arastus to house a person of ill luck makes a lot of people nervous. If you really loved your dad, you'd leave so he can lead us with confidence. So long as you remain, you're a chink in the armor of Valdenia."

Raine's blood surged as Olan bleated his vile nonsense. Until his cousin's taunts cracked through his own armor. In three clipped strides, he closed the gap between them.

Too ignorant to recognize his peril, the dimwit opened his rancid mouth, as if to spew more insults. Cocking his arm, Raine delivered a solid punch to Olan's jaw, shutting the oaf up with a rough clack of his teeth.

Raine massaged his knuckles as his cousin fell back on his ass. Scrambling to his feet, Olan spat blood. A thin, murky string of saliva clung to his chin. Baring his teeth in a lipless snarl, Olan's mouth glistened pinkish red. Then, he charged like a bull. His arms banded Raine's midsection, tackling them to the ground.

They tussled through the grass in a flurry of wild limbs. Raine's head smacked against a sharp corner of the bleacher's frame. He scarcely felt it. His rage was a fog blotting all rationality and pain. He wanted—no. He *needed* Olan to hurt.

Olan spiked an elbow, driving it into the corner of Raine's eye. The move left his cousin's face open and unguarded. Raine swung his left arm and smashed his cousin's nose. A satisfying crunch and collapse of cartilage met his blow.

"That's enough, boys," a voice called.

Neither man listened. Dark red rivulets flowed from Olan's nostrils, splashing wetly across Raine's naked chest. He cringed as Olan's noxious blood pooled between his pectorals. In his stupefaction, Raine nearly missed the vicious right hook aimed at his face.

Raine flung his left arm up, clumsily blocking Olan's fist, then threw a brutal jab to his cousin's throat with his free hand. Olan choked and wheezed, attack ceasing as he clutched his windpipe. Taking advantage of his cousin's preoccupation, Raine landed two more blows, hopefully fracturing his eye sockets.

Powerful arms seized Raine's waist from behind, hauling him upright before he could deliver a third. Raine turned, fist cocked and face contorted. Only to be brought up short by the incredulous expression of Nyx.

"I dare you," Nyx said after a beat, dark brows upraised.

Raine's arm dropped faster than an arrow-struck goose. He sputtered, speechless, then launched into Nyx, squeezing with all his strength.

"Can't … breathe," Nyx croaked. Raine released him, beaming. The older man chuckled and mussed Raine's pale braid. "I missed you too, kid."

Olan struggled to his feet, massaging his throat. After a baleful, bloody sneer at Raine, as if to say, *this isn't over*, he turned and stalked off.

Nyx glanced from Olan's retreating form to Raine. "All this time and that guy's still on your case?"

Raine shrugged. He could give a shit less about Olan. Especially with Nyx here. "It's been over a year, asshole," he complained, then hugged Nyx again, this time mindful of his strength.

"I'm sorry," Nyx said as they drew apart. "I would visit more frequently if I could."

Swallowing against the sudden tightness in his throat, Raine's voice was gruff as he said, "I know."

Per usual, Nyx was in mission mode. A black cloak draped his figure, hood drawn. If Raine wasn't nose-to-nose with the man, he wouldn't recognize him. It was intentional, since Nyx's mission was top secret, his orders directly from the Nine themselves.

A gliding shadow flickered the sun, drawing Raine's gaze back to the sky. He pointed. "You see what these idiots are trying to do?"

Nyx looked in the direction Raine indicated and went still, observing the spectacle.

Thatcher had ceased his screams, though that was more likely from his throat going hoarse than the absence of terror. Ruby toyed with him. Arrowing into the sky, she flew long, lazy circles that kept Thatcher clinging like a burr to her back, arms snug around her wing joints for extra purchase.

"That's repulsive," Nyx muttered from beneath his hood. Raine couldn't agree more. "Does Arastus know about this?"

"I don't think so."

Ruby soon tired of tormenting Thatcher. Her wings beat a vigorous downdraft as she landed in the distance. A gusting current rippled the training yard. Nyx clutched his hood to prevent it from falling back on the breeze.

"Thatcher and Bulloch want to surprise my dad with the idea. They purchased some horse saddles in town, then modified them. Ruby is their first test mount."

Nyx shook his head. "Arastus is going to skin them alive for saddling a dragon."

"It's better than they deserve," Raine said severely.

Thatcher tumbled off Ruby's back and flopped boneless to the ground. Rising to his palms, he vomited, ejecting grayish sludge. Bulloch stepped around the indisposed handler to unbuckle the saddle from Ruby's back.

A fat bee buzzed lazily in Raine's ear. He waved it off, then motioned for Nyx to join him on the bleachers. Nyx sat beside him with a long sigh. Raine located his discarded tunic in the crabgrass under their bench and slipped it on before asking, "What's up with you?"

He hated going years between visits with Nyx, a man he considered more brother than friend. He hated it even more that something was bothering the man.

Nyx had shown up at Chambrin Keep as a gangly teenager, back when Raine was a babbling tot in leading strings. Raine's father, a semi-retired Guardian master, had whipped Nyx into shape for the guild, as he still took apprentices back then.

Before long, Nyx had become like family. After a brutal training session with Arastus, Nyx would pick wildflowers with a small, childish Raine and braid them through his hair. Other days, they performed mock sword fights with sticks. When Olan had convinced the other children to pick on Raine for his strange hair and eyes, Nyx was the only one who could soothe away his tears.

After Nyx finished his apprenticeship and joined the Guardians of Vale—the elite shadow guild protecting their country—he remained close with Raine and his father, visiting Chambrin Keep every chance he got over the years. A beloved constant in Raine's life, Nyx was the only person who felt like family besides his father.

"I'm just weary of my mission. Don't get me wrong," Nyx added hastily, glancing sideways at Raine. "I am honored by the services I perform. But there are serious crimes being perpetuated in our country. Crimes which make my mission necessary. I've been living for the day that changes. For the day my task is obsolete because the world is better."

Raine's heart grew heavy as his friend relayed his troubles. Embroiled in a covert operation for the past decade, Nyx's current mission was abnormally long. Extraordinarily so.

"I'm sorry," Raine said, frustrated by the inadequacy of his apology. "Is there a way the guild can give you a break? I know a captain doesn't rest until his mission is complete, but it's been so long."

Nyx's shoulders sank on a new sigh. "There are no breaks, not for this."

Raine bit down the wave of questions rising to his tongue. As a child, he had agonized over the mysterious mission that pried his only friend away. An obsession that trailed him to adulthood, but no amount of wheedling unveiled the particulars. Both his father and Nyx were obstinate in their secrecy.

"I really miss my family," Nyx said quietly. "I haven't seen my little brother since he was ... *fifteen*. Divine Father, I can't believe it's been so long. He's a man now." His voice thinned with amazement. "My little stinkbug is a man. He could have a wife and children."

The choked longing in Nyx's words settled like a leaden mantle over Raine's shoulders.

"Your mission doesn't ever take you near home so that you can sneak a visit?"

Sporadic wind tossed Raine's braid as the other war dragons descended at Bulloch's signal. The dragon handler snapped an order, and servicemen beckoned the dragons into the bathhouse, a structure built specifically to accommodate their vast size.

"Never," Nyx said. "My family lives south, in Vesper. It's over a fortnight's journey on horseback, but takes you to another land entirely. Everything is different there. It's warm all year, the summers sweltering hot. The food, trees, and flowers are all unique."

A pang hit Raine at the name of Nyx's home city. Vesper. One of the furthest cities from Chambrin, it was tucked into the southernmost region of Valdenia. Raine only knew of it through his studies, the extent of his own travels being abysmally small. Essentially nonexistent, considering he'd never gone far enough to lose sight of the keep.

Most days, he yearned to get out and explore. But the homesickness in Nyx's voice made Raine grateful to be right where he was. He wondered which aspect of Nyx's mission brought the man to Chambrin Keep every so often, but knew better than to ask. Instead, he inwardly thanked the Divine Father that Nyx's mission returned him to the keep, even sparingly.

Raine couldn't stomach the idea of not seeing Nyx for ten years, couldn't imagine how Nyx's family felt. It was strange to think of Nyx's family, of people who loved Nyx as much as Raine did whilst remaining total strangers.

He didn't even know the name of Nyx's brother. Vague thoughts of inviting the man to Chambrin teased the edges of his mind. Perhaps Raine could arrange it so the two crossed paths? Nyx would be elated.

"What's your brother's—"

Raine broke off as the world started shaking.

The bench vibrated against Raine's bottom as earth and sky trembled, rattling remote mountain peaks like loose teeth. A deafening roar rocked the land, welling up from belowground. In tandem, Raine and Nyx—and everyone at Chambrin Keep, most like-ly—cupped their ears against the disturbance.

The collective cries from the Cavern occurred at random, though never more than once a year. Raine did not know what angered the breeding dragons, setting them off like this, but he wished whoever or whatever it was would cease. His skull crushed with the sound, a hellacious headache brewing.

An eternity later, the earth stilled, breeding dragons silent. Nyx dropped his arms and stood. "I must depart." The hood of his cloak cast his features in shadow.

"So soon?" Raine stood, as well. "But you've only just arrived." Nyx typically lingered a couple days before leaving.

They embraced tightly. "I wish I could stay longer," Nyx said, thick with regret.

"Maybe next time, I'll be the one visiting you," Raine said myste-riously.

A thrill darted through him at the prospect. If things went accord-ing to plan, Raine would join the Guardians soon. It was too much to hope he was placed with Nyx's unit, but who knew? He was the Wolf of the Vale's son. It might come with some perks.

Nyx startled, far more than his comment warranted. Stiff as a board, he jerked from their embrace and gripped Raine's shoulders. "What has your father told you?"

"Nothing," Raine said slowly, eyeing Nyx up and down. "Why?"

"No reason." Nyx cleared his throat and stared over Raine's head, avoiding his eyes. "Stay out of trouble, kid. I'll return as soon as I'm able."

Raine stared after Nyx's retreating form, his mind pouring over the man's odd reaction. He had meant to drop a hint about his application to the guild, but Nyx obviously conceived an altogether different implication. One Raine could not puzzle, try as he might. His neck prickled with unease. Nyx had never lied to him before.

CHAPTER TWO

R aine knelt and stoked the flames beneath his oversized iron tub, then fed it several more logs until the water reached a rollicking boil. Straightening, he shed his silk dressing gown and slid inside the steamy basin. Water too hot for any other human encased him with blissful, searing heat.

He knew it was bizarre—his ability to withstand such extremely high temperatures. Even the metal tub felt pleasantly warm, though it should have been hot enough to fry his flesh like bacon.

Regardless of how strange it was, Raine had no answers as to why he was this way. His father was so tight-lipped on the matter, Raine wasn't sure if it was because the man knew and didn't want to say … or if he was just as baffled as his son and loath to confess his ignorance.

What his father *had* shared was that Raine's various oddities, combined with his pale appearance, put him in extreme danger.

Valdenians were a superstitious lot. Blanches were already considered bad luck. Their pallid coloring was likened to ghosts, and made them unwelcome in most communities. Chambrin Keep was no exception. If people learned how strange Raine truly was, they could react violently out of fear.

Thus, since the tender age of three—when Raine's babbling speech began to grow more competent—his father had taught him to keep his boiling baths, among other things, absolutely secret.

Floating on his back, lavender scented bubbles gently rocked him as he stared at the exposed cedar rafters. There had been no word today. *Again.*

Raine had submitted his application nearly a season ago. Delays were common, he knew. And the Guardians of Vale were operating on a backlog of candidates thanks to a population spike twenty years prior. Many strapping young warriors were coming-of-age and sought the prestige of a position within the guild's ranks. Raine included.

As his bathwater fell to a simmer, he stood. Skin flushed pink, wafting steam, he exited the washtub, then grasped one of the thick cotton towels stacked along a shelf and chased the moisture from his frame.

Once dry, he sat at the vanity, folding the towel over his naked lap. His nose wrinkled at the shaving supplies and whisker fragments littering the blue-veined countertop. Doublechecking his hairbrush to ensure none of his father's facial hair was lodged within its bristles, he gently brushed his damp mane until it gleamed in the lamplight.

Raine loved his hair. It seemed cream white on a cloudy day but came alive in the sun. As if moonbeams and crushed jewels interwove the strands.

The door opened, admitting a rush of cool air. Raine yelped.

"Oi, shut the door. It's freezing," he said from his seat before the mirror. He heard General Arastus Chambrin's distinct chuckle as the door latched. Twisting in the chair, he greeted his sire with a smile. "You're home at a decent hour. I take it the annual visits went well?"

His father's sigh was so long-suffering, Raine felt an irrational urge to apologize.

"I spent three hours negotiating a property line dispute between Bunty and Drooger. It was miserable. And all over a few heads of lettuce and a damn goat."

His father massaged his temples with a toilworn air. Raine wanted to mention Thatcher and Bulloch's dragon-saddling idiocy from earlier, but decided it could wait. His father required cheering, which wouldn't be accomplished by tacking on more problems.

"On the bright side, you're back early." At his father's flat look, he added, "And you're just in time to help me with my hair. I know how much you love to braid it."

It sounded like a tease, but it was true. His father's expression was always at peace when he brushed and plaited Raine's hair. It was a nightly ritual of theirs, spanning Raine's entire life.

"How lucky for me," his father drawled, already crossing the room.

Plucking the brush from his son's hand, he worked Raine's tresses into a heavy braid with quick, practiced fingers. Raine's hair was dry enough to sparkle in the lamplight, and his mouth curved appreciatively as he watched the colors dance beneath his father's ministrations.

"You are so vain," his father teased. His sharp general's eyes missed nothing.

"I am a god among men," Raine responded with dramatic stoicism, meeting his father's twinkling stare in the half-fogged mirror.

"Is it vanity, then? Or simply acknowledging the truth and appreciating my status?"

A broad grin stretched his father's face, framed by a neatly trimmed beard. The skin around his eyes crinkled with humor. "You are pretty enough to be a god-*dess* among men, perhaps. The Divine Father knows you primp enough."

Raine scowled at his father's reflection, but the playful slant of his lips betrayed his mirth as they bantered.

"Really, Father, one does not have to look like a troll to be considered manly. I do understand why that belief gives you comfort, however." He raked his silver eyes up and down his father's figure with patently false sympathy.

Arastus Chambrin's head tossed back on a laugh. "I take my comforts where I can, son. You should, too." He draped Raine's thick, white braid across his shoulder. "I have something to discuss with you," he continued, looking more serious.

Raine's stomach fluttered at his father's tone. Whenever his father spoke like that, words heavy and stiff, it meant he was gearing up for a "tough parenting session."

He followed the general of Chambrin Keep into the spacious sitting room that anchored their bedchambers and private bath. Raine nipped into his bedchamber to dress, throwing on a cotton tunic and almond tights before joining his father.

Settling onto a slouchy leather sofa, Raine angled to face his father, who was straight-backed and tensely alert. There was a tightness to Arastus's face and shoulders that was only present while he was cloaked in his commander's persona.

Or when he was about to give his son a stern lecture.

Raine wracked his brain for what he might have done to warrant his father's consternation. Perhaps this was about him pummeling Olan? If so, he would not apologize. The arsehole had gotten off easy, thanks to Nyx's intervention.

"I received word from Chieftain Eddic that you applied for a position with the Guardians of Vale."

A gasp escaped Raine's throat as bitter betrayal coursed through him. Of course, they would tell his father. Applicants were supposed to possess complete anonymity, for national security reasons if nothing else.

But Arastus Chambrin was a highly esteemed general, charged with the most crucial task in the entire country: breeding and training Valdenia's war dragons. The nine Chieftains were more than the ruling oligarchy of Valdenia; they were also the commanders-in-chief of the Guardians of Vale.

As a rule, the Nine kept Raine's father close and vice versa. It was no surprise they broke their code of secrecy where Arastus Chambrin's son was concerned.

Apprehension warred with anger at the violation of his privacy, and Raine glared defiantly at his father. "What of it?"

His father extracted a scroll from his boot, offering it to him. Raine swallowed hard before his fingers closed around the parchment. The wax seal was broken. He sucked air through his teeth, outraged anew at the invasion of privacy.

Hands trembling, he unfurled the scroll to reveal a formal rejection of his application. The parchment shook in his grasp. His nose burned with unshed tears. Raine choked them back roughly.

"You," he hissed, meeting his father's steady gaze. "You had something to do with this. I am an *outstanding* candidate. What did you do?" Raine crumbled the scroll and tossed it at his father's feet, features twisting with rage. "What did you do?" he repeated, jabbing a finger at his father's firm chest, teeth bared.

A storm raged where Raine's heart and lungs should be. His blood was thunder and lightning, crashing through his veins and burning him up from the inside.

"Son," his father began tenderly, his gentle calm a stark foil to Raine's calamity, "I have told you countless times. You cannot be a Guardian. It's impossible—"

"Bullshit." Springing from the sofa, he hovered over his father. "I have told you countless times. I will be a Guardian. It's my dream. It's what I am meant to do. What is wrong with you? Why do you keep doing this? I've worked for this my entire fucking life, and you act like I'm not good enough. Nothing I do is good enough."

His father stood, rising several inches higher than Raine, who jerked his chin to meet his sire's eyes. The Wolf of the Vale did not intimidate him, and not solely because he was Raine's father. Of Chambrin Keep's two thousand soldiers, no man could best Raine. His strength and dexterity were a league of their own, another of his abnormalities.

Liquid mercury eyes clashed with coffee brown. Tension crackled, the storm in Raine's chest escaping through flashing eyes and snarled lips, flooding the space between them.

"You are not meant to be a Guardian and you cannot join the guild. I've told you repeatedly. You are to assume my duties here one day. Why are you fighting this? You love the dragons more than anything."

Wrong. I love you more than anything, he thought, almost savagely. "I am nineteen summers old, Father. I know what I want better than you. Most men have already left their homes to seek employment or apprenticeships by my age. I've delayed myself because of you. I don't want to upset or disappoint you, but I must be true to myself, or I will never be happy," Raine implored.

He willed his father to understand, though it felt like treading quicksand. A hopeless endeavor. This was an old argument that always ended the same.

Arastus Chambrin, the Wolf of the Vale, had actual *ballads* sung about his feats in the guild. Raine grew up listening to tales of his father's masterful feats and selfless deeds. From his earliest memories, his heart was fierce with the desire to follow in his father's footsteps. To join the guild and serve as an instrument of peace and protection.

Arastus crossed his arms over his olive duster coat, straightening to full height. Raine's back stiffened, familiar with the signs of his sire's stubbornness.

"I'm sorry, son," the interfering bastard said, without contrition. "I've made up my mind and the Nine agree. You cannot become a Guardian without their vote, and they will not accept you."

"Out of some fucked up deference to you," Raine spat. "All you had to do was leave it alone. I know my application was good. I would be a great Guardian. But you stuck your shitty nose in my business and made them reject me."

Arastus flinched. Then glanced sideways, jamming his fingers through the crown of his short dark hair. A nervous gesture they shared when feeling guilty, Raine noted through the haze of his anger.

"It's true. The Nine know I have no desire to see you serve the guild. They rejected your application as a personal favor." Arastus refocused his gaze on Raine. "Son, I know you're upset but you must trust me. If there was any way for you to join the Guardians, you would have my full support. There are things you don't know, things I cannot tell you yet. It's too dangerous."

Raine saw red and almost lashed out at his sire. He had never struck his father before, and his entire frame shook with the effort to contain his violence.

"This keep is filled with assholes who think, because I'm a blanch, I must be cursed." Raine spoke through his teeth. "I never thought you were counted among them."

Tears spilled unchecked down his cheeks, the glutted storm within finally breaking.

His father moved to speak but Raine threw out a hand, stopping him. "I know being a Guardian isn't easy. That men and women give their lives to protect Valdenia. It is a risk that every Guardian assumes at signing. But I spent my entire fucking life training to become as skilled as possible. I can beat you with blade, bow, and hand-to-hand. I am the fastest, strongest, most accomplished—"

"And modest," Arastus interjected wryly.

It caught Raine off guard, and he issued a broken laugh. Damn his father for knowing him so well. Humor was the best way to pierce his defenses. Another trait they shared. Raine and his father looked nothing alike, but there was no denying their relation once anyone knew them.

"Best looking," Raine added, sniffling as his tears slowed.

"You are stunning." Arastus rolled his eyes playfully before sobering. "Raine, I am not saying it is too dangerous for you because you can't handle it. I know how incredible a warrior you are. I am so proud of you."

His father engulfed him in a bearlike embrace. After a prolonged moment, Raine relaxed into the hug. He was still livid, but he adored his father.

"Son, there are things you do not know. About yourself. About the Guardians."

This was the second time his father alluded to Raine's ignorance, and he frowned. Their age-old argument was taking new twists and turns, his father hinting at something he had concealed in previous disagreements. *My application to the guild is the only thing that's different. Father must be taking me more seriously because of it.*

"What are you talking about?" Raine asked. He took a step back to meet his father's gaze.

Arastus's hand raked his hair again. Avoiding his son's eyes, he said, "I cannot tell you yet. There is something I must do first, but it's taking more time than I like."

Raine's chest inflated as a fresh wave of anger crested over him. "You had my application to my dream job rejected, and you aren't going to tell me why?"

"I will. I just can't yet. Son, I have been working on this situation since you were born. I am not going to fuck it up to satisfy your curiosity."

"*My curiosity?*" he shrieked. "I worked my entire life for this, only for you to come along and rip it away like some dream-killing busybody. I have a right to know why. Tell me the truth or stop interfering with my life."

"I will do neither," Arastus said grimly. "I am your father, and you need to trust me. This is for your own good."

"No. I refuse—"

"That's final," his father roared, patience spent.

Raine felt the blood drain from his face. His father had never yelled at him like that before, as if riding a current of black rage. Ears ringing, composure wrecked, he shoved past his father and out of their chambers, running blindly through a haze of unshed tears.

Yip's hot breath puffed into Raine's stomach. The heat felt liquid as it sank through his sweater, into his flesh. Fang shifted beside him, curling more snugly against his side.

It was like being snuggled by two scaly boulders. Raine all but disappeared beneath the two dragons' combined bulk. Any other man in his position would suffocate, but he bore their crushing weight with ease.

Shadows veiled the Roost, thick cloud cover blanketing the stars. Slumbering war dragons, jewel bright in daylight, were dark, indistinct shapes in the night. Raine had trekked the Roost's thirty flights of stairs in search of solace after the blowup with his father.

This place was Raine's private oasis. He had been sneaking into the dragons' vast tower since he was nine summers old; since the day Nyx announced his promotion to captaincy and tenderly explained he would be gone on assignment for at least a year. Devastated by the prospect of not seeing Nyx for so long, Raine had instinctively sought comfort from the only other friends he possessed. The war dragons.

Leaning against the rounded stone wall, he closed his eyes. Anger, as blazing as sunfire, scorched his veins. The too-recent disagreement with his sire left him bitter and burning.

The Wolf of the Vale should have been *honored* his son wanted to follow his path. His father's excuses were maddeningly vague and weak. Raine could not fathom any secret that would bar him from the Guardians.

Hideous suspicions crawled through his mind like spiders. That his father was ashamed of him. Embarrassed to have produced a blanch: a colorless offspring. An ill omen. A curse. Blanches were rare enough that Raine had never met another. Olan's cruel words echoed in his ears. Images of pale, helpless babies strangled or drowned assailed him in the darkness, and he shivered.

Yip puffed another breathy exhale. Her head was larger than his torso, but he clutched it closer, relishing her heft and heat. Resting his cheek against the bridge of her snout, he blinked against fresh tears. Fiercely glad for these dragons and the inexplicable connection they shared.

For many long moments, Raine absorbed the tranquility and peace of belonging. Until rage bled to exhaustion and a silent yawn cracked his jaw.

Scrubbing his eyes with his fists, he stared out the arched opening in the tower wall opposite. Nearly invisible in the darkness, it led to a deathly plunge for humans, but soaring freedom for the dragons.

It was just after midnight. His father would be asleep. Raine could return to their quarters and slip into his room without any further confrontation until morning.

He wriggled out from beneath the war dragons on all fours, loose rushes crunching beneath his palms. Yip lifted her head, snorting her displeasure as he stood. He gave her pointy lilac ear an apologetic scratch, then ambled down the many staircases climbing the war dragons' perch. The Roost—a massive spire—was an addition, like the dragons' bathhouse, and not an original outbuilding of Chambrin Keep. A cylindrical tower over four-hundred feet high, it was the tallest structure in Valdenia. Perhaps in the world.

Raine couldn't speak for structures beyond Valdenia's borders, as Valdenians had become excruciatingly xenophobic after Gargantha's invasion two centuries prior. Rokeshin Pass, the only way in or out of Valdenia by land, had remained closed ever since King Normund of Gargantha's ill-fated campaign to "pick the pocket."

Valdenia was a rich country, stirring no small pride in Raine and his fellow countrymen and women. Mines of gold, silver, and all manner of precious gems littered the bases of the Dragon Fang Mountains. Historically, Garganthans referred to Valdenia by any number of monikers. The Pocket. The Vale. The Crown.

Raine preferred the Crown best. His father liked to tease him, claiming arrogance drew Raine to its preening regality. Which was absurd. Firstly, one did not have to be arrogant to appreciate a well-crafted ornamental headdress. And secondly, he most appreciated the Crown for its dual reference to Valdenia's material splendor as well as the breathtaking peaks encompassing their country on all sides—like a spiked coronet.

The Dragon Fangs had inspired a youthful Raine to imagine a dragon the size of the earth itself, maw gaping wide as it balanced Valdenia on a grassy tongue. He had been a child urgently horrified and shocked at the people who carried out regular, everyday lives. As if an enormous mouth couldn't snap them up at a moment's notice.

Raine's lips twisted wryly at the recollection, envisioning the grief his father would give him if the man knew his adult son still looked outward across the land and saw an open mouth.

Reaching the base of the Roost's many stairs, he stepped silently through the rear exit. No one knew of his time spent here and he intended to keep it that way, avoiding the guards posted out front to secure Valdenia's greatest military asset.

Indistinct conversation drifted as he skirted the Roost's precarious sandstone curve. Only the tips of his boots fit on the ledge, his heels hanging over a sheer cliff drop. He clung to the tower, fingertips digging into mortar to prevent a fatal fall.

Chambrin Keep rested on a plateau. From afar, the grounds resembled a mountain with its top sliced clean off. The Roost was erected at the very edge of the mesa, beyond the keep's curtain. Much like the archway hundreds of feet above, the rear exit was designed for dragon use only, hence its lack of guards or flat ground. It was a path Raine had taken countless times over the years, and he reached a broad stretch of land without issue.

The scent of sweet tobacco wafted on the summer night breeze. His gut clenched. *Olan.*

Raine was surprised the man was fit for duty. His cousin's black eyes had swelled shut after their brawl. The self-important prick had probably pestered Wylan—the keep's steward—for healing salve and ice. Raine tossed a quick but heartfelt prayer of thanks to the Divine Father for the abundant clouds above. In the darkness, he could evade discovery so long as he avoided the footpaths and lamplights.

He might be General Arastus Chambrin's son, but Raine was technically trespassing. Olan would be within rights to detain him. Eels writhed in his belly as he considered that scenario, the abuses his cousin would inflict. *Hard pass.*

Voices carried from the guarded entrance at the front of the Roost. Satisfied he would remain undetected so long as he stuck to the shadows, Raine tiptoed away, listening halfheartedly to Olan and Garth's conversation.

"—have to figure their shit out without me. I go above and beyond for these assholes. They're about to find out how much shit I really do around here."

Raine suppressed a snort. Olan was so delusional, he crafted his own version of reality. It would be frightening if he wasn't so pathetic.

"I can't believe you got into the guild," Garth moaned enviously.

Raine froze, mouth agape. Without conscious decision, his trajectory altered, bringing him closer to the guards. The imbeciles had hung a torch at the Roost entrance, effectively blinding them to any movement outside the firelight's umbra.

Tucked against the tower's curve, Raine watched Olan pull a long toke from his cheap clay pipe, hamming up the moment. Garth looked on worshipfully, the dolt.

"Believe it," Olan said on a smoky exhale that formed a dense, pale cloud around his face. "Tomorrow, my ass is gone. I might stop by here and there to visit between missions but who knows? I will probably be too busy with Guardian business."

His lofty, conceited tone dug under Raine's skin like iron pins. The Guardians of Vale rejected him, but they were going to let Olan, who possessed the intellect of a worm and the work ethic of a house cat, defend land and country? He stood motionless behind them, near breathless at the damnable irony.

"How do you know where to go? No one knows where the guild is. They keep it secret from, like, everyone." Garth took the pipe and sucked eagerly, with too much lip. Olan didn't seem to care.

"It is all in my acceptance letter. I guess the letter doubles as my ticket through their gates. I must present Thursday morning for my entrance exam, which I am going to ace."

Raine ceased listening to their conversation. His mind, bombarded with rapid images, quickly supplied how simple it would be to nick that acceptance letter and go by the name of "Olan" for a bit. Just until he passed the entrance exams and proved to the Nine that their rejection had been a mistake.

His father was right, damn him. Raine *was* vain. That the Nine rejected him as a corrupt favor to his father was immaterial to his wounded pride. Rejection in any form stung.

He tried to pretend the decision was difficult, tried to imagine a war with his conscience. The truth was, his conscience purred in its sleep, turning over to get more comfortable.

Raine knew, logically, it would be immoral to steal Olan's acceptance scroll. But that was as far as it went. And logic never won against a whole heart.

The guild was his life's ambition. Besides, anyone with a sane mind would rest easier with Raine guarding and protecting Valdenia over Olan. He was the cream of the pail. The best. Stealing Olan's scroll was downright patriotic. Valdenia needed what Raine had to offer. Valdenia needed an intervention when it came to Olan being placed in such a critical position.

He crept away as silent as a dream. There was much to do.

CHAPTER THREE

*B*ang. Raine jerked awake, clutching a scratchy quilt to his chest. Another loud bang sounded from the bedside wall, followed by a muffled curse. Footsteps pattered down the hallway outside his room. Conversations carried through the thin, paneled walls on all sides.

With a groan, he sat up. There was no falling back asleep in this racket.

Last night, he had purchased a bed at Buckwheat Inn, named for the acres of white sprigged crops encompassing its bucolic village. A neighboring mill attracted lodgers to the inn, as travelers ventured from distant homesteads to grind their grain for cereal and flour. Many opted to spend a night at Buckwheat Inn and set off for home in the morning.

Climbing out of bed, Raine grimaced at the powder coating his pillow. Baths were a luxury service not provided at rudimentary countryside inns.

The crackling crush of grindstones drew him to the window, the gristmill's owners already hard at work to secure their living. He was met with the view of billions of buckwheat blossoms, burnished buttery yellow beneath the half-risen sun. The window's angle didn't permit a view of the gristmill, which sat further back and to the left of the inn, built over the winding river that powered the mill's heavy stones.

Plucking his favorite boar-bristle brush from the nightstand, Raine gently combed out his sleep-mussed braid, now long enough to graze his buttocks. Though his hair was unwashed, enough powder had rubbed away during his slumber to reveal pops of rainbow. Reweaving the alabaster strands into a thick, ropey braid, he tamped down a sigh.

His haversack hung on a blunt, wall-mounted hook that resembled something out of a barn. Raine's arm disappeared to the elbow as he fished its contents, producing a round, silver disc the size of his palm. It opened like a clamshell, holding a cake of compacted rice powder. His soul screamed against masking the gemlike brilliance of his mane, but his father was adamant.

You can't ever show anyone your jeweled hair, son. You will endanger both of our lives should anyone lay eyes upon it unpowdered.

His father had been grave during that discussion. And Raine, a mere seven summers old, had been in full tantrum from being denied permission to swim in Drooger's pond with the rest of the keep's children. But the pondwater would have rinsed the rice powder from his hair, so it was a no-go. Raine had even sworn to keep his head above water while he swam, but his father remained unmoved.

His peculiarities had gotten really old and really annoying by that point. Raine had started to care less and less about why he was so different and more about how it hindered his life.

There was nothing more limiting than a secret, and sometimes, it felt like he was born with twenty.

Gritting his teeth, Raine dutifully massaged the silky white flour into his braid and crown. It pricked his vanity to dull his precious hair. He usually made a point to wash it nightly, brushing it to its full, jeweled splendor before retiring. But given the accommodations he'd encountered on his journey thus far, he wouldn't see a bath until his return to Chambrin Keep.

A shot at the guild was worth far more than a few missed baths.

Blood zinged through his stomach as he repacked his rice powder and brush, preparing to leave. In a matter of hours, he would be taking the entrance exams for the Guardians of Vale. It felt impossible, like a dream turned to life.

Raine's room opened to a long, carpeted corridor with many doors on either side. A maid walked towards him, carrying a pile of clean sheets stacked higher than her head. He stepped aside, back pressed against the wall so she could pass unobstructed in the narrow hallway.

Lowering her arms, she froze as she saw him. Her features washed bone-white and she clutched her sheets harder.

Wonderful. Raine could add her to the ever-growing list of people who abhorred him on sight. Since he never left home, new faces were few and far between. It had been a while since he encountered another like Olan or Moranda. It was inevitable, he supposed. Yet it pricked him, like a wasp sting to the chest.

She stood there shaking, as if dragons roared beneath her feet. Raine pressed harder against the wall, trying to create as much space as possible while appearing non-threatening.

"Please, after you." Raine indicated the direction she'd been heading.

If she remained frozen, he would have to walk past her to reach the inn's exit. Something he was loath to do. The maid was petrified now, but great fear made for greater violence. She might run screaming. Or she might lunge at him. He was familiar with both reactions, more's the pity.

The maid stared down the hall as if eyeballing her final destination. Her features wrenched with dread as she visibly girded herself. *For the love of the Divine*, he wanted to snap. *Passing by a polite stranger is not a test of mettle.*

She charged for all she was worth, her skirts swishing wildly. Her eyes screwed shut as she passed him, as if she couldn't bear to look. Which was unfortunate, both for the maid and for the lodger who exited his suite at the worst possible moment. They tumbled into a heap, scattering the maid's sheets.

Raine shook his head at their floundering limbs and walked in the opposite direction. As he stepped into the reception area, tempting aromas assailed him. Bacon, freshly baked biscuits, and something sweet. He peered through the open doors of a breakfast parlor. Buckwheat Inn served its guests family-style, and the spread looked amazing. Eager lodgers piled their plates with enough food for a week and Raine found himself edging closer.

The sun's angle cast sharp beams in his eyes through the high lobby windows. He squinted against the glare. It was morning in earnest, and he wasn't certain how far he was from the exam site.

With a lingering look at the rapidly diminishing feast—damn, were those maple cakes?—he adjusted his haversack and left the inn on a sigh.

Clipping down the gray cobbled street, breath fogged his face in steamy white puffs. It was the time of year when the seasons muddled like tea leaves. The days were mild, but the nights—and early mornings—grew cooler as summer made room for autumn. The brisk morning air didn't faze him, however. He scarcely noticed, his thoughts whirling like pinwheels.

This was it. He was actually going to take the entrance exams. For the *Guardians of Vale.*

Would he be taking the same test Nyx took? Or his father? Raine wondered if he would perform better than they had. Was there a way to find out? If so, he would rub it in their faces. Lovingly, of course.

An echo of his last argument with his father played in Raine's mind, and he scoffed aloud. As if he would ever be content to take over his father's duties as Valdenia's dragon breeder. Did his father even *know* him?

Raine had been obsessed with joining the guild since before he could form sentences, for Divine's sake. It was inevitable. The two people he loved and idolized most both served as Guardians. His father had been promoted to master and retired a legend. And Nyx was on an assignment so long and so covert, Raine suspected it was something huge. Momentous. The sort of task that shaped history.

Where would Raine fit in the guild? What would he accomplish? He had no clue, but he was itching to find out. Eager to make his father and Nyx proud. To be worthy of standing beside them.

Desperate to permanently silence all the whispering doubts that crept through him at night, when he was alone. Low, cruel voices

Raine couldn't block out no matter how hard he tried. They said he was an abomination. That his father deserved a normal son. That his oddities were a burden on his loved ones.

Enough. He tossed his head, banishing his thoughts like an agitated carthorse shaking off flies. It was bad enough he dealt with those apprehensions when trying to sleep. They weren't going to torment him now, in broad daylight.

Raine was going to *prove* he wasn't a burden. Quite the opposite. He was going to be a hero. Like Nyx. Like his father. The guild was his destiny. He stroked the bit of scroll peeking out from the side pocket of his haversack, almost reassuringly.

Olan's acceptance scroll had been absurdly simple to steal.

With his cousin on the guard schedule all evening, Raine had crept silently into the cramped barracks for basic infantry. Beds were assigned alphabetically, and he had located Olan's without issue. The mattress stank like body odor and stale tobacco. Plugging his nostrils, he rifled through the backpack conveniently placed atop his cousin's sour blankets. Olan's clothes were crusty, the acceptance scroll pinched between stiff socks.

Upon departing Chambrin Keep, Raine ran the entire night and the whole of the next day before stopping at Buckwheat Inn.

It was mid-morning now, the hours passing swiftly. Nerves buzzed his sinew as he drew nearer to the "X" on the scroll's map, illustrated in miniature beneath the paragraphs detailing Olan's conditional acceptance.

While Chieftain Eddic referred to the "X" as the guild's headquarters, Raine knew better. The Guardians were the eyes and ears of Valdenia. The shadowy watchers protecting their country. Mere applicants would never be offered the true location of the guild's headquarters before they sat their entrance exams.

It was undoubtedly a false headquarters, existing for superficial functions. He recalled Olan's belief that the scroll led to the guild's actual base of operations and snorted. Truly, Raine could only take his cousin's contempt as a compliment. If someone that stupid hated him, he was doing something right.

As Raine progressed, orderly buckwheat crops yielded to rugged lowlands: patches of dense forest interrupted by tangled fields. Angular boulders littered the countryside—fragments of the white-capped Dragon Fangs sawing the sky to the north and west.

Reaching a road sign, he paused.

A staked, wooden arrow followed the cobbles. "Pashun" was painted in neat, block letters.

Raine gazed wistfully down the road. One of the nine cities of Valdenia, Pashun was renowned for its lush gardens and even lusher nightlife. He'd always wanted to go. Perhaps after his exams, he would go and spend a night there. That wouldn't delay his return home too much. Probably.

Even if it did, it would be worth it. Excitement welled through him, bright and fluid like quicksilver. This day kept getting better and better.

He quieted his feet, which had begun bouncing without permission, and forced his attention back to the road sign. There was another arrow further down the pole. It pointed toward a dense row of conifers on the right side of the road. The sign was blank other than a few scribbled, inkless gouges. It looked like nonsense at first glance, something carved up by a bored drifter.

He cocked his head, unable to make sense of it.

Incredibly, this new angle revealed the gouges as an overly simplified version of the guild's emblem. Nine shaky humps were the sweeping mountains that served as the emblem's backdrop. Three tight scribbles beneath the mountains represented a Guardian unit.

Raine surveyed the copse of pines and couldn't detect a single break in the trees.

The ground was unworn, showing no signs of travel. It was the exact opposite of the marked path promised in Olan's letter. It was no path at all. Worried he was wasting time, Raine wedged himself through a snarl of pokey branches and pushed through to the other side.

To his astonishment, a path appeared. Well-trodden and too broad to mistake for a game trail. Rectangular boulders wrapped in moss framed the offshoot on either side. Aged bronze glinted through the spongy lichen. He crouched and scrubbed at a boulder with his thumb, fraying the moss to reveal stamped metal.

His heart slammed his ribcage. It was the guild's emblem, rendered in exquisite detail. Raine adjusted his haversack and jogged the shady path. Pure giddiness infected him like magic. He was as light as a feather, brighter than a falling star. He wondered if he would ever trust this was really happening. Surely, he was dreaming.

Blinded by elation, he tripped over a felled birch tree and smashed through rotten bark, half-eaten by wooly beetles.

Thousands of fat, wriggly grubs and shiny, armored beetles spilled over him. With a high, terrible screech his father would have never let him live down, Raine lunged upright and smacked frantically at his chest, arms, and face.

Divine Father, he hated maggots. Ever since he had snuck a honey melon from the kitchen and hid in a cupboard, prepared to devour the whole fruit down to its rind. But when he'd split it, a mass of writhing white spilled over his lap. To this day, he could not abide maggots, grubs or even caterpillars. And the sweet smell of honey melon made his gorge rise.

Even after he knocked the last of them off, he could still *feel* them. The creepy crawly sensation didn't abate until the path brought him to a clearing.

He halted. Awe flooded him. Arms slack at his sides, he swallowed hard, his mouth drier than a sun-crisped fly on a windowpane. This was definitely the place. Pale limestone walls formed a forbidding barrier around the exam site, concealing it from view. There were no known castles or fortresses in this area. It could only be a covert guild property.

Raine followed the narrow path until it butted into a plain, uninterrupted brick wall—as if to admit specters and ghosts. There were no handles, hinges, or levers. He looked closely for the edge of a gate, where the curtain wall might draw apart to permit entry, but he was unable to detect a single stone gap. It was solid, immovable rock.

He cleared his throat. "Hello." No answer. He tried again, more loudly. "Hello! I'm here for my entrance exams?" He felt silly yelling at a curtain wall without a soul in sight, but he would gladly look a fool if that's what it took to gain access to the guild.

A slot no wider than his hand opened in the brick to his right, several steps removed from the path. "Insert your scroll."

The command was snappish, almost haughty. Olan's scroll jutted from the side pouch of his haversack, as he had anticipated the necessity of producing it for admittance. Carefully, he angled the scroll through the tiny opening. A small, hairy hand yanked it from his grip and slammed the slot shut, heedless of any fingers in hazard's way. Raine scowled, relieved his cautious maneuvering had spared him injury.

Patience was one of his "areas of opportunity," as his father said. A loving way of stating he possessed an abysmal lack of it. His father's observation was accurate, per usual. Less than thirty seconds of waiting, Raine tapped one foot against the dirt, then the other, hands on his hips. The tights chosen for his excursion were snug and comfortable. He wore a fine lawn shirt, tucked neatly into his waistband, and a well-worn pair of padded leather boots, borrowed without permission from his father.

Raine possessed no suitable footwear for long distance travel, and his feet thanked him for electing comfort over fashion. Even appropriately shod, his feet ached from hours of walking. He shuffled where he stood, waiting for the voice to return or something to happen.

A long, loud gurgle sounded from his abdomen. He recollected the towering platter of maple cakes at Buckwheat Inn and his stomach complained anew. Attention bouncing between his ravenous belly to the sorest parts of his soles, he growled, "Are you going to open the gate or what?"

The rock wall shuddered. A moment later, stones groaned and separated, scraping the earth in a laborious trek to permit passage. Raine stepped through the gap once it was wide enough to accommodate his frame. Turning, he spied the gears and pulleys cleverly concealed from the curtain's exterior.

A squat, bald man stood on a rickety platform against the wall, where he shifted a lever. The gate rumbled to a halt, then began another lumbering progression, this time to seal itself. The gateman approached Raine, squinting up at him with a thin mouth. He was cloaked by a loose brown cassock that might have been a shirt on a taller man, and his pant legs were rolled up several times, creating thick bands around his shins.

"Olan Chambrin, follow me." The gateman turned without introducing himself and scurried toward an imposing set of iron-riveted doors pressed within an austere building. A dreary, square structure of gray stone and paltry windows.

They entered a great hall. Its uncarpeted floors were made of the same stone as its walls and ceiling, creating a monochromatic effect that was striking, if not to Raine's taste. A nice mahogany floor or broad-loomed rug would warm up the space and offer better definition.

Three men sat like a panel at the far side of the room. The gateman scuttled across the chamber and presented them with Olan's wrinkled scroll. Raine loosely followed, his own stride long but unhurried.

As he approached the oblong wooden table, he studied the men facing him. They were three of the nine chieftains of Valdenia. Each chieftain represented one of Valdenia's nine cities.

The nine cities were originally settlements of the nine tribes. The tribes unified beneath the mantle of Valdenia only two centuries prior—opting to form an oligarchy wherein each tribe held equal representation in their new government.

No one chieftain possessed authority over the others. They ruled Valdenia equitably, issuing an era of peace, prosperity, and advancement that made them beloved by all. Even as the nine chieftains aged and died, passing their titles and responsibilities to ensuing generations, Valdenia continued to flourish.

The three chieftains before Raine were older, their faces creased with age, and dressed in jet black robes.

Brown eyes and dark hair were the predominant coloring of Valdenian people. Raine found most brown eyes richly warm, a pleasant contrast to his own cold, pale orbs. But as three sets of identical eyes focused on him, the hairs on the back of his neck prickled.

Their yellow-brown irises looked like piss and shit muddled in a garderobe. Revulsion corkscrewed Raine's innards. His pulse rioted at the base of his throat. Faster and faster, until his heartbeat was a rabbity thrum of alarm. An electric shock spiked down his spine and went straight to his heels, as if compelling him to flee. His reaction was as primal as it was irrational.

Is this how people feel when they see me?

The thought ripped through his hysteria, leaving him stunned and profoundly ashamed. It was unjust to hold a person's appearance against them. Something Raine had sworn he would never do. He never wanted another person to feel as he had, let alone be the source of such cruelty. Besides which, these were three of the nine great leaders of Valdenia. Raine's distaste was sacrilege, both to himself and them.

"Olan Chambrin," the chieftain seated center addressed him. Stomping his aversion like a redback spider, Raine resolutely offered the chieftain his undivided esteem and attention. "I am Chieftain Eddic. To my left is Chieftain Vanwert. To my right, Chieftain Tyrus."

The other two nodded respectively at their introductions. They were a somber trio, faces lined as though they spent most of their lives unsmiling. Neat stacks of paper sat before each of them. Eddic lifted his sheath of documents and rifled the pages.

"Your application is most impressive. You are fluent in Valdenian, Garganthan, and all nine dialects of the old tribes?"

Eddic's salt-and-pepper brows knitted in a mockery of amazement. Heat bloomed across Raine's cheeks. Damn it all, it was the blithering idiot Olan who had lied so blatantly on his application, not *him*.

But for today, Raine was Olan. And he felt like a dimwit.

Before he could comment on his unlikely gift for so many languages, Chieftain Vanwert shot him a derisive smirk and said, "I look forward to observing your skills with a bow." His head bent to survey his papers, revealing a freckled, hairless patch at the center of his scalp. "You've set a record, did you know? Landing a bull's eye at a thousand paces."

Eddic gave a low whistle. "The longest bull's eye ever recorded was during an archery tournament seven summers back. Covan Smyth took home a prize boar when he hit dead-center from just under eight hundred paces. You've blown his record out of the water, it seems. Our exam course is spatially limited, regrettably. The longest shot, a mere four-hundred paces. Child's play for *you*. I do hope you aren't too bored by our tests."

"Alas, the entry exams are meant to be quite challenging," Chieftain Tyrus chimed. "But once in a while, we find ourselves confronted with a magnanimously skilled candidate such as yourself and are confronted with the deficiencies of our little obstacle course."

Unlike the other two, Tyrus's hair remained thick on his head, but it had the opposite of a youthful effect by having gone full gray.

Eddic cracked a genuine smile. "The Wade brothers." The other chieftains heartily agreed, inspiring a spirited reminisce amongst themselves.

"Pity we lost the eldest." Vanwert.

"Ah, at least we have the younger." Tyrus.

"Never saw an arm like Sidian's." Eddic.

"His marksmanship is impeccable." Vanwert.

"He just completed his eighth level five assignment. Not a single casualty." Tyrus.

"Just remember, I chose him first."

That last remark came from Eddic, and Vanwert scowled. "We know," he said with a huff.

They seemed to recall Raine's presence at length, and Eddic addressed him once more. "Your entrance exam is a series of tests designed to evaluate your suitability as a Guardian. Please join us in the bailey. We won't waste your time with further delay."

Raine nodded, privately certain they didn't wish to waste any more of their own time and could care less about his. Eddic stood as he finished speaking. Vanwert and Tyrus followed suit, and the three chieftains led Raine through the archway behind their table.

Passing through a cramped kitchenette, they entered a large, comfortable study. A handful of armchairs faced a crackling hearth where a vat of stew simmered. Broth boiled over, sputtering as flames licked the drips to smoke. Aromatic garlic and parsnips plugged Raine's nostrils. His belly cramped painfully as he eyed the frothy overspill.

Striding toward an oaken door, the chieftains' path took them nowhere near the enticing cauldron. The door led outside, judging by the meager windows positioned on either side of its arched frame.

"That's an awful lot of soup," Raine observed wistfully. The chieftains ignored him. They were almost at the exit, and he tried again. "I'm positively famished from my long journey here. It could interfere with my performance during the exam."

Eddic opened the door and gave him a hard look over his shoulder. "It's a good thing you are such an incredibly skilled warrior. Even in your weakened state, you will certainly outshine most others."

Raine bent on a sigh. The chieftains were outright contemptuous of Olan's obscenely boastful application. Any other time, he would delight in their palpable disdain for his childhood tormentor. Just not when he was pretending to *be* the limp prick.

CHAPTER FOUR

Raine assessed the exam course as they filed into the bailey. There was indeed a section for archery. A handful of targets, spaced along the defensive curtain, were so far away that they would require both a longbow and better-than-fair skill to land any arrows.

A table laden with potted plants sat alongside the fortress wall to his left. Another area was seemingly devoted to knife skills, a dozen straw-stuffed dummies erected on posts next to an array of bladed weapons.

A long, winding strip snaked the grassy lawn opposite the archery station. It glowed a hellish red-orange, as if lava seeped from a crack in the earth. Raine's empty stomach ceased groaning, unease curdling his appetite.

Hot coals.

The coals unnerved him, though not for fear of pain. Flames neither blistered his skin nor scorched a single hair on his head.

A fact he couldn't reveal to anyone, including the chieftains.

Raine's imperviousness to fire was just one more oddity his father made him safeguard.

The stretch of burning coals was undoubtedly the most daunting task for any other candidate. But to Raine, they would be nothing short of pleasant. He had nearly given his father an apoplexy the first time the general of Chambrin Keep awoke to find his young son curled up like a kitten inside a blazing hearth, fast asleep and unscathed by the flames licking him on all sides.

If Raine's assumption was correct, he would have to walk the coals. Without a clue what it felt like for fire to hurt instead of soothe, he would have to pantomime pain and discomfort at every step. Raine doubted his ability to perform properly, especially on such a protracted path.

What if it's not meant to be completed? Raine's anxiety spiked at the thought. He didn't want to stand out conspicuously for being the first applicant to ever make the entire trek across the coals.

But what if it was not unusual for a candidate to complete the path? Then Raine would look weak and incompetent. Olan had already turned the chieftains—his judges—against him by being an obtuse, overreaching liar in his application. An insult to the chieftains' intelligence which they clearly took personally.

Raine stared at the coals and considered bowing out of the exams. This wasn't even his test. He was acting as Olan, after all. But his dream of joining the guild had roots far deeper than doubt or fear. He yearned to pass the exams with a desperation that fairly leaked through his pores. Raine couldn't back out, not when he was this close.

Vanwert directed him to the archery corner. Raine's shoulders eased as he swapped his haversack for the yew longbow dominating a nearby bench. Considering Vanwert's earlier jibe at Olan's patently false longshot, Raine was unsurprised archery was his first task.

Imagining Olan in his place, as his cousin rightfully should be, Raine almost wished he had allowed Olan to keep this appointment. His lips twitched as he pictured his below-average bully floundering to hit targets at even half the distance he had claimed. *A thousand paces. What an idiot.*

The bowstring was taut, freshly waxed, and possessed a punishing pull weight. Raine nocked an arrow, careful not to show precisely how little effort it took to draw back the string. Accustomed to concealing his abnormal strength, he was confident in this imitation, at least.

Turkey fletching tickled his cheek as he aimed at one of ten targets, little more than specks along the distant curtain.

Thwack. It buried into the innermost ring of the concentric target. His remaining arrows flew equally swift and accurate, striking their targets with unerring precision.

After firing the last bolt, he looked to the chieftains for direction. Vanwert's mouth was set in a grim line, but Eddic and Tyrus appeared pleased.

"I confess, I assumed your abilities were grossly exaggerated on your application," Tyrus said with a wide smile, the first friendly expression from any of them. "But *this.*" He gestured at the distant targets. "Remarkable! Talent like yours is what we strive to acquire."

Preening at the praise, Raine strove to contain his smugness. His father called him a showoff. Always teasingly, but perhaps rightfully so.

Raine frequently trounced warriors with decades more experience in all manners of exercises. What he lacked in skill or refinement, he made up for with his anomalous strength and speed. Advantages that frustrated Arastus, who believed his son should *earn* his wins. As if, by utilizing his innate abilities, Raine was somehow cheating.

It was nice, being lauded without censure for a change.

Tyrus escorted him to the plant table, beaming all the way. Eddic and Vanwert walked ahead of them and framed the table.

Eddic gestured broadly, indicating the table as a whole, and said, "This test is straightforward. You must identify as many plants as possible. Describe their uses, as well, should you know them."

Two dozen plants cluttered the table, with dirt and fallen petals dusting the spaces between pots. Raine recognized several straight away thanks to Wylan's extensive herb garden.

"Those are ramps," he said, indicating the leafy green tuft brushing Vanwert's elbow. "Their purpose is, er, to make eggs taste better?"

Tyrus squeezed his bicep with a chortle, but Eddic and Vanwert peered at him flatly, unimpressed. The tips of Raine's ears warmed, and he rushed to name as many plants as he could. He knew aloe was for pain and healing. And that many of the herbs could stave off infection as well as season food.

Unfortunately, he didn't recognize a single flower. They were all unfamiliar. He wondered if they even grew around here. Their lissome stems were exotic shades of green, and their oddly shaped petals seemed foreign compared to the daisies and wild roses around Chambrin.

"That is oleander," Eddic said, coming to Raine's rescue as he wavered over a starry, magenta bloom. "Ingesting the root will kill you in hours."

Oh. While Raine hated appearing ignorant before the chieftains, it was nice to know the keep's steward didn't intend to stuff a roasted pig with oleander and murder the entire keep over supper. Or if he did, he was wise enough not to grow it in his garden.

The chieftains took turns explaining the remainder of exotic plants, nearly all of which were lethal. Raine fought to keep his confidence levels high as they moved toward the practice dummies, but it was difficult. He'd only known half the plants. That was fifty percent, a failing grade. He didn't realize he groaned aloud until Tyrus spoke.

"You did very well," Tyrus said consolingly, bringing an arm up to rub soothing circles on his shoulder. "I can tell your mind is flexible and absorbs knowledge well."

Raine grimaced at the chieftain's overly familiar touch but swallowed his objection. It wasn't necessarily a bad thing that Tyrus considered them friends. At least Raine had one judge on his side, so to speak.

Tyrus misinterpreted his expression. "No, I speak the truth. Think of it this way: you knew all the edibles. We've had applicants who couldn't identify so much as a radish."

That actually did make Raine feel a bit better. Not about the invasive fingers *still* massaging his shoulder, but about his performance. He had recognized the radish, after all.

"This task is weapon of choice. You may use any one, or all, of them," Vanwert announced as they reached the table near the dummies.

Vanwert caressed the pommel of a flamberge sword, its wavy blade sharpened for real use. Not practice. "We will evaluate your form and proficiency with each blade you select."

Choose wisely hung in the air like a dire omen.

Raine blinked at the floppy straw dummies and felt the insane urge to laugh. Vanwert made it seem like such a grave decision; as if this was a fight to the death against battle-hardened black-guards and not petty vandalism against birds' nests with clothes.

The table was spread with everything from throwing stars and hatchets to daggers and rapiers. He imagined bludgeoning a straw dummy with the spiked mace and smothered a protest. This exercise was worse than absurd. It was demeaning. How much skill could anyone demonstrate against straw dummies?

Resigned, he opted for a set of identical claymores. They seemed the most dignified option. Better than the freaking mace, at any rate. With a sword clutched in each fist, he circled the dummies. They were faceless, dressed in mismatched castoffs, and fastened to wooden staves. Motions stilted by embarrassment, he raised a sword and slashed the nearest dummy's throat.

Like some juvenile delinquent slicing up farmer Habbard's scarecrows, he grit his teeth and kept swinging. Naturally, there was no resistance. The dummies fell one after another to a flurry of flashing steel. As the last dummy collapsed to the ground, Raine turned to the chieftains.

"You are outstanding! Every bit as amazing as you sounded in your application," Tyrus said, approaching. Bits of straw clung to his hair and robe like fallen snow.

Raine failed to see how amazing he could have looked while hacking away at scarecrows. Put a real opponent before him and then he could really show them.

Stopping in front of him, Tyrus took Raine by the shoulders. The chieftain's fingers were firm and weirdly assessing as they moved down Raine's biceps and forearms, feeling along bone and sinew.

"A worthy candidate indeed." Tyrus's tone was musing with an undercurrent of excitement. "Your eyes are sharp. Your mind is keen. And your body is well-formed and honed like a weapon. You, Olan Chambrin, are the full package."

"Thank you," Raine said stiffly, extracting his arms from Tyrus's hold as politely as possible.

That was creepy. It hadn't felt friendly, at all. More like a buyer examining a prospective horse's body composition. Raine stepped away before Tyrus decided to wedge a finger in his mouth to inspect his teeth, too.

Hot coals were the final task. Butterflies erupted riotously in his belly as he trailed Eddic and Vanwert to the burning path across the lawn. Inwardly, he cursed himself for rushing through his weaponry test. He should have taken his time and ruminated on a plan instead of blindly butchering the dummies as fleetingly as possible.

A heavy palm slid down his braid, pulling Raine from his self-reproach. "You know, I've never found blanches to be beautiful, but I could get used to this."

What. The. Hell. Raine snatched his braid and whipped around. His lips parted to deliver cutting, outraged censure.

The words dried up on his tongue. Mustard brown eyes gleamed possessively, tracing the lines of his body with off-putting avarice. As if Raine was a thoroughbred hound or finely cut jacket or some other such thing Tyrus wished to own.

Tyrus nodded, as if Raine had spoken. "Nvek is up next. He'll try to pick you, if only to spite me. But I'll—"

"Tyrus," Eddic called sharply.

A splotchy flush enveloped Tyrus's features as he glanced toward Eddic, who awaited them with Vanwert near the coals. "Forget I said anything," Tyrus muttered without looking at Raine. "A moment's confusion. It was nothing."

Raine frowned at Tyrus's retreating back. That most certainly hadn't been *nothing*. The man was deranged. Or crazy. He had touched Raine as though he were an animal or possession. Not with lust, but with an air of ownership and entitlement. *Socially backwards berk.*

Dragging his braid over his shoulder, Raine smoothed both hands down his mane to chase away the ick of Tyrus's pawing. If it happened again, he was going to deck the bastard, consequences be damned. Trailing after Tyrus, he halted at the edge of the coals. The tips of his boots were inches from the path. Even up close, it resembled a massive fissure seeping lava.

"I don't have to walk on this, do I?"

The chieftains interpreted his reluctance as fear of the fire. Vanwert crossed his arms, nodding toward the coals with a sagging chin. "It takes discipline of the mind and body to walk these coals. There are no rules regarding the quickness of your pace or the length of your stride. However, your feet must be bare, and you must make it to the end of the path without stepping off."

Raine relaxed ever-so-slightly. That was one worry diminished. Completing the path was a requirement to pass the entrance exams. Success would not risk exposing his unnatural tolerance for fire.

His father's leather boots were a size too large and easily removed. Raine tucked his socks neatly inside the insteps before setting the boots aside.

Eddic and Vanwert waited like solemn priests with their dark robes and wrinkled faces. Raine didn't look at Tyrus. When the chieftains offered no further instruction, he lined himself with the start of the path. Springy grass peeked through his toes.

Raine drew a deep, steadying breath. He could do this. He just needed to feign a regular person's discomfort at their naked flash touching hot coals. Now that the chieftains considered him a great talent, he hoped they would attribute any underreaction on his part to stoicism or grace through pain.

He felt like a stringed puppet, his extremities light and jittery. Delaying the inevitable would only fray his nerves further. Gathering courage, he leapt upon the coals and walked briskly, without pause. Normal people would not mosey through the path, after all.

The coals crumbled to powdery ash as he progressed. It was heavenly, like a warm massage. Raine wanted to dig his toes into the ashes and seek the red-hot stone beneath.

One, two, three. One, two, three.

He counted his steps, using an inner chant to keep his pace steady. His concentration was so complete, he faltered as his feet hit a patch of stiff, spry grass.

After the pleasant warmth of the coals, the ground was uncomfortably cold against his skin. He hurried back to the chieftains, mindful to avoid the coals.

They smiled as one at his approach. "Excellent performance," Eddic enthused.

Tyrus extracted a small, terra cotta jar from his robe pocket. "Please have a seat. I will apply salve to your feet." Tyrus motioned to a nearby garden bench, and Raine's heart leapt in alarm.

He couldn't let them see his uninjured feet. His soles, like the rest of him, were satin soft and uncallused from his nightly routine of boiling baths and the warm, scented oils he massaged into his skin. Any person with such soft feet would be afflicted with burnt, blistered skin after that final obstacle. Raine knew his own feet were perfectly smooth and unmarred.

"No, thank you," he said quickly. "My feet are fine."

"Such pride." Tyrus wagged a finger. "Everyone receives this salve upon completing the coals. We will not think you weak. It is necessary for safe healing."

Tyrus sat on the bench, jar in hand. Apparently, Raine was meant to sit beside him and what? Lift his feet into the man's lap? He wouldn't permit that creep to rub ointment on him anywhere, injured or otherwise.

"I am not being proud, Chieftain Tyrus," Raine assured him. He turned to grab his socks and boots, desperate to cover his treacherous soles. "My feet are covered in thick, hideous calluses. The skin is so hard and rough, it did not melt from the heat." He sat on the grass to pull his socks on.

A hand shot out and clamped his ankle. Raine sucked in a breath and yanked his leg to escape Eddic's grip. The chieftain bent, holding firm to Raine's leg. Spindly fingers turned white as they dug into his shin. For a frail elder, Eddic was surprisingly strong.

"Cease your struggles, Olan," Eddic barked. Raine stilled, his breath coming in short, quiet puffs. "The salve is not optional. Whether you require the treatment or not, it can do you no harm to accept it. As a member of the Guardians of Vale, you will obey us in all matters. Unquestioningly and without hesitation."

It was a rebuke as well as a warning.

Raine swallowed a lump of mounting panic. He slowed his breaths and tried to convince himself it wasn't that serious. What did it matter that his feet weren't burned? It was a fluke, nothing more. Even if the chieftains decided he was a cursed blanch, the worst they would do is reject him from the guild.

The prospect of being twice-rejected was rough on his pride, but Raine would manage. Besides, it was technically Olan being rejected this time around. The thought bolstered him, because *fuck Olan.* He relaxed his leg.

"You're right, of course," Raine said. "Although I don't require the salve, receiving it will cause no harm, merely sticky toes." He forced a smile.

Eddic held his ankle a beat longer, sickly sallow irises intent upon him. Slowly, one finger at a time, the chieftain released him. Vanwert hovered behind Eddic, gaze narrowing on Raine's black, sooty soles.

That's right. The ashy coals had coated his skin with a greasy residue. He had neglected to consider the potential camouflage the soot offered. Nobody could detect his burns—or lack thereof—on such filthy feet.

An ember of hope flared. Raine plopped onto the stone bench beside Tyrus with an ease he did not feel, an attempt to conceal his nerves. Tyrus grimaced as Raine dropped a blackened heel directly upon his lap, smearing soot all over the chieftain's robes.

Vanwert produced a muslin cloth along with an ewer of water and passed them to Tyrus. Raine tensed. So much for sooty grime masking his lack of blisters. There was nothing for it. He could only cross his fingers and see what happened.

Balancing the ewer against his thigh, Tyrus soaked the cloth. Raine's foot was bathed without ceremony, then Tyrus smeared thick, opaque salve across his sole. The chieftain's strokes were gentle and, Raine decided, overly thorough. The man's fingers combed between his toes, for Divine's sake.

At the precise moment Raine could endure no more, Tyrus released his foot. His spirits sang as the smoothness of his sole went unremarked. Raine quickly swung his opposite leg up, wordlessly conveying urgency. *One down, one to go.*

Tyrus dipped the filthy cloth, squeezing excess gray water over the grass before wiping Raine's left foot. The chieftain treated him to the same long, discomfiting salve application. Raine tensed to pull his foot back, and Tyrus gripped his ankle tightly.

Raine had somehow managed to go his whole life without being grabbed by the ankles until today, and it was already getting old.

"Aren't you finished?" Raine gave his leg a futile tug to emphasize his point. *You can let go now.*

Tyrus frowned thoughtfully at his left sole. It was angled more toward his face than Raine's other foot had been thanks to their positions on the bench. He quelled a wince as understanding dawned. The cause for Tyrus's scrutiny was exactly as he feared.

"How is this possible? Your foot is undamaged from the coals." Tyrus glowered down the length of him. "You are a cheat."

Raine reared back at the accusation and jerked his leg, this time successfully freeing himself from the man's ointment-slicked grip. "I didn't cheat. You all watched me walk those stupid coals barefoot. What do you think I did? I obviously didn't float across. My damn feet were black."

Raine shot up from the bench and found Eddic and Vanwert standing too close for politeness on either side of him.

"Show me your feet," Eddic ordered.

Raine's stomach bottomed out. He nearly smacked himself in the face for his stupidity. Tyrus's accusation had been a way out. Raine had no clue how he could have cheated the test, but had he feigned guilt, the chieftains would be none-the-wiser to his inexplicable firewalking ability. Instead, he had backed himself into a corner and would now suffer the consequences.

He toyed with the idea of forcing Eddic to his knees to peer at the pads of his feet from the ground. The air was tense, the chieftains still and grim like tombstones. Raine thought better of antagonizing them, a feat his father would claim him incapable of. Straightening on the bench, he leaned backwards and lifted his legs. The chieftains surveyed the exposed bottoms of his feet. Eddic stooped for a closer look.

"Such thick calluses you have," Vanwert said, lips scarcely moving as he spoke.

Raine regretted a lot of things he said in his efforts to avoid the salve and their suspicions. They were now aware, unequivocally, that he was a liar. That he had attempted to hide his unscathed skin through objections and deceit.

"I grew up in a neighborhood with a blanched chit," Eddic announced, still inspecting his feet. "Her skin was ghostly pale except where it was pink. She could hardly abide the sun. She burned so easily."

Raine lowered his legs and met Eddic's yellowish stare as the chieftain continued. "You are the very picture of health and vitality. Your skin seems to be on good terms with the sun. And you can apparently stroll across burning coals with baby soft feet without suffering the slightest blister. What a mystery."

Eddic's tone suggested it was not a delightful mystery. Cold sweat trickled down Raine's spine.

Tyrus recoiled, then flung himself off the bench. He backed away without turning, as if Raine was a rabid wolf bent on attack. Vanwert and Eddic, while more circumspect, were visibly ruffled as they joined Tyrus by the shredded practice dummies.

Assembled over the straw-strewn grass, the three judges convened in private discourse. Their postures were rigid, gestures agitated.

Raine jammed on his socks and boots, then eyed the oak slab door that would take him back through the fortress and spill him out front, where he could commence his journey home.

This exam was a shit show. Raine had fucked himself when he walked those coals. He had foreseen his expulsion in that fiery pathway like a soothsayer reading a palm line. He was clueless why his various oddities had to be so closely guarded, as if it were a matter of life and death, but here was proof that his father was right. Yet again.

Eddic stepped from their group and approached with a terse smile that did not reach his eyes.

Halting a healthy distance from Raine, he said, "My fellow chieftains and I agree your performance was commendable, despite the circumstances. We are prepared to offer you a position with the Guardians of Vale."

Raine gaped.

CHAPTER FIVE

Raine shifted on the hard, stubby chair in the subterranean room where the chieftains had deposited him. He was still dazed from his admission into the Guardians of Vale. His father was wrong, after all. Raine might be odd, but he was not inferior. He was worthy of being a Guardian.

The chieftains might revoke his admission if they discovered his true identity. That had been Raine's original plan: show up as Olan, best the exams, then reveal himself as Arastus Chambrin's son.

But the barest sip of success, of acceptance, made him unconscionably thirsty for more. Raine couldn't imagine revealing himself now, only to have his dream stripped away. He didn't have a uniform or assigned unit or anything yet. Couldn't he pretend, just a while longer?

Perhaps he would never relinquish his impersonation of Olan.

His cousin was a lumbering lout. Was it possible to retain the use of Olan's identity while his cousin pursued a dead-end career as a foot soldier?

Raine shifted again. The low-backed chair was miserably short and rigid. A stool, really. He considered sitting flat on the dirt floor and leaning against a wall. It would be more comfortable.

The chieftains had left him here, advising they would return shortly. But that was an hour ago. They had muttered something about paperwork and maintaining secrecy before leaving. Both his father and Nyx had impressed the guild's paranoia upon him, so Raine had not questioned the chieftains' request to await them.

More time passed, however, and Raine's unease grew in tandem with his discomfort. He stood from the chair of torture, careful not to upturn the oil lamp on the floor beside him. Massaging the sore globes of his bottom, he paced the squalid room. Belowground and the size of a closet, it contained two chairs and a mounted bookshelf with several dusty tomes, their titles bland and pedantic. Grungy cobwebs congested the ceiling corners, crusted with the desiccated husks of unlucky insects.

After his tenth circuit of the sparse chamber, Raine was through waiting. Secrecy be damned, he could not remain in this cell-like room a moment longer. As he went to turn the brass doorknob, it held tight. Raine frowned at the handle, wriggling it experimentally. It didn't turn.

Dread crawled through him like a thousand icy silverfish. There was a reason this space felt like a prison cell. Because it was. The chieftains had locked him down here.

He shivered as he jerked the knob, heedless of breaking it. The latch was unnaturally secure, so he shoved his shoulder against the door. Over and over, he rammed the door with all his strength. It didn't budge. *Shit.*

Raine spun and surveyed the room, panic scouring his entrails. The chieftains hadn't accepted him into their guild. No, they had fed him lies to keep him docile, then trapped him in this pit.

They had to know he would be mutinous upon their return. Whatever they were doing, it wasn't paperwork. Raine needed to escape before they returned, wielding weapons or worse.

The door was immovable and there were no windows. Raine paced the chamber anew, agitated eyes darting for a way out. Reaching the end of the room, he pivoted sharply. His boot scuffed up a spray of dirt.

Raine paused. And kicked the floor. Dirt sprayed. *That's it.*

He grabbed a chair by its legs and smashed it against the wall. Wood ruptured to splinters. Choosing the largest pieces from the wreckage, he collapsed to his knees before the door. Utilizing the jagged, broken end of a chair leg, he speared the soil loose.

For an indeterminate time, he tunneled into the floor. Sweat streamed his brow and stung his eyes, but he didn't pause. Not for breath or rest. He had already wasted a precious hour blithely awaiting his own execution.

It was an extreme assumption, but he felt its truth, its rightness, in the pit of his core. Something about his peculiarities had sealed his death warrant. He needed to *get out*.

Tightly compacted dirt yielded to his frantic efforts. Raine's torso bent into the ground as he scraped a tunnel. Employing fingers and wood fragments in equal measure, he was more beast than human. A wild badger, frenzied by the hunt that threatened him.

Phantom wolves nipped at his haunches as the clay tunnel compressed his shoulders like untried birthing hips. He pushed and clawed until the soil split and air hit his face.

Raine emerged by degrees, the tunnel greedy and unclenching. At last, he stood above the floor on the opposite side of the cell door. Filth matted his sweat-slicked skin, and his clothes were irreparably torn.

He was in the storage cellar he had passed through earlier, accompanied by the chieftains and blithely ignorant of their intentions. Weak light filtered through two small, seeded glass windows. The walls were lined with casks of wine, burlap sacks, and dusty wooden crates brimming with apples and turnips.

The cellar's entrance was concealed beneath a threadbare rug in the cramped kitchen above. At any moment, the chieftains could pop the hatch and descend the rickety ladder. There had to be another way out.

He dismissed the windows as a viable option. They were too snug for a child to squeak through, let alone a full-grown man. Keeping a wary eye on the ceiling hatch, he circuited the cellar. Nothing. Unless he was going to dig another hole, this time tunneling underneath the fortress's foundation to reach the courtyard, there was no other way out.

Raine deliberated. Blood drummed his ears in the musty, shadowed silence. To dig beneath the foundation would require significantly more time and effort than he could spare. It wasn't feasible.

His mouth hardened as he realized his only viable exit was through the kitchen. The instinct to bolt through the ceiling hatch welled within him, but he ignored it. His best shot at escape was to conceal himself. When the chieftains returned, Raine could sneak up the ladder and disappear through the hatch behind their backs.

It was settled. Raine rushed the cell door and fell to his knees. Shoving moist crumbles through the tunnel, he tightly compacted the dirt floor in front of the cell. It wasn't perfect, but it would fool any eyes unalert for recent tillage.

The hatch overhead creaked open, pouring light into the dim cellar. Heart seizing, Raine wedged himself in a gap between the two nearest crates, ducking low. Cobwebs ripped around his frame like felt swatches, trailing his arms like wraith fingers as he tucked deeper. While spiders were easier to endure than gross, wriggling grubs, he still shuddered as an untold number of spindly, eight-legged creatures crawled over his face and hair, skittering for the security of dark corners and packed crates.

His eyes tracked the descending figures from his hiding place. Three silhouettes moved with preternatural grace down the ancient ladder, their feet alighting upon the rungs like shadows. Dressed in inky black bodystockings, Raine recognized them as a Guardian unit. The Guardians of Vale operated in teams of three. A captain and two subordinates.

The first to descend was a captain, marked by the golden armlet encircling her bicep. Stamped into the metal would be a uniquely identifying serial number. Female captains were uncommon but not unheard of. Sable braids were piled atop her crown like a writhing snake pit. Her figure was lithe and silent as she stalked near the cell door.

A journeyman and journeywoman trailed after her. Just as silent. Just as lethal. All three held daggers with milky blades, viciously curved like the canines of an ancient predator.

Their arms were poised to put their strange weapons to immediate use. The chieftains followed last. Raine read fear in the stark lines of their withered faces, their hunched postures and hesitancy.

They were deathly quiet, careful to keep the awaiting Olan ignorant of their arrival. Once they were assembled around the cell door, Eddic produced a key from his robes.

Raine charged for the ceiling hatch as Eddic slotted the key into the lock. Not one sigh escaped the ladder as he ghosted up its battered rungs. For a split second, he contemplated barring the hatch behind him. But his momentum debated nothing as his body careened fast and faraway.

Pale and swift as a winter hare, he dashed through the great hall and exploded into the bailey. The gateman's face bleached with alarm as Raine sprinted for the curtain wall.

"I will not open this gate," he croaked, beady eyes bulging.

Raine pounded up the steps leading to the lever's platform, coming right up to the diminutive man, who shouted and shrank inside his brown cassock like a turtle shell. Raine grasped the lever and pulled, but not in the direction that would activate the gate. Snapping the handle ruthlessly, he rendered the gate inoperable.

Then, without a word, he sprang into the air. Powerful thighs propelled him up, up, up. Grasping the curtain ledge, he vaulted over in a high somersault and landed in a deft crouch on the other side. Raine didn't pause to savor the success of his escape. He ran.

It was full dark when Chambrin Keep came into view. Raine's lungs were scraped raw from his furious pace. He had stopped for nothing, racing home with the trajectory of a thrown spear. No inns would host him with empty pockets, anyway. His haversack, containing all his silvans as well as his hair powder and favorite brush, had been forgotten at the exam site.

Slowly, sluggishly, he traced the cracked dirt trail dividing Drooger's grazing pastures from Habbard's peas and beans. On his right, dark shapes clamored to all fours. The cows lowed plaintively before cantering further afield.

Most animals disliked Raine. It was just one more oddity, one more mark against his normalcy. As a child, he had cried torrents when all the keep's kids got to play with Drooger's baby goats. Except him. Whenever he tried, the creatures would scream and run. They became so distressed, in fact, he was sent back to the keep.

Solid blackness loomed ahead, the cliff walls of Chambrin's perch blotting stars and sky. Locating the slate gap through memory alone, he entered the cool stairwell that ascended the mesa. Sudden light stabbed his eyes. He flinched and squinted, recognizing the keep's steward.

Of course, Wylan knows I'm back. Guards, high upon the battlements, would have scouted Raine's approach from miles off and reported his return. Wylan lowered his lantern so that the light no longer blinded Raine.

Two guards occupied the shadows behind the steward, arms crossed and postures sullen. Wylan must've caught them betting dice while on duty again.

"Master Raine," Wylan exclaimed. Kind eyes curved like cashews in a face more wrinkled than a prune. "Thank the Divine you are back. And in good health! You've given us all a terrible fright, especially your father. He will be most anxious to see you."

Raine waved a leaden arm, exhausted. "I'm sure." Because this was Wylan, he mustered a smile. The keep's steward had slipped him many a sweet before supper and always provided Raine with false alibis when his childish misdeeds would have led to a whipping. "To be perfectly honest, Wylan, I am greatly fatigued. All I want is a hot meal and sleep."

Wylan stepped closer and winced. "Add a bath to that list, Young Master. You're riper than Drooger's dung heaps."

Raising an arm, Raine sniffed and gagged. Soapy, boiling water catapulted to the top of his priorities. Wylan drew back, waving a hand before his nose. Raine took no offense. His pungency was borderline toxic.

"Please, go ahead of me." Raine gestured up the steep stairwell. It was customary to walk by ranking order, and Raine was only outstripped by his father. Wylan's thousand-wrinkle stare tightened, immaculate manners rejecting such a breach of etiquette. "That is an order, Wylan." Softening his harsh tone, Raine added, "Please. I don't want to be responsible for killing my father's favorite steward. If you walk in the wake of my stench, you're liable to faint and break your skull on the stairs."

One of the guards snickered. Wylan glanced at them and sighed. Raine knew the steward wouldn't disobey an order with witnesses nearby. "Very well. Perhaps you will regale me with how you came to be so malodorous during our ascent."

Following the bobbing lantern, Raine kept several stairs between himself and Wylan. A necessary buffer, given his reek. This was why he needed to bathe daily. Maybe even *twice* a day. He'd forsaken his ablutions for less than a week and already, his stench was lethal.

Dragons had fire, flowers had poison, and apparently, Raine had the pits of hell itself beneath his arms.

"I made a mistake," he said, addressing Wylan's braided coattails. Far too tired to detail the sorry, sordid mess in its entirety, Raine kept his explanation deliberately vague. "There was something I thought I could do, but I was wrong, and I failed."

His eyes, red-rimmed and sore, remained dry. It was useless, weeping over a dead dream.

Even more pointless to weep for a delusion. A figment. A fantasy. His dream had never been attainable, which meant it had never truly existed. And a thing that was never real couldn't be crushed or crumbled. He just wished someone would tell his tattered spirits that.

Wylan halted and turned. Holding his lantern aloft, he regarded Raine in the flickering stairwell.

"Careful what you call a mistake, Young Master. Sometimes, what seems like failure is the Divine Father's hand altering your course, ensuring you arrive at your proper destiny."

Raine shook his head. "Father says a man makes his own destiny."

What would his future look like now? A quiet life, sequestered at his ancestral home, breeding dragons until he died ...

The vision drained what little energy he had left. While it was the life his father had chosen, it only represented bitter failure to Raine.

"I would not naysay General Arastus. But my own experiences are different." Wylan descended the stairs between them and wrapped an arm around Raine's shoulders. He smelled like mint and sweet basil. Raine crossed his arms and pressed his hands against his armpits, even more self-conscious of his stench. "If a certain avenue does not lead where you wish, that is only because you are meant for a different path. A destiny as unique and exceptional as yourself. And hopefully—if you'll forgive me, Young Master—with a bit more soap."

Impossibly, Raine's lips twitched. "In that, we agree."

They parted ways at the curtain wall's access. Hurrying through the keep's corridors, Raine reached his private quarters without encountering another soul. Which was fortunate, since he would have then been forced to throw himself from the battlements in abject humiliation. It was bad enough Wylan had gotten a whiff of him.

The sitting room was unlit, his father absent. Limbs weakening in relief, Raine darted for his washtub. He wasn't looking forward to the inevitable confrontation with his sire. If he hurried, he could be abed and feigning sleep before his father retired.

Thirty minutes later, Raine was boiling in his bath. Outwardly, he appeared as placid as a potato, buffeted by bergamot-scented bubbles. But his mind was a maelstrom of bewilderment, depression, and a bitterness that seeped like poison through his veins.

So much for following in Father's footsteps. His own heroes had tried to slaughter him. The sheer outrageousness of it was all that prevented him from falling apart.

He had been *so close*. To fulfilling his dream. To proving himself. The chieftains had genuinely accepted him into the guild. Or, they had. Up until they glimpsed his stupid feet. Did the chieftains truly think blanches were cursed? Pale harbingers of ill luck? Had his unblistered soles somehow confirmed it?

The door flew open, cracking against the wall like struck lightning. Raine whipped a startled glance at his father, who blazed with anger.

"You," General Arastus snapped, prowling into the bathing chamber. The door slammed shut so forcefully, Raine marveled that it didn't splinter into toothpicks.

"Me?" he squeaked, scooching away from the iron tub's edge.

Thankfully, it was a luxuriously oversized bath. Raine was out of arm's reach if he stuck to the backside of the washtub, which he did. His father had no special tolerance for boiling water, unlike his son. Raine was safe from his father's ire, at least for a short while.

His father stormed across the room, halting at the rim of the tub. "Where were you? You've been gone for days."

His father's words boomed and echoed in the small chamber, pummeling Raine's sensitive ears like thunderclaps. "I left you a note," he said weakly, sinking lower into the water.

"Oh, yes. You certainly did," Arastus said with scathing brightness.

Reaching into the breast of his olive coat, Arastus produced a sorely abused scrap of parchment.

It was so worn and crinkled, Raine knew his father must have read and re-read his note a hundred times or more. He sank deeper inside the tub, water boiling his chin.

His father smoothed the thin, wrinkled page and read aloud. "Father, I have gone on a spiritual journey. Be sure to stay sharp and spry in my absence. It would devastate me to discover you in a crippling dotage upon my return. While you are advancing in years, I have heard one can abstain from senility with consistent exercise and mental stimulation. Your adoring son, Raine."

Raine offered a sheepish smile. "As it says, I do adore you, father. And Wylan told me it is crucial for middle-aged people to stay active both mentally and physically if they wish to retain a quality of life when they are elderly. It is only my extreme love for you which causes me to say these things."

"It is only my extreme love for you that keeps me from strangling you." His father scowled down at him.

"I'm too old to be whipped," Raine pointed out hurriedly.

Arastus looked ferocious, every inch the general who ruled Chambrin Keep and commanded Valdenia's dragon battalion. His scowl lessened, and he raked his hands over his face.

"I don't have time for this. I must return to the Cavern. The entire keep has been on the lookout for you. My orders were to be notified immediately if there was any news. Wylan got word to me directly, but we have guests that I cannot ignore." General Chambrin's face softened. "I had to see for myself that you were back."

Raine's heart squeezed at the naked affection in his father's eyes and knew his own gaze mirrored that love back. Guilt jabbed him for causing his father such worry.

"I'm sorry, father. I truly did not mean to distress you. What guests did you take to the Cavern?"

The Cavern, where the breeding dragons were kept, was not a social site. It was a maximum-security pen with strict protocols to keep its precious contents safe and sequestered. Raine knew every square inch of Chambrin Keep, as only a spirited boy could, and he had never set foot in the Cavern. It was absolutely forbidden to him.

Typically, forbidding Raine anything guaranteed his fascination and recalcitrance. Yet, the Cavern was a mystery he gladly ignored. The very thought of delving that far below ground put his back up. Besides, they were *breeding* dragons. Which meant they were up to procreation-type activities. Not a sight he cared to see.

Arastus blew out a long breath. "Three of the Nine have come to inspect the Cavern. It has been too long since their last visit, and we have much to cover."

Raine raised to his knees in his bath, water sluicing down his chest. Alarm bells rang in his head. "Eddic, Vanwert, and Tyrus." It wasn't a question and his father's brows rose, either at Raine's grim tone or his uncannily accurate guess.

"They are Chieftains Eddic, Vanwert, and Tyrus, to you," his father corrected reflexively. "How do you know which three are here?"

Fuck. The chieftains possessed the advantage of horseflesh and must have used it.

The main roads, a much more direct route to Chambrin Keep, were used by riders and horse-drawn carts and conveyances. Horses bucked and bolted whenever they scented Raine, so he had kept primarily to the old, meandering trails reserved for foot-travelers. Even sprinting pell-mell across the countryside, he had not beaten them here.

Raine drew a deep breath. "I have a bit of a confession to make."

His father's face grew ashen as he explained all that had taken place.

Arastus tugged at his short, dark locks and groaned. "You have no idea what you've done."

Raine's hackles rose. He probably would not have *done* anything if his father had been more forthright. "I don't understand what the big deal is. My white hair didn't bother them until my feet failed to blister. Does being a blanch and immune to fire make me cursed? Do they think I'm evil?"

"Son, I need you to listen to me carefully and do exactly as I say."

The stark urgency in his father's voice gripped Raine's attention. It was a tone he had never heard before, raising gooseflesh down his arms despite the boiling water. If the situation was dire enough to strike such fear in his father, it was more dire than Raine realized.

He gave a faint nod, and his father continued. "There is not time for me to explain everything. The chieftains will complete their tour of the Cavern with or without me. Then, they will find Olan. Once they discover he was impersonated, the slightest questioning will lead them here."

Raine winced at the truth of it. Locating him as the false Olan would be no hardship. Almost any vague descriptor of his general appearance would point them to Raine. Olan, the treacherous rat, would put two and two together the instant the chieftains confronted him.

"The Cavern is vast, and they are being thorough with this inspection, which should grant you time to get far away before they emerge and search for Olan."

Raine rose from the tub and took the outstretched towel from his father. He dried off haphazardly, then rushed to his bedchamber, his father tight on his heels.

"But why are they here? Do they want me dead that badly? I don't understand *why*," he burst, popping his head through his shirt collar.

He finished dressing while his father rifled through his armoire. Arastus's arm moved with the repetitive strike of an asp as he loaded a haversack with his son's clothes. Raine swallowed a protest—there wasn't time to argue—and waited for his father to speak.

Once his father was satisfied with the amount of spare clothing tucked into the canvas bag, he sat heavily on Raine's goose down bedspread. Raine stood before him, hands fisted at his sides, and resisted the impulse to demand answers. After a beat, his father's large, callused hands encased his shoulders, squeezing. Raine looked into his father's coffee-colored eyes and froze as he spoke.

"Son, you are not evil or a blanch. They know that. But they also know what you really are, and they will kill you for it."

"What I really am?" Raine couldn't believe there was something *this* wrong with him. Something so terrible, it inspired three of the Nine to hunt him like wild game, with a single-minded goal of extermination.

Arastus raked his hand nervously through his hair, skewing it to one side. "I found you," he rasped, voice thick with emotion. "I found you in the Cavern. In the brood room."

"Brood room?" Raine's mind raced. "What do you mean, you *found* me?"

"I mean precisely that. We isolate and drug the dragonesses, then take their eggs once they are laid. The eggs are kept in the brood room until they hatch. The hatchlings imprint on the first life form they meet, and we have a trained staff that raises them through infancy."

"Why can't their parents hatch and raise them?" he asked, skirting the more obvious question. He didn't want to ask about being *found*. Not yet. Not while his knees were putty and his heart smacked his ribs like a fist.

"Because their parents despise us and for good reason. Dragons are intelligent from birth. The hatchlings would pick up on their parents' animosity and regard us with similar disdain. Think about it. We breed them for military use. It would be pointless if the hatchlings refused to cooperate. By having humans raise and nurture them, the war dragons are taught to care for us and be protective. They eagerly train with their human handlers thanks to our current methods."

"O-kay. I guess that makes sense," Raine said dubiously. It didn't. It really didn't. The breeding dragons despised humans? He'd never heard of such a thing. The battle dragons were so devoted, so loyal. He couldn't fathom a single dragon hating people, let alone the entire Cavern.

His father lifted the haversack onto the bed, reminding Raine he was practically being shoved out the door. A criminal on the run. He wasn't going to leave without knowing why. He couldn't. Squaring his shoulders, he met his father's stare head-on. "So, you found me in the egg hatching room?"

"The brood room, yes."

"What, then? My real parents didn't want a blanched kid, but felt too guilty to drown me and left me in a clutch of dragon eggs instead?"

Raine's face crumpled as the implications sank in. Arastus Chambrin might be the father who raised him, but he was not the man who sired him. The thought felt wrong, unreal. Raine wondered if he was trapped in an elaborate nightmare. His father's next words confirmed it.

"Raine, you were not abandoned in the brood room. You hatched there." Raine blinked and his father continued, "You are not human, son. You are a dragon."

"Father, did you forage wild mushrooms again? Or smoke Grover's skunk weed? Whatever you're tripping on, it has addled you. I am clearly a person and not a giant flying lizard." Raine waggled his arms in front of his father's face to emphasize his point. "See? Arms. Fingers. Not talons and wings."

His father offered an indulgent smile and stood from the bed. "I am not addled, you dimwit. You are indeed a dragon. And you are my son."

General Arastus crushed Raine to his chest, squeezing until Raine's lungs constricted. His eyes stung, the tenderness of his father's hold peeling back his defenses and pushing emotions to the surface.

"Never doubt it," his father whispered, pulling away slightly to meet his gaze. "You are the child of my heart, and I could not love you more."

Unable to speak through the knot in his throat, Raine nodded.

All his love was in his eyes, glimmering like fresh raindrops as he held his father's stare. A sudden pounding on their entry door shattered the moment.

Raine startled like a hapless deer, but his father jolted into action. Snatching the overstuffed haversack from the bed, Arastus grasped Raine's arm with his free hand and dragged him to the bathing room. Raine frowned as his father shoved the haversack into his arms.

Arastus spoke in a hushed, urgent tone. "I slipped some coins into the main pouch beneath your shirts. Enough silvans to get you by until you reach Sinopel. As soon as you get outside, run as far and fast as you can. The second you can rest, there's a bottle of ink inside your bag."

Raine sputtered a protest, knowing precisely where his father was going with this. There was no way in hell he was smearing ink all over his treasured mane.

"Use it," his father snapped, cutting him off. "Damn it, Raine, they will be looking for you. They have eyes everywhere. Your hair gives you away for miles. Tell me you'll do as I say."

Raine huffed a breath but agreed at his father's insistence. Arastus gave a terse nod. "Good. Stay off the main roads and trust no one.

If you hear horses or men, hide. No matter what. Don't stay at any inns. Don't use your name."

Whoever was in the hallway banged on their door once more. Each *boom* echoed like cannon fire and Raine feared they were using a battering ram. His father spoke louder so Raine could hear him over the insistent blows.

"There is a jewelry shop. Jaska's. Go there and find the owner. Talk to him and no other. There's so much I haven't told you. Son, it is crucial you do not trust the guild. They are not your allies."

A torrent of thoughts and confusion muddled Raine's mind, tying his tongue. Before he could react, his father shoved him to the stone floor.

"Take the chimney to the roof." His father gestured at the large space beneath the tub, where Raine's bath fire had burned to embers.

The tub was specially designed so Raine could indulge in the merrily boiling water he loved so much. Fire necessitated a chimney. The back part of the tub was tucked into an enormous hearth. The only way to access the flute was by climbing under or over the washtub. Under was the better option if he didn't want to get sopping wet, considering there was no time to drain the tub.

With his eyes, he measured the gap between the dying fire and the flute opening, ensuring he wouldn't catch his clothes on fire as he crawled through. His pulse drummed his ears, louder than the forceful blows against their entry door, and he hesitated.

Looking up at his father helplessly, he asked, "What about you?"

Would the chieftains punish his father for raising a "dragon" as his son? Not that Raine was a dragon. He wasn't. It was impossible. But although he didn't believe it, he was certain his father did. Perhaps the chieftains did, too.

"I must remain. I will be fine. I have a reputation since my guild days for defending the downtrodden. I will play on that; tell them I thought I was taking pity on a blanched child."

The sound of wood splintering reached them. "Go, now," his father hissed, shedding his coat.

Raine could not remain to learn more of his father's plan. He squirmed beneath the tub, crawling on his elbows and chest, and managed to skirt the fire with nary a singed sleeve. Upon reaching the flute, he deftly pulled himself up and out of sight before another crash echoed from the sitting room, their door caving to the intruders.

He was tempted to loiter in the chimney, out of sight, but acrid smoke stung his eyes and burned his lungs. Silently, Raine scurried up the chimney. His unnatural strength and dexterity made the climb more novelty than challenge. Emerging through the cap, he gulped crisp, clean air for several long minutes.

The midnight sky was clear and glowed with a glutted moon. Unlucky, but not the worst of obstacles. Raine padded across the slate roof tiles with slow, cautious steps, seeking the best angle to descend. He elected a steep slope that would dump him beneath a thatch of trees, where the laundresses liked to hang-dry the wash.

He descended effortlessly down the keep wall, using window ledges as footholds. Wind whispered through the treetops, an ominous rustling that made him glance up. No one was there. All else was quiet. Not an owl or cricket to be heard, as if the very night looked on with bated breath.

Beneath the deeper shadows of the small canopy, feet firmly upon the ground, he inspected his braid and found his white locks coated in chimney soot. *Thank the Divine.* Stealth was a real bitch to pull off with glowing white hair. Even still, part of him pouted at having his beloved strands matted with filth.

Sentries studded the battlements, their gazes fixed outward for approaching threats. Although Valdenia was at peace, Gargantha's invasion had left scars spanning multiple generations. The keep's scrupulous guard schedule was a remnant of wartime. The interior guards were his father's men, but the sentries atop the curtain wall worked directly for the Nine—which meant Raine would have to take particular care in avoiding them.

He had lived in the keep his whole life, so it was nothing for him to spot the sentries as he darted through the shadows and huddled against the curtilage. On the opposite side of the curtain wall, a forbidding cliff edge plunged. Below, dense woodland butted against the escarpment.

He needed the nearby sentries to clear out. Thinking quickly, Raine ducked behind a broad oak and mimicked the keening grunt of a Garganthan moose bull in rut.

A perpetual mystery of Chambrin Keep was the random appearance of Garganthan moose on the property. While the moose were a common enough sight throughout Valdenia, they couldn't climb cliffs. But the conundrum was too deliciously meaty to perturb the men atop the fortified mesa. They were as giddy as farmers' daughters on courting day whenever one appeared.

Excited whispers reached Raine's ears. Raine ceased grunting and shook his head. If a moose was anywhere near those loud-mouths, it'd take off at full bore from their racket.

He rounded two more trees and circled back to the inner curtain. Moonlight revealed the abandoned post of a sentry. Raine spied two shadowy figures further down the battlements. They were crouched together, both intent upon the oak tree he abandoned.

Raine grinned as he raced toward the now unguarded section of curtain wall. He didn't require a ladder or convenient tree branches to make the climb.

Instead, inhumanly powerful haunches propelled him a dozen feet into the air. Hands as clever as a racoon's dug into brick and clung. He positioned himself and sprang upwards. The motion carried him over the battlements, and he sailed like an arrow, diving hundreds of feet to the dark woodland below.

It was blacker than pitch beneath the summer-thick canopy. He hit the ground running and sent a fervent prayer to the Divine Father he wasn't about to do the chieftains' job for them by tripping on a tree root and breaking his neck before sunrise.

CHAPTER SIX

R aine blinked blearily at the too-bright sun, brows puckering. For several long seconds, he couldn't fathom why he was lying in a millet field. High, reedy stalks curled above him, tipped with feathery bran clusters. Observing their indolent sway in the mild breeze, he groaned as events of the last few days barreled through his oblivion. *That's right. I'm on the run for my life from my childhood heroes. No big deal.*

He hobbled to his feet like reanimated roadkill. Everything hurt. He had run through the night and all of the next day before collapsing. His haversack had served as a decent pillow despite its coarse cloth, and he tugged the strap over his shoulder before limping toward the trail.

As Raine trudged down the dirt path, the musical rush of a stream grew louder. Rounding a bend where the trail skirted a thicket, he was met with a small footbridge. A clear brook babbled underneath. With a sigh, he stepped off the pathway and rolled his shoulder, depositing his haversack next to the stream.

Raine dug into the bag, his first time inspecting its contents. He whooped with delight, startling a pair of nesting sparrowhawks into flight, as he discovered the items tucked below his clothes.

A hairbrush, a knife, some silvans, and a map. Raine ached to use his brush at once. But the onerous task of dying his hair loomed like a storm cloud, halting him. Not wishing to get ink all over his hairbrush, he reluctantly packed the precious instrument away, along with the money and knife.

The ink, corked tightly in a clear glass vial, was sinister. He tilted the bottle in the sunlight and his gut clenched at the awfulness of it. The ink would be sticky and dry out his hair. It would also stain his lovely, iridescent locks, converting them into a flat darkness. Like a sky without stars.

He unstoppered the vial and shuddered as a drop of black smudged his thumb. Balancing the ink in one hand, he dunked his other hand into the cold stream to rinse the ink off his thumb.

After a minute of vigorous scrubbing, he pulled his hand from the stream and surveyed the digit. His skin was pinkish and glistening from the brisk water, but that damnable smudge clung insidiously.

Raine shuddered anew as he pictured the ink on his hair. What if it never rinsed away and his hair forever lost its unique hue and radiance?

As he leaned over the water, he caught sight of his reflection, the dull dark color of his hair. Recoiling, he threw his hand over his head and frantically patted it.

Then relaxed, recalling his sooty escape through a smoking chimney. Bending forward once more, Raine inspected his hair. It was plenty dark with the soot. He didn't need to dye it with ink.

His father had demanded he dye it, but his father hadn't accounted for the soot. It wasn't a perfect cover. Bits of white were detectable. But it was altogether too preferable to dousing his head with nefarious black goop. Raine stoppered the ink, then tucked it into a side pouch where it couldn't ruin his belongings if it leaked.

The map was an absolute treasure. Due to his abrupt, unexpected departure from home, Raine had anticipated charting stars to reach Sinopel. In his youth, he had enjoyed learning astronomy from Instructor Brenk, a gangly man with lank hair and a weak chin.

Thanks to his childhood tutor, Raine knew which stars to follow to reach Sinopel. It was daytime now, no helpful stars in sight, but Raine also knew heading in a general southwestern direction would lead him toward the city.

Stars and a good sense of direction would not enable Raine to avoid the main roadways, however. Gently unfurling the map, he placed fist-sized rocks upon its corners to keep the parchment flat on the ground for his perusal.

The main roads, identifiable by their width and cobbling, were solid lines on the map. The backroads, consisting of narrow dirt paths, showed up as dotted lines. Mostly used by local traffic, they were just as far-reaching and interconnected as the main roads. Being lesser trafficked—with meandering routes that dug through woods and fields—there would be plenty of hiding places for Raine if he detected oncoming travelers.

Raine studied the map thoroughly, tracing and retracing what he thought was the most ideal route. He rolled up the map scroll and tucked it carefully into his bag, then reconvened his journey to Sinopel, one of the nine cities of Valdenia.

Sinopel was home to nearly twenty thousand souls, according to Brenk. Raine couldn't fathom that number of people or what a city hosting them might look like. Anxious excitement electrified his sore limbs, and he picked up his pace.

The weather was cool but fair. The only souls he spied were Guardians in lookouts, otherwise known as sky watchers. Everyone knew of them. They were the most visible Guardians of Vale. Stationed all throughout the country in rickety, elevated platforms, the sky watchers surveyed the land.

At the first sign of trouble—be it fire, invasion, or some other disaster—each platform was equipped with a huge signaling torch. Lighting one would summon the nearest sky watchers: multiple teams of Guardians who were prepared to provide whatever assistance was required to safeguard Valdenia and its citizens.

One of the sky watchers kept her gaze upward and outward. The two others Raine passed glanced his way and offered a pleasant wave. He returned the gestures with an ounce of misgiving. His father's warning rang in his ears. *Do not trust the guild. They are not your allies.*

It was, to be frank, a mindfuck of epic proportions. What the hell did his father mean, *do not trust the guild*? His father was the most famous, decorated master the guild had ever produced. Arastus Chambrin was the Wolf of the Vale. Their country's fiercest protector.

If Raine couldn't trust the guild, whose sole purpose was safeguarding Valdenia, what did that make him? An enemy? It made no sense. Even less sense than Raine being a damned dragon.

Father is mistaken. Raine had ruminated upon his father's revelation for the past two days and was certain it was hogwash.

Most likely, his birth mother or father worked in the brood room and abandoned him there, eschewing the shame and scorn of producing a blanched offspring.

This explanation still didn't satisfy the Nine's blatant assassination attempt after he had completed the guild exams. What on earth made him their enemy? Whether they believed him a dragon or not, nothing justified their gross hostility.

On the third morning of Raine's travels, the unpaved trail emptied into the main, cobbled roadway leading to Sinopel. Raine had no choice but to take it for the last stretch of his journey. It was quite early, only an hour after sunrise, and he was surprised at how crowded the main strip was.

It was jarring to see so many people after days of isolation. They all walked in the same direction, all headed to Sinopel. Women carried sacks of flour and bolts of cloth. A man balanced a basket of brown, speckled trout over his head, a fishing rod slung over his back. Merchant carts and farmers' wagons, drawn by an array of horses and donkeys, congested the street's center. Raine kept to the furthest edge of the road, so as not to agitate the creatures.

As he progressed, elevated walking paths lined either side of the thoroughfare, dividing foot traffic from wheels and hoofs. It was Raine's first time seeing such a thing and he was amazed at the cleverness of it.

Soon after the sidewalks appeared, Sinopel's juniper gates grew in the distance. The crowd thickened to a crush as a multitude of small trails converged outside the city. Hundreds of people milled about. Raine felt like an ant in an anthill, unremarkable and safe as he threaded through the masses, passing through the gates without issue.

Sinopel's architecture was simple but striking: straight lines fashioned of wood painted varying shades of green, so that entire streets seemed lined with verdant foliage instead of buildings. Raine struggled not to gawk as he meandered down the walkways, surveying pubs, inns, and a dizzying array of shops.

He paused at an enormous window revealing intricate furniture pieces. Back home, people crafted their own sofas and tables with wood, leather, and worn tools. In Sinopel, one could visit this shop and simply buy what they liked. Raine admired a set of armchairs, upholstered in pea green fabric with beaded leaves. They were gorgeous, but then his attention was captured by a clock shop. Then a dollmaker.

People looked at him askance, and he felt self-conscious at the image he made. Less a country bumpkin and more a wild, homeless vagrant. His pale tunic was filthy from days of travel. His hair was a matted snarl of greasy black, as he refused to run his brush through it while it was coated in grime.

Worst of all, he *smelled*. His father had not tossed a lick of soap, shampoo, or scented oil into his bag, items Raine would've never left without. He sighed. He and his father had always held different versions of what constituted necessities.

Raine could not begin to speculate how many hours he stared through windows. He'd originally moved as one with a massive throng of pedestrians. As the sun slung low on the horizon, his eyes swept the rapidly emptying streets. He needed to find that jewelry shop before they closed for the day.

Standing on a street corner in the center of Sinopel's market square, Raine spun a hopeless circle. He hadn't encountered any store called Jaska's.

Stragglers peppered the sidewalks, people heading this way or that. Raine approached a middle-aged woman in a blue dress patterned with polka dots of a deeper hue. She was the closest to him and walking his direction.

"Good afternoon, ma'am. Do you know where Jaska's jewelry shop is?"

The woman stopped short and drew her purse up under her arm. Raine took no offense, aware he resembled a vagabond criminal.

"It's off the beaten path, several blocks from the main strip." She gave him brief but simple directions.

He smiled, thanking her, then followed her instructions carefully, locating the establishment after half an hour of hasty walking. Jaska's was a narrow shop with pinched windows. Most shops possessed wide windows, with glass constituting as much of their storefronts as possible. Raine guessed it was to lure prospective customers with teasing glimpses of the wares within. Jaska's was closed off and uninviting, by comparison.

A tremor shook Raine's hand as he reached for the knob. He had no clue who the owner of this store was, knew nothing about them except that his father had directed him here. Raine trusted his father implicitly, but that trust did not necessarily extend to his father's mysterious contacts. He only had to recall the chieftains' behavior to be leery of the shop owner.

But Raine had nowhere else to go. That, and he wanted to be where his father could find him.

He felt like an intruder as he stepped into the shop. It was as dark and private as a bedchamber.

Beeswax candles burned throughout the space, but they were a poor substitute for natural light or a hearth. Shelves lined the walls from floor to ceiling, encasing a library of gems and jewelry. Each shelf was piled with rings, brooches, bracelets, and more. There were chains and necklaces and ornate treasure boxes.

A counter sat in the darkest corner of the shop. A man was positioned on a low-seated stool behind it. Raine approached the shopkeeper, who held a small, silver instrument in his hand and was delicately setting a precious red stone into a striated gold ring.

"Good afternoon," Raine said politely, trying not to startle the man who appeared lost in his craft.

The shopkeeper's hand went still as he looked up. His eyes were as green as Oxlip kale. Raine gasped as they focused on him.

Hundreds of years ago, foreign merchants and travelers had been welcomed by the nine tribes. Some of those foreigners never left, choosing to settle down in Valdenia permanently. While brown hair and eyes were Valdenia's native coloring, remnants of the foreigners carried through occasionally, like with the shopkeeper's eyes.

Silence dragged for several heartbeats. Until Raine decided the man would not be offering a return greeting.

He shuffled nervously. "Is the owner of this store available?"

There was a closed door behind the man, which customers could not access without vaulting the counter. Raine guessed it contained the owner's private office or workshop. It might also contain the owner.

"What do you want?" the shopkeeper asked. His voice was rough with impatience.

Raine stiffened, then diligently reminded himself he was a bedraggled and smelly stranger in a shop filled with expensive things. The shopkeeper's brusque demeanor was downright cheery, considering.

"I was told to seek the owner of this store by my father. There is an urgent matter I must discuss with him."

The man sat his dainty tongs and the etched ring to the side with a small clink. Then, he lifted the counter. It bent straight up, swinging on a hidden hinge. "Come on, then."

Raine stepped through the opening. The man leveled the countertop before leading him through the back room. An office. The shopkeeper positioned himself behind the desk, sitting in a plush chair patterned with brushstrokes of crimson against deepest black. Raine admired the fabric and design of the chair, still awed by Sinopel's ornamentation of utilitarian objects.

Unlike the main shop, the office was well-lit by lamps. The man had short, dark hair and strong features set in a face too sharp to be handsome. Raine sat in the closest chair, an unpadded wooden seat, and silver eyes locked with green. Either the shopkeeper was also the owner, or he was playing at it.

"I am Jaska, current owner of Jaska's Jewelry. I do not know you. Who are you and who is your father?" His curt tone was tinged with suspicion.

Raine swept his gaze over the stark office. The desk was bare. The walls were bare. Jaska was bizarrely without frills considering he sold expensive luxury goods that were nothing but frills and frosting. He eyed Raine as though he were a threat, dark green eyes steady on his face.

Raine hesitated, causing Jaska's eyes to narrow. "My father's name is Arastus," he said slowly, offering his father's first name to see if that sparked recognition in the standoffish jeweler. "I am Raine."

"I am familiar with neither of you. I fail to see how you could have an urgent matter which pertains to me, given we are strangers." Jaska leaned back in his seat, hands falling to his lap beneath the desk.

Raine fidgeted in his chair, not sure how to proceed. Half of him wanted to leave without further comment, but trust in his father compelled him to remain. He drew a breath, debating how much to share.

"The urgent matter is that I am wanted by the Nine. For something outside my control. My father is not in a position to help me, so he bade me to come here. I had presumed an acquaintanceship between the two of you, but I can see I was mistaken."

As much as Raine adored his father, he was going to kick his ass the next time he saw him. Regardless of how pressed for time they had been at their parting, the man could have found a way to slip in that Jaska had no fucking clue who either of them was. *Why the hell did Father send me here?*

Jaska took a moment to digest his words and said, "There are several jewelers in Sinopel. Did your father name mine specifically?"

"Yes," Raine said, then frowned, wondering if that was the issue. Perhaps his father misremembered the jeweler's name. Three jewelers occupied the main city square alone.

Jaska picked up on Raine's doubts, shifting forward and regarding him unblinkingly. "Why are you so sure my shop is the right one?"

Raine admired Jaska's midnight green eyes. Eyes so purely green, he had never seen their equivalent.

Wait. Yes, he had. Realization dawned as bright and vivid as a new day, and he almost smacked himself for ever attributing Jaska's irises to a foreign ancestry.

"Because I know your eyes. I've seen their likeness. Only they did not belong to a human."

Dazzling green war dragons flitted through his mind's eye. Raine was a blockhead for not putting it together sooner. His father must have happened upon Jaska's in the past and known immediately what the shopkeeper's secret was.

In a blur of motion, Raine was shoved from his chair and pinned to the wall, cold metal biting his neck from a milk-white dagger Jaska produced from seemingly nowhere. Raine swallowed, feeling a prick as the blade cut deeper when his throat bobbed.

Nobody had ever gotten the jump on him before. Raine was fast. Jaska was faster. The thought perturbed him more than the immediate threat to his life.

The man didn't loosen his arm, and the knife continued pressing into his flesh. Raine fought to stay utterly still, unable to speak without aiding in the cutting of his own throat.

Jaska stared hard into his eyes before trailing over his face, spying the pieces of cream white hair protruding from his sooty braid. A drop of blood beaded down his neck. Jaska leaned forward. Raine held his breath as the man *licked* him. Jaska's tongue was hot and wet, right on his pulse where the blood dripped.

The knife pulled away and Jaska released him, stepping back and regarding him as if *he* was the odd one.

"Where I come from, you buy a man dinner first." Raine rubbed his neck, wiping away saliva and blood. "Is there a reason you attacked me like a psychopath?"

Jaska held the knife loose at his side. "You are one of us," he said accusingly, which Raine thought was a bit ironic considering his only offense was sharing something in common with the man. "How did your father know where to find me? What is your family name? Is this a trap?"

That last question was laced with so much menace, Raine went to take a step backwards and bumped into the wall he'd been so recently thrown against.

"A trap for who, you? I'm being hunted down like a fucking criminal by the Nine for committing virtually zero crimes." Which was technically untrue. He was pretty sure it was a serious offense to impersonate a candidate of the guild and take the entrance exams in their stead, but that wasn't really the point. "If we are people of a similar circumstance, are you going to help me in the spirit of brotherhood or some shit, or am I on my own?"

Jaska tucked his odd, white blade into his boot and scowled. "It is not up to me. You can tell your story to the elder. She can decide what to do with you."

Raine waited as Jaska extinguished the lamps and candles, then positioned a "Closed" sign in a small window. Jaska paused with his hand around the doorknob and met Raine's gaze.

"If you try to run, I will kill you."

Raine swallowed his automatic retort. *I'd like to see you try.*

If being a dragon was a death sentence, Jaska couldn't risk Raine escaping with the knowledge. Besides—Raine's mind flashed back to the knife at his throat—for the first time in his life, he didn't know if it was a fight he'd win.

CHAPTER SEVEN

S inopel was a mind-boggling maze of streets and alleyways. Raine trailed behind Jaska as early evening ticked into twilight. *Left. Left. Right. Left. Right. Round-a-bout?* That was new. *Left.*

The city's streets constricted as they moved deeper into its center. Buildings grew smaller, the shops fewer, until they passed through a singularly residential district with no shops or public buildings nearby. The houses were small, but in good repair, and made of wood. In the countryside, most homes were built from stone, but he could see how this massive city would need to draw upon other resources to house its thousands of residents.

They didn't speak, which was fine by Raine. After another turn caused them to double-back on their progress, he wondered if Jaska was trying to confuse him by picking a circuitous path he couldn't hope to retrace. If so, the surly jeweler succeeded. The enormity of Sinopel overwhelmed Raine. He had ceased attempting to memorize their route after the first few turns.

Jaska led him to a nondescript house on a narrow street lined with similar-looking structures, all painted meadow green. Raine imagined frequent confusion as people mistook their neighbors' houses for their own, so alike they appeared. The thought made him homesick. No two houses were the same where he came from, the way it ought to be.

Jaska opened the door, ushering him into a foyer. A round chandelier hung high overhead. The walls were decorated with thousands of tiny painted flowers. Raine fingered the wall to their right, marveling at the display, and realized the flowers were not painted. Well, not on the walls themselves. They were covered in some sort of bumpy, patterned paper.

Blatantly fascinated, he inspected the intricate, perfectly repeating design more closely. It was gorgeous and clever. The more he stared, the more he noticed. The way pink faded to blue on every third flower, or how all the white ones had wispy leaves.

Jaska cleared his throat. Raine flushed, dropping his hand. He followed the jeweler into a spacious dining room. The table was a glossy, cherrywood oval with flowering vines carved around its edges.

The residents of Sinopel treated everything like art. It was enchanting. Back home, the Divine Father was the artist, painting the world with natural beauty. Things like walls and tables were plain and functional. They didn't have pretty carvings or delicately curved table legs and other fripperies that existed purely for pleasure.

A woman entered the room while speaking. "You're home earlier than—whoa! Who are you?"

She halted as she noticed Raine, and they observed each other briefly. Her hair was vividly red, the color of a lover's rose. She was as pale as plaster, as though her skin had never felt sunlight. Her eyes widened in surprise. They shone like garnets. She looked young, around his age. Probably not the elder Jaska had referenced earlier, then. Her brown dress had long sleeves and a modest bodice. One fair hand clutched at her breast, an unconscious motion done as she'd glimpsed him.

"Aly, please gather everyone and ask them to meet us here at once, including Mother," Jaska said.

Her porcelain features creased with concern. She nodded and left, hiking her skirts to hasten her stride as she scampered from view. Jaska settled into a chair facing Raine. Waving an arm, he indicated for Raine to join him. The table was lavishly sized for a single family, fitting twelve identical cherrywood chairs. Grooved etchings brushed his fingertips as he pulled a chair. Their high backs were carved with the same vines as the table edge.

Aly returned with four others in tow. She sat at the end of the oblong table while the others filed opposite Raine, which left him alone on his side of the table. A woman with blue hair took the seat directly across from him.

She was breathtaking, her exquisite features a match for his own. He tried not to stare, but her perfection was too striking. It pulled his gaze like a magnet. Staring into her eyes was like falling through the sky. He gripped the sides of his chair to steady himself.

"My name is Evin," she said, her voice sounding both musical and ancient. The fine hairs on his arms rose as she spoke. Raine felt as though he was being addressed by a goddess or some other eternal, ageless being.

"On my right is Lukor, then Jaska," Evin said, indicating as she spoke. "To my left is Savere, then Oka. Aly is at the end. Might we learn your name and the circumstances which bring you to our den?"

"My name is Raine and the reason I'm here is ... complicated."

"Uncomplicate it," the man beside her, Lukor, growled, fists smacking the table. His plum-colored irises contracted with an ugly emotion and his hair, deepest purple, was tied back in a severe knot.

"Lukor," Evin said mildly, and he flushed as though she chided him. He murmured a response too soft for Raine to hear, then fell silent. A half dozen sets of gemstone eyes trained on Raine expectantly.

He swallowed. Then began detailing the events which brought him to Sinopel, starting with his impersonation of Olan at the guild's entrance exam.

Nobody interrupted him. They listened with rapt curiosity except for Lukor, who glared belligerently the entire time. Raine resisted the urge to snap at him—the guy clearly had issues—choosing instead to focus on his more welcoming audience.

"Your father did not dissemble, youngling. You are a dragon, through and through," Evin said as Raine completed his tale.

His doubts about his dragon status must have seeped into his story. Even surrounded by humanoid versions of the lustrously hued dragons he'd been raised around, Raine could scarcely grasp this new reality.

The beauteous Evin was evidently in charge of their group. Her face was unmarred by time, yet Raine had no difficulty accepting her status as "elder". She was not ancient like a wizened crone. She was ancient like the mountains and forests.

"I know my father believes his words," Raine said slowly. "I can tell you guys believe it, too. But I'm familiar with dragons. They are massive creatures with wings and scales. Why does everyone keep saying we're the same as them?"

Evin smiled. The expression warmed him like a large mug of hot chocolate, sinking through his chest and soothing him to the tips of his toes.

"I can answer your question with a bit of dragon history. Do you know how dragons came to be, youngling?"

Raine shook his head mutely, and Evin nodded as though expecting such. "A great, slumbering dragon rests in the heart of the earth. We know her as the Dreaming Mother. The Dreaming Mother, being thusly confined, creates entire worlds within her sleep to pass the time. Her dreams are not like mortal dreams. They contain the power of true creation. And one day, a curious creature slipped out of her dream and into reality. That was Myrrah, the first dragon."

She paused to clear her throat and Jaska stood. "I will get you some water, Mother." Evin graced him with her warmth-inducing smile, thanking him before she faced Raine to continue.

"Myrrah was a singular creature, and while she loved this world, she was incredibly lonely. After years of seeing others find love and create families, Myrrah yearned to experience the same. One day, she noticed a human caught in a powerful river current. She flew down and saved him from drowning. They became friends. Then, they fell in love."

Jaska returned with a glass of water and handed it to Evin, who thanked him once again and took a long swallow. As she resumed, the other dragons listened as raptly as Raine, though this could not be their first time hearing this tale.

"The human, Darrok, prayed incessantly to the Divine Father for a solution, that he may be with his love. Myrrah prayed likewise to the Dreaming Mother. The Father and Mother met to discuss the predicament of their beloved children. The Mother could not make

Myrrah human. The Father could not make Darrok a dragon. But the pleas of the mortal lovers affected them deeply, so the Father gifted Myrrah a human form, as humans are his craft. The Mother gifted Darrok a dragon form, as dragons are her creation.

"The Mother and Father's magics cannot overpower each other, so Myrrah and Darrock retained use of their dual forms all their lives. They were dragon and human combined. Their offspring were similarly gifted and so it continues. Dragons are, and have always been, creatures of two forms," Evin finished.

Though her story was told in the fashion of old lore, Raine felt the truth of the tale and believed it must have happened exactly as Evin said. But wait. "Does that mean I have a dragon form?"

"Oh, youngling. You absolutely possess a dragon form. As do we all." She motioned her hands to encompass the table. Raine's head spun at the fantastical turn his life had taken.

"We can continue this conversation over supper," one of the green dragons said. Oka? He stood, mallard green hair brushing his shoulders, and left the room. Aly and Jaska scooted their chairs and followed closely behind.

"Where do I go from here?" Raine asked, cursing the vulnerability of his position. The uncertainty.

He had successfully located the secret dragon family his father meant for him to find, but they owed him nothing. Indeed, they might not be able to aid him if they wanted to.

His question incited an eruption from Lukor, who had apparently reached his breaking point.

"You can go hang yourself. You are trash," he spat, chair toppling as he stood. Looming over the table, his lips curled back in a sneer. "You are no better than the pestilent humans you flee from. You are a pig. Arastus Chambrin is a pig. And everyone who serves in that miserable, hellish fortress is swine and filth and unworthy of life."

Evin stood and faced Lukor, her expression serene though her eyes were blue flames. "Lukor, you are dismissed."

Lukor trembled, searing hatred warping his features while looking daggers at Raine. The male's vehemence shocked him, but shock yielded to icy rage as he held Lukor's stare. The tenuousness of his circumstances would not prevent him from decking this prick if Lukor uttered one more insult about his father.

Lukor's lips parted but no words came. The purple dragon's mouth audibly snapped shut and he stalked from the room.

Jaska, Oka, and Aly filed in bearing large trays of meat on the heels of Lukor's retreat. Aly gave him a tentative smile beneath her thick lashes. Prior to meeting her, Raine would have imagined red eyes on a woman's face as ghoulish. On her, they were darkly beautiful, like the brilliance of a poisonous frog's skin.

Pewter platters were spaced across the table, and Oka pulled wooden plates and flatware from an elegant sideboard. Tiny vines carved along its edges declared it a matching set to the table and chairs.

"I apologize for Lukor's outburst," Evin said as everyone served themselves.

Raine's stomach twisted at the food. He had not eaten since sunrise, polishing off the pears he'd plucked from a roadside orchard. But the dragons' meal was raw and wet with blood. The others filled their plates without hesitation, lending the impression this was a typical meal in their home.

Raised not be rude, he placed two small slivers of the raw, bloody meat on his plate but made no move for his knife and fork.

"His feelings about me and my father are very strong for a complete stranger," Raine observed, not hiding the question in his voice. In Lukor's absence, Raine's offense had relinquished to curiosity.

Savere, who had yet to speak in Raine's presence, addressed him. "Lukor holds no affection for Chambrin Keep or any of its human residents. I believe the best manner for us to proceed is with absolute honesty between each other. And in the spirit of that honesty, Lukor is not alone in his feelings."

Oka *hnn'd* through a too-large mouthful of raw meat and waved his hand to interject. After a painful looking swallow that made Aly wince, he said, "Wait a minute. You're going to give Raine the wrong idea. The thing is, our fellow dragons are being held prisoner at Chambrin Keep, suffering the Dreaming Mother only knows what torture."

Savere leaned back in his chair. "Not to mention, the dragons who evaded imprisonment at Chambrin have been hunted to extinction by the Nine these last two centuries. We're all that's left. Our numbers were a thousand strong before the massacre. Less than one hundred survived and escaped."

Jaska's mouth pressed into a grim line. "The reason I was so suspicious of you is because the Nine are eager to eliminate any remaining wild dragons. They formed their hunters' guild and seek our kind mercilessly. I thought you could be an evolution of their tactics to flush us out."

Raine frowned. "Hunters' guild? Do you mean the Guardians of Vale?"

Several snorts sounded around the table. "They termed it that," Jaska replied, "but we don't call them guardians. To us, they are hunters."

Oka nodded emphatically. "The Nine use their hunters for all sorts of things. They act as spies, assassins, watch dogs. You name it. We don't care about the details of their corrupt human activities. All that matters is, one of their primary objectives is to find and eliminate rogue dragons."

"That would be us," Aly said.

The atmosphere of the room darkened as Savere added, "The guild is at war with us. And they're winning. There used to be an underground thunder in all nine cities, consisting of the dragons who evaded capture after the massacre. Now, we're the last thunder remaining."

Raine's mind raced as he tried to absorb everything. "A thunder is a dragon family?"

"Yes and no," Evin answered, using a piece of meat to mop the blood on her plate, closing her pink lips delicately around the morsel. "A thunder is traditionally grand-dragons and their immediate family. Our population was decimated two centuries ago. Humans slaughtered most of us and stole the rest. In the aftermath, we fashioned our thunders from the survivors."

And now, these dragons were the sole survivors of those survivors.

Raine knew about the wild dragons of old. Everyone did. They'd been a scourge and constant threat. The original Nine had contained them with the help of elite warriors from every tribe. Those warriors had become the first Guardians of Vale.

But he hadn't known how bloody it was, had never learned of an all-out massacre. Lukor's grudge began to make sense. From the purple dragon's perspective, Raine was aiding and abetting atrocities against their kind. He observed the downcast eyes of the dragons across from him, each lost in memories horrible beyond comprehension. Guilt gouged his chest.

"The people of Valdenia are ignorant of your plight," he said gently. "The public isn't aware any wild dragons remain. They are taught the dragons were feral and dangerous, a plague upon the land and its people a long time ago."

He couldn't bring himself to say the rest. That capturing the dragons and breeding them in the Cavern was considered a mercy. That the Nine were lauded for their clemency and cleverness. Because the next time Gargantha or any other northern territory tried to seize Valdenia's riches for their own, the invaders would be met with battle-ready dragons and an elite guild. The people of Valdenia couldn't be more proud of the Nine's accomplishments.

As the son and heir of the illustrious Chambrins—the family blessed with the opportunity to breed and train dragons for Valdenia—Raine had counted himself amongst the proudest. Mere weeks ago, at that.

His current shame eclipsed all else. It suffocated him. Raine had been *proud*. Of something abominable. What did that make him? What did that make his father? His father, who *knew*. Raine's heart flinched from the pain, and he forced his mind back to the present. The dragons were as stiff and still as statues.

"I never questioned it," Raine admitted. "I certainly didn't know dragons possess human reason and intelligence. Hell, human *forms*, even."

"We believe you," Aly assured him. Her crimson locks, falling to her waist, were fluid around her shoulders as she leaned forward, bracing her elbows on the table. "From what you've said, Arastus Chambrin raised you as his son, not as a prison ward or any role that's harmed our kind directly. Nobody here blames you for anything." Her garnet eyes were earnest and kind.

"Except Lukor," Oka pointed out with a crooked grin. His green eyes crinkled, shaped like the leaves of an apple tree.

Aly hissed, "Oka."

"Well, it's true." Oka raised his hands defensively.

Evin stood and offered a smile to the room. "Speaking of which, I am going to go check on Lukor. Aly, please show Raine to a guest room when you're finished here." Aly agreed and Evin looked at Raine. "You are welcome to stay with us. We may have been poor at showing it, but we are overjoyed at welcoming a new member to our thunder. We'll talk more tomorrow. There remains much to discuss."

It was like having a boulder rolled off his back, so profound was Raine's relief at their acceptance and welcome. He deserved neither.

"Thank you," he said, rough with emotion.

Upon Evin's departure, Oka abandoned all pretenses of table manners. Using both hands, he shoveled so much raw meat into his mouth that he couldn't close his lips. Blood and spit dribbled down his chin.

"Gross." Aly mimed a gag. "Chew your food, freak."

In response, Oka crammed another piece of meat into his mouth. He leaned forward and gnashed the meat inches from Aly's face, taunting her. Seconds later, he made a strangled sound and fell back in his seat. His neck veins bulged as he pounded his chest.

"You going to help him?" Jaska asked, addressing the green dragon next to Oka.

Savere's placid features didn't shift as he surveyed Oka's purpling complexion. "If I do, how will he learn?"

Contrary to his dispassionate words, Savere stood and moved behind Oka. Wrapping his arms around Oka's waist, he cupped his fists and positioned them below the choking dragon's ribcage. He applied three rapid upward thrusts and a wad of raw, mangled steak ejected from Oka's mouth. It landed on the table in a wet, glistening mound.

"Thanks," Oka rasped.

Massaging his throat with one hand, Oka reached for his half-masticated meat wad with the other and popped it back into his mouth. A chorus of disgusted exclamations erupted, Raine's among them. His stomach rebelled as Oka moaned, chewing harder.

"You're a savage." Aly snagged his plate with a finger and dragged it across the table. "Nope," she said when Oka gestured for its return. "You can have it back when you learn how to eat."

Oka couldn't speak through his prodigious mouthful, but his message was clear as he went to reclaim his plate himself. With a squeal, Aly shoved the plate to Raine. As Oka rounded on him, Raine didn't think. He snatched the plate and ran.

With a garbled shout, Oka chased him around the dining table. Once. Twice. Jaska scooched his chair out as Raine made his third loop, forcing him to draw up short.

"Interference," he cried as Oka tackled him.

The platter flew from his hands as he hit the floor. Instead of retrieving his plate, Oka wrestled with Raine, trying to pin him. They tussled like wolf pups, shouting with laughter. Above them, Aly and Jaska debated who would win.

"That's enough," Savere said. "You'll disturb Mother."

Abashed, Raine and Oka drew apart and stood. The green dragon flashed him a toothy grin, his mouth now empty. How Oka had managed to chew and swallow a clump of meat the size of a chicken—while holding his own in an all-out wrestling match—Raine would never know.

"You're good," Oka said approvingly. "Someone competent taught you how to fight."

"My father," Raine said shortly, then braced for censure. When Oka merely nodded, he relaxed. They rejoined the table, and Raine pushed his untouched plate toward Oka in recompense for spilling his on the floor.

"Mother's presence will be required more often," Jaska remarked to Savere. "We'll need her to keep these hatchlings in line."

There was something in Jaska's tone that made Evin sound imposing. Like a strict, no-nonsense general who made her troops quake in their boots. "Evin seems so sweet," Raine said, almost like a protest. "Is she really that strict?"

"She's our den mother," Oka said around a reasonable-ish mouthful. "Knowing nothing of dragons, I guess you probably need an explanation." Raine confirmed his ignorance. Oka swallowed, then continued. "Every thunder is ruled by a den mother. The den mother is always the eldest female dragon in the family."

At Raine's amazement, Aly said, with no small amount of relish, "Thunders and storms are matriarchal. A storm is a dragon community. Humans have cities. We have storms. The leader of a storm, a storm mother, is the eldest female within an entire community."

The concept of female authority was nearly more surprising than discovering dragons possessed dual forms. Human women weren't permitted to own property or hold government office in Valdenia. A household was male led, always. Only very recently were females permitted to captain Guardian units. The change had caused quite a stir, too.

Perhaps Raine *didn't* want to join their thunder. Once a man reached the age of seventeen, he was an adult by Valdenian law and master of his own destiny. Raine recalled how enraged Lukor had been. And how the slightest command of Evin's was obeyed by the virulent dragon without protest.

The power of a den mother was considerable, then, to curb that situation so easily. It was enough for Raine to understand a male in a thunder obeyed the den mother unquestioningly. And while Evin seemed beyond wonderful, Raine was not there to be controlled by anyone.

"So, to fully answer your question, we behave like total sticks because our den mother, any den mother, sets the tone and social norms for her thunder," Aly said. "Crude language and roughhousing don't go over well. Evin prefers us to be polite and proper, so we are."

Raine was used to being proper and polite when certain company necessitated it. That didn't perturb him nearly as much as the idea of forced subservience.

"Enough about our thunder." Oka folded his arms on the table and leaned forward. "Tell us about the dragons at Chambrin."

"We still don't know who all was captured after the massacre," Jaska said, zeroing in on Raine, too. "Or how many. I've been wanting to ask after them, myself."

"I've never met the dragons in the Cavern," Raine admitted.

Jaska's dark eyes shuttered, but not before Raine glimpsed his agonized disappointment. Aly and Oka's shoulders slumped. Savere stared unseeing at his hands. They had been counting on Raine for news of their loved ones. His inability to offer a single scrap of consolatory information made him feel lower than dirt.

"But I'm very close to the war dragons," he said, trying to ease their dejection. It worked. His audience perked up like wilted flowers after a substantial rainfall. They faced him, listening.

"Twenty-three dragons have been born since ..." he trailed off uncomfortably. They knew since when. "The oldest is Fern, a green female. She's fast but sweet, letting the other dragons win any time they race. Yip, the youngest, is the one I play with most. Probably because we're so close in age. She's sixteen, with lilac scales, and insanely funny."

Raine spent hours describing the only childhood friends he possessed—other than Nyx—to the rapt dragons of Evin's thunder. Mayhem, a red male who started fights for fun. Fang, whose crushing bite could crumble granite. Clover, who liked to blend in with the grass and ambush the unsuspecting for sport. Ruby, who glittered like a billion crushed jewels.

As he spoke, Raine wondered if the powerful connection he shared with the war dragons was due to his own secret heritage. It was an odd thought, but no odder than being on the run for his life from those sworn to protect him.

"I can't believe you didn't realize you were a dragon sooner," Aly said after he ran out of dragons.

Raine arched a brow. "How could I have? I had no way of knowing dragons possessed human forms. You wouldn't have guessed it, either, in my shoes."

"Are you kidding me?" Aly snorted. "Ruby? Clover? Fang?" She stared at him intently, as if waiting for something.

"Um, yes? Those are some of their names," Raine said slowly.

"Come on." She rolled her eyes and looked at Jaska. "You know what I'm trying to say, don't you?"

Jaska's thin lips twitched as he took in Raine's bafflement. "What are *our* names?" he asked instead of answering.

Raine blinked, now even more confused. "Jaska, Savere, Oka, and Aly?"

"Dreaming Mother, get this kid a brain," Aly cried. "The dragons at Chambrin Keep are all named like pets. Not people. *Pets*. There's this human lady next door with, like, thirty-seven cats—"

"Five," Savere interjected.

"Whatever." Aly waved a hand, as if the difference between thirty-seven and five was trifling. "My point is, the gray one is named Smoky. The orange one is Pumpkin. *Your* name is Raine. And you have really pale, silvery eyes. I'm guessing your hair is pale, too. It's hard to tell through all the grime."

Raine frowned. "My father said he named me Raine because—" He broke off, blushing. There was no way in hell he was finishing that sentence. *Because my eyes are like pools of rain suspended in the sky.* Fucking hell, his father had named him like a pet.

Aly's smirk was smug. "Exactly," she said, as if he'd spoken aloud.

A clock somewhere in the house chimed the lateness of the hour. Jaska stood. "I should retire. Unlike you louts, I work to secure our living."

"Oi, no fair," Oka cried. "How many times have I been the sole provider of food on our table?"

"And I always ask if I can run the shop," Aly said. "You won't let me."

"I'm the darkest dragon here," Jaska said. "A human would have to be too dense to breathe not to notice something off about you."

Aly's lower lip jutted outward. Raine mentally ceded the point to Jaska. With hair and eyes a green so dark they bordered on black, Jaska easily passed for human in the jewelry shop's poor lighting. With Aly, there was no mistaking those brilliantly red orbs for human.

She turned her pouting gaze to Raine. "Looks like it's bedtime."

CHAPTER EIGHT

Aly led Raine up two separate flights of stairs. The second set, behind a door, rose steep and narrow. The landing opened to an attic. Aly cranked the oil burner of her lamp, bathing the space with soft light. There were two beds within, pushed against opposite walls. One had pink blankets messily bunched at the end. The other was haphazardly made with a skewed quilt and flat pillow.

"My guest bed is in here, with you?" Raine arched a brow.

Aly arched a red eyebrow, playfully mimicking his expression. "Is that a problem? I'm sure we could set you up with Oka or Jaska, but fair warning. Oka's a slob and Jaska stays up all night crafting jewelry. Which is miserable if you are light-sensitive and need complete darkness to sleep."

Raine slung his haversack on a bedpost, then settled onto his mattress. It gave a squeaky bounce. "But you're a woman." She grinned and he frowned. "A young, beautiful woman," he elaborated.

It's not that Raine was a prude, per se. But when did anyone ever put two passionate young adults of the opposite sex in a shared bedroom if they weren't blood-related or married?

"And you were definitely raised by humans." She laughed. "How old do you think I am, anyway?"

Raine cocked his head, studying her carefully. She couldn't be more than, "Eighteen summers?"

"Oh, my." She shook her head with a teasing grin. "I've seen two hundred and seven summers."

Raine's mouth fell open. He knew, logically, that Evin and the others were centuries old. Hell, the eldest war dragon at Chambrin—Fern—bordered two centuries of age. But it was still startling to learn the precise age of Aly while staring at her impossibly smooth countenance. Raine was used to thinking of human faces and ages in a certain way. It would take time to assimilate two centuries as young.

"Dragons live to be a thousand years on average," Aly revealed, then analyzed him for a reaction. If she expected a greater display of shock, she was disappointed. Raine might have been slow on the uptake, but he was up to speed now.

"I'm the youngest. Everyone here thinks of me like a kid," Aly went on after Raine's expression remained even. "I was in my mom's egg when the humans attacked our storm. Our community," she added, in case he'd forgotten. "Not that I've ever lived to be part of a true storm. In many ways, I'm as ignorant of dragon culture as you. My whole life, I've spent in hiding, living among humans. I've heard the stories, but they feel like fairytales. Life is so different from what they describe."

Raine nodded his understanding. Dragon tales and history lessons were one thing. But they paled to reality.

"How old are *you*?" Aly asked, eyes narrowing. "You only just discovered your dragon heritage. Human lifespans are a fraction of ours. You must be fairly young if you haven't picked up on the discrepancy."

"I'm almost twenty years old."

"You're a baby," Aly screeched, then glanced at the stairs in alarm. "I've got to be quieter," she murmured. "Mother will be very displeased if we disturb her."

"Evin is your den mother. Are you related beyond that? Any of you?"

Raine kicked off his boots and splayed across his bed. The mattress was thin with coils that dug into his back, but it was heavenly compared to sleeping on the hard ground outside, which was how he'd spent the past several nights. With summer tipping to autumn, the nights were uncomfortably cool. Raine pulled the cotton quilt snugly around his shoulders. This was much preferable.

"Savere and Oka are brothers. Savere is the older of the two. He's also the more serious one. They are the only direct relations in our thunder. Evin's mate died defending her and their children. She'd lost all will to fight and was about to surrender when she spotted my egg. My family's thunder neighbored Evin's, and she had watched my parents die. She grabbed me and got away. I hatched the very next day. My mom never got to meet me."

Aly's eyes glistened and she blinked back tears. "We all call Evin 'Mother.' In a traditional thunder, the den mother is referred to as Mother by everyone, but I mean it as more than just a title. Evin raised me as her own and it feels wrong to call her by name. She'll always be Mother to me, even when I find my mate and start my own thunder."

Aly placed the lamp on her bedside table. Kicking off her slippers, she boldly yanked her dress overhead, standing naked in the room.

Raine squawked in alarm. "What are you doing?"

"Preparing for bed." She pressed a hand to the generous curve of her naked hip.

Raine regarded her suspiciously. Women had played this game with him before, feigning guilelessness as a seduction method. "You're trying to entice me into making love to you," he said archly. "This isn't the first time I've had something like this happen, and while I'm flattered—"

"Oh, puh-lease!" Aly marched over to Raine's bed, breasts swaying with each step.

Raine bolted upright, shifting away at her approach. She stopped directly in front of him, and he pointedly kept his gaze above her neck. No easy feat when her breasts were eye-level and inches from his face.

She held out one hand and began counting with her fingers.

"One, I sleep naked. Your presence here has no bearing on that. Two—and I guess this is my fault since I never got around to answering why nobody cares that we're sharing a room—but two, dragons are not like humans. Lukor says they bugger anything that takes their fancy once they reach sexual maturity. That's not how dragons operate. Do you have any attraction to me? Any feelings of arousal or desire?"

Raine shifted on the mattress, putting more space between them. Aly's breasts swayed with her agitation, and he was strongly averse to them brushing him.

"No," he answered honestly. "I am not attracted to you at all."

He didn't conceal his confusion. Aly's build was lushly sensual with generous hips and breasts. He should have been salivating at the every-man's-fantasy on display before him, but he felt nothing.

Raine had never experienced the primal urges that seemingly ruled everyone around him. When he turned fourteen, he had watched his peers with bewilderment as they rutted in hay lofts and linen closets. Anywhere with a modicum of privacy and a tupping surface, really. His father insisted he was merely a late bloomer, but Raine was nearly twenty. No one bloomed *that* late.

Aly appeared to recognize his need for personal space. She backed off, collapsing onto her own bed, still nude.

"I got *the talk* when I was about forty-four, which is far older than you are now, so I guess this is one dragon lesson you'll be getting sooner instead of later," Aly said cheerfully, grabbing a pillow and cuddling it to her center.

Raine's shoulders lowered as tension eased from his frame. Laying back down, he curled onto his side so they faced one another. He guessed "the talk" Aly referred to was the dragon equivalent of a human sex talk. How different could they be?

"You already know we live to about a thousand years old, or so. Our bodies mature rapidly in comparison to our lifespan, and we can mate and have children as young as fifteen."

An image flashed through Raine's mind. Himself at fifteen, already at his full adult height, without the lankiness that plagued other boys who sprang up prematurely.

"But even though we reach adulthood early, our sexual maturity is a whole different matter."

"You just said we can have children at fifteen," Raine interrupted. That seemed to imply sexual maturity to him.

"It's not that simple. Our sexuality is dormant until we meet our mates. If you're lucky enough to encounter your mate that young, then yeah. You can mate and start a family. But mates aren't guaranteed to have the same hatching days. It can take decades, even centuries, for your mate to be born. Until you meet your mate, your sex organs are deader than Oka's meat jerky."

"I thought something was wrong with me," Raine burst, stunned.

His adolescence had been rife with turmoil. The sense of isolation, of being different from everyone else. At times, it had bordered on torment. Being so exceptionally strange, both internally and externally, had made it that much worse.

It might have gone more smoothly had Raine known he was perfectly normal, merely a dragon instead of human. Relief and disgruntlement warred within him at Aly's revelation. His father had a lot to answer for.

Replaying Aly's explanation in his mind, his brow furrowed. "Do you mean we don't choose our mates?"

"Nope. We sure don't. Your mate is a fated match, a gift from the Dreaming Mother."

Raine's eyes widened in horror. "But ... What if they die before you meet them? Or they are born after *you* die?"

"Then you live a life devoid of sex and sexuality, and you never have children. Same goes for them if it's you who dies first."

"That's fucked," Raine sputtered.

Making his own choices mattered to him. His father had taught him that's what defined someone as a person. Yet arguably the most important decision of Raine's life, selecting his partner and the bearer of his children, was out of his hands entirely. Being a dragon came with setbacks beyond a murderous guild, apparently.

"Tell me about it," Aly said. "Why do you think we're so obsessed with the dragons at Chambrin? Especially the newer generation. Any one of them could be my mate. Same for Savere, Oka, and Jaska."

Raine closed his eyes and brought each dragon to mind as Aly spoke. Savere and Oka—brothers by blood, they sported identical shades of duck green hair and leafy eyes. Jaska, with his greenish-black kale coloring that helped him pass for human.

Then, he thought of Evin with her sky-blue eyes and hair, who had lost her family when the Nine went to eradicate the dragon blight, then decided at the last minute to spare some for a breeding experiment. Raine tried to piece the big picture together based on all he'd learned, but there remained gaping holes in his knowledge.

"Two centuries ago, the dragons were attacked," Raine murmured, sensing this was the key. He turned it over in his mind like a puzzle cube. "That was around the same time the Garganthans invaded, and the nine tribes united to defeat them."

But how could the Nine have assaulted the dragons so soon after their depleting battle with Gargantha? With fewer numbers and no formal military, the tribes' victory against Gargantha had been a miracle. One that should have taken them decades to recover from.

Aly snorted. "The tribes didn't defeat the invaders. Dragons did."

Raine sat up with a frown, blankets pooling in his lap. "What do you mean?"

"The humans who invaded to pick the pocket? They marched through the heart of dragon territory, where we lived peacefully and a respectful distance from human settlements. Savere said they attacked our storms with a brutality he hadn't thought humans capable of. There were terrible losses on both sides, but the dragons were the victors, in the end. Although I don't think they felt like it. Not after what it cost them."

His mouth opened and closed but no words escaped. He had none. Aly's version of events was obscene. The Nine's sweeping defeat of the Garganthans was the founding of Valdenia. They'd been fortunate, as the Garganthans had underestimated the tribes and brought insufficient numbers and resources.

"That doesn't make sense," Raine said, frowning. "If Gargantha's army ended up in the dragons' land and decided to attack, they would have been decimated. I swear, it would take fifty humans to match a single dragon. At *least*."

"The invaders' army was a hundred thousand strong," Aly whispered. Raine's heart stammered. "They outnumbered the dragons a thousand to one. Still, the dragons triumphed. But like I said, it cost them dearly."

It couldn't be true. But Aly's somber stare held no deceit. Only sorrow and grief. *A thousand dragons*. He should have put it together sooner. The Nine could never have taken on that many dragons, no matter how good their warriors were.

The atmosphere turned heavy, as if discussing the past had stirred departed souls. Raine shivered, drawing his blanket up to his neck. "If the dragons defeated the Garganthans, how did so many end up in the Cavern?"

Aly's smile was laced with bitterness. "An army of a hundred thousand can't march in secret. Word of their invasion spread like fire throughout the land. The nine chiefs arrived with their greatest warriors to assess the situation. They discovered dragons battered and broken from battle. They discovered the remains of a vast enemy army. And they discovered an opportunity."

Her red eyes gleamed like fresh blood as her voice darkened. "Many dragons were severely wounded from the battle, incapable of flight or resistance. The human chieftains had them bound and carted away. They saw the might of dragons and seized it for themselves. They hunt the rest of us like vermin, so that the only dragons alive will be the ones that serve them."

Truth rang from her words with the dismal clarity of a death knell. Raine's throat pinched at the atrocity. "Some 'thank you,'" he rasped.

Aly loosed a humorless laugh. "You got that right. If the dragons hadn't engaged with the invaders, they would have turned the tribes' pockets inside out. And instead of gratitude, they were betrayed."

Raine rolled onto his back, staring blankly at the exposed rafters of their attic suite. "What about Lukor?" Raine whispered, feeling a sense of dread. "What happened to his mate?"

"His mate's name is Naiah. She's a blue, like Evin."

"Where is she?" Raine somehow knew as soon as he asked his question.

The answer slipped from Aly's lips and gutted him like a knife. "The humans took her. She's locked in the Cavern."

CHAPTER NINE

R aine woke late the next day, drool on his chin and mattress springs digging into his side. *Still better than the ground.*

Aly's bed was empty. Her sheets and blankets formed a twisted heap where she had slept. Raine carefully made his bed, smoothing the threadbare quilt over the mattress and making it altogether neater than it was before he used it. Years of having a general as a father made him excessively tidy. He pulled on his boots and hesitated as he eyed his haversack, its strap slung over a pinewood bedpost.

Evin had welcomed him into her thunder with open arms. But Raine didn't think he could accept her invitation. Funny how it had seemed a desperate imperative to find these people and gain their aid, yet now that he had it, he wanted to leave. They seemed wonderful—barring Lukor—and he had no justification for his impulse to run.

Except that he absolutely refused to obey anyone, even an angelic den mother who only wanted his safety and the happiness of her thunder.

There was no coming-of-age in a thunder, granting one freedom of choice upon reaching a certain age. Joining a thunder meant the obligation of obedience. The den mother spoke, and her thunder obeyed, period.

Even if Evin never demanded anything that Raine felt was unfair or unreasonable, the fact that she *could* bothered him. Humans emphasized a man's freedom and responsibility to manifest fate through his own actions. By obeying some higher authority, Raine could not truly make his own choices. Therefore, he'd never be able to attribute his successes, or even his failures, to himself alone. It went against everything his father had instilled in him, and he could not endure it.

Decision made, he plucked his haversack and looped it over his shoulder before navigating the house. Now brightly lit with midmorning sun, it was a warm, welcoming place. His progress was delayed as he inspected all the different wallpapers he encountered. Some rooms were painted instead, vivacious hues so different from the gray stone walls he was used to. Sinopel treated their homes as canvases for art. Raine was mesmerized.

"Are you lost?"

Raine looked up as Savere entered the parlor he had recently discovered. Its ceiling was painted like a starry sky, the walls papered to resemble a moonlit forest. So far, he'd located two barn owls hiding in trees, a doe nosing through the brush, and a raccoon poking its head out of a bush. It had become a game, attempting to spy all the cleverly concealed creatures. Raine had entirely forgotten his mission to locate the resident dragons.

"I got distracted," he said with a sheepish grin.

Savere's mouth ticked upward, not quite a smile but friendly enough. He led Raine down the hall and into an open kitchen. A round card table sat at the center of the room. There was a cutting board on top where Oka butchered a hefty slab of meat. Aly stood with her back to him, washing dishes at a sink.

The cupboards were rows of buttercup yellow. The tiled floor was black-and-white checkerboard with thick, mismatched rugs. Three rectangular windows were open, permitting a breeze lush with gardenias and roses. Raine glanced through the nearest window and found a small flower garden, well pruned and resplendent with aromatic blooms.

There were several empty chairs at the small table. When Savere took a seat, Raine joined him. They idly watched Oka work the meat, his butchering skills apparent as he expertly broke down the carcass.

Aly sat beside Raine once she finished her morning chores. She was wearing a similar dress to the one she wore yesterday. Plain with the sleeves rolled up, this one a clay red. It should have clashed with her crimson eyes and hair, but it emphasized her exotic coloring instead.

She wrinkled her nose at him. "You smell so bad."

Raine's cheeks flamed redder than her hair or dress. "I haven't had a proper bath in days. Not to mention, I've been on the run for my life. Considerable sweat is involved in outlawism."

"Your hair is dreadful. Is that soot all over you?" Oka asked, glancing over as he carved uniform steaks from a roast.

Raine grit his teeth. "I was forced to escape my home suddenly and through improvised means. Since my natural hair draws attention, I left the soot to disguise my appearance."

"Stinky, sooty, and filthy. That's gotta be rough," Oka tutted.

"Your hair is super tangled, by the way," Aly said. "It looks like a lark's nest is buried in the middle. Don't you have a brush?"

"Yes, I have a brush," he snapped. "But the soot dried my hair out and I have no soap or oils to clean or detangle it. I left it alone since I already look crazy with my dirty clothes and great black smears on my face!"

"Knock it off," Savere said, giving Oka and Aly a chiding look. To Raine, he said, "Dragons are incurably vain. Some more than others, to be fair, but we're all easily riled when our appearance is criticized. Oka and Aly are baiting you."

"We were not baiting him," Oka protested.

"Maybe just a little." Aly smiled ruefully as Savere crossed his arms, staring flatly. She twisted in her chair to face Raine. "We were only teasing, Raine. I was about to say so and ask if you'd like a bath before Savere butted in."

"Hatchlings," Savere scoffed. "You will refrain from *teasing* our guest while he acclimates. He is in a place filled with strangers and has suffered multiple shocks in a short time."

Oka and Aly looked suitably chastised. Savere's rebuke made Raine sound fragile, and he wanted to insist he could handle their trifling taunts, but something far more pressing gripped him. He jumped on Aly's offer of a bath like a kitten on a cricket.

An hour later, Raine felt like himself again. He hadn't realized how much his grimy appearance lowered his confidence. The dragons' bathing room was freakishly like his own, and he basked in the roiling heat of an oversized tub. If he shut his eyes, it was like being home.

A cedar chest of soaps and oils sat at the foot of the tub. Murky water sluiced around him as he dove through its contents, grinning as he located sandalwood and jasmine oils. He lathered, scrubbed, and rinsed until his bathwater was black. Then, he drained the tub and began anew.

By his third bath, the water remained clear, and he finally felt refreshed. He toweled himself dry and massaged creamy lotion into his skin before brushing out his thick, shimmering hair. It had been deplorably matted before his bath, almost requiring scissors.

It took more time for Raine to detangle his hair than it had to wash the dirt and grime from his figure. Throwing his damp locks into his customary braid, he dressed in a clean—if wrinkled—lawn shirt and tan tights. With fresh wool socks and leather boots to complete his ensemble, he went to find the dragons.

The kitchen seemed to be their hangout space. Aly and Oka played a board game while Savere whittled a piece of wood that fit inside his palm. Raine tossed his stained, smelly clothes into the blazing woodstove in the back corner of the kitchen. The fabric melted to ash in seconds.

Satisfied, Raine turned to rejoin the dragons at the card table. His stride faltered at their gob smacked expressions. Aly, Oka, and even Savere stared at him as if he was a chieftain in a tutu, sashaying to the plucky tunes of a country dance.

"The clothes were all natural fibers that burn cleanly," he assured them. Did they think he was nuts for getting rid of his clothes like that? The soot had hopelessly stained his shirt and breeches. There'd been no saving them.

"You're beautiful," Aly breathed. Her eyes mapped his face, as though she couldn't look at him all at once and had to savor him in sections.

Raine lifted his nose, smirking as he slipped into the chair he vacated earlier. "I know."

"Well, we don't have to ask where your vanity lies on the dragon spectrum," Oka said through a chuckle, taking one of Aly's pawns on their gameboard.

"At least my high self-opinion is justified," Raine said with a shrug.

"It certainly is." Aly's lips formed a pout. "I was relieved yesterday when I didn't spark with you. You looked so haggardly, I couldn't imagine desiring you if you *had* been my mate."

"Oi," Raine protested, flicking one of her game pieces.

Aly straightened the piece and offered a gamine grin. "I assure you, my mind has entirely changed. Now, I wish I'd sparked with you."

"Sparking occurs when a dragon meets their mate," Savere said for Raine's edification. Before Raine could ask what sparking entailed, Savere added, "You'll know when it happens. Trust me."

Huh. He mock-glared at Aly as her message became clear. "Shallow much? I'm more than just a pretty face, you know."

Aly boldly swept her gaze from his feet to his face. "I can see that," she said throatily.

"I'm going to retch," Oka muttered to Savere, who continued his woodcarving.

"Turn your head from me when you do, little brother," Savere replied, not looking up as his pocket blade bit into the chunk of wood he held.

"Where is everyone else at?" Raine asked.

He had been in the bath awhile, yet there remained no sign of Evin, Jaska, or Lukor. Not that Raine was terribly put out regarding the latter's absence. He might better understand the purple dragon's antipathy after learning his mate was imprisoned in the Cavern.

But knowing why Lukor was so viciously hostile wouldn't make enduring his company any more pleasant.

"Jaska runs a jewelry shop. He's there every day until closing. Lukor is typically gone all day, too. He walks the city, keeping tabs on things so we have some warning if there are hunters nearby," Oka explained.

"How does Lukor blend in?" Raine wondered aloud. The purple dragon had dark amethyst hair and eyes. His exotic coloring would be easily concealed at nighttime, perhaps, but it was broad daylight.

"Dragon vanity is strong in that one, too," Savere murmured. "He wears a hooded cloak."

"*How*?" Raine asked, incredulous. "One strong gust of wind and it's game over."

"We sew two loops inside our hoods. They hook around our ears and keep our hoods secure." Well, wasn't that a kick in the balls? Why hadn't Raine thought of that? Savere's lips twitched at his expression. "I have a spare cloak with a modified hood you can have."

"You do?" Raine beamed his gratitude. "Thank you. Seriously. I'm so glad I didn't dump ink on my hair. My father insisted it was the best way to disguise myself, but I swear, my soul curdles like sour milk just thinking about it."

"Ink? No way. I'd rather be dead first." Aly shuddered, hugging her loose red tresses closer.

"As you can see, we all balk at altering our appearances," Savere said. "Hence the modified hoods. The only dragon who ever shows their hair is Jaska, and that's only while he's indoors at his shop. It would be a dead giveaway to the hunters, if they heard of a shop-keeper that concealed his head and face."

"They'd at least be curious and check it out," Oka agreed.

"I'm one hundred percent using hoods from now on," Raine declared. Caking cosmetics or filth onto his hair brutalized his spirit. He didn't know what aspect of his dragon's nature shuddered so deeply at altering his appearance, but he intended to heed it. "Even before I was on the run, my hair glimmers iridescently in direct sunlight, so I've always been made to dust it with women's face powder to conceal that aspect of it."

"I've never seen a white dragon before," Aly said. "Mother says they are of the rarest of our kind."

"Is that what I am?"

There weren't any white dragons at Chambrin Keep that Raine knew of. Though, he was only familiar with the war dragons. He pictured white dragons, trapped in darkness hundreds of feet below soul-crushing earth, and sucked in a breath.

The horrifying implications of his origins penetrated at last, a hideous truth he had been running from since the moment he discovered he was a dragon. His mother—and real father—were locked in an underground prison. Could there be a white dragon down there, lamenting the loss of her precious egg?

He shivered in his seat, pulled from his bleak reverie by a hand waving in his face.

"Anybody home?"

Raine gently pushed Aly's hand away.

"Sorry," he said, still shaken. "It occurred to me that my parents ... They're locked away, too."

"Hey, it's okay," Aly whispered, taking one of his hands into hers and squeezing.

But it wasn't okay, not by a long shot. He thought he could understand Lukor's rage earlier, but now his eyes were wide open. It was a wonder Lukor hadn't ripped his throat out.

Wanting to change the subject, Raine inquired after Evin. So far, he'd only learned how Jaska and Lukor spent their days.

"Mother is in her room." Aly's voice lowered, as if she was answering a forbidden question. Raine arched a brow.

Savere, who had ceased whittling at Raine's query, shared the details Aly seemed reluctant to vocalize. "Mother remains in her rooms much of the time. Her presence at the evening meal yesterday was unusual. It takes something extreme—like a strange dragon appearing on our doorstep—to draw her from her bedchamber."

Raine privately wondered how Evin could be a den mother if she secluded herself so severely and was never around to lead her thunder. He sensed pressing for more details would be unwelcome, given Aly's obvious discomfiture, and held his tongue.

Oka crowed in triumph as he captured one of Aly's game pieces. She shrieked her outrage as she tackled the much larger male to the checkered tile floor. They rolled across the tiles as they wrestled. Aly was small but scrappy. Her arms and legs were a blur, jabbing at any potential vulnerability of the dragon above her. Oka captured her wrists and pinned her.

Raine threw himself on the floor and began slapping his palm against a black tile. *One. Two. Three.* "You're out!"

Oka released her, his victory secured. Aly yowled like a feral cat and threw herself at Raine, knocking the wind out of him. He narrowly dodged an elbow to the nose and pinched her side in retaliation. Before long, they were laughing breathlessly as they engaged in a prolonged wrestling match.

Like Oka, Raine was stronger and should have been able to pin her. Only, Aly somehow discovered he was agonizingly ticklish. Her wriggling fingers ruthlessly sought his sensitive underarms and stomach.

Tears streamed down Raine's face, and he begged, "Mercy!" through heaving laughter.

The back door opened, and Aly took pity on him at last, rolling over and offering her hand to help him stand. He accepted her outstretched palm gracefully, all the while plotting payback. Jaska entered the kitchen. Oka offered the jeweler his chair and went to prepare the meat he butchered earlier. The dragons moved with the fluidity of routine, Oka and Aly filling serving platters for supper.

It had been over twenty-four hours since Raine last ate, and he winced as it appeared raw meat would be the only thing on the menu once more.

"I don't suppose there's any fruits or vegetables to go with that?" he mumbled loud enough to be heard, sounding as pathetically hopeless as he felt.

Jaska chuckled at him. "That's right, you were raised as a human. Dragons like to hunt and eat their kills hot and bloody like nature intended. Since we're in hiding, we never shift into our dragon forms, let alone hunt in them. So, we do the next best thing, buying the freshest meat from the market each morning and carving it up for dinner."

"You eat *vegetables*," Oka exclaimed, aghast. "Dreaming Mother only knows what's wrong with you." He cradled a platter laden with bright red meat strips protectively. As if Raine's perversion of vegetables was going to somehow turn his steak into broccoli. Raine would have laughed if he wasn't so damned hungry.

"Do you mind if I cook mine a little?"

Oka shook his head at him, frowning. "You can burn your meal if it suits you. Just know you'll be committing a crime against nature when you do, and that I'll be judging you for it."

"I can live with that." Raine grabbed an entire tray and carried it to the woodstove.

He pushed up his shirt sleeve before pinching a slimy steak in his fingers and plunging his arm directly into the flames, cooking it to a perfect medium rare. Over and over, Raine did the same, plunging the meat into the fire until it was perfectly seared before swallowing the hot, scorched strips with minimal chewing. He was starving and it tasted divine.

The others elected to eat in the kitchen, watching Raine like he was putting on a performance. He ignored them, too hungry to care.

Once his platter contained nothing but pinkish meat juice, his belly achingly full, Raine brought it to the kitchen sink. He washed his platter as well as the arm he used to cook the steaks, the flames having left a sooty residue on his skin.

"You already know we're impervious to fire, then," Jaska observed as Raine approached.

He sat gingerly, full to bursting. The pain was deliciously satisfying compared to the gnawing hunger that had plagued him for days, scavenging little to no food as he raced to Sinopel in search of safety and answers.

Savere completed his carving, placing an elaborate figurine of a crowned king on the table. Raine picked it up and examined it, awed by the detail Savere achieved. The game piece had perfect little ears and his beard looked soft to the touch though it was made of wood.

"Savere made our chess set," Oka declared proudly. He gestured to the game board and chess pieces he and Aly played with earlier, now tucked onto a shelf along the wall.

Jaska held out his hand and Raine deposited the king into his palm. "He's making this set for me, to keep at the jewelry store," Jaska said, a smile softening his sharp features as he turned the figurine in his hand to study the craftsmanship.

Jaska complimented Savere profusely and Raine swore the staid dragon swelled with pleasure. A kiss of pink tinged Savere's cheeks as he muttered, "It's nothing."

The kitchen door cracked open. A towering, hooded figure swept inside and kicked the door shut without turning. He tugged his hood down, revealing dark purple hair, styled in a severe bun, and a wild expression.

Lukor's gaze focused on Savere. "We have a problem."

CHAPTER TEN

They were back in the dining room, which seemed to be the official meeting place for Serious Discussions. Evin remained composed as Lukor filled them in. The situation was dire and worse, it was all Raine's fault.

"They have wanted posters everywhere, seeking *him*," Lukor railed.

Raine shifted in his seat, feeling as foul as his filthy black bathwater for causing these dragons grief and stress simply by being there. The solution was obvious. He would depart at once. Lukor's vitriol was immaterial to his own tattered conscience.

"There is a planned door-to-door search, which will commence at dawn. Furthermore, a reward has been announced. Five thousand silvans for any information leading to Raine Chambrin's arrest."

"I will leave," Raine interjected. Aly gasped a protest. Raine shushed her with a look. "I didn't come here to jeopardize your safety. You've been hiding successfully for two hundred years. I'm not about to fuck all that up for three hots and a cot." This was not the time to mention he'd been planning to leave regardless.

Lukor's lips peeled back in a snarl. He surveyed Raine like a rat he'd found burrowing inside his winter grain. "Humans saw you. They will put two and two together. Your hair may have been matted with filth, but your eyes were clear and silver. Did you tell anyone where you were going?"

Raine froze. Because he had told one person where he was going, in order to get directions. Divine Father, he'd fucked up.

Lukor pounced. "I knew it," he spat. "The damage is done. You have condemned us to death. They will come here looking for you, and they'll find a house full of dragons. They'll slaughter us the same way they slaughtered Carisha's thunder."

"Enough," Evin said calmly.

It was as if she screamed it. The dragons visibly straightened to attention, all eyes on her. A muscle ticked in Lukor's jaw, but he obeyed Evin as well, falling abruptly silent.

Her sky-blue eyes found Raine. "Lukor has one thing right. The damage *is* done. However, we have more than one safehouse. We will be fine." She craned her neck to survey her thunder. "Pack your things. We leave tonight." She eyed Raine once more. "You, too, Raine. Please join us. To remain here or strike out on your own is a death sentence. With so many of our kind gone, we need every dragon we can get. Come with us. Learn more about yourself and your heritage. Live and grow stronger."

Evin was keen. She'd picked up Raine's intent to separate from her thunder. He squirmed beneath her kind, knowing gaze.

He *could* join them, he supposed. It didn't mean he was joining their thunder. And anyway, he owed Evin. His presence was uprooting their lives and endangering them in the process. If all Evin desired of Raine was his company, it would be unpardonably churlish to refuse.

He nodded and she smiled, warming him to the tips of his toes. As if her smile held the love and warmth of his father's embrace.

Raine and Evin's thunder filed outdoors and huddled beneath the nearest lamp post, drawn like moths to its pulsating light as they awaited the den mother. Lukor hovered outside the house, waiting like an anxious parent for Evin to emerge. Everyone's packs were stuffed overfull for a long journey with no return date.

Raine's bag made a slight clinking sound as his weight shifted, and he smiled. He had tucked a dozen glass vials of scented oil into his haversack as well as three fat bricks of sweet soap. He loved his father dearly, but the man needed to straighten his priorities. Soap was a non-negotiable travel necessity.

He might have over-compensated a little, but he'd endured a very recent, very smelly trauma, damn it. He'd barely refrained from plucking the entire ungainly chest of bathing products and fashioning a strap to carry it alongside his haversack.

Lukor edged the door open, as if to see what the holdup was, but Evin's slender figure emerged, hood securely fastened over her head. The sight reminded Raine to throw his own hood on. It was attached to a new-to-him cloak, courtesy of Savere. Just as the green dragon claimed, there were two stretchy circles sewn into the hood's lining.

He popped his ears through the tabs, ensuring his hood wouldn't drop by accident.

Evin locked the door behind her, then she and Lukor approached.

"Lukor, you have point," she said quietly. "I will take the rear. Everyone, keep your hoods up and try to move quickly but casually."

"This city's walls are yet unguarded," Lukor added. "That changes at dawn, and soon for every city in Valdenia. No one will be admitted without inspection. Tonight is our only chance to leave undetected. Keep your backs straight and face forward at all times. We should not be stopped or questioned so long as we do not call attention to ourselves."

With that, Lukor took point. Although they hadn't discussed how to organize the middle, the dragons moved into place as if it was second nature. Jaska followed Lukor. Oka and Savere followed Jaska. Raine stuck with Aly, trailing Oka and Savere. Evin brought up the rear and they were off.

Raine felt conspicuous beneath the glow of so many streetlamps. Sinopel blazed brightly, even at night as its residents slept. He tried to avoid the lights as they moved, but it was difficult. Lukor seemed to actively seek them out as they progressed.

"Do not dodge the lamps, hatchling," Evin murmured as quiet as the night, startling Raine. He hadn't realized she was so close. He remained silent but glanced questioningly over his shoulder.

"Innocent humans do not hide from the lamps. They seek the light for its illumination and safety."

Ah. When the den mother put it like that, Raine felt foolish. He nodded to show he understood and forced himself to walk directly beneath the splashes of light that spilled from the hanging lanterns lining the street. While it felt counterintuitive, he muffled his instincts with Evin's logic.

In the darkness, every sound that reached Raine's sensitive ears felt ominous. The scraping near a shadowed alleyway was a Guardian drawing their blade. A faint *clink* across the street was another plucking an arrow from a quiver. A patter of mercenary feet sounded behind them. Raine's heart seized, and he turned to spy a chubby raccoon darting into a gutter.

Aly grinned and crooned, "Poor baby, I won't let the raccoon get you."

"That makes me feel better, thank you."

It was the last time Raine spoke for hours as Lukor directed them out of Sinopel, through the same juniper gates Raine had entered less than two days prior. It was a trader's route, which explained the large, overburdened wagons that had congested the street when he arrived.

The lateness of the hour ensured it was significantly less busy now, but even near midnight, a couple carts creaked along the cobbles and weary merchants marched with bent backs on the sidewalks.

Lukor chose the busiest exit. It was another counterintuitive move, boldly striding down the most popular thoroughfare in the city. They needed to be as unremarkable as possible, a challenging feat with a group of seven, all with cloaks drawn on a fair evening. If hunters were present and watchful for suspicious activity, they were more likely to question a strange, cloaked bunch if they appeared furtive. Abstaining from the shadows, keeping their necks straight, taking the popular route ... All these things helped them appear aboveboard. And further demonstrated just how long these dragons had been hunted.

The road ahead was as black as pitch with the city lights at their backs. The orange glow of a thousand streetlamps faded as they progressed, and Raine's night vision developed over the distance. By the time they branched off the thoroughfare onto a smaller cobbled road, Raine could discern the shapes between trees.

They kicked up their pace once they blended with the night, no humans in sight. Guilt plugged Raine's chest as they jogged, their steps whisper-soft even as they sped up. Evin's thunder truly had no choice but to leave. The chieftains had branded Raine as an enemy of Valdenia. He was wanted for treason, of all things. It was as brilliant as it was damning.

There wasn't a single citizen who wouldn't turn him in with pride. Valdenia was still cold-shouldered to outsiders since the outsiders had come *inside* and tried to steal their wealth away. Believing Raine was somehow working with Gargantha, plotting another invasion, the woman who'd provided him directions to Jaska's would be compelled to report their interaction. He was screwed. And so was Evin's thunder.

A horse-drawn conveyance clattered in the darkness ahead. Lukor paused, creating a standstill as their group halted behind him. Raine strained to see ahead, but the roadway curved left, blocking the view.

The carriage rounded the bend abruptly. Its driver spotted them before they could duck into the woods. Oka uttered a curse. It was the middle of the night, and they were seven cloaked figures standing upon a stretch of road far between towns. They were conspicuous as fuck.

Raine realized the others had their hoods down and felt a stab of envy through his mounting apprehension. In the darkness, the other dragons' hair appeared vaguely dark and satisfyingly human.

His own hair was too pale to be mistaken for the typical brown or black locks of native Valdenians, even in the dead of night. He was going to seem invariably suspicious to a passerby. They all were.

Lukor started walking. "Act natural," he hissed in a tone that carried.

Aly reached for Raine's hand in the darkness and gripped his fingers painfully tight. They walked. Four horses pulled the coach, dark manes dancing along their glossy, russet necks as they cantered down the lane. The carriage was black and gleamed expensively in the wan moonlight.

Not a typical traveler, which spiked Raine's trepidation. It would have been better to encounter a sleepy family taking advantage of the lighter traffic at nighttime. Or an enterprising merchant tirelessly burning the midnight oil.

As the carriage clattered closer, Lukor moved to the grassy side of the road, creating a wide berth for the conveyance to pass. Raine and the others followed suit. The horses pinned their ears, jerking nervously as they drew even with Raine's group. The carriage stopped.

"Good evening." Evin stepped up to the carriage, approaching in a manner that kept her behind the team of skittish horses.

The driver bent away, rifling with something at his feet. As he straightened, his arm raised a small lantern. Orange light illuminated the shadowy features of his face. His forehead creased as he regarded them.

"Good evening," he said, returning Evin's greeting.

"Is there something we can help you with?" Evin's tone was open and courteous.

"Indeed so, ma'am. I've been instructed to pause and give notice whenever we encounter passersby."

Evin offered a small smile in the pulsing light of the driver's lantern. "Oh, dear. Whatever for?"

The carriage door swung open, and three figures emerged. They wore tight, form-fitting clothes that transformed them into shadowy silhouettes. Raine suppressed a shiver.

The Guardians of Vale were known as the shadows of Valdenia, their legendary black uniforms immediately recognizable. It was a Guardian unit, or as Raine now saw them, an elite team of dragon hunters.

If Evin realized their predicament, she gave no outward sign. Turning, she offered the Guardians—the hunters—a politely confused smile.

A woman stepped forward. "Greetings, travelers."

Her immodest uniform clung like a second skin, starkly outlining her small, high breasts. A golden cuff banded her bicep, marking her as the captain of her team. Her straight, black hair was pulled into a high ponytail that reached the backs of her thighs.

An impractical length that Raine eyed with approval. Too many Valdenian women were turning to traditionally male hairstyles, shearing themselves instead of bothering with the upkeep of long tresses. Raine went to finger his own substantial mane reassuringly but encountered a rough spun hood. Slowly, he dropped his arm.

The other two guild members positioned themselves on either side of Raine's group. Like living bookends, they locked them in place on the side of the road. The female captain addressed them as a group.

"I am Captain Lyka Vithier of the Guardians. We are enroute to Sinopel, where a full search of the population has been ordered. Every man, woman, and child must be inspected as we search for violent subversives believed to be hiding among our people."

Captain Lyka Vithier took the lantern from the driver's out-stretched arm and marched toward Lukor, who was the furthest away at the head of their group.

"My orders further require us to inspect all passersby as we travel to Sinopel. I will be brief so that you may continue your journey with minimal interruption."

Raine held his breath and Aly squeezed his hand so tightly, he was sure his knuckles were confetti beneath his skin.

Lyka held the lantern just above Lukor's head. She leaned in, tilting the lamp back and forth as she inspected his face intently.

Without a word, she lowered the lantern and moved to Jaska.

Alarm bells rang in Raine's head. Something was not right here. Lukor had purple eyes, for fuck's sake. That was not normal.

Beneath the lantern, Lukor's dark purple hair might be mistaken for the blue-black hair common in many Valdenian families. But there was no mistaking his large, plum irises for human.

Jaska's green eyes were rare but not impossible. The night turned his kale hair black, even beneath the orangey glow of Lyka's lantern. The captain spent considerably less time examining his features.

Raine shifted on his feet as she reached Savere and Oka. The other dragons were motionless.

Savere and Oka's eyes were much more vividly green than Jaska's, their hues startlingly bright like dewy young grass. Their hair gleamed unmistakably emerald under the lantern's light. The captain's features remained shuttered, neither surprise nor recognition alighting behind her even stare.

Lyka's fingers flicked as she stepped before him. Raine's stomach sank. It was a signal. She was counting the dragons; ticking them off to her journeymen as she identified them so they could prepare. Her arm stretched above his head. Fire danced in the lantern, splashing whorls of light and shadow across her features.

"Lower your hood."

He froze, arms stiff at his sides. Blood roared like a ravine in his ears as she reached out to yank his hood down herself.

The thunder exploded into action. Lukor tackled the journeyman standing guard at his shoulder. Evin simultaneously attacked the other at their rear.

The journeymen reacted swiftly, as though anticipating the attacks. Both hunters grappled out of reach and extracted long, pale blades from belted sheaths. Jaska and Savere rushed to aid Lukor and their den mother, forcing the journeymen to fight two-against-one in either skirmish.

The captain whistled a sharp, piercing signal. Six more shadows spilled from the carriage. Raine cursed their miserable luck of encountering not one, but *three* hunter teams traveling together.

His neck snapped toward the sound of shattering glass. Lyka had tossed her lantern to draw a long, whiplike rapier from her hip. She lunged, her thin blade whizzing in a lethal arc meant to slash his throat. Raine jerked back and sidestepped her charge.

Her strange, milky blade spliced the air, coming within a finger's breadth of his neck.

Breath sawed out of Raine at the near hit. Loose stones skittered as Lyka corrected her angle for another swing. Sword upraised like a lightning rod, she bore down on him. Raine ducked left, then skid on his knees to avoid a journeyman's dagger.

The scene erupted into total chaos as the six other hunters joined the skirmish. The hunters had the advantage of numbers and darkness, their uniforms blending seamlessly in the shadows while the dragons stood out, particularly Raine.

Two journeymen and a male captain surrounded Oka, wielding crooked, milk-white daggers. Oka's yelp of pain tore through Raine's battle haze, and he narrowly evaded the slash of Lyka's rapier as his eyes sought Oka reflexively.

The sound of fabric ripping overrode the din of blows and grunts. Raine halted as the moonlight disappeared, as if swallowed by an enormous cloud. In the deepened darkness, massive dragon wings unfurled overhead.

Oka batted his wings, flinging the hunters at his sides helter-skelter. Raine stumbled and fell backwards on a powerful wind burst as Oka surged into the air. His back scraped the cobbles as he gaped at the sky.

Oka's huge dragon form glided overhead. Raine soaked in the sheer power and beauty of him, awed by his transformation. He had heard the story of Myrrah and Darrok. He knew that dragons were creatures of dual forms. But witnessing the sheer, undeniable reality nailed the truth home in a way nothing else had. *Divine Father, I'm a dragon.*

Around him, the other dragons leapt to their feet, jarring Raine from his stupor. He bounced to his heels in time to observe the hunters recover. They formed a line, putting their backs to their carriage. A collection of swords and daggers pointed at the dragons, milky blades shimmering against the waning moon.

Captain Lyka Vithier's teeth flashed as white as her rapier in the dark. "Dragon scum," she spat.

Raine and Evin's thunder mimicked the hunters, lining the roadside opposite with the woods at their backs. Oka descended, leathery wings gusting as he landed behind them, presenting a united front.

Evin said, "It takes at least three hunters to take down a dragon. There are seven of us. If you continue to engage, you will not survive."

Before tonight, Raine would not have believed Evin. He thought a dragon could take down dozens of humans, regardless of their skill. Sparring with Captain Lyka had been revelatory. She displayed a breadth of mastery with her odd blade that kept him too busy evading her attacks to formulate his own. Whatever training the guild offered was no joke.

"Perhaps not," one of the other captains said, a man with a pencil-thin moustache, "but we'll take some of you with us before we die."

As Raine shifted, his back brushed against a solid wall of scaly muscles. Scaly muscles that belonged to a huge, winged Oka. Raine frowned. The dragons didn't have to suffer any casualties. They could simply fly to safety, as Oka just demonstrated.

Shit, the dragons could fly to the end of Valdenia and back in a single evening. Why were they walking at all?

"We will retreat," Lyka announced. Her black clad arm motioned the other hunters back to the carriage.

Outraged protests exploded from several subordinates, but the other two captains interjected sharply, siding with Lyka. Without any further acknowledgement of the dragons they had attempted to slaughter, the hunters piled into their carriage. Captain Lyka entered last, a hateful sneer painting over her features before she slammed the door.

Their driver, who had remained in his seat throughout the ordeal, snapped the reins, launching the horses into motion. In moments, the carriage disappeared around the bend, its rumbling wheels fading to silence.

A hundred knuckles cracked behind Raine. He whirled to find Oka stark naked and human. Savere tossed his brother a backpack. Oka knelt on the shadowed grass and dug through it, retrieving a tunic and trousers to dress.

Aly broke the silence. "Why did they leave? The hunters never leave dragons alive. Even if it's a fight to the death."

Lukor crossed his arms and scowled. "Because they possess knowledge of us that is too precious to die with them. When they reach Sinopel, they will report directly to its chieftain and relay every detail of our group."

Oka slipped into their huddle as he buttoned his trousers. "So, who's going with who?"

CHAPTER ELEVEN

Aly's eyes widened. "What do you mean?"

Evin held up a hand, and her thunder looked to her as one. "There are seven of us. Hours from now, that information will be distributed to every chieftain, hunter, and officer in the vicinity. It is too notable a number. Oka has correctly surmised we must split up."

"Before we cover that, is anyone hurt?" Savere asked.

Oka showed him a large cut along his side. "It looks worse than it is," he assured his brother.

Savere dismissed his brother's protests, shedding his pack. He knelt and extracted cloths and salve to bandage Oka's wound.

While he worked, Evin said, "Raine, you are the most distinct in appearance—"

"You have *blue* hair," he objected, and she gave him a patient smile.

"That is true. However, I don't have thousands of drawings of my face littering the country. Even without the posters, your features draw attention."

"You're the prettiest princess," Aly simpered.

Raine hooked a leg behind her ankle, unbalancing her. As she fell, Aly clamped onto his arm and yanked him down. They landed in a heap of limbs, wrestling for dominance.

Savere called out, "Hatchlings!"

Reluctantly, Raine and Aly drew apart and righted themselves. Evin's eyes sparkled as she regarded them with a tolerant smile. "We will not separate permanently. But we must break into smaller groups if we hope to travel safely. I want us spread as far apart as possible, so that if any of us are discovered, it will give the hunters no clues to our destination. Raine and Aly will be one group."

Lukor hissed. "Mother, I do not think that is wise. They are hatchlings, too drawn to mischief and carelessness—"

"I appreciate your insight, Lukor, but my decision is firm. Raine requires minimal companions to remain undetected. Aly is the only other female among us. They can pass as a young married couple, a common and unremarkable traveling pair."

Jaska's brow creased as his concerned gaze found Raine and Aly. "I don't mean to question your judgement, Mother, but they are both so young. One of us could accompany Raine in the guise of a brother or other such relative just as easily."

Evin issued a soft sigh, the most overtly exasperated gesture Raine had observed from her. "That is quite true. Except humans, unlike dragons, are promiscuous beings. Two attractive males traveling together will draw attention. In order to make Raine as unremarkable as possible, he should be paired with a young wife."

Raine and Aly had no objections and nodded. Raine tried to look extra serious since everyone was acting like he was a reckless puppy.

"Our destination is the safehouse within Hollyhock Forest," Evin continued. "Oka and Savere, you will take our usual route there. I will travel with Lukor and Jaska via East Road. Aly and Raine, you will go north and follow the Pash-Ox Trading Route toward Pashun."

Pashun was a vacation hotspot for honeymooners. Raine's lips pursed appreciatively at Evin's cleverness.

Evin looked at him. "That route will solidify your cover as newlyweds. Before you reach Pashun, take the Joltar Trail junction. It will lead you straight to the safehouse. If you pass Campion Village, you've gone too far. Don't worry. Aly knows what to look for."

Savere shrugged on his pack. "Looks like this is where we part ways, then."

Oka grabbed his pack by a torn strap. It had ripped from his frame during his transformation.

"Be careful," Jaska said sternly. Savere gave him a flat look and Jaska smiled. "Fair point," he said, as if the taciturn dragon had spoken. The dragon brothers bid their farewells and walked slowly in their original direction.

Raine and the remaining thunder reversed their progress, the atmosphere tense. These dragons were essentially strangers to him, yet he felt the absence of Oka and Savere keenly and knew the others felt the same anxiousness for their friends' safety as he did.

Their altercation with the Guardians replayed in Raine's mind, leading him back to the moment Oka shifted; his leathery wingspan was as broad as five horses from snout to tail. Dragons flew as swiftly as wind in fair weather. Hell, the war dragons at Chambrin Keep covered over a hundred miles in a day's practice.

The mystery was intolerable, loosening his tongue in the dreary silence. "Why are we walking? It will take over a week for us to reach your safehouse on foot. You could arrive in a matter of hours if you flew."

Jaska adjusted his bag. Tilting his head upward, he stared at the stars. "One word, hatchling. Watchtowers."

Raine frowned his confusion. The watchtowers peppered Valdenia's countryside at random. He had passed two on his way to Olan's entrance exam and several more as he traveled to Sinopel. They were manned by the guild. New recruits typically served at the towers, rotating shifts so that a team of three shared the watch equally.

"What about the watchtowers?" Raine asked. Valdenia had erected the lookouts in response to the invasion. They had nothing to do with dragons.

Lukor snorted. Raine tensed, anticipating one of the purple dragon's abrasive tongue lashings. When Lukor spoke, his tone was gruff but even.

"The watchtowers were built for us. Evading the hunters was child's play with our wings, so they grounded us."

Jaska nodded. "The towers are spaced so no matter where we land, a sky watcher will spot us. They dispatch their units and hunt us from there. Many years ago, dragons were cocky and took to the air again. And again. They didn't learn." His head swiveled to stare at the ground, as if a great weight pressed upon him.

"What do you mean?" Raine didn't try to mask his confusion. He would have done the same as those cocky dragons. Who cared if hunters spotted him when he could shoot across the sky and land on the other side of the country?

Lukor sighed. There was no anger or impatience in the breath he blew out. Only sorrow. "The watchtowers leave no blind spots. The dragons that refused to walk flew themselves to exhaustion, until they could no longer flee."

Raine didn't trouble his imagination to finish the grim picture. The dragons who didn't walk didn't live. That answered why Oka had kept low, hovering below the highest trees during their encounter with the hunters earlier.

Aly elbowed his ribs. "Besides all that, we wouldn't leave you behind. You haven't learned to change forms yet."

Raine bit his lip. "I'm not sure I can change forms."

Aly and Jaska burst into laughter, dispelling the somber air. Even Lukor flashed a smirk.

Raine threw his hands on his hips. "I fail to see what's so amusing."

His face grew hot as they only laughed harder. Evin must have sensed his fraying temper because she silenced their amusement with a quick word. Her gaze softened at whatever she saw in Raine's expression.

"Every dragon thinks the same thing, youngling. Your position is reversed from the norm, but every dragon experiences the anxiety of never discovering their other form. Jaska and Aly are laughing at themselves as much—if not more—than they are laughing at you."

Aly grabbed his arm and looked up at him with wide, unblinking eyes. "It's true and I'm sorry for making fun of you." She appeared genuinely abashed. "It took me years to change into a human. Mother began teaching me when I was eleven and I finally managed it at twenty-six. It's really, *really* hard."

"My father taught me how to change," Jaska said as they continued moving. "I hatched earlier than I was supposed to and almost didn't survive. My mom and dad spent every minute of my first ten years taking care of me. I got sick easily and had less energy than other hatchlings my age. My dad began teaching me how to change forms when I was about fifteen. It's older than when hatchlings typically start learning, but I was behind in most things so that wasn't unusual."

Jaska slowed, flanking Raine's other side. A rueful smile traced his lips. "It took me almost fifty years to transform, longer than any other dragon. By the time I was forty, I was sure it was never going to happen. I wanted to give up. My father wouldn't allow me to stop trying, though, and one day, it worked! I was sixty-one."

Lukor made a sympathetic sound. Raine hesitated a moment, then asked, "Did it take you a long time to learn?"

The purple dragon smiled, though Raine attributed it to whatever memory he recalled and not from looking at him.

"I was twenty-four when I changed. I was in a bad mood because my best friend Yurrow mastered his change and rubbed it in at every opportunity. One evening, I went to bed as a dragon. When I woke up, I was human. I told my mom the Dreaming Mother must have taken pity on me and taught me in my sleep. She said the Dreaming Mother must have taken pity on *them*."

Their group continued to exchange stories from before the invasion, adding dimension and color to Raine's fuzzy understanding of typical dragon life.

All too soon, their party reached Joltar Trail's turn and were forced to make their final split. It was still full dark, sunrise not due for a couple more hours.

"All right," Jaska said, examining the signboard. He pointed at Raine. "What is your route?"

"Why me? Aly's coming, too."

"Because he asked you," Aly sing-songed.

Raine rolled his eyes but dutifully parroted Evin's earlier instructions. "We need to head toward Pashun, then take Joltar Trail down to the safehouse." Raine frowned. "How far down the trail is the safehouse, exactly? I know it's before we reach Campion, but I'm not familiar with that village or where it is."

"Campion is a small farming community on the outskirts of Joltar," Jaska said. "The safehouse is concealed in an uninhabited section of Hollyhock Forest. It's close to Campion, maybe two days' travel outside of Joltar."

Lukor, of all dragons, seemed worried as he glanced between Raine and Aly. Troubled lines creased his brow. Raine half-expected the male to insist on accompanying them. He wouldn't, would he?

"They don't even know where they're going," Lukor said tersely, eyes darting from Evin to Raine. "One of us should accompany them."

"Hang on," Raine blurted. An idea came to him, inspired by pure dread.

He dropped his haversack and dug through vials of scented oil and folded shirts for his father's map. The nine major cities were marked, as well as most roadways. But small towns ...

Nope. It was just as he thought. There was Pashun and Joltar, spread far apart on the map but connected by a winding line: Joltar Trail, colloquially referred to as Lightning Road. But Campion wasn't marked anywhere.

The insidious black ink was right where he'd left it, in the side pocket of his bag. Raine popped the cork and dipped a finger. Using his knees to keep the map spread open on the ground, he waved at Jaska. "Show me where Campion is, and I'll mark it. We'll make our way to the safehouse, no problem."

Jaska crouched and poked the map several inches from the bold dot labeled Joltar, right off the main trail. Raine dabbed the spot, scratching a quick, smudgy "X" to mark Campion as their guide.

"That's that," Raine said, in a tone meant to convey the matter was settled.

He tucked his map away and stood. Jaska and Evin appeared satisfied, but Lukor eyed him dubiously and opened his mouth. Raine's stomach knotted. The purple dragon wasn't appeased. Their trip was going to be miserable with Lukor accompanying them, he just knew it.

"I know how to find the safehouse entrance," Aly announced, appearing beside Raine. "We stayed there about thirty years ago, or so. I remember it perfectly. I don't need any map to show me how to get there. You just turn left after crossing Drakkus River. Everyone knows that."

Thank the Divine for Aly's quick thinking. She'd picked up on Lukor's objection and stalled him, strengthening their case while she was at it.

Evin remained silent, neutral. It wasn't her style to let anyone posture authority, which meant she was willing to indulge Lukor's verdict. Raine held his breath, too horrified to exhale as Lukor mulled over Aly's reasoning.

"You need to get on a daytime schedule," Lukor said at length. "Walk through the night and well into tomorrow before resting."

A relieved sigh whooshed out of Raine like a bellows. Lukor was sending them off.

"That doesn't make any sense," Aly protested. "We left Sinopel at night because it's the best time to travel."

"It was the best time because we had to exit the city before dawn," Lukor corrected. "Night is never preferable when sneaking a large group." His purple eyes trained on Raine's hood. "Your coloring requires you to cover yourself no matter the hour. Wearing your hood at night will draw the scrutiny of hunters."

"And newlyweds prefer to spend their evenings sharing a bed," Jaska added with a salacious smirk.

Raine and Aly recoiled with exaggerated looks of disgust.

"Do not embarrass the hatchlings," Evin admonished Jaska, though her cheeks were pinched with a smile. She embraced them tightly. First Aly, then Raine.

"I trust you to stay safe. We will see you shortly." She eyed them for a long moment, then turned south onto a small, country lane would take her group toward East Road.

Aly and Raine feigned a dignified walk up the forked path that angled north, toward Pashun.

The moment they lost sight of the den mother and other dragons, they dropped all pretenses of solemnity and whooped with delight.

"I cannot believe they let us go alone," Aly crowed, dancing a jig in the middle of the street.

"Evin gave us the best route to take, too," Raine said with relish, skipping a circle that turned into a triumphant dance of his own. "The Pash-Ox Trading Route goes directly to Pashun. Do you know what that means?"

"No." Aly wasn't put out by her ignorance. Swishing her skirts, her dance grew even more silly.

"Pashun is called Carouse Town. Or, that's what Nyx told me. My friend," he added, realizing she'd have no clue who Nyx was. "It's a place where people party all night, every night. There's lots of dancing and music. It'll be super easy to blend in with the crowds with so many people."

Raine had never gone to Pashun, of course. But plenty of others had. Soldiers and guards went off on honeymoon and came back with the wildest stories. He had always wanted to go and see for himself what the fuss was about; but, like every other proposal that involved Raine leaving Chambrin Keep, his father had thwarted it.

Being a criminal on the run had one perk, at least. He could finally see parts of the world heretofore barred to him.

"Wait. Are you thinking what I'm thinking?" Aly asked, her skip halting.

"That maybe our trip to the safehouse takes a little bit longer than expected." He waggled his brows meaningfully. "We can always claim we took longer because we were being extra cautious."

"Oh, yes. Extra cautious." Aly stifled a giggle with her palm. "Not at all because we stopped in Carouse Town for a little recreation."

Raine's face contorted in mock offense. "Never would we dream of doing something like that. Yes, our return was delayed from excessive caution." He began walking excitedly. "Come on. If we hurry, we can enjoy a few days in Pashun and still make good time to the safehouse."

CHAPTER TWELVE

Pashun, aka Carouse Town, was the northernmost city of Valdenia, tucked into the mountains on the far western side of the border.

Evin had been correct; newlyweds were a common sight on the roads leading to Pashun. It was Raine and Aly's second day traveling as a pair, and they had encountered dozens of couples. As an extra stroke of luck, drawn hoods were common. Many young lovers strove to preserve their skin from freckles and sunburn along the Pash-Ox Trading Route.

Pashun was rumored to be the most romantic place in Valdenia, resplendent with gardens filled with lush arbors and private picnic areas. Couples could rent a cabin for an extended weekend or however long they liked, soaking up idyllic scenery curated to enchant newlyweds and romantics.

It had sounded boring as hell to Raine as a kid. But when he got older, he learned of Pashun's more lurid reputation as the best place to party in Valdenia.

While he balked at sex and had no desire to engage in the elaborate mating rituals humans favored, he absolutely loved getting hammered and dancing all night at the seasonal festivals hosted at Chambrin and its neighboring villages.

Amid Pashun's soft, romantic scenery was a downtown area known as the pleasure district. Young visitors picnicked at the park beneath rose arbors during the day and at night, they went clubbing. Aly was not as familiar with Pashun's blood pumping night scene, so Raine filled her in on the road.

"I'm not kidding. Dozens of clubs where all you do is dance and get shit-faced." He grinned as he spoke. "They stay open all night and the lighting is dark on purpose. Nobody will be able to recognize us in a lineup the next morning, let alone discern the color of our eyes."

"It sounds awesome," Aly squealed. "I've never been away from Mother or the others. This is so crazy. I've never even been drunk," she confessed as they walked.

Raine issued a dramatic gasp, throwing a hand to his chest. "A travesty we will be rectifying multiple times over," he declared, and she snickered. "Seriously, how do you reach two hundred and seven summers old and never get hammered?"

He recalled his first inebriation. He'd been eleven. It involved a lot of apple ale at a late summer festival. Nyx, who had visited the entire week, got equally foxed. They danced along the battlements and received the scolding of a lifetime from his father when he found them.

"It's called growing up with Evin as your den mother while hiding in a world filled with hunters seeking to eradicate your species," Aly said dryly. "I almost never leave the den. When I do, it's typically because we are moving from one safehouse to another, like now, or meeting with the other thunders to discuss plans and things."

Raine side-eyed her skin, pale as porcelain where her features peeked from her hood, and understood why Aly always tilted her face away from the sun. The brightness probably stung her eyes after so many years remaining indoors. By contrast, Raine's countenance followed the sun like a flower. He habitually tilted his chin and closed his eyes to bask in the radiant warmth of the sky's hearth as they walked.

"Even when you met up with the other thunders, it was all business? You never had a party or celebrated anything?"

"No," she said, as if the idea was ludicrous. "Meetings with the other thunders were depressing more than anything. Everyone was always sad. Even in our own thunder, Oka likes to joke around and play a bit, but the others are so serious. Evin is trapped in grief from losing her mate. A part of her died with him and her children, I think. Sometimes, I imagine what she must have been like before. I think she probably laughed a lot."

Raine was silent as she spoke. Passing clouds blotted the sun, matching their deepening gloom.

"Lukor is always so angry," Aly continued. "He went crazy when the humans took Naiah—his mate. I still don't think he's entirely sane, but he gets by. I think the only thing that keeps him going is the chance that he might be with her again someday. Like Evin, he isn't whole, if that makes sense. The rest of us have never met our mates so, mercifully, we don't have that pain."

Raine considered the unmated dragons of her thunder. Savere with his carvings, Oka with his meat, and Jaska with his jewels. They didn't know Evin or Lukor's pain, but Raine saw how they kept themselves obsessively busy. They seemed achingly lonely, which was its own kind of suffering.

Aly sucked in a breath and grabbed Raine's arm. "Don't look now, but there's a watchtower on our left," she hissed. Raine couldn't see her face as she drew close beside him but imagined it was strained like her voice.

He put a hand over hers comfortingly. "It's okay. I passed three on my way to Sinopel. The hunters watch the sky, not the travelers."

Just then, a crunch of footfalls came from the woods to their right. Aly's grip on Raine's arm intensified painfully. He winced as a hunter stepped from the tangled undergrowth. It was a man dressed in the traditional black costume of the guild. His lack of a captain's cuff marked him as a journeyman.

The man straightened, rubbing at his eyes. "Good afternoon," he said politely, blinking to alertness. He pointed at the watchtower on the other side of the road. "On my way to relieve my fellow captain. How do you fare?"

Aly choked, the sound wet and loud and ridiculously suspicious. Raine thumped her back as if she was genuinely choking and grit his teeth in a smile. The journeyman's smile faded at the edges. Raine had seconds to put the hunter at ease before things went south.

"Don't mind my wife," he said. His mouth separated from his brain and spun a yarn consisting of pure, panicked desperation. "You happened upon us right after she revealed a longstanding fantasy to make love with a Guardian."

Aly let out a strangled cry. Raine ignored her. "We are newly-weds, and I was teasing her about already not being enough to satisfy her, then you popped out of the bushes." He shook his head with a self-deprecating grin, then spread his hands with an expression that said, *can you believe the timing?*

The journeyman barked a laugh. "The Divine Father must have been listening in." He smiled at Aly. "No need to be em-barrassed, miss. Us Guardians are fodder for all sorts of fantasies. How do you think I snared my wife?" He gave a broad wink.

Raine squeezed Aly's shoulder in warning, and she chuckled, albeit weakly. "She's a lucky woman," Aly wheezed.

"Oi, so are you," Raine cried in mock offense, nudging her shoulder.

"On your way to Pashun, then?" The hunter's feet, shod in the guild's standard-issue black boots, shifted against the crushed stone path. Raine saw the movement and relaxed. The hunter was not suspicious, at all. Merely impatient to get to his post and too polite to dismiss them.

"Yes," he answered, then gave a small foot shuffle of his own. "We only have a few days to enjoy ourselves before we have to return to my family's farm and assist with the harvest."

The polite hunter read their eagerness to continue. "My wife and I honeymooned in Pashun, as well. You're going to love it. Safe travels."

A massive archway appeared ahead of them, resplendent with millions of bold, exotic flowers. Vines draped across the city's whitewashed walls with delicate blue and pink blooms studding the bricks. Against a backdrop of turquoise sky, it looked like the entrance to the Divine Father's palace itself.

Raine and Aly were not alone in their gawking. All around them, travelers made their way to the stunning gates of Pashun. Even the road was beautiful. Bricks of varying hues were inlaid amongst the orange clay to create a blooming mosaic beneath their feet as they approached the city.

Drawing closer, Raine noticed the lushly flowered gate was guarded by a portly man in a navy officer's uniform. The man was part of Pashun's municipal staff and not a Guardian, then. Raine watched as two couples ahead of them were stopped by the guard and questioned before entering.

"I forgot that every city got the decree for mandatory security checks," he muttered from the side of his mouth.

Raine took Aly's sleeve, prepared to retreat, then dropped his hand with a soft curse. They were too close to the gate. If they backtracked suddenly, it would draw the guard's suspicion and they might be forced to offer themselves up to his scrutiny anyway.

"Me, too," Aly hissed back. "What do we do?"

They were getting closer, and both had their hoods drawn. Covering one's head wasn't exactly a crime, but refusing to lower their hoods for inspection was. One glimpse at their uncovered heads and they'd be swarmed by hunters.

The foot traffic worked both ways, and a youthful couple approached on their left upon exiting the floral city. The woman was buxom with eyes like melted caramel. She looked Aly up and down as they passed and said, "The guard is a disgusting pervert. You should fasten your cloak if you don't want him drooling over your tits."

Raine's eyes narrowed as he thought quickly. They were almost to the guard station. He grabbed Aly's elbow and forced her to stop, his mind spinning. Leaning in, he pretended to be overcome with passion for his young bride and moved his mouth to hers.

Surprise jerked her away and he cupped the back of her cloaked head, preventing her evasion. Raine made sure to seem like they were kissing as he hushed her. He worked his fingers deftly as he whispered over her lips.

"I opened the top buttons of your dress. Hopefully, the guard will focus on your chest more than our faces. Flirt with him, promise to meet him later. I don't care, just keep him more interested in you than doing his job."

Pulling back, he observed his handy work and gave her a cheeky grin. Aly's modest gown was most immodest with five buttons unfastened. He could see the tips of her dusky areolas as her heavy breasts strained to pop out. The sight did nothing for Raine, but he'd been around long enough to know what brought blood rushing to a man's cock.

She gave him a sour look. "If that human touches me, I'm going to kill you."

An eager queue of waiting couples pressed into their backs. Raine looked up in time to watch the guard finish with the couple immediately ahead of them. The guard turned his blunt, ruddy nose to inspect the next couple—for everyone seemed to arrive in pairs—and his eyes riveted to Aly's bountiful display.

Raine was certain she should be charged with public indecency. But the guard would have to look away long enough to send for a ticketing officer, and Raine didn't believe there was a remote chance of that happening.

"State your names and business," he ordered Aly's breasts, somewhat breathlessly.

"Me and my little brother came here to find our sister." Aly spoke in a low, sultry voice that sounded so outrageously come-hither, Raine sank his teeth into his tongue not to laugh. "She eloped with a fortune hunter, and we just received word they are staying in Pashun. Our mother is incredibly distraught."

The guard took a moment to process her words. Raine felt a rush of pride at Aly's quick-thinking. The lecherous guard might have flicked his gaze to the husband of the woman he was salivating over. But a little brother was a nonentity. The guard managed to drag his eyes up sufficiently to glance near their heads.

"You have to lower your hoods."

Aly gasped, her breasts welling dangerously in her unbuttoned gown. The guard's eyes dropped like anchors to her chest.

"Sir, please. I beg you to make an exception. Our sister will bolt from this city if she catches sight of us. I cannot be sure, but I think she is walking the town square just over there. Our plan might be crazy, but it can only work if we catch her by surprise."

She kept her voice husky with the promise of sex and leaned over, grasping the guard by his upper arm. Her new angle spilled her breasts even further from her gown, a feat Raine would not have thought possible without them flopping out of her bodice. The guard flushed puce, on the verge of apoplexy, Aly's nipples a mere whisper from brushing his chest.

"You have a big ... heart to come all this way to save your sister," the guard croaked, sweat dampening his brow.

He appeared to be trying to summon the remainder of Aly's breasts from her bodice by sheer will of concentration. She took full advantage, bless her big heart, and drew a deep breath that heaved her chest enticingly. The tips of her nipples peeked out. It was farcical how hot and bothered the guard was. Raine wrinkled his nose at the man's lack of dignity. *Divine Father, spare me a mate if it will make me act anywhere near this stupid.*

A little more wheedling and the guard caved like lake ice during the spring thaw. As Aly bounced up and down in genuine joy, the guard was near fainting. Raine dragged her along before she killed the man.

After they were several blocks from the gate and out of sight, they ducked into a narrow alley and erupted into gales of laughter.

"I have got to get me a set of these," Raine said playfully, tugging up her bodice and redoing the buttons. "They are like magical pillows."

Aly burst into a fresh peal of laughter. "Puh-lease! You have magical everything else. Have you looked in a mirror?"

Raine snorted. "And where has it gotten me? Not into Pashun, that's for damn sure. Now that you aren't committing a crime of public indecency, let's go. I want to see everything!"

Pashun was a city of heavenly beauty. The streets were bricked with floral designs ranging from the size of Raine's palm to the size of a house. No two blooms were alike, each one newly delightful.

"What do we do first?" Aly asked, spinning a circle to take it all in.

"I'm not sure." Raine scratched at his head through his hood, wishing for the thousandth time it wasn't necessary. The weather had warmed recently and made his hood uncomfortably hot and itchy. *Still better than the ink.*

The buildings were the same white brick as the gates. Baskets hung from various hooks and awnings, exploding with flowers. Boxes of exotic blooms lined windowsills. Vines crawled across clay-tile rooftops and draped decorously down white stone walls.

As they turned a corner, a towering water fountain stole his breath away. It was huge, taller than any of the buildings. A marble carving of the Divine Father stood high and proud, an enormous copper watering can in his hand. Out of the can poured water, cascading gorgeously over an intricately sculpted stone garden containing over a dozen varieties of flowers.

Raine trailed his fingers through the cool, glittering basin that somehow collected the fountain's water but didn't overflow, designed to maintain a desired fullness. At the bottom, beneath the clear, glittering water, were hundreds of silvans. A wishing well.

Beyond the fountain was a flowering archway with a sign. "Blooming Passion: Single entry, two silvans. Couples' entry, three silvans."

Digging through his haversack, he brushed the soft velvet of a coin purse. Raine carefully extracted three coins and grinned at Aly, who was cupping the water as it cascaded from the fountains' enormous watering can. "We can't visit Pashun without seeing the gardens."

Two hours of wandering the pristine gardens of Blooming Passion later, Raine and Aly were over it. While the gardens were stunning, with massive sculptures of animals and historical scenes crafted from lush shrubbery and flowers, they had arrived after days on the road absorbing the untamed splendor of nature. Handmade gardens were lackluster by comparison.

"I want to see the shops," Aly said as they exited the garden.

They retraced their steps since the shopping center was on the opposite side of the city gate. Raine held Aly's shoulder at the edge of the plaza and eyed the guard. There had been a shift change during their garden exploration. The new guard was a different man, his bald head shiny and red in the sun.

"All clear," Raine said, patting her back.

Aly wasted no time, springing forward. She sprinted the length of the plaza, weaving through a throng of newcomers, then followed an arrowed sign which read, "Marketplace."

Raine chuckled as he chased after her, thanking the Divine Father for the hidden bands encircling their ears. Aly practically begged for a hood slip as she galloped like an eager pony through the first door on the left.

He caught the mouthwatering aroma of pub fare on her heels. *Yes.* Apparently, the market district hosted a few restaurants in the mix.

Raine wasn't very enthused about shopping. Unlike Aly, *he* considered how they'd have to lug any purchases across the country. But he could seriously get behind a hot, delicious meal.

Aly loitered in the entryway, looking lost. Raine tucked his arm through hers and guided her forward. A wrap-around bar floated in the room ahead, crowded with chatty diners and day drinkers. The pub's dining area extended beyond the bar with rows of tables and booths. Only half of them were occupied.

A serving girl with twin braids tucked an empty tray under her arm to greet them. "Hello. Take whatever seats you fancy, and I'll be right with you. My name's Tisa."

"Thank you, Tisa," Raine said, then led Aly away from the busy bar, selecting the dimly lit corner booth furthest from the other diners.

"I've never been to a restaurant before," Aly whispered across from him as she sat.

Raine was heartily sick of eating dried meat. Oka's passion for crafting different types of animal jerkies made for convenient travel rations, but he was desperate for bread and cheese and everything else that wasn't the culinary equivalent of shoe leather.

Tisa brought them each a draft of mead, then rattled off the daily specials. Aly looked helplessly at Raine as the woman waited for their order.

He smiled and said, "We will have two shepherds' pies, an order of buttered rolls, a crock of garlic mash. Oh, and we'll do the roasted corn with cream. Two ears."

She beamed at them both. "It'll be right up."

As she left to fill their order, Raine took a swig of mead. It was crisp and bright. He moaned into his mug, quaffing it to the dregs. Plunking the empty tankard onto the table, he snickered at the horrified disgust on Aly's face.

She looked from him to his mug, then to her own. "This isn't water."

"It's mead," Raine explained. "Perfectly delicious mead. Try it."

With the grim yet resolute expression of a prisoner being executed, Aly brought the tankard to her lips and took the barest sip. Her garnet eyes brightened beneath her dark hood, and she tipped it back, much as Raine had, draining it neat. Then loosed a loud belch that made Raine laugh.

She grinned, unrepentant. "Do you think Tisa will bring me another?"

Tisa arrived on the tail end of Aly's question, two fresh drafts in hand. Raine smirked. "Wait 'til you try the pie."

Ten seconds after their food arrived, Aly's eyes rolled in the back of her head on a moan. Raine deliberately suppressed his mind's treacherous comparison of the sound to the noises that occasionally escaped his father's bedchamber. The man was entitled to his comforts, but Raine liked to think he was similarly entitled to his sanity.

"So, I take it you like it," Raine said, lips twisting wryly as he wrapped them around his own bite of pie. *Mmm.* Buttery, flaky crust. Scrumptious gravy. Generously stuffed with pheasant and root vegetables. Perfection.

Aly's vigorous nod made her fork bob like a metallic frog's distended tongue. She grasped the handle and removed it, tines sparkling clean, then immediately dove back into her pie, spreading the crust to get at its gooey middle. Steam billowed thickly but heat did not faze a dragon; she was scraping an empty pie tin with the side of her fork before most humans could have taken a bite.

"Oka is so wrong about food," Aly said, reaching for a generously buttered roll. "I want the years of life back that I wasted not experiencing gravy. Oh, Dreaming Mother, gravy is everything."

"Say that once you've had pudding." Raine sat his fork down and patted his stomach, too full to continue.

"I can't wait to check out the shops. This place is incredible." Aly bounced in her seat.

"I want to take a nap," he moaned, throwing his head back against the wall as he rubbed his stomach. "I'm too full to shop."

They squabbled back-and-forth and negotiated five shops. Then they would reserve a room at an inn for a few nights. Savere and Oka were probably already at the safehouse waiting for them, but Evin's group had a longer route. Even with their time spent in Pashun, Raine and Aly would probably arrive only a day or two after them.

Aly dragged a sullen Raine to a tea shop (where she checked over each blend in rapt fascination), a candle store (where she took forever dipping a wick into liquid wax at the shopkeeper's encouragement), a glassblower (where she knocked over an expensive vase Raine was forced to pay for), and a rug shop (where she tried out a loom and failed spectacularly, tangling up the coarse wool).

Finally, mercifully, they were at their fifth and final shop, Moll's Meats and Treats. Aly had decided to grab Oka several varieties of spiced jerky to sample. Standing at the checkout, she kept trying to convince Raine to visit *just one more shop*.

"I want to go to the inn," he said firmly, crossing his arms.

The shopkeeper, presumably Moll, was a pleasantly round woman with a streak of gray though her dark ponytail. She looked between them and chuckled knowingly.

"Newlyweds, then. As I figured. Always so eager." She gave Raine a sly wink, surprising a laugh out of him. She handed Aly a paper sack holding her purchases, then leaned in, whispering, "Take him to the store six spots that way before letting him take you to bed. You won't regret it."

Aly grinned. "Yes, ma'am."

As they exited the shop, Aly tugged his arm. "You heard the woman. Six spots this way."

"That was the fifth store. We agreed," Raine grumbled, but without much rancor. He thought he saw an inn this direction anyway, and the woman had stoked his own curiosity. It helped that some time had passed since their indulgent repast, allotting his stomach time to accommodate all the heavy foods he had shoveled down.

The storefront six spots over served a stark contrast to its white-washed neighbors. It was painted bright red with a big black heart on the door. "Love Play" was spelled in gilded, flowing script at the heart's center.

"We don't even have sex drives," he deadpanned, just to mess with Aly. She fairly vibrated with excitement to explore the mysteries of sex Love Play might contain.

She didn't bother responding, wrenching the door open and entering with or without him. He trailed behind her and learned more about "love play" in his brief perusal of their merchandise than he had in his entire life prior. And that involved not only awkward attempts at seduction from several women, but also possessing the misfortune of walking in on more than one ungodly erotic session wherein the parties involved hadn't considered bolting the damn door. *Thank you, Father.*

Aly was borderline obsessed with a wall of fake phalluses, carefully examining and feeling each one. She seemed particularly keen on a thick, veiny black cock. It looked more suited for a horse's pleasure than any person's. Was there a cock on either end of that thing? He shook his head and meandered off.

Nothing sparked Raine's interest—without the urge to have sex, it all fell a bit flat for him, personally—until he reached the erotic costume aisle. With glee, he snatched the most incredibly wondrous merchandise he'd ever beheld and pranced to the counter to pay.

The cost was criminal, but he shelled out the correct coinage and thanked the demure, cowled woman who ran the counter. He located Aly—predictably engrossed in the fake cocks—and she gasped when she spied the bag in his hand. "You bought something! What is it?"

He held the bag away as she reached for it. "I'll show you when we get to the inn," he whispered, making his voice an erotic promise in the same manner she'd done hours ago with the city guard.

Her cheeks turned pinker than the double-sided dicks displayed on the wall. As if she thought he planned some sort of sexual mischief. He might have taken pity on her if she hadn't just dragged him through all those shops without mercy.

And what did she honestly think was going to happen? To reiterate: *they didn't have sex drives.* Or, at least, he didn't. Aly was becoming something of a giant question mark in that category given her odd behavior.

CHAPTER THIRTEEN

Raine knocked back his sixth—seventh?—drink of the evening and was promptly twirled from the bar by a pair of pretty sisters. A band of minstrels played roisterous music while everyone either danced or tapped their toes to the rhythm. The lighting was dim, most areas of the club darker than outside. Raine and Aly took full advantage.

They each wore a realistic brown wig—courtesy of Love Play—but that was their only measure of disguise. Aly wore a scarlet gown with a plunging neckline she'd bought from a modiste several blocks over. Raine preferred his own clothing and wore a soft, lawn shirt tucked into tan tights. His only splurge had been a pair of new boots. Supple buckskin molded perfectly to his calves, ending just below the knee. Padded, comfortable and sublime, they didn't force him to forsake style for comfort like his father's boots.

They had explored every club in the pleasure district and were presently enjoying Debauched, a mutual favorite due to its younger crowd and extra dark atmosphere.

Many of the clubgoers wore deliberately garish clothing and skin was *in*. Raine could write an essay about the varying shapes and sizes of women's breasts after two nights of clubbing. The men didn't show quite as much, but he'd seen several sets of pectorals strategically displayed.

Raine kept his own shirt buttoned, but it didn't stop women from liberally smoothing their hands down his front. He'd almost snapped a dozen wrists, whenever the more daring females sought a handful of something south of his stomach.

The sisters were great fun. He'd danced with them the previous night, too. They didn't touch him like they owned him. They were kindred spirits, seeking nights of drunken merriment and dancing until sunrise.

A svelte woman, with sleek dark hair and one of the racier costumes he'd seen, wrapped her arms around his shoulders, cutting off the sisters mid-twirl. Her skirt was trimmed so short, it threatened to show the club how babies were born.

"Your shoulders are so strong," she purred in his ear, wrapping her arms around his neck. Her palms trailed boldly down his back and clasped the two globes of his rear. "Mm. Your ass is delicious. I want to bite it."

"I have raging diarrhea," he yelled over the minstrels' lively tunes, refusing to put his mouth close to her ear. "And I think I just shit myself."

Her painted lips parted in shock as he pulled away, and he had to turn before she saw his silly grin. He'd been making up lies for days to put women off. It was a tie between diarrhea and a strange rash for first place as most effective.

Raine elbowed his way through the throng of dancers and sat at the bar. He angled himself in the chair to get the bartender's attention and gestured for another drink. The stool next to him was occupied and his head jerked at the flash of white hair. Debauched was a youthful scene and his heart slowed as he realized it was an elderly woman and not ... well, not another of *him*.

She glanced his direction, then reacted almost as Raine had. Her head jerked back, and she stared. Her cloudy eyes seared through his skin. He swallowed and forced himself to hold her gaze, though he wasn't sure why.

The woman was ancient, her face carved like the Dragon Fangs. Long, sweeping lines and deep gouges. She flashed a smile, all gums and no teeth. It made her mouth resemble a black hole in the dimness. Then she lifted a stout glass and drained the amber liquid neat.

A bartender deposited Raine's preferred drink on the counter, a fruity concoction topped with ripe strawberries. He scarcely noticed, his focus intent upon the strange old woman. She pushed her stool out and stood, all while staring at him. The hairs prickled on the back of his neck as she leaned forward and whispered into the shell of his ear, "You will fly again."

Before Raine could fully register her parting message, the woman dipped into the crowd and disappeared. He searched the spaces between dancers but found no trace of white hair. With a sigh, he faced the bar and took a deep swallow of his pink-and-yellow drink, the colors swirling like a sunset. *You will fly again.*

Somehow, that old woman knew what Raine was. She knew and seemed kind. Try as he might, Raine could discern no negative meaning behind her words. Her message had been a reassurance.

The minstrels switched to a song played with strings and drums. It was a rousing tune, summoning several of the bar's patrons to dance as a feminine arm slung around his shoulder. He reached out to steady Aly without having to turn and see that it was her.

"I can't believe you turned her down," Aly yelled in his ear, entirely plastered. "She looks dangerously sexy, you know?" She hiccupped.

For a wild moment, he thought Aly referred to the shrunken elderly woman. His mouth fell open, then he recalled the female with the scandalous skirt.

Raine yelled over the music, "She wants to bite my ass!"

"Most men would probably pay for her to bite their ass." Aly plucked his drink from his hand and downed it.

Raine snatched his now-empty glass and scowled. "Oi, get your own drink next time. I'm not letting her creepy mouth near my sweet ass."

Aly thought this was hilarious and collapsed into giggles. Fortunately, Raine's strength was not affected by his inebriety. He managed to keep her upright when she would have fallen to the club's grungy floor, littered with grime and debris concealed by the poor lighting. He loosened his grip once she appeared steady. She immediately toppled over.

"All right, back to the inn we go," he sing-songed after catching her again.

If Aly couldn't stand unaided, there was no point remaining. He wouldn't be able to dance or enjoy himself if he was busy playing babysitter.

It was their third and final evening in Pashun. Staying another night would delay their arrival to the safehouse long enough to make the other dragons worry. Not to mention that old crone's unsettling words. *You will fly again.*

It didn't matter how well-meaning the woman had seemed. No one was supposed to know what they were. While Raine tended to see the good in others, it was too much to put his and Aly's lives in the hands of a complete stranger, which is what they'd be doing if they stayed any longer.

Raine thought he'd be disappointed to leave the fun-loving dance club early, but as they walked back to the inn, him half-carrying Aly, he was surprised at how relieved he felt. Instead of carousing until daybreak and hitting the road directly after, they could sleep off the night's excesses and even grab a hot bath in the morning before exiting the city.

The prospect of bathing never failed to perk Raine up, and he joined Aly in caterwauling the bawdy songs he had taught her on their journey from Sinopel.

"A second son is always fun,
But only after the eldest is won.
If neither one tickles your fan,
Have a go with their old man."

"Damn, I wouldn't mind two brawny brothers and their old man," Aly hummed, leaning into him heavily.

"Why are you so sex crazy?"

It was something that had been perplexing the hell out of him since they arrived. Aly was acting like any hot-blooded human woman on the prowl. Not that Raine cared. More power to her. But it didn't jive with what he had learned about dragons.

She snorted, hot breath blowing into his neck. His nose wrinkled at the unpleasantly moist heat, but he didn't shove her off him. Mostly because he'd have to peel her off the sidewalk when she fell.

"I'm not sex crazy." *Hiccup.* "I'm just curious."

Raine kept silent. Curiosity was normal, and he easily accepted her explanation. Aly took his silence as encouragement to continue.

"Mother." *Hiccup.* "She's so great. And the others are, too." *Hiccup.* "But they treat me like a baby. I'm two-hundred and seven, damn it."

He grunted sympathetically. If anyone asked Arastus Chambrin, Raine would always be his precious baby. And the man definitely treated him like it, when he wasn't being a bastard, forcing him up at the ass crack of dawn to inflict new and increasingly sadistic training regimes.

Aly halted under a streetlamp. Raine turned to see what the holdup was and stifled a groan as her bottom lip trembled. Given his piss-poor luck, it made sense Aly was one of *those* drinkers. The kind that got maudlin after too many pints.

"I'm never going to have sex," she cried in a confessional rush. *Hiccup.*

"Aly, relax. It's like you said—"

"No," she shouted. "You don't get it. I hadn't hatched yet. Jaska, Savere, and Oka? They didn't lose their mates." *Hiccup.* "They'd already met every dragon before the massacre. Their mates weren't among them. But I *hadn't hatched yet.*" Her eyes glistened, voice breaking as she added, "One of them might have been my mate. And now they're dead."

"By that reasoning, *my* mate could be dead," Raine said patiently. "I've met the war dragons, you realize? And I didn't spark with any of them." She blinked slowly, as if emerging from a stupor. Raine nodded grimly. "Exactly. At least you still have a chance of sparking with a war dragon. I'm all but out of options."

"Oh, Raine. I'm so sorry." Aly went to hug him and tripped into his chest. "We're doomed to spinsterhood, but at least we'll have each other."

Raine moved Aly to his side, hooking arm around her waist when she started falling. "You're being ridiculous, and I want to get back to the inn. Start walking before I leave you here."

Aly wasn't the only one who'd drank too much. Raine's body was heavier than normal, as if his skeleton had turned to lead. Except for his skull. His head felt lighter than dandelion fluff, in danger of floating away on the chilly night breeze.

Mercifully, Aly resumed walking. If one could call it that. Her feet shuffled and tripped, forcing Raine to half-carry her. Tucking her face into the crook of his neck, she sniffled. Wetly. He shuddered at the moist heat of snot and tears against his skin.

"Knock it off," he groused, bouncing her head up-and-down with his shoulder. "Your mate isn't dead." She sniffled even more wetly, and he growled. "Look, we can get that black monstrosity from Love Play before we leave, if that's what you need. But hear me now, I'm not sharing a room with you anymore after we buy it."

Aly's gloom shattered on a peal of drunken laughter. Her puffy eyes and red nose lifted from his neck so she could smirk at him. "Are you sure? It has two ends. We can use it together."

"I just threw up in my mouth."

Aly only laughed harder. She was still tittering when they reached the Sleepy Bear Inn. Raine tripped through the door while trying—and failing—to balance his increasingly unsteady companion. They ended up sprawled on the floor of the lobby, Aly laughing hysterically. Raine found himself chuckling beside her, his good humor restored now that a hot bath was imminent.

The nightshift innkeeper barely glanced at them. Inebriated couples arriving at all hours was the norm in Pashun. Somehow, they managed to climb the three flights of stairs to their room. The top floor only had two suites, one on each side of the hallway. The room opposite theirs had been vacant when they checked in. It was vacant no longer.

As Aly and Raine reached the landing, the world slowed to a crawl. If time was a river, it turned from water to molasses as two men clad in tight black uniforms exited the suite. The hunters froze when their gazes found Raine and Aly, the latter tripping as she cleared the final stair.

She looked up at Raine with a crooked smile, leaning against the rustic banister. Her head wobbled on her neck, as unsteady as her feet. "You lost your wig," she slurred. "Your hair is so beautiful, like moonlight and rainbows."

She slumped over and promptly lost consciousness, leaving Raine to face the two hunters alone and drunk off his ass.

One of the hunters was a captain. His golden armlet flashed as he reached behind his back and withdrew a longsword. The journeyman gaped at Raine in stunned disbelief while the captain charged with a savage snarl that did absolutely nothing to mar the utter perfection of his exquisite face.

Still caught in a syrup-thick timestream, Raine traced the slashing brows that arched above dark brown eyes. Stunning eyes which possessed the same velvety richness of a fawn's. The man's hair was midnight black and appeared feathery soft, its short length teasing his neck and falling over his broad, noble forehead. The captain's cheekbones were high, his chin firm. His mouth was wide and dusky as it curled back to reveal straight, white teeth.

Every inch of him was sculpted with equal parts strength and beauty. He was too perfect to be real. Raine wanted to fall to his knees and worship every inch of the divine perfection hurtling toward him.

The sinfully gorgeous captain raised his sword arm. Dazzling flakes of color imbedded in a bone-white blade glimmered in the light. As Raine's eyes flicked from the captain to the blade arcing overhead, time jolted back to normal.

Raine dodged too slow and shouted as pain lanced his right shoulder. Had he reacted a second later, the sword would have cleaved his skull.

The captain came at him again and again, his sword fast and lethal. Raine ducked and scrambled to stay alive, stumbling further down the hall. The captain was the cobra and he, the hapless grouse.

Blissfully unaware of their peril, Aly rolled to her side and loosed a snore. With her wig snug on her unconscious form, the hunters didn't spare her a glance.

Envy and relief scored Raine in equal measure. If he had to defend himself *and* protect her prone form, he might not have pulled it off without the incensed captain's blade skewering his chest.

Dodging the captain's brutal thrusts, which seemed fueled by a hellacious fury, Raine backed into the other hunter. The journeyman snapped out of his onlooker daze and threw Raine to the floor before producing a dagger.

Raine rolled once, twice. The journeyman's blade bit the floor, gouging a thick line through the beaten wood. The captain appeared above him and swung his sword in a smooth line meant to rend Raine's head from his shoulders. He tucked in his legs and somersaulted backwards, landing on his feet.

With both the captain and journeyman intent upon him, Raine's concentration was split between two opponents.

He remained entirely defensive with the captain, only dodging the man's swings as he bounced around the hallway, leaping at the last second each time the sword slashed. But when the journeyman came at him again with the dagger, Raine snatched his knife and snapped the man's wrist. It was a clean break. Agonized screams flooded the inn.

Raine threw himself into his and Aly's room to avoid the captain's next slice. It came hair-raisingly close to gutting him, the captain having gained ground while Raine was busy debilitating the journeyman.

He zigzagged through his and Aly's room, struggling to evade the crazed captain's hacking slashes. The man was hotter on Raine's tail than if he had caught him abed with his wife. It was fortunate Aly had finished Raine's last drink at the bar. His reflexes were so dulled by intoxication, those six ounces may have been the difference between survival and death.

The captain's snarl was so bloodthirsty, it helped sober Raine a little, too. Enough to keep moving, keep dodging, as the captain worked him over with the expertise of a master swordsman.

Raine's calves butted against a bed frame as he narrowly avoided a slice to the throat. Murder raged in the captain's eyes as he corrected his swing. Raine flipped through the air. The captain's sword whined like a bee in his ear, narrowly missing him. Feathers exploded as the blade split the mattress.

Raine continued to jump out of the blade's path, panting for lost breath as he said, "What do you say ... we call it a tie? You seem ... like a great guy. I'd hate to embarrass you ... by kicking your ass."

Speaking was a mistake, Raine quickly surmised. The captain became a whirlwind of metal and fury, his movements twice as fast. In no time, the man backed Raine into a corner and plunged his pale sword through his left shoulder.

The only sound was their labored, intermingled breaths. The captain paused with his sword buried in Raine, its tip skewering the wall behind him. Their gazes met and held, unblinking. Raine lost himself in the man's velvety eyes. Not for a second or a minute. What passed from him to the man bent upon slaying him was infinite. Eternal and irrevocable.

Whatever he'd done to hurt this precious soul was unforgivable. If the captain had to kill him to find peace, Raine would throw himself onto the sword. He kept his eyes open, memorizing every detail of the man's perfect countenance, needing to spend his last remaining seconds of life staring at this angelic being who—

Crumpled to the floor.

The captain's eyes rolled to the back of his head as he slumped unconscious. Aly stood before Raine, brown wig askew and an empty bottle of spirits in her hand. It was the grain alcohol they had polished off before heading to club Debauched, wanting to be buzzed when they arrived. The cost of drinks in Pashun's pleasure district was criminal.

"Thanks," he gasped. "Mind pulling the sword out?"

She gripped the hilt and yanked it free. He staggered against white-hot pain. Blood ran down his chest, soaking his shirt. Aly's hands flew to her mouth as her eyes widened.

"It looks worse than it is. He didn't hit anything vital," Raine assured her, gingerly stepping over the captain's prone form.

Raine purposefully kept his head up. His mind turned to fucking mush each time he laid eyes on the captain. An alarming phenomenon best examined far away from the Sleepy Bear Inn and the deadly assassins it currently housed.

Raine tensed, looking beyond Aly, toward the hall. "Where's the journeyman?"

"Fainted, I think," Aly said, turning a slow circle to take in the total destruction around them.

"Good. Let's get out of here."

They scrounged their belongings from the wreckage of their room and booked it to the inn's exit before either hunter roused.

The innkeeper did look at them this time, his face ashen. Raine's eyes fell onto his wig. It sat on the floor of the lobby where he and Aly had drunkenly collapsed earlier. He seized it on their way out, tugging it sloppily over his head.

They hurried down the sidewalk, abandoned due to the lateness of the hour, and made their way to the city's exit.

As they neared the enormous arbor gate they had arrived through, Raine's stomach leapt like a grasshopper. A public notice board sat next to the guard station, illuminated by a lamppost. They hadn't spotted it during their slapdash performance to gain entry. They were noticing it now.

"That's *you*," Aly exclaimed, sounding worlds more sober than she had an hour ago.

Indeed, it was. Raine's likeness dominated the noticeboard. Sketched with damning accuracy, it detailed his name, age, and physical characteristics. Beneath an exorbitant reward for his capture was a list of outrageous crimes, ranging from espionage to insurgency.

His wanted poster was in Pashun. It had to be in every city of Valdenia, by now. It was absolutely, unequivocally time to leave.

The city guard sat with his arms folded, head nodding as he battled sleep. His chin didn't leave his chest as he waved Raine and Aly through. Leaving Pashun was a lot easier than getting in.

CHAPTER FOURTEEN

Raine jerked upright with a gasp. Molten blood seared his veins. His pulse thundered as if he'd been sprinting. Dream fragments winked and faded like dying embers. Soft sheets and silken, tanned skin. Velvety fawn eyes. A lean, hard body slightly taller and broader than his own.

He had awoken in this heated state each night since they left Pashun. Always with an aching erection.

Something tickled his neck. He pinched near his collarbone, gripping the smooth, unyielding carapace of an insect. A pale green spider writhed its legs, trapped between his thumb and index finger. He gently flicked it into the high, tawny wheatfield.

Aly's mouth parted on a snore several feet away. Raine scowled at her deep slumber. His own sleep was ruined. For the third night in a row.

Groaning quietly, he rose from his makeshift bed of flattened wheat. Fire raced up his shoulders, his wounds punishing him for the motion.

Grain stalks rustled and crunched beneath his boots as he surveyed the coming dawn. It was disconcerting, looking outward and not seeing the Dragon Fangs. They were in the heart of Valdenia, deep in a forested valley. Too low and too far to spy the distant mountains.

Swift, dark shapes tore through the wheat stalks. Field mice. One skittered across Aly's face, jolting her awake. Silent laughter shook his shoulders, further agitating his wounds, as she whipped around, seeking the source of her disturbance. The mice were long gone. Clamoring to her feet, she patted down her face and figure, ensuring no creepy crawlies clung to her.

Raine wiped his smirk as she faced him. Her crimson brows knitted. "I thought we were waking after sunrise."

Pink and gold framed the rim of the world, where the sky bent out of sight. Sunrise was an hour off, perhaps.

"I woke early," he said with a shrug.

Her gaze immediately fixed on his groin, visibly protruding with his arousal. Raine wasn't prepared to confide the bizarre sensations the captain evoked. Aware that, for a dragon who hadn't met their mate, he was exhibiting some serious signs of a rapidly burgeoning sexual maturation. He shuffled awkwardly and angled himself so his bulge didn't face her.

"I live with four male dragons. I've seen morning wood." She laughed and went to relieve herself in the rustling privacy of unflattened grain.

Raine glared down at his tented tights before adjusting himself to alleviate some of the pressure. It was strange how he had awoken with a stiff cock more times than he could enumerate, and it had never felt sexual. Just a mundane physiological phenomenon, easily and routinely ignored. Not once had he experienced the inclination to *touch* himself. But ever since fucking Pashun, it was all he could do not to dry hump his haversack.

He really ought to tell Aly what happened, if only to see if she possessed any insight for him. Raine had opened his mouth repeatedly to do just that, but something always stopped him. His body's reaction to the captain felt private, and he instinctively rebelled at sharing the intimate and perplexing thoughts plaguing him.

The captain had acted like a blood-thirsty lunatic. Raine should want to kill the man. That, or never see him again, since it surely meant death.

But he *did* want to see him again. Raine's heart didn't beat twice between thoughts of the captain. He wanted to touch the man's soft, black hair and see if it was as silken as it looked. He wanted to—

Fucking hell. It was madness.

When Aly returned, he tossed her a wig and tucked his long, white braid beneath the other. They could do nothing about their exotic eyes, but they passed as an ordinary Valdenian couple so long as they kept their wigs on and heads down.

Errant crimson locks poked out beneath Aly's wig. Raine tucked them away, then turned so she could do the same for him. Their wigs were medium brown. His, an upside-down bowl style more commonly seen on boys than men. Hers, shoulder length and slightly wavy. Both were plain and utterly unremarkable.

"Let's pick some more apples before we go," Aly said as she scrutinized his head, double-checking for any stray hairs. Satisfied, she grabbed her knitted tote bag and marched for the orchard.

Raine settled his haversack strap over a shoulder, wincing at the pain. The wounds on his shoulders were healing nicely, given that he'd received no medical attention. Aly claimed dragons healed twice as fast as humans, but the pain had yet to fade.

He trudged after her, neatly hopping the drainage ditch that ran the length of the field. Aly was already on her tiptoes, plucking the reddest and sweetest fruits from the orchard they'd slept near. Her bag was so full, he didn't see how she would be able to walk without toppling a trail of apples in their wake.

Snickering, he plucked the low-hanging fruit, their whirls of yellowish pink reminding him of the berry tart drinks at Debauched. His shoulder complained the higher he reached, and he finished with room to spare in his bag. The strap bit brutally into his shoulder from the added weight.

The captain had skewered Raine twice, once on each shoulder, ensuring there was no comfortable way for him to carry his pack. The strangest thing was, Raine didn't mind. It was unpleasant as hell, yes. But he attributed it to the price he had paid. To see that face, to meet the captain? He'd suffer worse. He'd suffer anything. And that thought was as terrifying as it was confusing.

"Should I get the map out?" Raine asked.

They had yet to consult the smudgy "X" denoting Campion's general location on his map. Joltar Trail began outside Pashun and was a straight shot to their destination. So long as they didn't waltz past the safehouse without realizing it, they wouldn't miss their turnoff.

Thus far, there were no signs of civilization. There hadn't been for a while. They were surrounded by forest. Thick, misty woods teeming with songbirds and wild game. It felt like a mystical, isolated place, not a famous route between two massive cities. No one had passed them on the road in ages.

"No, I've been here several times. The trail crosses over the Drakkus River. Once we clear the bridge, we turn left and follow the water into the woods. The safehouse is hidden near there."

Raine imagined a large house in the middle of an otherwise uninhabited section of Hollyhock Forest. "You realize, for a safehouse, that is conspicuous as fuck?"

Aly elbowed him in the ribs. "Give us some credit, bonehead. We've managed to stay hidden for how long? Oh, that's right. Ten times longer than you've been alive. Obviously, we know a little something about what makes a proper safehouse."

Raine flicked her wig off in repayment for the jab and kept walking as she scrabbled for it. He called back, "It's obviously been pure luck based on your bad decisions. And you should stop rubbing in how old you are. Don't you know we men enjoy youthful maidens, still fresh and dewy like the mornings in spring?"

Rapid footsteps pounded behind him. Raine bolted into a dead sprint, laughing. Aly chased him, shrieking threats on his manhood. He had only recently begun to appreciate his manhood and was reluctant to permanently lose use of it. Thusly encouraged, he maintained his breakneck pace, turning left after the river crossing thanks to her earlier directions. She didn't catch up until he was deep in the woods.

Panting, he spun a circle and examined every angle of the forest. The river remained visible through the trees nearby. "I don't see a house. How far in is it?"

Aly waggled her eyebrows. "What's the matter? The little baby dragon can't find the safehouse? I thought it was conspicuous as fuck, sweetheart."

Raine smiled angelically. "There's a spider on your head."

She ripped her wig off with a shrill scream and smacked her hair with short, frantic slaps. Raine fell to the ground, laughing helplessly. Tears streaked down his face, and he only laughed harder as she launched into a tirade, sharply kicking his side to emphasize her insults.

"Aly, stop."

Raine and Aly froze in surprise before turning in unison toward the source of the command. Evin and Lukor stood a dozen paces away, hovering near the curtained vines of a weeping willow. Evin's delicate features pinched in reproval, but her glare was focused on Aly.

"He started it!" Aly aimed a finger down at Raine. He stood and made a show of rubbing his side where she kicked him.

"It's okay. Aly's right. I was teasing her." He gave an exaggerated wince as he felt along his ribs.

"We will discuss this back at the den," Evin said sharply. When his father used that tone, it meant he was going to feel a belt on his bottom.

Aly scowled so viciously, Raine braced for a blow. But under Evin's firm glare, her shoulders sank. The instant Evin and Lukor turned, he stuck his tongue out.

"I'm going to suffocate you in your sleep," she mouthed at him.

"If you do, I'll tie you up and dump you in the river," he mouthed back.

They exchanged silent and increasingly creative death threats as they followed Evin and Lukor deeper into the woods. The rushing river disappeared behind them, fading to silence. Prickly, verdant foliage encased them on all sides as Evin stopped before the hugest tree stump Raine had ever seen. He fought the tangled undergrowth, tripping as he reached her.

"Welcome to our new den." Evin smiled warmly as they gathered before the stump.

A thorny branch poked his back as he stared at the stump. It was broad, flat, and enormous. The remnants of an ancient atmos tree that must have stood as high as a small mountain. It was impressive. A historic relic. But not a safehouse.

Nobody had told him Evin was a nutcase. Then again, they *had* gone on about how severely reclusive she was. Didn't she go, like, six months without once leaving her bedchamber?

"That's a tree stump," he said gently when nobody else spoke.

Concealing their den mother's insanity was sweetly protective of them, but didn't they think he had a right to know? The woman was supposedly in charge of them all. Not to mention he was being actively recruited into their thunder. It seemed unwise to take orders from a barmy dragon lady.

Aly burst into a gale of obnoxious laughter, then shoved him aside. She crouched and pressed her fingers inside a knot low on the stump, half-concealed by detritus. A soft, metallic snick sounded, not unlike the tumblers in a lock disengaging.

Lukor reached down as if to wrench the stump from the earth.

It lifted easily, and Raine saw at once it was a door, its underside rootless, sanded flat and smooth. Beneath the stump was a round, dark hole tunneling straight into the earth.

Aly was entitled to the triumphant smirk she shot him, and he grinned back good-naturedly while inwardly thanking the Divine Father he hadn't made any comments out loud regarding Evin's mental state.

It was genius.

And huge. The vertical descent was deeper than all their combined heights. Lukor was the last to enter, shutting the stump door and latching it back into place. Sunlight cut off from above, amplifying the dim glow of lamplight at the ladder's base.

Raine could somehow smell the hush in the air, the staleness of a world below earth and sky. As he reached the bottom, Evin took the lantern in hand. She led them down a brief, horizontal tunnel. Roots peeked through the rocky, dirt-crusted walls, tickling his fingers as he felt along the narrow passage.

It dumped them into a massive chamber, bigger than the average cottage and twice as tall. Thin straw mattresses lined one half of the space, enough to sleep twenty. Travel bags were piled along the other wall. They trekked the wide path through the center of the chamber and entered another short tunnel. It forked in three directions. Evin veered left and they followed.

Savere, Jaska, and Oka sat around a broad, wooden table. It was unvarnished and roughly hewn with a thousand concentric rings. It must have been fashioned from the very atmos tree which formed the stumped entrance. Raine imagined a mighty giant plucking the tree like a weed, its rended roots leaving crumbled, hollowed spaces that became these very tunnels and chambers.

Short, fat logs sat flat-side up against the dirt floor to be used as chairs. The trio of green dragons flew from their seats as Raine and Aly entered behind Evin and Lukor.

"We were starting to worry," Jaska said, clapping Raine on the back, close enough to his injured shoulder that he tensed.

Oka enveloped Aly in a bear hug, spinning her around in a manner that made Raine's injured shoulders ache by merely watching. When Oka dropped Aly and reached for Raine, he took a step back, not in the mood for untold agony. Oka didn't look offended in the least. He grinned and plucked Raine's wig off, tilting it in the air as he inspected it.

"This is the most hideously beautiful thing I've ever seen."

Oka tried tucking his mallard green hair beneath the wig. His hair was short, only to his shoulders, but it was unbound. More hair stuck out of the wig's edges than ended up beneath it.

"How do I look?" Oka asked the room at large with his arms outstretched.

"Like an imbecile," Savere said dryly. Oka jerked his head in outrage, sending the poorly secured wig to the floor.

"It works better if you tie your hair back first," Raine said as Oka scooped the wig up and offered it back to him.

"I look forward to hearing how you came to possess those hairpieces," Evin said with the slightest edge. *Uh oh*. She had clearly put it together and wasn't pleased. "Lukor and I have guard duty until nightfall, so we will speak with you then."

He didn't mistake her parting words for assurance. That had been pure warning. *Damn*. Aly's stare met his and she made a face, bugging her eyes.

He laughed despite himself. They were in for it later and they both knew it. But maybe getting his ass reamed with a friend would make it bearable.

The remaining dragons ambled back to the enormous table. Raine settled next to Jaska while Aly took the empty log between Oka and Savere across from him.

"How was your trip?" Jaska asked. He stared with an unsettling intensity at Raine.

He fidgeted, both at the strange expression he was receiving and because there was no way he could tell the truth.

The panic burgeoning in his chest must have shown on his features. Aly took one look at him and said, "How was *yours*? You guys finished before us, after all."

Jaska's expression flattened, as if he knew they were stalling.

Oka's chest puffed up beneath his carob tunic. "We smeared onion juice all over our skin and kept the peels in our pockets. Even the hunters avoided us." He pointed a thumb at his brother with a shit-eating grin. "Savere made two humans puke."

A slight twitch of Savere's eyebrow sent Raine and the other dragons chuckling. Excepting the unflappable Savere, who resumed carving his wood piece with a dismissive air.

Jaska, Evin, and Lukor's group had experienced the most uneventful trip to the safehouse. Opting to remain in the woods as they followed East Road, they hadn't encountered any hunters, officers, or otherwise suspicious citizens.

When the conversation returned to Raine and Aly's trip, he was slightly more prepared. Aly caught his eyes meaningfully and he nodded.

They opened their mouths and answered, "Nothing much," and "It was boring."

"Where'd you get the fake hair? It's awesome!" Oka's eyes roved reverently over the frizzy brown locks concealing Aly's crimson mane.

"We stopped at a few shops on the way here," Aly said with a vague flick of her wrist.

Savere's thin carving knife pointed to the low, dirt ceiling as he glanced shrewdly from Aly to Raine. "The cities are crawling with hunters. Nobody can get near a human settlement without passing guarded checkpoints."

"I know. We were really lucky," Raine said, wide-eyed with exaggerated earnestness. Aly nodded. Very carefully, they avoided each other's gazes, mirth too close to the surface.

Savere placed his carving on the table, a half-formed horse mounted by an armored rider. "Nothing happened on your way here?"

"No. Well, nothing worth mentioning." Aly shrugged.

"You're absolutely certain?" Savere pressed, looking hard at Raine.

He concentrated on making his features as innocent as possible. No small task with Savere's eyes boring through him like metal screws. Raine felt more and more like a naughty child. Pressure built in his chest until he was compelled to say something—anything—to appease Savere's silent interrogation.

"We saw a herd of pink whiffy pigs. Seriously, there were droves of them. Pinker than raspberries—"

"Your shirt is soaked with dried blood, moron," Jaska cut him off.

Oops. Raine's aching shoulders should have served as a constant reminder to craft a credible cover story. But whenever he had dwelled upon his injuries, obsessive thoughts of the captain took over instead.

"Oh, did I say whiffy pigs?" he asked, scraping the recesses of his skull for a lie. Any lie. "My mistake. It was a pack of pink wolves. The craziest shit I've ever seen. We got away but I did have to fight them off and give Aly a chance to get away. She's much slower than me," he added confidingly, leaning across the table.

"That is quite a tale," Jaska deadpanned.

Aly buried her face in her palms and Oka's shoulders shook with suppressed laughter. Raine could well recognize when he was being laughed *at* and not *with*, thanks to many debasing encounters with his cousin Olan. His cheeks burned, undoubtedly rosier than his imaginary wolves.

"Your ignorance is showing," Oka said between chortles.

Savere interjected, before Raine could inquire as to which salient dragon fact he blatantly lacked. "Your wounds indicate a clear run-in with hunters. Haven't you ever wondered why no sword or blade can pierce you?"

"No," Raine replied slowly, unsure if Savere's question was rhetorical. "I try really hard to avoid the pointy ends of sharp objects."

He was usually quite proficient at it, too. While Raine was a decent swordsman, his speed surpassed his technique. Raine wasn't the best, but he was always the quickest. Until Pashun.

That captain was *good*. Raine wished he could blame his blundering ineptitude on whiskey. But he knew damned well his preternatural obsession with the captain was what had gotten him skewered like street food.

"Traditional weapons cannot penetrate dragon hide," Savere explained. "Even in our human forms, our flesh retains its resistance. Can you recall bleeding from a wound before those?" He pointed at Raine's shoulders with his whittling knife.

Raine's brow furrowed. Surely, he had scraped a knee once or twice as a child? Gotten scratched by a cat? Nicked by a weapon? "Jaska," he said at last. "He cut me when he met me. With that knife he keeps in his boot."

Jaska nodded. "Dragons bleed as red as any human, but our blood tastes markedly different. It burns the tongue like firebasket peppers. Licking your blood was the fastest way to determine if you were a dragon or not."

"You have no idea what Jaska's blade is made of," Savere remarked. Raine shook his head, though his confusion was written all over his face. "The only thing that pierces dragon flesh is bone. Our bone."

Raine stared blankly. Did Savere mean …

"The hunters take the bones of our dead, from the dragons they slaughter, and craft weapons from them," Savere explained.

Jaska's features darkened with what looked like pain. "That blade I keep in my boot? I found it at the site of a large-scale hunter attack. Where they located and exterminated an entire thunder. One of the hunters must have lost it in the slaughter."

"Oh," he said weakly.

His mind flashed to the captain. A seething tornado of enmity and bloodlust, armed with a long, white sword that glittered as it slashed. The man Raine fixated on was a creepy, psychopathic dragon killer and maker-of-swords from their corpses. *Wonderful*.

If the captain was his mate—and he was really beginning to suspect this was the case, though he had no fucking clue how it was possible—Raine imagined they were going to require something stronger than couple's counseling to overcome their differences.

"So," Jaska drawled, his eyes clearing, "would you like to tell us what really happened?"

Raine and Aly fabricated a simple cover story of encountering a Guardian unit along on the Pash-Ox Trading Route. They spun their acquisition of the wigs into events, neither keen to admit they had spent multiple evenings partying in Pashun.

Savere stood. "Your wounds require attention. Let me get my medical kit."

Aly yanked her wig off and tossed it onto the table, next to Raine's. Her crimson braids were a matted mess, and she began working out the bulbous knots with her fingers.

"Shirt off," Savere said, moving behind him. Raine tugged the white cloth over his head, gritting his teeth as phantom wolves mauled his shoulders.

Savere cleaned the wounds and applied a thick, bitter-smelling herb paste before bandaging him. All the while, Raine cringed at Aly's ropey tangles. If his hair looked like *that* after wearing a wig, he would rather endure a hood, regardless of how hot or itchy it was.

Once Aly's hair was as straight as it could get without the benefit of a brush, she flipped the mass behind her shoulders and turned a frown on Jaska. Busy fitting a gold band with a brilliantly faceted ruby, the evergreen dragon didn't notice until she addressed him.

"What's up with Lukor?"

Jaska's tiny tongs paused its task of turning the jewels on the table, seeking the perfect gem for the piece he crafted. Oka's features pinched as if he got a sudden stomach cramp. The sounds of Savere repacking his medical bag stopped.

Raine blinked at Aly, as nonplussed by their dramatic reactions as she was. He understood why she'd asked. Lukor wasn't a quiet guy. He was loud, with a shitty attitude. But the dragon hadn't breathed a word since their arrival.

"Yeah," Raine piped into the unnatural silence. "What's up with Lukor?"

His reiteration jarred the green dragons back to life. Savere started rustling behind him once more. Oka looked at Jaska. So did Aly. Raine followed suit, adding his stare to the mix.

Jaska rolled his eyes but answered. "He's been arguing with Mother. He wants to ... Well, you'll hear about it soon enough. Lukor's not letting it go and a decision needs to be made."

A light of comprehension shone in Aly's eyes. As she looked at Raine, her expression shuttered. Nodding gravely, she said, "I agree. A decision needs to be made, once and for all."

CHAPTER FIFTEEN

If Raine thought Aly or the others would fill him in on Lukor's mysterious disagreement with Evin, he was sorely mistaken. He was stuck living with a bunch of people who were all in on a secret except for him. Being the odd one out, in a group where he finally fit, hit Raine square in his childhood. He tried to shrug it off, but as time went on, the sense of isolation suffocated him like a snowdrift.

While his father was equally guilty of keeping secrets, it wasn't the same. Arastus Chambrin had changed his nappies. Told him bedtime stories. Rocked him through nightmares. Raised him. Their relationship would survive his father's misguided methods of protecting him.

He couldn't say the same for Evin's thunder. They were essentially strangers to him. And vice versa. Any kinship or camaraderie developing between them ground to a halt.

Their infernal secret crept through the tomblike den like invisible smoke, poisoning every interaction. Gazes shifted. Words were stilted. And Raine just wanted to go home.

It didn't help that he absolutely loathed living belowground. After three days in the new safehouse, the walls began to push in on him from all sides. At times, his eyes tricked him so completely, he would curl up into a ball and tremble, waiting to be crushed.

On the third night, Savere took him aside and taught him how to take slow, measured breaths to calm himself out of all-consuming panic attacks.

"My mantra is 'One.' Breathe through your diaphragm." Legs crossed and back straight on a straw mattress, Savere demonstrated. "Fill your lungs as full as you can. Hold it for a beat. As you breathe out, you say or think your mantra. It will balance your mind and quiet your panic."

It took practice and his progress was frustratingly slow. But Raine did as Savere instructed. His mantra was, "Fawn."

The other dragons were similarly tense and grim, appearing to enjoy their new den as much as Raine. They argued over who got guard duty, everyone equally desperate to get the fuck out.

"We're creatures of the sky," Evin told him when yet another bickering session devolved into a nasty argument over who got guard duty. "It is ironic because our Dreaming Mother sleeps deep in the earth, yet we are unsettled the more we draw near."

It turned out claustrophobia was a condition of their species. "Maybe that's why she gave us wings," Raine replied. "Because we're meant to show her the things she cannot see. And we can't do that if we're down here with her."

Evin's brow furrowed, her finger coming up to scratch at one cheek. "You know, youngling. I think you're right about that."

Lukor was no longer overtly hostile to Raine, but their interactions were the stiffest out of everyone. They kept to opposite guard schedules, which told Raine their efforts of avoidance were mutual. With different guard and sleep schedules, they seldom occupied the same space.

By the sixth day, Raine understood why humans thought hell was beneath their feet. Because that's where he was. Literal hell. He massaged his stiff neck, awakening from another fitful sleep on the thin, scratchy pallet he had claimed.

Raine cracked a yawn, more tired than he'd been prior to resting. Deep sleep was impossible to achieve. He had woken every fifteen minutes to shift position, but his efforts to get comfortable were in vain. A pile of rocks would be more pleasant to lay on than this abysmal excuse for a bed.

At least I no longer suffer those dreams. It was quite possibly the only positive aspect of the whole wretched experience. The dreams were too intense, too confusing. He couldn't fathom enduring them and this terrible tomb of a safehouse at the same time.

The vast sleeping area was empty except for Raine.

He stood from his pallet and walked the short tunnel on his left, heading to the table room where the dragons tended to congregate. A brief survey from the threshold revealed Aly and Savere had guard duty. Raine nearly backed out as he glimpsed Lukor's presence, but he was sick of dodging the older dragon as if he were contagious. It wasn't sustainable and Raine had nothing to feel guilty about.

He hadn't trapped Lukor's mate in the Cavern. That unfortunate incident took place over two centuries ago, the wretched details omitted from human history. Lukor was entitled to his feelings, but he wasn't entitled to treat Raine like shit over something he hadn't even done.

As Raine crossed into the room and took a seat between Oka and Jaska, he decided the kid gloves were off. He'd given Lukor enough time to adjust to his presence. If the dragon came at him again, Raine wasn't going to hold back. He was as gorgeous as he was deadly, and anyone who wanted to mess with him was going to find that out the hard way.

Evin and Lukor sat across from Raine and the green dragons. Both glanced at him, expressions taut, before Lukor refocused on the den mother.

Aggression charged the stagnant air, his words a low growl. "We're their last hope. The others are gone. We have no thunders left. This is it. This is our final chance. We can rot in this hellhole, or we can try to save them."

Word to the hellhole. It was a fitting name for their miserable lodgings, and Raine was quietly astonished at how kindred he felt with Lukor over something so minor.

Evin placed a palm on his arm. It looked like a child's hand against Lukor's large, muscled bicep. "I know how you feel, Lukor. But it's a suicide mission. We can't do them any good if we're dead. We must remain hidden and wait for the right time."

Lukor shrugged her hand off, pounding one fist against the table. The foot-thick, petrified atmos slab was rock solid beneath his blow.

"I'm done waiting," he roared. The room froze as Lukor raged. "In two hundred years, there's *never* been a right time. There will never *be* a right time. We lost eight thunders waiting. Had we done what I suggested at the beginning, we would have over fifty dragons at our backs. That cursed fucking keep would be burnt to cinders and our families would be free."

Evin flinched and shrank away. In the echoing silence of Lukor's outburst, Jaska said, "I'm with Lukor." As one, they turned to the dragon whose green eyes were as dark as a midnight pond. "He's right. There's never going to be a good time. Waiting costs too much. If we keep waiting, we'll die waiting."

Evin shook her head, blue eyes mournful with regret. "My decision is unchanged."

"I'm with Lukor, too," Oka cried. He jumped to his feet, jostling Raine's left shoulder. He tensed, expecting pain out of habit, but none came. His wounds were nearly healed.

The den mother looked dejectedly from Oka to Jaska. Her gaze settled on Raine. "And what of you, young one?"

All eyes turned on Raine and he blinked.

If he had it right, the mysterious, ongoing argument was Lukor's desire to free the breeding dragons at Chambrin Keep. It was no wonder the dragons had been reticent to enlighten him. Chambrin was his home. And, well, he *had* abetted the incarceration of those very dragons, albeit ignorantly.

He lifted his chin, meeting Lukor's challenging glare. "I'm with Lukor," Raine stated firmly.

The purple dragon's eyes widened slightly, the only sign he'd surprised him.

"But I swear to the Divine Father, the Dreaming Mother, and every holy relative in between, if you talk any shit about my dad, I will punch you in the fucking face until all your teeth fall out and Savere will have to carve you dentures."

The urge to beat the shit out of Lukor for the vitriol he had spewed weeks ago resurged with a vengeance. Raine consciously lowered the pugnacious set of his shoulders. This wasn't the time to fight, and he'd already decided to let Lukor slide that one time due to the terrible situation with his captured mate.

Crimson splotches mottled Lukor's neck, slowly overtaking his visage. He didn't speak. Raine wasn't sure if the purple dragon was too furious to form words or if Lukor was genuinely heeding his threat.

Raine forced his gaze away and landed on Evin's grave expression. And as everything he'd overhead rushed back to him, he tilted his head and asked, "But why *didn't* you try to free the dragons sooner, back when there were more thunders to help?"

"At first, we didn't know where the chieftains had taken them," Savere said from behind. Aly and Savere moved to stand at the edge of the table where he could see them, their faces ruddy from the brisk evening air outside.

Nobody spoke as Savere continued. "After they were initially taken, we scoured the lands openly, seeking the captive dragons while the hunters sought us. Soon, the hunters expanded their guild. Flight became a death sentence once they littered the country with sky watchers, all equipped with bone-tipped spears and arrows."

"The Allium thunder thought it safe to fly if they reserved their wings for nighttime or cloudy days," Jaska said. "But the hunters spied them during takeoff and landing. They narrowed their perimeter until they knew precisely where Carisha's den was located."

The jewelry-obsessed dragon's countenance darkened. Staring at the center ring of the table, his eyes shone with fear and horror, as if a venomous snake was curled there. "It was a massacre. More hunters than I've ever seen in my life. They entered everywhere. The doors, the windows. Dragons were slaughtered in their beds before they could stir, before they even knew what was happening."

By the Divine, Jaska had been there.

"How did you get out alive?" Raine breathed.

One captain in Pashun had been too much for him. As many hunters as Jaska described ... It was a death sentence. A massacre, as he'd said.

Jaska swallowed, his throat bobbing long beneath his ruby cloak clasp. "I was not a part of Carisha's thunder. The Allium dragons were the most determined of us to locate the captive dragons. I arrived seeking an update on their progress. I almost walked right into the bloodbath but hid at the last second, ducking into the hedges out front."

His fists clenched and unclenched. "I had no choice but to wait. It lasted for hours. First, the hunters slaughtered every last dragon. Then, they loaded their corpses onto massive wagons, concealing them with tarps before carting them away."

Jaska trembled, and Raine impulsively grasped one shaking fist between his hands. The midnight green dragon's skin was a shock of ice, but he relaxed his fist and squeezed Raine's hands tightly.

"Once the hunters grounded us, our search fell to a crawl," Oka said. "The humans began boasting of a dragon army they were raising. By the time they finally unveiled the secret site of their breeding program, we were only four thunders strong. That's when Lukor demanded we attack."

Oka's gaze flicked to Lukor and the purple dragon took over seamlessly. "We knew it was a trap. The hunters hadn't uncovered anymore of our thunders in over two decades. They must have been confident there weren't enough of us left to overtake Chambrin Keep. I wanted to prove them wrong. I wanted to turn their dragon dungeon into their gravesite."

Lukor paused and took a steadying breath. His rage pressed visibly close to the surface, like spring water trapped beneath thin ice. "Not everyone agreed with me. Many were too frightened by the threat of a trap to act. But I persisted and the remaining den mothers agreed to gather their thunders and put it to vote."

Raine's pulse raced in his ears. He flicked his mercury eyes from Lukor to the others. Each face was bleaker than the one before it. "What happened?"

"Only three thunders made it to the vote," Evin whispered. "Rokeshin's thunder never arrived."

Raine was able to fill in the blanks himself. Fearful and grief-stricken, the remaining dragons had balked at attacking Chambrin. That it was obviously a trap was the last nail in the coffin of their burgeoning revolution.

"When they voted it down, I went by myself," Lukor said. Raine whipped his head to stare at him, wide-eyed. "I encountered a militant castle sitting high on a plateau. Over a hundred hunters encircled the keep, the bones of our loved ones sharpened to fine points that glinted against the sun as they awaited us."

Raine flushed with shame, dropping Lukor's stare. He had always considered the number of sentries stationed around Chambrin Keep inexplicably excessive, a flagrant waste of soldiers and resources. It made a dismal sort of sense, now that he knew the threat they anticipated was not Garganthan. Not even human.

And his father must have known the sentries were a type of Guardian, all along. General Arastus Chambrin had served three terms in the guild himself. Once as a journeyman. Then, as a captain. And finally, as a master.

Raine's feelings toward his father were becoming as murky and complex as a wetland's ecosystem. Too many secrets. While Raine would decimate any ignorant ass who spoke ill of his father, a black kernel of doubt lodged inside his chest. Doubt that made him feel equal parts despicable and irate.

A wild confrontation brewed in his gut. A teeming stew of all he'd discovered since the night he was forced to flee his home. And if they went to rescue the breeding dragons, Raine would have the chance to see his father and get those answers once and for all.

"Raine grew up at Chambrin! He has insider knowledge that could help us free them," Aly said. *Pro-Lukor, then.*

Evin must have realized they all were, because her shoulders sagged. "Lukor mentioned something to that effect before you joined us," she said, looking at Raine. Worry lines creased her eyes. "But unless you know of a secret entrance that leads directly into the Cavern, I do not believe it will make a difference."

Raine sprinted through the halls of memory, chasing every scrap of knowledge he'd gained about the Cavern throughout his lifetime at Chambrin.

The entrance to the Cavern *was* a secret. Not even Raine was supposed to know how to enter the subterranean dragon prison.

Except he did. A desperate plan took shape in his mind, a four-legged shape with a tantalizing rack.

He looked at Oka. "We're going to need a Garganthan mountain moose."

CHAPTER SIXTEEN

Raine stalked lightly through the dusk-lit woods. Leaves rustled and twigs snapped as he picked a discreet path, occasionally startling a critter from the brush. Birds were active and everywhere. Finches and warblers, wrens and geese. They busily fueled themselves for their southern migration, where they would outwait Valdenia's gelid winter in comfort.

This sprawling woodland butted against one of the forbidding walls of Chambrin Keep's mesa. The very sheetrock cliff he'd dove from when fleeing home a month ago. *A month*. Each week had seemed a decade.

Six dragons and one mountain moose trailed his wake. They had entered the woods at dawn, miles away, where none of the keep's sentries would detect their approach.

The sentries loved moose. Thought it was the greatest thing since toffee pudding. Raine had taken advantage of that fact, combined with the convenient timing of the seasonal rut, when he evaded the sentries the night Eddic, Vanwert, and Tyrus came calling.

Although the sentries had already proven how derelict in their duties they could be at the prospect of a red, juicy steak, Raine didn't trust they'd wander far enough from their posts with only the bellow of a mountain moose to draw them. Which was why Oka currently led a massive moose bull by a thick rope knotted into a harness. The beast was huge. It could rest its chin atop Raine's head and possessed a broad-fanned rack as wide as he was tall. A veritable behemoth.

As far as bait went, the moose was supreme. It had taken Oka two days to find a specimen suitable for their purpose. Most of Raine's plan was risky and had a low—*all right, zero*—percent chance of success. But when Oka had presented him with this moose, he had no doubts they'd pull off the first phase of his plan.

Unfortunately, the moose's prize-worthy size made directing the creature through the woods markedly challenging. The beast did not fear dragons like traditional prey. It was aggressive and struggled, occasionally lowering its head to charge their backs.

Progress was further hindered as Oka picked a protracted path that didn't get the moose's antlers hung up. At least ten times, Oka had backtracked to maneuver the recalcitrant moose around a too-tight section of trunks and branches.

Thankfully, they'd begun early. Even with the moose slowing their advancement, they reached the cliff wall just as the last fingers of daylight gave a parting wave.

Hovering against the outermost canopy, Raine placed a palm flat against the forbidding sheetrock wall. This section of cliffside beveled out before receding in a lazy limestone wave that concealed the ground immediately below the keep's curtain.

It wasn't *impossible* to scale. An astute selection of the right tools and rope could get the job done. But the addition of the defensive curtain, rimming the mesa and concealing the keep from view, had always struck Raine as absurdly redundant. If someone was going to climb a sheer, lethal cliff to reach Chambrin, what was a few more feet of stone?

Well, it all made sense now. Because the curtain existed to protect the keep from soaring dragons, not rock-climbing humans. High above his head, upon Chambrin's battlements, dragon slayers were stationed as sentries. Raine had been surrounded by humans wielding the bones of his own people as weapons his entire life and never knew it.

His father must have wielded such cadaverous armaments, too. A fact his mind shrank from like a wounded animal. The thought was too hideous to contemplate.

Raine turned toward the dragons waiting several paces back, gathered between shadowed elms. They stared at him beneath long, hooded cloaks, blending seamlessly with the early darkness.

It was halfway to shift change, and the sentries would be bored and restless.

He made a broad gesture with his hands to signal Oka, not chancing a whisper. No one had spoken since they entered the woods hours earlier. The hush that overfell them contained the weight of two centuries of strife. The air was loaded with apprehension, grief, determination and, most importantly, hope.

Oka issued a loud, piercing moose scream. Then another. His bellows were immaculate, putting Raine's imitations to shame. He couldn't detect Oka's movements, the dragon too deeply ensconced in the forest, back where the tree trunks blended in a solid shadow.

The moose gave a sudden, sharp cry, indicating Oka had cut the ropes and smacked it hard on its rump. Hooves thundered across the ground. The moose bulleted across the clearest path in its agitation, charging between two lines of dragons as they shrank out of its way.

At the mesa's dead-end, the moose veered right, away from Raine, galloping the bosky trail between sheetrock and forest canopy.

Twack. Twack. Two arrows split the wind and buried into the moose with hair-raising accuracy. The beast staggered with an acute, braying cry. Branches snapped like firecrackers as it fell, crashing through undergrowth. Then, silence.

The sentries above whisper-shouted in exalted tones that quickly faded. Raine counted in his head. He reached one hundred as the bushcrickets began chanting their night music in earnest.

"They're good and gone. We have to hurry."

Several hundred feet above their present location, the curtain was unguarded. They had to move fast. The sentries would take the quickest route to the fallen moose: a concealed stairway carved into the mesa, the keep's sole access to its outlying lowlands.

Two guards were stationed at the ground-level entrance, round-the-clock. The sentries, bent upon retrieving their prize, might ask one of the stairwell guards to man the battlements in their stead while they harvested the moose. Unlikely, but too risky not to consider.

Lukor stepped from the woods and Raine blinked before jerking his face to the night sky. The male was stripped nude in anticipation of their next step. A little warning would have been appreciated. Raine pressed a balled fist to his forehead, wishing for selective amnesia to scrub the image of Lukor's junk away.

The sounds of knuckles cracking and bones popping drenched the darkness as Lukor shifted. Purple scales were best for blending with the night, for whatever reason. Raine had originally thought Jaska would fill this part of their plan, given his extra dark coloring. Evin had kindly shot him down, explaining Lukor would be better.

As he lowered his chin, Raine saw she was right. Lukor's hulking frame erased the moon and stars like a patch of blank midnight. Jaska knelt by Lukor's side, cupping his hands. Evin stepped into Jaska's linked palms like a makeshift mounting block and climbed onto Lukor's back. Clutching the knobby ridges of his dragon spine, she perched directly between his folded wings. Jaska climbed up behind her.

Raine waited until everyone was on before clamoring after Aly, wrapping his legs securely around her waist. He felt Lukor breathe beneath him, a gentle rise and fall that crested through his thighs and buttocks like rolling waves.

Twin wings expanded, rocking them sharply. With a cliff before them and a forest wedged at their backs, there was no room for Lukor to maneuver his gigantic wings, no way for him to get the angle he needed for flight.

Muffling a curse, Raine tensed to dismount when Lukor abruptly shoved his wings against the jutting branches. Wood bent, split, groaned. Then, *whoosh*.

His stomach somersaulted as Lukor kicked up from the ground. Raine scrambled to hold on, gripping Aly's midsection hard enough to break ribs as the earth fell away.

As Lukor ascended, his sickly feeling dissipated. Aly's hood flew back, loose wisps of sweet-pea scented hair tickling his nose. Wind caressed him from all sides. A roaring well of ecstatic joy burst through him as Lukor hurtled at the moon, swifter than a spear.

He was flying. And it was glorious. Exhilarating. Intoxicating. Raine would never again identify as a creature of the earth. Wind was his blood. The sky, his soul. How could he have ever doubted it?

Lukor eclipsed the battlements and landed hard. Raine's wonderment evaporated instantly, the impact pinching his nut sack against a spiny ridge along Lukor's back. He hissed through his teeth, clutching his lower belly. Aly, oblivious to his agony, asked him to move twice before his crippling pain subsided sufficiently to breathe.

Very gingerly, he dismounted, fantasizing a brutal scene where he turned Lukor into a eunuch. The others followed suit. Raine was appeased as Oka cradled his own groin with a grimace. At least Raine's precious sack wasn't the only casualty.

"Lukor, fucking asshole. You crushed my nuts," Oka snapped.

Lukor shifted to his human form and Raine looked away while he dressed. There was a scowl in Lukor's voice as he said, "I would like to see you land softly with that much weight on your back."

It was after sundown on a weekday, the lights of the keep diminished as soldiers and servants slumbered. Chambrin was a hardworking military base. Its residents worked hard, played hard, and mercifully, slept hard.

Sentries stared outward, diligently scanning the night horizon for threats. So long as the dragons remained silent, the sentries wouldn't glance backwards and detect them.

Once the dragons were all cloaked human shapes in the night, Raine led them to the keep. The bailey was deserted, and they sidled to a corner where two outer walls met inward. Deep shadows shrouded the niche beneath an awning.

The keep's stone walls were too well-tumbled to grip for purchase. Instead, he pushed his hands and feet against the angled walls, locking himself in the hollow space. Navigating to the rooftop was as easy as climbing a ladder. The other dragons imitated him without pause, ascending on his heels. Slowly, they slinked across the slate tiles of the keep's many-level rooftops.

It was time for the part of Raine's plan which had caused the most contention, namely from Lukor. Raine would have knocked the bastard back into the dreams dragons came from if he maligned Arastus Chambrin. Wisely, Lukor hadn't. Not directly. But his ire and disgust at involving Raine's father were an insult all their own.

Evin had diffused their hostilities by calmly asserting that they had placed Raine in charge and must therefore trust his judgment. And Raine's judgment insisted they needed his father. While he knew where the Cavern entrance was, he'd never actually been down there. He had no clue how the dragons were secured or what would be required to release them. Arastus Chambrin's aid was necessary if they hoped for any chance of success.

And if Raine was being honest, he didn't give a fuck if they needed his father or not. Nothing was going to keep him from seeing his dad.

A bright half-moon starkly illuminated the dragons as they trekked sloping slate. It felt like a slitted eye on his back, watching them. Illogical paranoia crept through him, and he forcibly reminded himself they were at a vantage where only the Roost overlooked them.

Raine's gaze flicked to the massive spire reflexively, but the tower was dark and still. The war dragons worked just as hard, if not harder, than Chambrin's human residents. He pictured them as they were every night, piled up like a hoard of living jewels, slumbering soundly amid piles of loose, clean rushes.

He threw out a hand to Evin's thunder as they approached a particularly steep gradient. Several chimney crowns peered over the other side of the ridge. Only one fireplace was unlit, the one to his washtub. Raine motioned for the others to wait, then walked a tight line to the smokeless chimney, throwing his arms wide for balance. He slipped down the narrow, brick flute and landed as silent as a cat in the firebox below, rolling his knees to absorb the impact.

His fingers stroked the edge of his beloved washtub wistfully before he crept into the darkened sitting room. The window shutters were open, filtering enough moonlight into the space for him to pick around the furniture and avoid tripping on a pair of discarded boots as he made his way to his father's bedchamber.

Soft, sawing snores grew louder as he eased open the door. His father hadn't been asleep long. A bronze oil lamp burned at his correspondence desk in the corner and the hearth was alive with a fire consuming fresh logs. Arastus Chambrin's large, powerful frame was softly illuminated in the orangey glow, tucked beneath a goose down coverlet identical to Raine's.

Joy surged through him, stinging his nostrils, as his father's lips puffed a snore. Raine cracked a watery smile at the breathy duration of his father's exhale, as if he was blowing on hot soup in his dream.

Whenever Raine overslept and his father was in the mood to devil him, Arastus liked to pounce atop his son's prone form and wake him with a smattering of obnoxious, wet kisses. The tables were turned. Raine's haunches tensed to spring, his father's slumbering vulnerability a magnet for mischief.

He took a step forward before reason prevailed, halting him. Stealth was paramount to their success. And as much as Raine would relish the high, startled scream it would provoke, he couldn't risk his father waking the entire keep, blasting their covert mission to smithereens before they set foot into the Cavern.

Feeling like a paragon of maturity and virtue, he walked to his father's bedside and gently shook his shoulder instead.

Arastus Chambrin jerked awake, recoiling as he beheld Raine. His father's fist dove beneath his pillow, where his paranoid ass had kept a sword all Raine's life. Belatedly registering the cause of his father's averse reception, Raine yanked his hood down as cold steel touched his chin.

Recognition and a tenderness that stung Raine's eyes flooded his father's gaze. He tossed his sword down the mattress and yanked Raine down on top of him.

Raine buried his face in his father's neck, savoring scents of sandalwood and home. Prickly whiskers rasped his skin as his father crushed him closer, cradling his head as if he were an infant. With a final, tight squeeze, his father rolled, making room for Raine to stretch beside him on the bed.

The hilt of his father's discarded sword dug into his back. Raine fished the sword out and tossed it further down the bed before parting his lips to speak.

A large, callused hand clapped over his mouth. His father's eyes flashed white in the dimness as he shook his head vehemently.

Raine frowned as his father leaned forward, whispering against his ear. "You should not have come. They've been waiting for you. There's a Guardian unit camped outside our quarters, in the hallway.

Another unit waits in your bedchamber. It's been like this since you left."

Raine twisted, staring at the wall separating their bedrooms. It hadn't occurred to him to stop at his own room before seeking his father, thank the Divine. The hunters would have gotten the jump on him, likely cleaving his head from his shoulders before he could perceive his peril.

Angling his mouth to his father's ear, he whispered, "I found the jeweler. He took me to his th—family. They're waiting for us on the roof."

"You're here to free the Cavern. It is impossible." Raine opened his mouth to argue. His father reached out a hand and pinched his lips shut between his fingers with a grim smile. "My sole ambition since the day you came into my life has been releasing those dragons. They are kept in cages with bars that do not bend, break, or melt. Without a key, they aren't going anywhere."

Raine pried his father's fingers off his mouth. "Where is the key?"

"Unreachable."

"Where."

His father blew a sigh. "There are two keys. Chieftain Eddic took my personal key. The other is in the Cavern."

Raine made an impatient noise. "That sounds like the opposite of unreachable."

"It's guarded by two Guardian units. The grounds are crawling with them. The chieftains anticipated your return and are leaving nothing to chance. It's a miracle you've made it this far, but you must go. Every minute you're here increases your chance of discovery."

Raine shook his head. "If I don't manage to free the dragons from the Cavern, I'm going to die trying. Will you help us or not?"

His father closed his eyes for several long heartbeats. When he opened them, he nodded once, grimly resigned. "I love you so much." He stretched his hands to cup Raine's face, smoothing his thumbs over his cheeks. "It was selfish of me to keep so many secrets from you. I was trying to find a way to free your real parents first, so that you would not bear the pain of their confinement once you knew the truth."

His father's voice was hoarse and Raine felt his own throat plug with emotion.

Leaning in, Raine pressed their foreheads together and closed his eyes. "I love you, too," he choked. Thoughts and emotions too complex to sort or comprehend sped through him. "I don't really want to meet them," he admitted. "I already have you. I don't need a set of strangers for parents."

It was a selfish sentiment, unworthy of utterance. But Raine had always confided in his father. His father, whom his heart insisted was his one and only parent.

Strong arms wrapped around Raine's shoulders and squeezed. "Son, it's okay if you don't love them yet. You will come to know them with time and feel differently, I promise. We must get started if you're still determined to see this through."

Raine nodded against his father, who could feel it if not see it. His father released him and stood. Trailing behind him, Raine hovered near the armoire while his father dressed. A scrap of woolen fabric draped over a wicker basket snared his attention. He grasped the cloth and unfolded it against the firelight. Aghast, Raine nearly flung it to the floor.

Finished dressing, Raine's father turned. He was outfitted in a matte black bodystocking. The official uniform of the Guardians, it was featherlight, form-fitting, and functioned like fine chain-mail, insulating the wearer from damage.

His father's arm extended, offering Raine a spare uniform. He ignored it, shaking the offensive cloth at his father's face.

"*Moranda*?" he mouthed. Both question and accusation.

The dress was snatched from his grip and tossed into the wicker basket. "I've been stressed," his father whispered intently.

Raine's mouth opened and closed several times. "But she hates me," he sputtered at last.

A roguish grin tugged his father's lips. "Well, she doesn't hate *me*."

Rolling his eyes, Raine's gaze caught on his father's rumpled bed. His jaw dropped as he pointed. "*You* ... You dragged me onto that defiled mattress."

A billion maggots writhed on his skin. Raine would never be clean again. He needed a bath. No, he needed a fire. Surely fire was the only method of cleansing that could purify this taint.

His father, the unrepentant bastard, scoffed. "If you're finished castigating me for the sole crime of being a man with needs, perhaps we can continue your mission?"

Swallowing several choice expletives, he gave a grudging nod. Not because he forgave his father, but because his sanity demanded he forget all knowledge of it lest his brain explode.

He refused the uniform his father proffered, deciding to remain solidary with Evin's thunder. One person garbed as the enemy would make them nervous, as it was.

Raine's bedchamber door was secure, the faintest trace of light beneath the crack. Goosebumps washed across his arms at the thought of what awaited on the other side. His father took his arm and steered him to the bathroom, where they shimmied up the chimney flute without issue.

Hoisting one leg over the cap, Raine shivered at the chill breeze. It was officially summer's end. Already, autumn's colors were painting the tips of leaves amber and gold.

Evin and her thunder sat along a high, slate ridge, legs dangling above a lower-level roof. They positioned themselves with alternating backs, observing all directions as they waited.

Gripping the mortared cap, Raine stepped silently from the chimney. Turning, he gave his father a hand, half-pulling the older man out of the chimney with a grunt. A jibe about his father's weight danced on his tongue, but their need for extreme stealth forestalled his teasing utterance.

Evin's thunder crossed the roof to meet them. High on the keep's rooftops, no shadow touched them. Moonlight illuminated expressions naked with relief and nervousness. And malice, if one counted the ugly look Lukor gave his father.

Raine bared his teeth like an animal, silently warning Lukor to back the fuck off. He didn't have the luxury of words to communicate his threat, but his visage was vocal enough. Lukor looked away.

CHAPTER SEVENTEEN

His father guided them across the keep's intricate, multi-level rooftops until they faced the northeastern edge of the grounds. A beautifully manicured garden was sequestered below, ostensibly for the lord of the keep's personal pleasure. An elaborate maze of hedgerows concealed a well at its center. Except it was a well no longer, now serving as the hidden entrance to the Cavern.

"The entrance is unguarded on this side," his father said, pointing for the benefit of the other dragons. "The well has a false bottom. When you descend, the wooden boards at the bottom will tilt beneath the weight of a man. Allow it to open beneath you and you will be deposited into a stone cellar. A Guardian unit waits on the other side."

Putting his back to the ledge, his father faced them. "If things go poorly, you need to know how to find the dragons."

Raine stiffened. His father paused to give him a stern look that said, *don't interrupt me*, before continuing. "The cellar has two doors. Take the one on the right. That will lead you down a hallway lined with doors on each side. Take the fifth door on the right. It opens to a stairwell you will descend. It is a long descent but keep going until you reach the end. The stairwell empties into the Cavern where the dragons are kept."

"Thank you, Father. We will take it from here," Raine said, approaching the awning to descend. A heavy hand gripped his shoulder, stopping him.

Raine met his father's amused smile. "Did you think I told you all that so you could go alone? I will take us as far as I can, using the weight of my authority. The real trouble will be when we reach the Cavern and the two units guarding the key. I have no control over the Guardians beyond keeping them out of my private rooms. They are zealously loyal to the Nine." His father dropped his hand, looking away as he added, "I suspect they are here to watch over me as much as they are here to wait for you."

Evin moved forward and placed her hand on his father's shoulder. "If we succeed, we will owe our success to you. Thank you for helping us."

His father's eyes shone like glass in the moonlight. He covered Evin's hand with his own. "Don't thank me yet," he said gruffly.

His father selected a lower roof with a steep pitch for their descent, where an ancient sycamore brushed the keep, providing shadowy cover above and below. His father went first, and the dragons swiftly followed, disappearing one after another over the drip edge.

Raine went last. As he approached the jump-off, his boots glided frictionless across a patch of slick mildew concealed by the ever-present shade of the tree. His stomach seized as he slid.

His supple, buckskin boots were crafted to look and feel good, not keep him upright on slippery, sloping surfaces. *This is what I get for not checking the outsoles.*

Shifting his feet to slow his fall, Raine sank to his knees and turned, gripping the roof tiles as his legs dangled. A slimy wet patch licked his palms as he lowered himself over the drip edge. He snatched his hands from the offensive ooze, forgetting his precarious position for a split second. That was all it took. He scrambled futilely, grasping naught but air, and fell. The whole of his breath *whooshed* on a brutal exhale as he smacked the earth, flat on his back.

Just as the stars blotted out, his struggling lungs seized oxygen. He dragged air through his open mouth as several hooded figures and one ex-Guardian master stared down at him.

"Seriously, nobody could catch me?" Raine scowled up at his companions.

"You're not exactly dainty, princess," Aly whispered with a smirk in her voice.

"Dragons are stronger than humans. I don't have to be dainty for someone to catch me."

"Not *that* strong. It was a long fall and you're heavy as fuck."

"Yeah, it was a *long* fall. That's what makes it so fucked up you didn't try—"

"Enough," his father hissed, glaring between Raine and Aly. Raine grasped an outstretched arm, and his father pulled him to his feet. "You *are* heavy as fuck," his father murmured, and Aly snickered.

Raine rolled his eyes, wishing he'd issued his earlier taunt about his father's weight, stealth be damned.

He trailed the rear as their group darted into the tall hedges that formed a garden maze around the wishing well. The maze was short but would confuse a stranger, especially in the darkness. Raine's father guided them unerringly to its center.

The maze garden was deceptively unguarded. A shiver trailed Raine's spine like a skeleton finger. The hunters wanted them in the Cavern, and the dragons were playing right into their hands. If Raine and the others didn't come out on top in their task, it meant the Nine would have solved their little dragon problem overnight. In that event, would the chieftains kill them? Or keep them for breeding?

I will die before they cage me. The prospect of captivity—subterranean captivity, at that—made sickly saliva pool in Raine's cheeks.

They rounded the final hedgerow, spilling into the heart of the maze. Placed dead center was a wishing well. Old but solid, with sunken mortar that made its smoothly polished stones pop like corn kernels. A diminutive roof leaned over the well's opening, equipped with a rusted rope-and-pulley.

The Cavern was once part of an underground spring, hosting a reservoir of clean drinking water. It had been blocked off and drained two centuries prior by obsequious Chambrin ancestors, all too eager to assist the original Nine by securing their fire-breathing loot.

Those aware of the well's existence thought it was a decorative prop from an age gone by. Its status as the access point to the Cavern was privileged information, provided on a need-to-know basis. The Nine were aware of its location as well as select guards and workers.

And, apparently, several elite Guardian units. They were down there, lying in wait like spiders. Relying on their prey to come to them.

A fresh wave of foreboding seeped over Raine like a raw egg as his father climbed into the well. He rushed silently to the opening and peered inside. Rusted metal rungs, bolted down the inner well, served as a ladder. His father gripped them with familiarity as he descended the rungs.

It was too late to back out, he realized, surveying the grimly determined dragons around him. His father disappeared through the floor, which tilted vertically like a trap door at the slightest pressure of his boots. Raine climbed in to follow.

Nerves jangled like coins in his viscera. This could be the last time he ever saw the sky. He tilted his head for one final glimpse of the moon and stars. And nearly rammed his nose into Lukor's hovering arse. The purple dragon must have descended right on his tail. *Go figure.*

The false bottom swung on generously oiled hinges. Once his head was below the door, Raine dropped from the footholds, landing in a crouch near his father. He did a sharp double-take at the man arguing with his father. A Guardian captain.

"The commanders-in-chief ordered us to apprehend any unknown persons who enter the Cavern."

"I am the commander-in-chief of this keep, Claytus. You are guarding *my* Cavern. If you wish to report me to the Nine for disallowing you to arrest my guests, that's your prerogative. But you will allow myself and my guests passage in my Cavern." His father's words were a threat masked as an order.

The unit captain, Claytus, was visibly affected. Wan with a sweaty upper lip, he said, "I mean no disrespect, General Chambrin. The Nine were explicit in their directives."

Tremors wracked Claytus's knees. Seeming ready to faint or piss himself, his gaze darted frantically to the growing group of hooded figures clustered beneath the Cavern entrance. And the most absurd, asinine thought seized Raine.

My captain would not be intimidated.

He conjured his captain in his mind, the man with a fawn's liquid eyes and the twisted, snarling rage of a honey badger. That captain wasn't *his*. Where the ever-loving-fuck had that thought come from? And it was a good thing this captain was so intimidated because he backed down, gesturing to his journeymen to permit them passage.

His father led them through the door on the right. The primitive stone hallway was dark and stale. Sconces burned intermittently against coarse rock walls, illuminating various doorways. Raine imagined them as little ants, marching in a straight line through an anthill. His father stopped at one of the doors and looked back at them. His lips pinched as he caught sight of Raine's goofy smile.

Wiping the expression from his face, Raine tried to project seriousness. He'd been creating wallpaper patterns in his head ever since Sinopel. He mentally added several ant patterns to the ever-increasing cache of designs in his head.

His father was grave. "I do not know the Guardians that met us below the well. The unit that I know well, the unit that I expected to see, was dismissed and replaced with strangers without my authorization." Arastus Chambrin looked at the dragons, then Raine. "Only the Nine outrank me in my own keep."

"Are you saying the Nine are here, now?" Jaska asked.

"No." His father frowned ponderously. "The Nine dislike the Cavern and prefer to manage it from a distance. Claytus was given an official scroll commanding the regular unit to step down. It does not bode well that he didn't report his orders to me first."

"Do you think we should retreat?" Raine asked, following his father's thoughts. This was looking more and more like a trap. Better to live now and fight another day than end up dead. Or worse, caged.

Lukor swelled beneath his cloak, hands forming fists at his sides. "I will not retreat."

His father's eyes bled sorrow as he surveyed Lukor, as if he knew the dragon's anguish. "I think you never should have come. We're here, though. We might as well give it hell." He sighed and flicked the door latch. "I was unaware of the guard change. I thought I knew what we were walking into, but now I have no idea," he warned.

"It doesn't matter," Lukor said in a tone sharper than a bone saw. "I will face death a thousand times to retrieve my mate from this pit."

The door swung inward, revealing a steeply spiraling staircase. "Then let's go," his father said simply.

The staircase coiled tightly around itself, running them in dizzying circles. Down, down, *down* they went, their path dimly lit by recessed lanterns in a central stone column. At each step, Raine's body grew stiffer. His very marrow howled at going deeper. It was like being back at the Hellhole, only a million times worse. He didn't have to turn to know the other dragons were similarly afflicted. As Evin had said, dragons were creatures of the sky.

He stumbled, missing a stair, as unadulterated reality smacked him like a battering ram to the chest. Two hundred years of relentless torment. That's what the dragons below had suffered. This Cavern was a coffin, a tomb. A place that could chew a dragon's sanity to cud in a matter of hours.

His heart palpitated in his throat, terrified of what condition they might find the dragons in. He'd just assumed they would be whole and unharmed. The Nine relied on them to be fit enough to propagate, after all.

But if the Cavern itself was torture ... Who or what could survive two centuries of relentless torture?

After what seemed like days, they reached the foot of the world's longest staircase. They were so far below the surface, it was like treading on the Dreaming Mother's back.

His father motioned them to stop. "Wait here. As I said, I have no idea what awaits us. Let me scope it out first."

Opening the door the barest sliver, his father slipped through and shut it tightly. Raine leaned against it, pressing an ear in hopes of listening to his father's confrontation. Ice kissed his skin. A metal door.

The other dragons crouched, eavesdropping alongside him. But any conversation on the other side was muffled by the thick walls of the insulated door.

"How will we know when we're supposed to provide backup? If he calls for help, we probably won't hear him," Aly whispered.

Raine pressed his ear harder, but it was no use. Even if his father bellowed for aid, they wouldn't hear him. They waited for several tense moments.

It didn't take long for Raine's notoriously threadbare patience to snap. Rushing in might ruin everything, but the fear of their delay resulting in harm to his father compelled him.

"I'm going in." He tensed, anticipating objections. Instead, the others agreed. Pressing forward as one, the dragons gathered at his back. On the count of three, they plowed through the door, poised for conflict.

The Cavern arched high overhead, going up and up, walls disappearing into inky darkness. Billions of sparkling gems flecked the glassy, jagged walls, like a facsimile of stars set in the blackest sky.

"No," his father groaned from the side.

Raine twisted, discovering his father crumpled in a heap beside the Cavern door. Judging by where his father had fallen, he must have been flush with the door when they'd thrust it open.

Arastus stood haltingly and leaned against a starry wall, his posture deflated.

The other dragons hurtled without pause, Lukor at the helm, toward a series of distant cages that appeared small in the hulking Cavern. Raine's attention split between the dragons' progress and his father's sagging form.

He stepped closer to his father. "What's wrong? Where are the Guardians?"

His father looked up, brown eyes large against his chalky pallor. "I didn't notice the door until I entered. It sealed itself behind me."

Raine glanced back at the metal door in question. Initially puzzled, but then he saw it. The absence of a handle. The door was perfectly smooth, tightly fitted in a section of flat wall. His eyes found his father, who continued.

"That is not the door to the Cavern. Or, it wasn't three days ago. It's been replaced without my knowledge. There are no Guardians down here. Just us. The Cavern is our cage. We're trapped."

The other dragons were deeply engrossed in their reunion, paying no heed to Raine and his father. He watched Evin and her thunder press themselves into the bars, arms clinging to their lost loved ones, sobbing a mixture of joy and relief.

He was too far to make out many details of the caged dragons, but they appeared sickly and thin. With coloring so dull, he couldn't discern their unique hues from his vantage. They were fifty paces or so away, near enough he should have been able to determine blue scales from green or red. But he couldn't.

Raine's attention fixed on Lukor. The dragon stood awkwardly to the side, not reaching for anyone. His expression was so ravaged with anguish, Raine sucked in a breath. It was a pain too raw to witness. Then the purple dragon turned to his father. Trepidation iced Raine's blood at Lukor's mask of bilious hatred. His maddened rage.

Lukor stalked across the Cavern, seething savagery. "You dung-eyed *pig*."

"Back off, Lukor," Raine said in a firm tone. He was miserable for Lukor's loss, but the dragon wasn't going to harm a hair on Arastus Chambrin's head.

Lukor ignored him. "These dragons are starving and sick and wallowing in their own filth. Is that how she died? Did you starve her? What happened, you pig! Tell me how she fucking died!"

Lukor's words boomed and crashed against the glassy, jagged walls. He lunged for Arastus and Raine leapt to meet him. The bastard was strong, shoving Raine aside like a doll.

He quickly recovered his balance and spun, leaping on Lukor's back. Cinching his arms and legs like iron bands around Lukor's throat and torso, he wrenched them to the gritty stone floor.

They grappled, too evenly matched. Thanks to Raine's frequent wrestling matches with Aly and Oka, he spied an opening. Faster than a viper, he struck Lukor in the jaw. The blow was solid and punishing. Lukor's teeth sliced Raine's knuckles as they split through his lip.

The fight left Lukor like a snuffed candle. The purple dragon went limp and didn't move. Raine carefully inspected him, ensuring he was truly unconscious before standing. Turning, he nearly walked into Evin. Jaska, Savere, and Oka hovered behind her.

Evin smiled, albeit wanly, as their eyes met. "We came to aid you with Lukor, but I see it was unnecessary."

"You're a fucking badass," Oka crowed. "Nobody beats Lukor." He held out a fist and Raine bumped it absently with his bleeding hand.

A frown puckered Raine's brow as he noted Aly's absence. He searched around but couldn't find her. Jaska jerked his chin, indicating the cages. Raine spun and froze.

Aly pressed her body flush against a dark metal cage. A dragon dug its head into the bars, the tip of its snout burrowed into her neck as they clung to each other. Raine's frown deepened. Aly didn't know any of these dragons. She hatched after they were taken, and Evin had watched her parents die.

Raine's confusion must have shown on his face, because Jaska offered him a weak smile and said, "Aly found her mate."

Raine whipped his head back around and scrutinized the pair more intently.

Aly's hood was down, crimson hair curtaining her back. She stroked every reachable inch of the caged dragon with a tenderness that bordered on reverence. Raine's throat tightened as he stared. Neither Aly nor the dragon appeared to harbor doubts as to their connection. It was pure and powerful and mutual. His captain's countenance—glittering with as much malevolent rage as Lukor's—sliced through his mind like an ice pick.

Raine shoved the image away, refocusing on the crystalline Cavern. "Where's the key?"

"Gone," his father said. He jabbed a thumb to the left, indicating a vacant wall hook. "Our only exit is sealed," he re-explained for the benefit of the others. "They've taken the key and trapped us down here."

Jaska and Savere approached the door and felt around its frame.

"One of us can shift and tear that door out like tissue paper," Oka said, making his way to the door, as well.

"No," his father said, gesturing upward, into the blackness above. "We can't risk impairing the structural integrity of the Cavern. It could start a rock fall and bury us alive."

Jaska, who'd been prying experimentally where the stone and frame met, ceased abruptly.

"They'll be arriving soon," his father said. Evin's blue brows knitted, and he clarified. "The unit we passed near the entrance will have sent a report to Chieftain Vanwert in Sinopel, as he's the closest commander-in-chief. We have hours before hundreds of Guardians arrive to either execute or imprison us."

"I've always loved how positive you are. Even when everything is going wrong, I can really count on you to find the silver lining," Raine groused in the bleak silence.

"Let's get our friends out of those cages," Jaska said. "We can worry about a way out after."

The dark green dragon strode across the Cavern, the others hurrying after. Raine moved the opposite direction, leaning against the wall at his father's side. In moments, Evin's thunder was clustered around the cages, carefully inspecting the bars and welds.

Jaska appeared to be questioning the caged dragons. Raine's brows climbed his forehead as the dragons grunted and chuffed, as if answering him in a beastly language.

An arm nudged his shoulder. "You should go." There was no need to ask where. Raine was unsubtly avoiding the dragon cages.

"I can't," he whispered. He was terrified of the cages, of what awaited him there.

"Yes, you can—"

"I never thought twice about their situation until I learned what I am," he said, cutting his father off. "I never cared about the immorality or unfairness of their situation. I never *once* asked if the breeding dragons were treated well. I should have known they weren't. How could they have been, when they have wings to fly but are buried like the dead?"

As his father enveloped him in his arms, Raine registered the dampness on his cheeks. How could he look those dragons, his parents, in the eye after years of ignorantly accepting the most brutally inhumane treatment of a gentle, intelligent species? If they didn't hate him, they ought to. He didn't deserve their forgiveness but was too cowardly to face their blame. He was loathsome, a spineless cretin as odious as Olan.

His father smoothed a hand over Raine's pale hair, cooing nonsense that his body subconsciously responded to.

Tears slowed as his calm was restored. Raine drew a shuddering breath and stepped from his father's embrace.

"Son, listen to me—"

"I can't talk about it anymore. *Please*." His father looked ready to argue and Raine loudly—and shamelessly—sniffled.

His father rolled his eyes, familiar with his son's overdramatizations. Just then, Lukor let out a guttural, choking snore, surprising a chuckle out of them. Raine glanced at the prone dragon and hoped Lukor slept until the damned Guardians arrived. He'd rather die fighting for his life and freedom than die trying to protect his father from someone who was supposed to be an ally.

Their situation was hopeless. Before dawn, he would be dead. His captain's face flashed in his mind with every beat of his heart. A cruel staccato that cut like a knife. *I never even learned his name.*

"Hey," Oka shouted, the sound echoing. "We need you guys."

Large, familiar hands squeezed Raine's shoulders. His father gripped him, gazing intently until Raine met his stare. "There are no white dragons," he said calmly. "Your parents will not know you on sight." The hands on his shoulders squeezed harder, nearly bruising. "I will be right beside you."

Trailing his father like a shy toddler, he stole brief glimpses of the gaunt dragons, heavy heads drooping like withered flowers. Halfway across the Cavern, a reeking stench stole his breath and frothed the acid in his stomach. His eyes watered.

"Breathe through your mouth," his father whispered, too soft to carry.

Lips parting obediently, Raine took shallow breaths. As they drew closer, he eyed Aly through the stinging moisture in his eyes.

She was oblivious to the miasma. Not one crease of displeasure marred her delicate features as she cradled her mate's muzzle, stroking his filthy scales reverently. If she could bear it, so could he.

"They said something in this room keeps them from transforming," Evin said, meeting them several paces from the cages. Her lips remained slightly parted, as if she breathed through her mouth, as well.

His father nodded. "The Nine supply a venom that prevents them from changing forms. We lace their drinking water."

Savere asked, "Does it ever wear off?"

Oka scoffed at his elder brother. "How would that change anything? Even if they could shift, our human forms are so much weaker than our dragons."

"It matters," Savere said dryly, "because the bars on the cages are wide set and the dragons are severely malnourished. They can probably slip through if they access their human forms."

It was a macabre observation, but a worthy one. The caged dragons' emaciation would be a blessing in disguise, were they able to shift.

Oka rubbed the back of his head. "Can't we just melt the bars?"

Savere closed his eyes in the slow, exasperated way Raine had seen his father do a million times. "If the bars could be melted, don't you think they'd have freed themselves by now?"

"The metal bars are infused with diamonds." Raine's father gestured at the gem-crusted cavern walls. "The melting point is somewhere around six thousand degrees. Dragons' fire burns at about three thousand." He paused, then added, "The diamond is also the reason the bars are so unyielding. These cages were designed to contain dragons."

His father raked his fingers through his hair and angled his frame away. Raine's silver eyes narrowed at the familiar tells. "What aren't you saying?" he demanded.

His father's hand dropped on a sigh. "Back when I took over the breeding program from my father, the dragons were wasting away. They looked much worse than they do now, if you can imagine. And ..." His father hesitated, then grimaced. "Long story short, I stopped lacing their water with the venom. It was meant to be temporary, but when I saw how much better the dragons looked a week later, I resolved never to use it again. It's been decades since these dragons have given up on changing forms, which is why they still believe they can't."

A guttural growl emerged from behind Raine. "And you didn't offer that information immediately because?"

Raine's spirit leapt from his physical body. Lukor was at his father's unguarded back. He whirled, finding the purple dragon's unblinking eyes trained on his father, not ten feet away.

"They are safer in their cages." His father's mouth flattened as he met Lukor's bellicose glare. "The guild is underway. Once they come charging through that door, it will be with the intent to destroy every perceivable threat. I brought you here to save these dragons, not get them all killed."

Lukor's upper lip curled back, revealing even white teeth. "That choice belongs to them."

Either this was a dream, or the world was ending. Because Raine agreed with Lukor.

It was Evin who said, "With all due respect, General Chambrin, I believe Lukor has the right of it."

His father grimaced. "I know." He continued looking at Lukor as he said, "Freeing these dragons has been my sole ambition for years. You have no idea what I've done for them."

"Done for them?" Lukor's poisonous laughter leaked through the Cavern. Raine tensed as Lukor stalked closer to his father, all the while uttering a menacing tirade. "Please, regale me with your mercies, dung eyes. Because I can't help but notice they are shrunk from starvation and knee-deep in their own waste. Your mercy didn't feed them. Your mercy didn't make them clean or comfortable or get them the fuck out of this festering pit."

Arastus Chambrin was the Wolf of the Vale—back straight and head high, his powerful frame confident and relaxed. "I could not unlock their cages and shoo them into the night. They would have been dead by dawn," he said calmly. "Their condition is reprehensible and you should be irate. But know that I could not offer a shred of kindness or pity without arousing the Nine's suspicions. I have made genuine progress that cannot be observed here. An operation spanning years, committing treason and risking my life daily. It is a long conversation, and I'll gladly fill you in if we somehow escape this death trap."

Lukor wasn't appeased. The hard line of his jaw flexed visibly. Evin moved to him, resting a hand on his bicep. It seemed to bring the dragon back to himself. Tension eased as the purple dragon's attention turned to the cages.

Raine tracked Lukor's gaze and found Jaska quietly conversing through the bars of the nearest cage. The three dragons he addressed were of indeterminate coloring, though now Raine knew it was actual shit encrusting their entire bodies that gave them their dull, dingy appearance.

Bathing was practically a holy ritual for dragons. His soul bled as he took in the thick layer of refuse that served as the dragons' floor and sleeping surface.

Crackling pops snapped his neck upward. The caged trio dissolved, scales giving way to skin. Shit flaked the air like brown snow as it sloughed from their diminished forms. The other caged dragons lifted their heads, visibly roused. In the span of several heartbeats, every dragon in every cage was human. Aly now clasped the arms and chest of a frail man through the bars.

In their human bodies, the effects of prolonged starvation were more pronounced. Hollowed cheeks, arms and legs like matchsticks, lines of ribs outlined beneath flesh as thin as gossamer.

"How ..." croaked a male from the end cage.

"No time," Savere said. "Can you squeeze through the bars?"

The skeletal dragons tried. Their sunken bodies could wriggle through the bars, but their heads were too wide. Oka and Savere grasped one bar on the cage nearest them while Evin and Lukor took the bar next to it. The four dragons pulled, each pair straining their bar in the opposite direction. After several moments of intense straining, nothing happened.

"We need to transform," Oka said, red-faced and panting.

The others didn't argue. Despite the seriousness of the situation, Raine grinned at his father's askance expression as Evin pulled her muslin gown over her head. "They don't want to ruin their clothes," he explained.

Oka's flesh rolled and twitched, as if the bones beneath his skin liquified. Faster than a blink, emerald scales exploded over thickly corded muscle. Green, leathery wings, slightly darker than his scales, extended beyond the cages.

Oka was a magnificent dragon. Vivid green eyes, the same hue as his human form, were now the size of ostrich eggs. His sheer mass and vitality served as a brutal foil to the caged dragons they'd come upon.

Evin's dragon was willowy and serpentine, her scales the pure blue of summer sky. Lukor was a beast, nearly as broad as he was tall and built thick everywhere. Savere was as green and beautifully proportioned as his younger brother.

Powerful dragon arms bulged as they gripped the cage bars with their taloned paws and wrenched. Black, glimmering metal yielded to their combined strength, beveling infinitesimally. The fingerbreadth gap they added was all the shrunken dragons required to eke out of their cages. They emerged slowly, weakly, and with a quiet dignity that Raine didn't for a second think he'd possess under their circumstances.

In minutes, all six cages were emptied. Twenty-one dragons. Frail, filthy, but unbroken. Raine saw the hesitation that rippled through the dragons, the uncertainty. The, *what now*?

He surveyed the Cavern with futile hopefulness, as if another exit might magically appear if he willed it hard enough.

It didn't. Their only way out was the way they came in. *Fuck*.

"Okay." He clapped his hands. "I think we're going to have to risk a rockfall. Do one of you want to try breaking through the metal door?"

In lieu of answering, Oka's massive body ate the distance to the entrance in seconds, tail whipping the air behind him. Without stopping, he rended the steel door from the wall in one swipe of his wicked claws.

The metal slab crashed to the floor, shooting sparks as it grated stone. It had insulated the stairwell so completely, they failed to detect the cacophonous din of an encroaching army. At least a hundred strong, by the sound of it.

Raine's stomach lurched. "Put it back!"

Oka didn't argue. He grasped the metal door and punched it back into place, wedging it back into its surrounding rock frame. The steel was roughly misshapen and wouldn't hold. Raine searched around for something to barricade the door. The only things in the Cavern were the reeking cages and dragons. *Dragons!*

"Oka, sit in front of the door and keep it shut." His dragon form had to weigh several thousand pounds. It was not an indefinite solution, but hopefully it would buy them enough time to think of something better.

Once Oka was in position, Raine snapped at Jaska and Aly. "Shift."

They did, not sparing a moment to shed their clothes. Fabric ripped, bones popped. As if they'd discussed it, Evin's thunder looked to Raine, awaiting instruction. Raine wanted to yell at them to stop, that he wasn't the leader here, his father was. Only, his father looked to him, too. *Well, shit.*

"That's real cute, putting me in charge of a doomed mission. I'm not a fucking fall guy."

The dragons stomped impatiently, and his father crossed his arms, looking amused. Raine shook his head, feeling sick as the hunters in the stairwell reached the door and began pummeling the steel. The Guardians were equipped with dragon bone weapons and sufficient numbers to annihilate every dragon in the Cavern without breaking a sweat.

The newly freed dragons were too feeble to fight. They would serve as liabilities in a skirmish and would be the first to fall. Which left Raine, his father, and six healthy dragons. Not enough.

Raine thought hard and fast, staring at the nearest wall. The glittering effect of the diamonds against black, glassy stone was breath-taking. Dire circumstances aside, he filed away several wallpaper ideas to examine later. If later ever came.

His gaze ticked absently upward, until he stared into the void above.

He blinked. Then, pointing overhead, he looked at his father. "What's up there?"

His father's neck craned to take in the inky emptiness above. "I don't know. It has remained unexplored in my lifetime, though I'm sure there are records of previous Chambrins inspecting the area."

Jaska was the nearest dragon. Addressing him, Raine said, "Fly up there and see what you find."

With a quick nod, Jaska beat his wings. Wind furled through the cavern, blowing Raine's braid back and offering a brief respite from the reeking cages. He clenched his teeth to keep from gagging as the cloying stink pooled around him in Jaska's wake.

The midnight green dragon was quickly swallowed by the void. As they waited, the incessant banging against the metal door frayed Raine's nerves. The others were equally restless, casting wary glances toward the sound. Oka held them off effortlessly, curled in front of the door as cozy as a reptile in the sun.

Raine was preparing to send Savere after Jaska, not sure what the holdup was, when the dragon finally descended, landing neatly on his hindquarters between Raine and his father.

In his claws rested a large, wooden panel, rusted iron nails sticking out in neat rows. Tossing it to the floor, Jaska popped back into human form. Heedless of his nudity, he shouted, "There's a way out!"

A crowd gathered to listen as Jaska relayed his discovery: a massive hole in the darkness that had been sealed shut. An ancient tunnel that led to the woods outside, the very woods they had traversed to reach Chambrin Keep.

As Jaska lapsed to silence, his father fisted the short, graying hairs at his temple. "I'm an idiot. The dragons can't fit through the stairwell. If I'd only thought about it, I would have realized long ago there was another entrance."

Raine tugged his father's arm down. "This is what you get for all those times you accused me of not having any common sense," he said with a sniff.

His teasing comment couldn't drain the well of guilt burgeoning behind his father's dark eyes, but it did make the corner of his mouth twitch in an almost-smile as he rolled his eyes at his son.

They quickly discerned the rescued dragons were too weak to fly, their wings atrophied by two centuries of disuse. The frail, gaunt dragons climbed shakily upon the backs of Evin and her thunder. Lukor fit seven, the most out of everyone, and took off directly behind Jaska. One by one, they launched themselves and their infinitely precious cargo into the blackness overhead until only Raine and his father remained.

They chose to leave last, with Oka. As they approached the green dragon, Raine noticed the banging had ceased. He wasn't foolish enough to suggest the hunters retreated. The silence was more unnerving than anything.

Oka stood, edging discreetly from his post. With any luck, they would be gone before the hunters tried the door again. Oka gestured toward his discarded clothes with the tip of his tail. Arastus caught Oka's meaning. He stooped and began gathering the dragon's discarded clothes when the steel door erupted from the wall.

The Wolf of the Vale froze mid-crouch, Oka's cloak and boots in his arms. The Guardians were similarly stupefied by their success. A teeming mass of black-clad warriors stood gawking from the stairwell, an array of eerily white-tipped blades at the ready.

Raine snapped out of his daze and yanked his father by his Guardian-black sleeve, sprinting to Oka. They scrambled onto the dragon's back as the hunters flooded the Cavern like a dark tide. A dozen Guardians charged them, spears and swords upraised. The pale blades which had once enchanted Raine were grotesque now, and he swallowed bile with his panic.

Oka spun, employing both wings and tail to knock the approaching horde back. Their attackers sprawled in a tumultuous heap. Several agonized screams echoed as Guardians fell on the outstretched blades of their comrades. The stairwell contained an endless host of Guardians. More hunters trampled the fallen as they hurtled themselves at their lone target: them.

Raine gripped Oka's broad neck as the dragon pitched and spun anew, taking out the nearest hunters, clearing space to launch. His powerful, shimmering body shot through the air on a gusty surge of wings. Raine craned his neck, watching the hunters below pool in their wake, swarming the space they had abandoned mere seconds ago.

He located the archer at the exact moment the hunter released the taut string of his bow, firing a white-tipped arrow directly at his chest.

Time slowed as Raine tensed. But he didn't try to evade the arrow. If it struck Oka and hit something vital, they would all die.

Braced for injury and possible death, Raine squeezed his eyes shut. Then flung them wide open, staring horror-struck, as his father released a soft, pained *oomph* and slipped away. Raine scrabbled to grab him, to keep his father mounted.

It was too late. His mouth opened on a silent scream as his father plummeted to the cavern floor, the arrow sticking out of his shoulder. Their eyes met and held for an eternity. The void swallowed Oka and Raine just as the hunters caught his falling father in their outstretched arms.

CHAPTER EIGHTEEN

Twenty-one rescued dragons. Twenty bedrolls. The Hellhole had officially exceeded maximum occupancy. It should have been uncomfortably cramped with so many dragons underfoot, but an air of exulted victory and elation perfused the once-dismal atmosphere of the underground safehouse.

The ex-breeding dragons were weak from their ordeal and rescue. For over a week, they did little more than sleep. Oka hunted game with a single-mindedness that resulted in rows of hanging carcasses in the salt-bricked niche where they stored food.

Aly did not leave her mate's side. Her appearance suffered for it, as the filth of her mate rubbed against her skin. Her hair grew lank and lusterless. She forced her own meal portions onto him, losing weight because of it.

Guard duty, once highly coveted and fought over, became a burdensome task overnight. Everyone wanted to be near the dragons, hovering like anxious parents with newborn babies.

Except Raine. He scheduled himself for guard duty every day, usually taking double shifts, like present.

Nobody complained, and Raine knew why. He was a lone, black cloud in a sky of jubilant rainbows, dampening the joyous, feverishly celebratory atmosphere. He tried to be glad about rescuing the dragons, but his spirit was crushed by what it had cost.

When his father leapt to take the arrow intended for Raine, it had punctured the area where his upper arm and shoulder met. Not a killing shot. His father was *alive*. Alive and in the clutches of the Nine. The sadistic commanders-in-chief of the guild and deceitful leaders of Valdenia could be doing anything to his father. He imagined his father hanging from chains, in a dark, moldering dungeon, being tortured or worse.

Hood firmly over his head, he leaned against the craggy, fissured surface of a black cherry tree in the dense, quiet forest. Breathing in the sweet-sharp smell of autumn, Raine plucked the darkest cherries from a branch, nibbling the overripe, brown-spotted fruit from their pits. The cherries should have tasted delicious, but anxiety soured his snack as he brooded over his predicament.

He could not leave his father in the Nine's custody. Every hour he tarried magnified his dread to a sickening degree. But he feared he couldn't save his father alone.

The prospect of requesting aid from the others, days after their poignant, centuries-awaited reunion, shriveled his stomach. Which left Raine waffling in circuitous indecision. He couldn't leave his father to a merciless guild. He couldn't ask for help.

A chill wind whistled through the surrounding branches. He secured the gap in his cloak, pulling the coarse fabric tight against the turbulence. A rustling crunch made him stiffen, then relax.

Aly and her mate, whose name he'd forgotten, picked slowly through the woods. Their hair was wet, lips smiling as they carried small bundles of soap and dirty clothes. Aly was neither tan nor plump, but she seemed downright stout and sunkissed alongside her mate. His pale limbs, little more than skin-wrapped bones, shook with the effort of their brief trek back to the Hellhole.

Lukor trailed their wake, the other dragon on guard duty. The purple dragon would follow them to the Hellhole's entrance and ensure they were safely ensconced below before resuming his post. It was nonstop, the traffic to-and-fro the river, now that the rescued dragons were strong enough to bathe.

Casually glancing at Lukor's features, Raine sucked in a breath, gripping his handful of cherries until wine red juice dripped from his fist. He'd expected to see a flash of annoyance. Or the purple male's features set in plodding resignation for the next pair of dragons inevitably bent upon a brisk wash. What he found instead was ... raw, naked envy. Lukor's eyes were fat amethyst drops of glittering despair and longing as Aly gently aided her weakened mate, who clung to her with aching trust.

A hungry starling swooped down for a cherry, trilling as it perched on a branch. Lukor glanced at the sound. His expression blanked as he caught sight of Raine, who hastily tore his gaze away. Heart thundering in his throat, as though he'd been caught doing something forbidden, he stared at the starling's bobbing branch overhead until the footfalls faded.

The solution was obvious. It had been all along. For whatever reason, it had simply taken a glimpse of Lukor's vulnerability to see it.

Raine couldn't ask anyone to help him. He had to go alone.

Now that his decision was made, guard duty dragged on in a way it never had previously. Why the hell did he always have to take double shifts? Each hour was an eternity until Savere relieved him after dawn.

Creeping through the communal sleeping chamber, he gathered his haversack and a few belongings. The dragons continued sleeping, their rest deep and deadened as they continued to recover. Raine's chest tightened as his eyes roved the shadowy figures tucked beneath thin, shabby blankets.

The mated pairs were easy to locate since they clung together, sharing pallets. Somewhere among them were his *parents*. Another thing had troubled Raine, and he thought of it as he eyed the unconscious forms of the dragons. Twenty-three war dragons served at Chambrin Keep, and only ten mated pairs lay before him, excluding Aly and her mate.

Which meant Raine didn't just have parents. It was likely he had siblings. Siblings he had unknowingly grown up with without ever realizing.

He'd always felt a special connection with the war dragons, but he had also thought of himself as firmly, undeniably *human*. While the war dragons always struck him as incredibly empathetic and intelligent, he had never imagined dragons possessed the same mental and emotional capacities as people. As himself.

Dazed by his revelation, he tossed one final look at the sleeping dragons. Quickly, before anyone came to check on them, he climbed the exit tunnel, slipping from beneath the broad stump that served as both doorway and disguise.

Savere and Jaska were currently on guard, but they wouldn't see him emerge.

Raine had learned during his first guard session that, as an additional precaution against discovery, they were to stand watch further away from the Hellhole. This way, if hunters or humans entered the forest and encountered them, they would not associate the stump with the dragons or pay it undue attention.

He made his way to the clear, quick-flowing river west of the Hellhole, brazenly trampling fallen twigs and leaves beneath his boots. He smiled as Jaska stepped from behind a nearby elm.

Gesturing to his haversack, Raine said, "Just going for a wash."

Jaska's dark hair and eyes allowed him to almost appear not only human, but like a native Valdenian. In his dragon form, his scales were a dazzling ombre of onyx and green. He was the darkest dragon Raine had yet seen, the black base of his scales only emphasizing their gleaming emerald tips.

"You walk like a herd of cattle. Be a little lighter on your feet," Jaska teased.

Raine grinned and nodded. His noisy steps had been intentional. He now knew where the western guard was stationed and could avoid running off where Jaska would witness his defection.

His shoulders sagged as he continued through the forest. *Father would have seen right through my bullshit.* The blessing of a parent who loved him so well was equally a pain in his ass, especially in his hoydenish youth.

The sky was an uninterrupted sheet of gray. A northern wind nipped relentlessly at his nose and fingers. Autumn was lovely, he thought, observing the scattered sunbursts of changing leaves, but it was also the beginning of many cold months.

As a creature of fire and sunlight, he'd always felt the chill more poignantly than others, bundling himself in thick-knitted sweaters before the first leaves fell. *It must be a dragon thing.*

After ten minutes of walking, he heard the stream before he reached it. The passing tree trunks became stained where the river flooded in the spring snowmelt. Raine was tempted to pause and bathe. His cover story had been so believable because of how frequently he washed, after all.

He felt the weight of the soap and scented oils in his bag and sighed. *Father owes me for this.* He'd neglected to secure the inner ear-loops of his hood, and the wind flung it back as he marched toward Joltar Trail. If he turned right, the lightning-shaped road would take him most of the way to Chambrin. He had no way of knowing if his father was still there, but it was the most logical place to begin his search.

He rounded the edge of the woods, nearing the oak bridge where the river cut across the main road. Drawing up short, he halted inches away from plowing into someone. He looked up and came face-to-face with the human who haunted the spaces between his heartbeats.

Raine froze, his jaw somewhere near his boots. The captain collected himself before Raine's mind could reconnect with the rest of his body. The man outstretched his arm, abruptly slamming a dagger handle into Raine's head. He crumpled, losing consciousness before he hit the ground.

Raine awoke in a hay-strewn barn, his wrists bound in chains fashioned from an all-too-familiar mixture of black metal and shimmering diamond. A milk cow lowed plaintively from its stall as he nestled against the strawbale at his back. He cradled his head, which throbbed from being brained by a fucking scabbard.

A bizarre mixture of emotions assailed him. An involuntary and intense adoration for the being that he also wanted to throttle. Nausea roiled his stomach, and he closed his eyes. Footsteps approached silently. Raine only sensed them by the faint vibrations beneath his bottom. Very gingerly, he raised his head.

The captain loomed before him, extending a canteen without a word. His velvety eyes were dark and his handsome, tanned face inscrutable. Yet Raine got the distinct impression the captain despised him.

A fact he should be indifferent to, only he wasn't. Not at all.

His muddled thoughts turned to the tainted water the dragons had been given in the Cavern, but he took the canteen, nonetheless. His eyes traced the captain's high cheekbones. Those graceful brows. The rigid line of a strong jaw that ticked under his perusal.

The captain's lips had been pulled back into a hateful snarl at Sleepy Bear Inn, so Raine wasn't able to picture them correctly all this time. They were brownish pink and shapely, though not as full as his own. They looked soft.

The captain frowned down at him and Raine cleared whatever expression was on his face, uncertain what he may have given away while staring.

"Drink," the man ordered. His voice was husky and firm, but quiet. He was used to having his commands obeyed, Raine decided. Men uncertain in their authority often raised their voices when issuing orders. The captain had almost whispered. *Drink.*

Raine looked down at the canteen in his shackled hand. The leather sack was heavy and cool to the touch. He pressed his lips around the opening and swallowed long, deep gulps until the canteen was empty. Damn, he had been thirsty.

He gave the captain a sheepish smile. "Thank you. My name is Raine. What's yours?"

The captain accepted the canteen, his neutral expression hardening with distaste. "I am Sidian Wade, captain of Guardian Unit One-Zero-One-Three. My orders are to apprehend the rogue dragon, Raine Chambrin, and present it to the nearest commander-in-chief for further instruction."

"Oh. I suppose you're doing very good so far," Raine mumbled. With a million questions clamoring on the back of his tongue, desperate to learn everything about this man—*Sidian*—he could have thrown himself off Moontop mountain for the one that made it out. "This is a bit of a personal question, but have you ever found yourself attracted to men?"

Sidian's features turned glacial. "Let there be honesty between us. Chieftain Morseth of Pashun ordered my unit to capture you alive. If his order had been phrased 'dead or alive,' we wouldn't be having this conversation."

His voice was smoky and sensual in his anger, sending heat through Raine's groin. His dick evidently lacked any connection whatsoever to his brain, which screamed, *my mate is a homicidal maniac, and I should run very far, very fast.*

He swallowed hard and nodded, since Sidian seemed to be waiting for a response. The barn door opened, admitting the other two members of Guardian Unit One-Zero-One-Three. The journeyman and journeywoman were outfitted in the same style as Sidian and all Guardians: skintight black hose that left nothing to the imagination. Indeed, Raine studiously kept his eyes above Sidian's neck to prevent an overt perusal of the man's attributes.

As Sidian's subordinates approached, Raine recognized the man as the same hunter he'd fought at Sleepy Bear Inn, when they had attacked him. The man wore a cast on his left arm where Raine snapped his wrist. Gazing down at Raine, his small eyes promised pain. *Guess somebody holds grudges.*

Raine inspected the journeywoman next and struggled not to react. He recognized her, as well. She was the scandalously clad female who'd propositioned him at the dance club, Debauched. Thirty minutes after she offered to bite his ass, he and Aly had gone back to the inn, where they ran into Sidian and the other guy.

Recognition flared across her face, but she didn't acknowledge him. "Captain Wade," she purred, placing a hand on his shoulder in a way that should have seemed friendly but was sexual somehow. "I have acquired the provisions you requested from town. We can depart with the creature when you are ready."

Raine felt something hot and ugly coil inside himself. An image of him stripping the flesh from the woman's torn limbs filled his vision, grotesque and darkly satisfying. He blinked it away, taken aback by the malefic fantasy.

"Await me outside." Sidian's quiet, smoky command was immediately obeyed. The two disappeared through the barn exit, closing it softly behind them.

The captain stared down at Raine for a long moment. "Stand."

Raine shifted to his feet, his cuffed hands lending awkwardness to the task. Sidian had him by about four inches, which meant he was *tall*. While Raine was tall for a human, he was of average height for a dragon. Many of the males at the Hellhole were about an inch taller than him, sometimes more.

A thought struck him like a lightning bolt, and he stared at the captain with new eyes. "Are you a dragon?"

Captain Sidian Wade was the size of them. He possessed the strength and speed of them. And Raine had ceased wondering if the man was his mate. It was denial, plain and simple. The instant he encountered Sidian in Pashun, his body had reset.

Raine's primal priorities used to be something like: oxygen, baths, food, sleep. Now his body demanded: Sidian, oxygen, Sidian, baths, Sidian, food, and then sleep, where all he did was dream of Sidian.

Raine's pleasure and purpose in life were inextricably tied to this man, indelibly and eternally.

Sidian's face twisted in a semblance of how it had first appeared to Raine, in Pashun. Lips curled back, baring his teeth in a silent snarl, he clutched Raine by the neck and shoved him against the wall.

Maintaining his punishing chokehold, the captain bit out, "I am not a dragon. I possess honor and reason. Your kind are rabid and spineless."

Spots danced between Raine's eyes as Sidian released him. He fell to his knees and wheezed as the captain continued. "The nearest commander-in-chief resides in Joltar. It is a day's journey. You will be compliant. You will not run. If you do, you die. This is your only warning."

Raine looked up at his mate. Sidian's blue-black hair was shorter in the back, growing longer in the front. Inky bangs fell over his eyes as he stared down at Raine challengingly. The captain's right-hand twitched, as though itching to unsheathe the sword on his back.

"I hear ya," Raine croaked, not sure if the captain expected a reply.

"Tayo," Sidian called in an authoritative voice that was controlled yet carrying.

The barn door flew open, and the journeyman stood at attention. "Captain Wade."

"Is the prisoner's wagon ready?"

"I just finished hitching it when you called, sir. We're ready when you are."

"Escort the creature to the cart." Sidian moved in a smooth, sure stride away from Raine, displaying no sign of apprehension or uncertainty at turning his back to his "enemy."

Raine clenched his teeth, hard, as his treacherous eyes took in the sinful lines of the captain's beautifully muscled backside. That skintight uniform was going to unman him.

Tayo swept across the barn. Standing straight, the crown of his head only reached Raine's neck. His brown eyes were duller than dirt as he looked Raine over, wearing a sneer that emphasized his round features.

"Move," the cretin snapped. Raine tried to emulate Sidian's cool confidence as he was forced to march with his back to the journeyman. Something blunt slammed into his back and sent him sprawling to the floor.

Raine fisted strewn hay beneath his palms as he attempted to calm his racing pulse. He had no doubt he could kill the walking turd behind him before anyone intervened, but he also knew Sidian's execution would be swift and merciless.

Even if Raine could physically overcome the captain, he wasn't certain his instincts would permit him to harm the man. Even to save his own life. It was an intolerable mindfuck.

He carefully stood, scowling at the hay matting his knees and forearms. Tayo refrained from shoving Raine again as they exited the barn. The door faced an expansive cabbage patch, where neat rows of leafy heads awaited harvest.

Tayo grabbed Raine's bicep, which was too broadly muscled for him to clamp his stubby fingers all the way around. The man dug his fingertips into the underside of Raine's arm, eager to bruise, as if punishing him for being fit. He gave a sharp tug. "Move, vermin."

Raine easily wrenched his arm out of the little prick's grip and walked left, as indicated. On the other side of the barn was a modest farmer's homestead. A worn, gravel path crawled from the roadside, sectioning off in a "Y" pattern. One arm branched to the house and the other, the barn. Awaiting them where the pathways converged was Sidian, the journeywoman, and a prison cell on wheels.

The thing was a monstrosity of iron bars and open air. It would be bitterly cold and uncomfortable. If Raine could ride in it, that was.

Two piebald carthorses startled as he neared. A high, agitated whinny greeted him as he stood next to Sidian and the female, both of whom were seated on a padded bench in front of the barred conveyance.

"Get in the wagon," Tayo half-yelled. A meaty hand pushed Raine's shoulder, directing him toward the rear cage.

The horses kicked and brayed. Another whinny, this time sounding more like a scream. Raine snorted but allowed the journeyman to usher him toward the cell's opening. The hunters didn't seem to realize this was doomed to failure, and Raine didn't see how it was his job to explain.

He climbed into the barred wagon. Raw, splintered wood irritated his palms, but slivers couldn't pierce dragon skin. Tayo locked the door with a nasty grin. Raine grinned back. The man froze, so Raine made a little shooing motion.

The journeyman punched the bars—a foolish move when he only had one good hand. "Think something's funny, dragon bitch?" he spat.

Raine just settled in, treating the wagon as if it were a throne instead of a cage. Tayo smacked the bars again, his dirt clod eyes plotting retribution as he moved to the front bench of the conveyance. Raine rolled his eyes to the sky and sighed.

Twenty minutes later, all three members of Guardian Unit One-Zero-One-Three rounded the wagon, glowering at Raine. As if he'd nefariously sabotaged their travel itinerary.

"It did something to the horses. I know it," Tayo said, pointing a stubby finger.

"Wow," Raine drawled. "What kind of Guardians don't know that horses are afraid of dragons? This cart won't budge with me strapped to their rears."

It wasn't limited to horses. Most prey animals seemed to possess an instinctive recognition and weariness of dragons. There were no stables at Chambrin Keep for that very reason. Knowing how warily cows, horses, and hoofed creatures in general had always treated him, Raine felt like a proper idiot for not piecing his lineage together sooner.

Raine's question brought Tayo up short. His neck flushed the pinkish red of an unfortunate sunburn. "How should we know? We kill dragon scum, not cart the living shitbags across town and country."

The implications of the Nine requiring Raine alive suddenly hit. They expected him to lead them to Evin's thunder. What's more, he was also their only hope of reclaiming the freshly liberated Cavern dragons. This realization should have eased Raine's anxiety. After all, if he died, invaluable information died with him. But instead of relief, pure dread iced his spine.

"That palfrey was fine when we transported the dragon here," the journeywoman observed, glancing sideways at a speculative Sidian. "Maybe the trick is keeping it unconscious. A spoonful of poppy serum should knock it out until tonight."

The smile that traced Tayo's doughy lips raised the fine hairs down Raine's arms.

"Great idea," he chimed, thinking fast as he sat up in the wagon. "I love poppy serum. It doesn't make dragons sleep the way it does humans," he lied with an insouciant shrug. "But it will make me super randy." He waggled his eyebrows at the woman. "I know you'll like that."

Her lips pursed primly even as she covertly surveyed his body with warm appreciation. The shape and definition of his muscles were concealed by his cloak, but there was no mistaking the size and breadth of him as anything other than toned, strapping warrior.

He refused to let his eyes take in the size and breadth of the other deliciously toned warrior of their group, though some treacherous part of him was all too aware of Sidian's proximity. His subconscious counted Sidian's every breath and measured the most minute shift of the man's weight on his feet. Raine somehow knew, without looking, how each feathery soft strand of that blue-black hair lay.

"We travel on foot," the captain announced. Raine's low belly clenched hotly as he met Sidian's narrow-eyed stare. "Not for your feeble lie, dragon." Raine's ears warmed as the captain called him out directly. "The serum is too risky. Some sleep for hours. Others sleep for eternity. We cannot chance the dragon falling into the latter category."

Sidian clipped to the front of the wagon. "Gather your packs," he ordered his unit. "I will fashion a lead from the reins. Tayo, you will tether the beast to your person as we travel."

"Hey, now," Raine protested, not liking where this was going. He pointed at the woman, though Sidian couldn't see him. "Why can't she tether me?"

Raine really wanted to be near his captain, but he wasn't stupid enough to state that preference.

Sidian was disinclined to please him, so Raine pretended he wanted the journeywoman to lead him in case it made Sidian decide to lead Raine himself. But truthfully, anyone would be better than Tayo the Turd, whose face had brightened with unholy glee when the captain mentioned tethering Raine to him.

Sidian returned with a pack on his back and stepped up to the wagon. He placed his face inches from Raine, whose breath hitched at the sheer perfection of the man. Raine wanted to wrap entire kingdoms in ribbons and lay them at Sidian's feet. He wanted to kiss every inch of him, starting with his wide, dusky mouth or the corners of his rich, velvet eyes.

"Tayo will bear the burden of you," he said in his low, slightly hoarse voice. Raine's most favorite sound in the entire world. "Because Rosa does not need to be subjected to your perverse lechery."

Raine blinked, absorbing the words more slowly than he should have. He liked to think his mental delay was due to his drinking water being laced, but he knew the only drug at play was his intense reaction to the intoxicating captain.

"What about you?" he asked, before Sidian stepped away.

The captain's eyes were as cold and remote as the distant, snow-capped mountain peaks. "I don't know if I can suffer a dragon's prolonged proximity without slaying it."

CHAPTER NINETEEN

The hunters took Joltar Trail, which made sense. The road's namesake was their destination, after all. The winding trail buried into Joltar like a bolt of lightning before disappearing.

It felt strange traveling a main thoroughfare without the stress of discovery. Mostly because he was already discovered, worst case scenarios and all that. Still, it took ages for Raine to stop tensing whenever they encountered other travelers on the road.

As they walked, Sidian led their group. Rosa took up a rear-guard position, walking behind Raine and Tayo. He surmised they kept him in the middle to stop him if he made a run for it.

Tayo was tame, at first. He jerked the braided leather lead sporadically, which was fastened to Raine's handcuffs. The first time the turd had done it, his timing was impeccable. Raine's disobedient eyes were feasting on Sidian's calf muscles, flexing against his Guardian hose in the afternoon light. A vicious tug had sent him crashing to the cobbles, skidding so hard that the stones ate holes in the knees of his pale almond tights.

The journeyman became preoccupied with reproducing that first fall. He yanked the tether repeatedly, though never catching Raine off guard like he had initially. Now that he knew the game, Raine was able to maintain his balance, only stumbling here and there.

While Tayo was fixated on him, Raine scarcely registered the vile worm's existence beyond a little extra care with his balance and footing. He was too caught up in his own private obsession, Sidian, along with quietly marveling at his newfound depths of stupidity.

Raine was likely being led to his own execution—by the one person he yearned to cherish and love above life itself—and his thoughts were as dimwitted as, *At least I'll die knowing his name* and, *He's incredible. Handsome, commanding, intelligent, strong.*

There was nothing Sidian said or did that eased Raine's wanting. His dragon instincts found something praiseworthy in the captain's every action. Sidian paused at a water pump to fill their canteens. *He has keen survival instincts and an eye for detail.* Sidian distributed rations to his human subordinates but offered Raine nothing. *He's smart to keep his captive weak with hunger.*

Rosa abandoned her rear guard to walk alongside Sidian, deliberately brushing their bodies together. The captain seemed to lean in participatorily. Raine's involuntary mental fawning finally malfunctioned.

He's a lecherous human pig. They rut with anything, like Aly said. Then, because the Dreaming Mother evidently loathed him, his admiration machine kicked in again. *He is virile and seeks release. He will be a lusty and attentive mate.*

Raine's eyes traced Sidian's snugly outlined shoulders, slightly broader than his own. His back was concealed by his pack, but his powerful, sculpted buttocks and thighs were still visible. The view endlessly pleased him, his half-hard cock swelling to full mast. The crude term *blue balls* had never made sense to Raine. Until today. His sack ached from the incessant heat in his groin.

Once again, Raine's lust-addled mind left him vulnerable and Tayo got lucky. The journeyman shoved him without warning, hitting his lower back. Raine tripped, chin smacking hard against the road. Fiery blood flooded his mouth where he bit his tongue.

His heart pumped pure adrenaline at the bursting pain, but Raine ignored it, calmly moving to his feet. The captain and journeywoman had turned at the sound of his fall. Once he was upright, they began walking once more, neither commenting on the blatant misconduct of their teammate.

Raine clenched his jaw and kept his gaze on the back of Rosa's dark head, where she'd pinned her braid into a high bun. His own braid hung long and heavy down his back, swaying as he walked. It was a delightful benefit of captivity, that he could walk in the open with his hood down, his hair without powder or wig. Iridescent pinks, purples, and blues glittered in dappled sunlight as the overcast sky broke apart.

Tayo's enmity was understandable, given that Raine had broken his wrist. But it was pathetic to attack a guy in handcuffs, from behind no less. He anticipated it when the man shoved him again, a full-effort jab designed to sprawl him flat on the roadway once more. Raine stumbled but remained standing. Clenching his jaw, he resisted the urge to tug on the tether himself and splatter the man's skull against the cobbles like a pumpkin.

It became clear, after some time, that Raine would not succumb to another fall. An hour passed while Raine enjoyed a peaceful reprieve from Tayo's petty attentions.

Unfortunately, the neanderthal was creative and eventually thought up another game. This time, he found a lovely rock the size of a potato on the side of the road.

Raine remained ignorant of Tayo's new toy until he whipped the stone at his back, bludgeoning the center of his spine. He bent on a shock of hot pain, legs threatening to fold. Sheer grit and refusal to give the fucker satisfaction kept Raine standing. Straightening, he walked stiffly. Muscles taut, braced for the next throw.

Tayo didn't disappoint. As Raine walked, the bastard whipped the stone into his back, over and over. He chucked it with as much strength as his soft body could muster, then picked it up wherever it rolled onto the street. Moments later, without fail, he whipped the rock again.

A mirror wasn't necessary for Raine to know his back was a solid bruise. The pain was brutal, borderline agonizing. But he refused to make a sound or acknowledge his tormentor; indifference was his only weapon.

Tayo got meaner, the rock striking more frequently. Raine became even less reactive, his stride unbreaking with each repetition. The captain and journeywoman ignored them, but as Tayo's rock clattered noisily to the street over and over, he imagined that they knew. Knew and were unbothered.

Raine was near his breaking point when the captain paused to disperse rations for a quick supper. He swallowed a groan as the captain handed Tayo two meals-worth of food, expecting him to share.

Sidian sat upon a fallen tree that had been moved to the side of the road so it would not impede passing carts and wagons. Rosa plopped down next to him, pressing their hips and thighs together. Raine grit his teeth and turned to Tayo.

"Oh, did you want this? Here you go, dragon." Tayo spat thickly on a crust of bread stuffed with cheese and tomatoes. There were two dried strips of meat, as well. The man threw it all at Raine's feet and stomped, grinding the heel of his boot for good measure before taking a seat on a flat rock to tend to his own portion.

Raine stared at his ruined food before moving away from the others, as far as his tether allowed. Gingerly, minding his raw back, he splayed across the grass near the roadside and stared into the sky. The clouds were fleecy and soft, riding the blue like tufts of raw cotton. They looked so soft and comforting, he imagined himself swathed in a cloud, sailing slowly to the edge of everything; a special place only clouds could reach, where they fell like dandelion wishes across the graceful, shining back of the Dreaming Mother, whispering to her of the things they'd seen.

Sidian's face blocked the sky as the captain stood over him. Silently, he dropped half of a cheese and tomato sandwich onto his chest as well as one strip of beef. Before Raine could react, he walked away. *He split his meal with me.*

He remembered how fiercely Sidian had proclaimed his honor, his implication that dragons had none. Respect filled him for the man who would be pleased if he dropped dead but wouldn't let him starve in his custody.

Rosa followed behind Raine for the rest of the day, and Tayo mercifully abstained from using the rock. At nightfall, they took a sudden turn from the road. Dense foliage scratched his face as he pushed after the light of Sidian's lantern, tripping on roots along the shadowed forest floor.

They came upon a rusticated cabin. Its roof was thatched, the windows crooked. Sidian knelt in a tangle of brambles near the door and plucked a stone. Raine watched curiously as he opened it, extracting a key.

"Tayo, gather wood and light the hearth," the captain said as they filed into a stale sitting room. Tayo gave an affirmation and left, tossing Raine's leash to the floor.

Placing his lantern on the mantle, Sidian grasped one of the half-burned tallow candles on a table and tipped the wick into the flame. Once the tiny wick flickered to life, he pointed at the dusty sofa. "Sit, dragon. Do not move or speak." Raine sat, fighting a grimace as his tender back touched the cushions. "Rosa, guard the dragon until Tayo gets the hearth lit."

"Where are you going?" she asked, hooding her eyelids.

"To bathe," the captain said shortly.

To bathe? The words reverberated through him, striking a chord in his very being. The corner of a bathtub flashed as the captain disappeared inside a room. A *nice* bathtub. The kind with functioning pipes, where water could be pumped into the basin instead of carried in cumbrous pots and buckets. Raine was not above begging for a bath, if it came to that.

At the sound of the bathroom door bolting, Rosa slid onto the sofa cushion beside Raine and angled herself to face him.

She arched her spine, thrusting her breasts outward as she leaned forward. Looking at Raine through heavy lidded eyes, she said, "Oh, yes. I remember you, delicious boy. Good enough to eat." Her teeth flashed an avaricious smile.

"Funny," Raine replied with a faint smirk. "I don't remember you."

Her face settled into the hot fury of a woman scorned before she barked a laugh. "Oh, baby. I see how it is. You're afraid I'm leading you on because of my history with the captain."

His heart shriveled in his chest. "The captain?"

Her sultry laugh stung like nettles. "Ancient history, darling. Captain Wade is too career-driven to settle down. We hooked up a few times while serving in the same unit. Then our captain retired and Sidian was promoted. He won't lay a finger on a subordinate."

A bold finger traced the center of Raine's chest as she curled further into him, damn near climbing on his lap. Warm breath fanned his face as she whispered, "Technically, we aren't supposed to fraternize with prisoners. But I'm making an exception." She leaned close enough to kiss. "Because you ... are ... exceptional."

Raine forced his jealousy of her intimate relationship with Sidian aside. As Rosa said, they were ancient history. Besides, Raine had no claim on the man. Sidian could do as he pleased. Dragon instincts gnashed and raged against those thoughts, but Raine wasn't a brute who thought he was entitled to his mate's body. Though a very dark, primal part of him blazed possessiveness.

Sidian was wrong about dragons. Raine had honor. And reason. And more courage than he could stare in the eye. The courage to let his mate go, even if doing so killed him.

Rosa trailed one hand across her breasts, peaking her nipples against the black fabric of her uniform. Her fingers edged lower, a loaded smile creasing her lips. While her confidence was admirable, Raine was as moved as a corpse at her display.

Her lips parted on a sensuous sigh as she leaned away. Raine relaxed, grateful for the distance. He was more grateful still as she left him alone, plucking her own body. An effort to entice him into replacing her hands with his own, he gathered.

The idea nauseated him. Saliva pooled in his mouth, and he shuddered. As if to console itself, his mind replaced Rosa on the sofa with Sidian. He imagined his mate's fawn eyes hot with desire. *For him.* Blood rushed to his groin so swiftly, it left him dizzy.

Rosa crooked a finger at him while her other hand disappeared between her thighs. He was morbidly curious about what her fingers could be getting up to with her guild hose in the way, but not enough to watch. He averted his gaze, shifting against the cushion to help disguise his erection. The last thing he needed was for her to spot it and think he was aroused by this nonsense.

She didn't appreciate him looking away, a fact he gleaned as she gripped his chin and turned his head to face her. "Playing hard to get? I like that." She licked her lips. Slow and deliberate. Then glanced at his groin, where his damned cloak had parted to reveal his bulge. "I like other hard things, too."

Raine's brief fantasy of Sidian reciprocating his desire had been incredibly ill-conceived. But how could he have known it would inspire such an unflagging hardness? Raine glared at his groin, willing it to *flag, damn it.*

Sidian did not return his feelings. The captain was not about to emerge from the bathroom and ravage Raine on this musty sofa. If he was truly Raine's mate, it was a mistake. Or a cruel joke. Either way, there would be no happy ending for Raine or his prick.

His cock, deaf to all reason, remained stiffer than a fire poker. Rosa's hand crept toward his lap. A wave of pure fury washed through Raine. His body belonged to a single person in this universe, and it wasn't the wanton woman making a fool of herself on a stranger's sofa.

He gripped her wrist, a scathing rejection on his lips. The cabin door opened. Tayo entered on a rush of cold wind, a stack of firewood slung over his shoulder in a leather strap. Rosa yanked her hand free and flung herself to the other side of the sofa, affecting an embarrassingly obvious air of ennui.

Tayo either possessed the wits of a troll or the observational skills of a blind man. Perhaps both. He proceeded to the hearth with ponderous, incurious steps and began to build a fire one-handed. Rosa tried to catch his eye, but Raine feigned engrossment with Tayo's fumbling efforts near the hearth. *Who the hell knew I'd be so glad to see Tayo?*

The journeyman fed his first log to the crackling kindling as Sidian emerged from the bathroom. He was fully dressed with tousled, damp black hair. Raine's heart swelled painfully at the sight.

He stood and skirted the room, nearing the recently vacated bathroom as Sidian moved to check Tayo's progress. Raine headed him off and gave the captain his nicest smile to make up for blocking his path.

"May I have my bag so I can bathe?" He posed his question with utmost solicitousness, blinking his wide, silver eyes in the manner that always got his father to yield.

Sidian turned without answering and stepped toward the entry door. Their packs were deposited in a small heap, Raine's haversack among them. That was another perk of being a prisoner. He wasn't trusted with anything, not even his own belongings. Tayo had been forced to carry Raine's haversack as well as his own pack.

Raine brightened as Sidian hefted the worn, canvas strap of his bag over his shoulder. There was a good chance he looked like a lunatic, but there was no containing the beaming grin that overtook his face as he reached for his haversack. Sidian gave him a flat look, making no motion to offer Raine his bag. Silently, the captain turned and reentered the bathroom.

Bemused, Raine followed the captain, though he'd not indicated for Raine to do so. The bathroom contained a hammered copper basin, designed to accommodate a full-sized man. Raine smiled, pleased that he wouldn't be cramped in a crockpot as he washed. He shifted to watch Sidian place his bag at the foot of the tub, then extract a key from his uniform.

Raine held his breath as Sidian released his handcuffs, avoiding any skin-to-skin contact as he did so. Twin bruises circled his wrists as the bands fell away. He thought Sidian stilled upon seeing them, but the captain resumed motion so quickly, Raine decided he imagined it.

Sidian sat upon a towel bench. The handcuffs dangled in his grip between spread knees. "Well? Bathe. Or don't. But make up your mind. I have better things to do." He leaned back against the wall, the epitome of cool indifference.

Raine's belly fluttered. "You're going to sit in here while I wash?"

Sidian gazed at him as if he couldn't fathom the existence of a more stupid creature. "You will not be left unguarded in my custody."

Beneath his cloak, his prick went from semi-hard to full-blown erection at the prospect of being naked, in a bath, with his mate right there.

The captain's dark eyes paralyzed him. They were so penetrating, Raine feared the man could see straight through his cloak. It was an absurd fear. Utterly illogical. Of course, Sidian couldn't see through solid wool.

Even so, Raine was unable to resist a single downward glance. He had to be sure his cloak was loose enough to conceal his humiliating condition. Mercifully, it was. But that hardly mattered if the man was going to watch him disrobe.

"Could you, maybe, turn around while you're in here?"

The irritated look Sidian shot him was as nonsensically arousing as everything else the man did. "You can take a bath under my guard or Tayo's. Or forfeit the bath. I really don't care."

The captain was getting impatient and Raine blew out a breath. He quickly shut the bathroom door, sliding the bolt to engage the lock. A brass pump emptied water directly into the basin as Raine worked the lever. Tepid water quickly filled the tub.

Raine removed his boots, then fiddled with the clasp of his cloak. "It's only that I'm deeply ashamed of my body," he tried again, his groin straining behind his cloak. The captain stared at him stone-faced. Desperate, Raine went on. "I have a micro penis." A beat. "I'm too embarrassed for anyone to see. It's bad. Like a blueberry cradled by two walnuts."

Nothing rattled his mate. Sidian blinked at Raine slowly, his features unreadable. Though Raine suspected his dark gaze was mocking.

He looked from Sidian to the tub to his groin and back. *Fuck it. Men have this sort of problem all the time. It is normal to be unaccountably firm at times. A sign of virility. Probably.*

He shed his cloak sullenly and yanked down his tights before he made a bigger ass of himself. His dick sprang free, and he studiously avoided looking at Sidian. Raine had encountered enough men in his condition to know he was enviably large and beautifully formed, both down there and everywhere else. He had nothing to be ashamed of.

His cheeks flamed in direct opposition of his inner mantra.

The captain received an unfiltered view of Raine's front, but he comforted himself that the man didn't see his backside. While his buttocks were round and firm, he felt strangely self-conscious of the captain observing his back, ravaged from hours of Tayo's rock pelting game. Some intrinsic part of him would shatter if his mate displayed pleasure at the damage he'd taken.

He slid into the bathwater, thoughts turning wistful for his custom washtub at home and its merrily boiling bathwater. After a minute of wallowing, he quashed his yearning. Raine didn't like thinking he was spoiled but there was a slight—*all right, all right,* a very strong chance—that he was rottener than last year's egg, forgotten in the henhouse.

He took a thin washcloth from a neatly stacked pile on a shelf above the tub and scrubbed himself from head to toe twice. In his own bath, it would have been three times with a long soak before and after.

But this water was too cold for comfort, and he could feel Sidian's stare burning a hole into his profile as he washed. The man took his guard duty seriously.

"You will stay away from Rosa," the captain said curtly, breaking the silence as Raine busied himself with a final rinse.

He jerked, wincing as his knee smacked the side of the tub. The washcloth slipped from his fingers. He searched for it before meeting the captain's stare for the first time since falsely professing an intimate deformity.

Sidian's soft lips were pinched, his glare flinty. It sounded like he was warning Raine away from ... "Are you implying I have a carnal interest in the journeywoman?"

Sidian's stare narrowed as his lip curled into a hateful sneer Raine was becoming all too familiar with. "Ten minutes alone with her and you're splitting your seams to fuck her. I'm not implying anything. My orders are explicit. You will not touch her."

To his horror, Raine felt his eyes sting. He splashed water across his face to disguise the moisture. Taking a steadying breath, he affected a jaunty air of male competitiveness entirely at odds with his emotions.

"Jealous I'll steal her from you?"

Sidian's eyes were black ice. "I will not allow one of your kind to sully the flesh of a human woman. Any woman. It'll be wise of you to remember this conversation if you find yourself tempted."

A fissure cracked inside Raine's chest, seeping pain and shame. The thought of Sidian desiring Rosa had hurt, but it was nothing compared to the agony of Sidian believing that Raine wanted another. He ached to correct his mate's assumption, to declare Sidian as his one and only heart's desire, now and forever.

Sidian would drown him in this tub if he told him they were mates. Raine clung to that truth, that brutal reality, and it grounded him enough to edit his response.

"If you're so worried about it, keep your precious human woman away from me. Furthermore, you're very ignorant of a species you regard so hatefully. If you're going to despise us, you ought to do so with all the facts. Dragons don't engage in casual affairs. We mate for life." Raine stood from the tub, water sluicing down his body. His stiff cock bobbed, boldly undermining his declaration.

Sidian eyed him up and down with a caustic twist of his lips. "I can tell you're entirely disinterested in casual affairs." Raine flushed as the captain threw him a towel.

Stepping from the tub, he worked the towel over his damp skin, chasing every bead of moisture. Not looking up, he mumbled, "My *problem* is not related to your journeywoman. I'm … going through some things. Puberty-type shit. Dragons are late bloomers."

It was more truth than lie. But when he finished dressing and caught the captain's gaze, Sidian's expression was coldly disbelieving. "Remember what I said."

CHAPTER TWENTY

*A*nother marvelous day with *Guardian Unit One-Zero-One-Three*. Except it really, really wasn't. It was the second and final day of their journey to Joltar. They had left the vacant cottage before dawn and would reach the city that afternoon. Tayo was assigned the rearguard, and Raine's leash, while Sidian took point with Rosa.

Raine knew the captain was ensuring he couldn't sink his unworthy dragon talons into the journeywoman. It would have been laughable if it didn't mean he was stuck with an increasingly bold, petulant sadist the entire time. Whenever Raine considered complaining about Tayo's escalating abuse, the fear of Sidian's indifference—or worse, pleasure—gouged the words from his throat.

Besides, the captain might view Raine's complaint as a feeble attempt to get closer to Rosa. Sidian's belief that he coveted another drove him mad. It meant Raine was failing his mate. The core of his very being railed against it. His instincts clawed to prostrate himself at Sidian's feet and swear his undying devotion and fidelity.

Declaring himself would be suicide. So, even though the desire to confess his feelings plugged his throat until it was too tight to breathe, he choked it down. He endured Tayo's little torments. And he studied Sidian obsessively, learning much about the captain in a short timeframe.

Sidian was quiet, authoritative, and sharply intelligent. He never smiled or laughed, exuding a gravitas that bordered on melancholy. He possessed a code of ethics and honor embedded within his identity and followed it with conscientious consistency.

Last but not least, Sidian absolutely despised dragons. His hatred was glacial. A thick rime of forbearing ice. Raine passed the time pondering its source. He suspected the sorrow his mate so carefully concealed was related to his dragon antipathy.

One day, Raine would discover the story behind those sad, serious fawn eyes. There was always a chance Sidian would choose to be with him. Raine just needed to be patient. Not his greatest strength, but Sidian was worth everything. A little patience was nothing.

Tayo's rock smacked his shoulder and Raine stifled a scream. His skin didn't split and his bones didn't shatter, but his raw, bruised back was a portrait of Tayo's methodical sadism. Tayo caught the rock on a bounce. Sidian's stride never faltered.

Raine kept walking, concentration split between his ravaged back and overfull bladder. He'd been holding his piss for hours. Until each step sliced his lower abdomen like a knife and his bladder threatened to explode.

Tayo had behaved strangely when Raine went to relieve himself earlier that morning. The journeyman had walked directly up to him, where he stood before a secluded tree. Then, he had pressed his barrel chest against Raine's side and looked down, waiting for him to release his prick.

The phrase *awkward* was not sufficient to describe the scene. Raine had silently moved back to the road, deciding it was better to wait for a time when Tayo wasn't doing ... whatever the fuck he'd been doing.

That had been several hours ago. The pain was unbearable.

Raine cleared his throat. "Excuse me," he called to Sidian and Rosa, who walked side-by-side about ten paces ahead. They turned as one. Rosa angled her neck, blatantly eye-fucking him, which she did whenever the captain wasn't in direct view of her countenance. Sidian eyed him dispassionately and waited.

"I have to pee." His hands squeezed his groin without conscious permission. He had to *go*.

The captain turned his gaze to Tayo expectantly.

"I'm happy to take the dragon," Tayo said with mock solicitousness before grasping Raine by his elbow with his good arm. "We shouldn't be long," he added. Something in his tone chilled Raine's blood.

"I'd really prefer if someone else accompanied me," he said through clenched teeth. He wasn't going to piss his pants in front of his damned mate, but it was going to be a close call.

"I don't mind taking the dragon," Rosa said eagerly. She stepped toward him with an exaggerated sway in her hips.

Sidian's eyes hardened. "Tayo will escort you."

Damn this woman. Raine closed his eyes against the violence that gripped him. If Rosa would cease acting like she was dying of thirst and his dick was a drinking fountain, Sidian might acquiesce to her escort. *Too late now*.

Raine stepped gingerly from the roadway and into the autumn-kissed woods lining Joltar Trail. Opening his cloak, he fumbled with the buttons below his waistband at the first suitable tree. The instant his dick touched air, a stream shot out, puddling at the gnarled base of a sycamore. He bit back a relieved groan.

A branch snapped behind him before a thick fist gathered the back of his cloak. "Turn around."

"Let me go." Raine jerked his torso inward, hunching his shoulders against the tree.

Tayo pressed his chest into Raine's back, pinning him to the sycamore. Raine braced his knees, preventing his vulnerable manhood from scraping against the bark. He was still pissing, and hot urine splashed across his hands as Tayo tried to bodily twist him from the tree.

Raine's strength was infinitely superior to his aggressor's, but his wrists were bound in unbreakable handcuffs. Tayo's wrist was broken, which helped even the score, but the journeyman was heavy. Using his brawn and heft, Tayo shoved Raine sideways. Raine's torso curled closer into the trunk, his body tottering as he fought the lean.

Tayo's sour breath blew across his cheek. "I want to see your micro dick. I'm going to pop it like a blister." His chest shook against Raine's back with cruel laughter. "You'll have to become a homophile and take dick up your ass if you ever want to fuck again. If you beg prettily enough, maybe I'll stick mine in you."

Finally, Raine finished pissing. He hastily tucked himself back into his tights and started closing the buttons.

"No, you don't," Tayo snarled, redoubling his efforts to wrench Raine from his deciduous shield.

Raine closed one button of his tights before Tayo succeeded in knocking him down. Landing on his side, he immediately rolled to stand but his attacker was already on him. Raine flailed beneath Tayo's weight but didn't have the range of motion necessary to buck him off.

They scrabbled across the forest floor. Fallen branches stabbed and scraped Raine's battered back, but the pain was secondary to his need to fight. He would die before Tayo's grubby sausage fingers closed around his dick.

Tayo pinned him heavily, straddling his thighs. He hiked Raine's shirt up to his chest and ripped his codpiece open, sending a lone button flying. Raine accepted the inevitability of his death. Because he was going to have to kill Tayo and that meant Sidian would kill him.

Raine went to wrap the chains of his handcuffs around Tayo's neck, fully intending on twisting the man's head off his bottle-body like a cork, when a dark blur slammed into the journeyman.

Tayo skidded through the brush, shouting in alarm. Raine sat up, braid askew, bits of forest detritus clinging to his shimmering alabaster hair. In a single bound, Sidian leapt upon Tayo. The man's confused cry cut off as Sidian punched him square in the jaw. Crimson bloomed across his knuckles as he drew back, then struck Tayo again. And again. The meaty, rhythmic sound of skin hitting skin grew loud in the silent forest. Raine's sensitive ears discerned each blow over his sawing breath.

The journeyman's face was gone. Only a mess of meat, wet with ruby bright blood, remained. Raine really didn't want to intervene, sensing how easily Sidian's fury might shift targets.

Sickened at the sight of Tayo's tenderized features, he swallowed his fear and timidly brushed the captain's shoulder.

Raine jumped as his mate halted. He had expected Sidian to ignore him, as lost to bloodlust as he was.

"Hey," Raine whispered, speaking on a razor's edge. "It's over. He's done."

Raine had almost said, *he's gone*. But a faint, moist rattle of life croaked through the journeyman's ruined mouth. He tried not to wish Tayo dead, in case it would disappoint his father. But it was especially difficult, and Raine couldn't summon anything beyond a small hope that Tayo drowned in his own blood as he laid there.

Sidian stood and faced him. His temples, cheeks and chin were speckled scarlet from the blood that had splashed beneath his hammering fists. Accusation burned in his stare.

"You did this," he said, low and hoarse.

Raine surreptitiously moved one foot back, then another. He trod as lightly as possible, as if the crunch of a single leaf might detonate the incensed captain like a bomb. Sidian's habitual frigid disdain was doting adoration compared to whatever this was.

"How exactly did I cause this?" He hoped his question would restore some semblance of reason to the ordinarily rational captain.

It only agitated Sidian's malevolence. "You came onto him like you came onto Rosa," he spat.

Raine halted, one buckskin boot frozen mid-retreat. "*What?!*"

"This has been your plan all along. Get my team chasing your tail. Turn us against each other. Destabilize our unit so you can escape."

Raine's survival instincts warred and lost a battle with righteous indignation at his mate's nonsensical accusations. He reversed his steps until his chest was inches from Sidian's.

For a moment, he took in the captain's features up close, resenting Tayo even more for the ruby droplets marring Sidian's perfect features. His lashes, as long and lustrous as Raine's, weren't the cause of the shadows beneath his lovely fawn eyes. No, the captain's face was lined with exhaustion. The delicate skin beneath his eyes was bluish purple, as if he had not slept well. Or at all.

"I asked for anyone other than Tayo to accompany me," Raine said rigidly. "I'm not sure how I planned to seduce that waste of fucking space when I've been doing everything possible to get away from him."

Sidian's dark eyes were pinpricks, hard and remote. "And yet you wasted no time working your wiles the moment you were alone with him."

Raine drew in a shuddering breath and stepped back. "You know what happened," he said, keeping his voice even. "You just can't reconcile that the villain in this situation was a Guardian and not the big, bad dragon."

Raine thought he was done. He had fully intended to spin on his heels and storm off. But his accursed instincts raged like a beast trapped in his chest. They roared and slashed and mauled at him to bellow reassurances.

His mate doubted his fidelity. Doubted his devotion. The pain of it savaged him and made his movements slow.

"Dragons are scum," the captain said to Raine's back.

No unbridled anger laced Sidian's words. They were spoken in the soft, husky timbre that haunted Raine's dreams. He halted. Knowing damn well he needed to get the fuck away from Sidian pronto, he halted. Very slowly, Raine turned and met eyes so velvety rich, simply gazing into them was an unholy decadence.

"You are scum," the captain continued evenly. "Tayo made a mistake. He can repent and improve himself. The only atonement a dragon can offer is their throat to a knife."

Raine wondered if Sidian would ever know how deeply he cut him just then. A slit throat was merciful compared to the soul-deep gouges bleeding out the light behind his silver eyes.

He breathed in through his nose, out through his mouth. Those calming exercises that had helped him cope with living below ground, in the oppressive deep. They helped him now, too.

Fawn. Fawn. Fawn. He took slow, meditative breaths until the warning sting of tears abated.

"You let your experiences color your perception of the world, Sidian. But your perception doesn't define reality. Do you know, in all my experience, I've never encountered a cruel dragon? Only cruel humans. Yet I don't use my experiences to castigate humanity as a whole."

He turned to stalk away and stopped, spinning round again. "I believed you when you said you had honor. But I also believe honor requires fairness. It is unjust to blame me for the memory that haunts your eyes. Whatever happened, whoever hurt you, I promise it wasn't me. It will *never* be me."

Raine grit his teeth against any more damning drivel. He was perilously close to declaring his feelings. Given Sidian's crackpot theory of him seducing his unit into discordance, proclaiming undying love would be the proverbial nail in his coffin.

With his luck, it would send his mate into another killing frenzy. This time, with Raine as his sole target.

CHAPTER TWENTY-ONE

The captain remained in the woods for an interminable duration before emerging. Long enough that Rosa propositioned Raine no less than five times. He made sure to perch on a rock only large enough for one as he waited, and Rosa was smart enough to distance herself as they detected Sidian's rustling approach through the trees.

Rosa craned her neck and scanned the woods over Sidian's shoulder. "Where's Tayo?"

"Discharged," Sidian said in a tone that brooked no further questions. Rosa's dark pink mouth pinched, but she heeded the unspoken command, gathering her pack in silence.

Sidian remained at the head for the remainder of their journey. One end of the leather lead was taut around his fist, the other end fastened in an elaborate knot around Raine's handcuffs. Raine followed the captain with a measured pace, ensuring the tether remained slack between them.

His mate's demeanor—usually cold, somber, and somewhat disconnected—changed after the incident with Tayo. Sidian moved like wildfire. Dangerous and unpredictable. Raine tried his best to be invisible, sensing the hell he would pay if he drew the captain's attention in any way.

Rosa brought up the rear, a respectable distance behind Raine. She was unnaturally quiet, picking up on Sidian's volatile mood. If Raine discounted the harrowingly tense atmosphere, the remainder of their journey was nearly pleasant. Nobody hurled thick rocks at his back. Or sucker punched his kidneys. There were no sporadic jerks of the tether to unbalance him.

The cold snap of the previous few days eased. The sun shone high and bright. It was as if the seasons themselves wrestled in the sky, and Summer had Autumn pinned. Raine wanted to take his cloak off and soak up the rays directly, but his handcuffs made him a prisoner of his own stifling layers. Sweat dampened his back and chest, but he didn't dare complain.

Traffic increased after an hour or so, with carts and wagons crossing both directions. Raine skirted the edge of the road, one boot in the grass. It was that or cause a riot of panicking horses. Sidian ignored him, though he moved closer to the roadside to enable his captive's equine avoidance.

Like all Valdenian cities, Joltar was originally a settlement. Its founding tribe was the Strowa. The zigzagging trail that buried itself into the city was also the city's namesake. Joltar was the Strowan word for lightning.

Residents of Joltar seemed taken with the title. Their city wall was sculpted to look like a thunderstorm. The top of the gray wall was carved like the pillowy edges of storm clouds. Etchings of rain and lightning flung from the clouds in an ornate design.

When they were right on top of the entrance gate, Raine noticed the raindrops were actually turquoise gems embedded into the stone. The lightning bolts were gilded and shone in the sun.

Sidian produced a scroll to the gatekeeper. The burly officer leapt from his seat as if his hindquarters had springs. He scraped a deep, obsequious bow, the blunt tip of his nose brushing the street bricks. "It is my honor to welcome you, captain, journeywoman."

He straightened tentatively, as if standing in the presence of Guardians was somehow naughty. The city officer's nut-brown eyes fell on Raine, and his expression warped from reverence to abhorrence.

It was a reaction Raine knew well, though the light of recognition in the gatekeeper's features was new and different. This wasn't the hate Raine was used to, fueled by superstition and ignorance due to his colorless hair and eyes.

No. The gatekeeper's hatred was personal.

And no wonder. Thanks to those damned wanted posters, Raine was one of the most recognizable persons in the country. And the most detested, since the posters proclaimed him a dangerous enemy of Valdenia and its rulers, who possessed the absolute trust and devotion of their citizens.

Before continuing into the city, Sidian wrapped the leather rope around his fist and elbow several times, shortening the gap between them. As if Raine was a vicious dog who must be kept close.

The captain's caution was rapidly proven unnecessary. The residents of Joltar gave Raine a wide berth. Men and women cursed at him, but only after crossing the street where he could not reach them. Some people threw rubbish. Spoiled food and empty bottles. Their aim was poor, fortunately, so he kept his chin up and ignored them.

Of all the damned lies the Nine could have put on his wanted poster, why did they have to choose offenses guaranteed to piss off the entire country?

Well, all right. The answer was obvious, wasn't it? By effectively turning everyone against him, the Nine had all but guaranteed Raine's eventual capture.

The Nine's deceit went a step further. Nowhere in Raine's wanted posters did they reveal him as a dragon. Considering it was the crux of why they hunted him, the omission was glaring. Glaring, but not surprising. After centuries of concealing dragons' dual forms, the Nine were hardly going to reveal it now.

But why all the secrecy in the first place?

Probably because the Nine didn't want the public to know that dragons weren't mere beasts. That they were *people*. Such a truth would reveal the Nine's dragon breeding program as morally repugnant. They'd be forced to relinquish their little dragon battalion, too.

Or would they? Perhaps the Nine were being overcautious in their secrecy, and nothing would change if the public knew. The guild knew, and they cheerfully exterminated his species like rats anyway.

Then again, the Guardians of Vale clearly believed dragons were coldblooded monsters that only *appeared* human. Sidian certainly thought so.

Raine was pulled from his bleak conjecture as a group of young children, the tallest reaching no higher than his waist, ran up to him on the sidewalk. He braced himself, expecting them to emulate their predecessors by throwing things or calling him names.

But the little girls' hands were empty. They danced around Raine and his two captors, dark eyes bright and black ponytails flouncing. They didn't hate Raine. They were fascinated by him. Chattering like excited squirrels, they gestured at his hair and eyes. Sidian surveyed them with the blank stillness of a sentry. Rosa cooed and petted their heads, asking their names and things like that.

Raine's gut clenched when a little girl with a wave of riotous black curls approached him. She eyed his handcuffs with confusion. Children obviously didn't keep up with current enemies of state, as she showed no recognition or fear of him. Only rapt awe and curiosity.

"I've never seen hair or eyes like yours," she said in a high, sweet voice. "You look like the moon and stars."

Raine's throat closed tight. He swallowed hard, trying to work it back open without being obvious. *Divine Father, don't let me burst into tears and scar this kid for life.*

"Thank you," he said in a near-whisper that was still somehow choked with emotion.

She smiled down at her feet. "I wish I looked like you."

Raine reached out to ruffle her hair, but a manacle snagged his wrist. He blinked at the restrictive chains, returning to his senses. Glancing over, he found Sidian observing them like a hawk; tense and motionless, his arm poised to give a brutal tug on his tether in case Raine tried harming the little girl.

Something ugly churned in Raine's stomach at how despicable his mate thought him. Raine looked away and his gaze fell onto the little girl. He didn't crouch down to her level, like he wanted to, and he didn't muss her hair the playful way Nyx liked to do to him.

But he did lower his neck and say, in a hushed tone that was just for her, "I always wished I looked like you." She looked up at him, wide-eyed and disbelieving. "It's true," he insisted. "I love your hair and eyes. You're like a little panther cub."

She beamed at his words, shining far too brightly to ever be compared to the weak pallor of moon and starlight. "I have to go now. But my new name is Panther Cub. Yours is Moonbeam, okay? Okay, bye Moonbeam!"

Raine blinked dazedly as she skipped away. The other children left, as well. A harried woman in a plain teacher's robe honked at them like a mother goose from across the street. He didn't realize he was softly smiling until he looked over and met Sidian's stony expression. His lips fell slowly as the captain stared. It felt like a reprimand, but Raine hadn't done anything wrong. The children had approached him, not the other way around.

"We should get moving," Rosa said, shattering their stare-off. "There's a mob forming a couple blocks behind us. I want to make it to Commander Pare's office before they riot."

Before the mob jumped Raine and tore him limb from limb, is what she really meant. Sidian's gaze flicked behind Raine. His jaw flexed at whatever he saw. "Come on."

Sidian led them away briskly, taking several quick, dizzying turns through Joltar's zigzagging streets. Several blocks over, Sidian's pace slowed. Raine chanced a backwards glance. The street was empty except for a pair of workers unloading a cart of green and yellow squash.

Another angular turn spilled them into a bustling market district. Raine's gut lurched, but the shoppers paid them no mind. They were engrossed in their errands—haggling over cheap shoes, common spices, and coarse fabrics. Many of the shops were simple tents wedged between alleyways.

Raine halted at one such market stall. A blue-and-yellow striped awning covered the merchant's shelves. An easel was strategically placed for passersby to admire—a detailed sketch of the Dragon Fangs, rendered in charcoal. It featured the same mountain section depicted in the guild's emblem, which included the Fangs' two most distinguished peaks, Snaggletooth and Draggair.

Raine stared at the sketch, thoughts whirling. He didn't see a landscape in his mind's eye. He saw all the whimsical wallpaper designs he'd been mentally constructing. He fingered one of the sketchbooks stacked beneath the awning, placed next to the easel. Its rich, smooth vellum begged for color and life.

Turning to Sidian, he found the captain watching him with the same cold, shuttered expression he'd worn since the Tayo incident. "I would like to make a purchase. I have silvans in my bag."

The captain's lips thinned but he reached inside Raine's haversack, slung over his shoulder, and produced several coins. Raine took them with a softly muttered, "Thanks."

It felt weird to thank someone for offering him his own money, but the man did have him handcuffed and wanted him dead. When Raine considered it like that, it seemed like its own brand of generosity, the captain permitting Raine to buy some art supplies.

As Raine went to make his purchase, Sidian hung back at the canopied entrance, unwinding the leather rope so he wouldn't have to trail his captive to the checkout stand.

The merchant attending the stall took one look at Raine, clutching a sketchbook and colored pencils, and spat at his boots.

"Get out of here, you fucking blanch. I don't sell my wares to traitors."

It was Raine's turn to wear a shuttered expression. He rejoined Rosa and Sidian empty-handed, brittle with humiliation and anger. They must have seen and overheard the interaction but neither commented, for which Raine was grateful.

Chieftain Pare's office was located between a library and a messenger station back on Joltar's main thoroughfare. Sidian directed them through side streets and alleyways until they spilled right out in front of it. The building was striking, made of smooth, polished stone, deepest violet with fracturing veins of creamy white. Like lightning in a storm.

The secretary was an older woman, her steel gray hair frosted with streaks of white in a manner that eerily echoed the building's exterior. She glanced up at their entry, paling as she beheld Raine.

"J-Just one moment," she said. Her chair squeaked against the tile. Scuttling toward a door with a gilded lattice window, she lunged through it as if being chased.

Raine shifted nervously. His clinking chains reminded him of his position, his defenselessness. Ten minutes ago, he'd tried to buy a fucking sketchbook, and for what? Chieftain Pare was probably going to put him down like a pestilent coyote.

Not if I escape.

Raine balked at the thought like a hot knife. Absolute refusal reverberated through him, his dragon instincts repudiating any plan that involved leaving Sidian. Abandon his mate? *Never.*

But if he didn't do something soon, he was going to *die*. Surely survival instincts trumped all else? His legs were unshackled. At full bore, he was swifter than a deer. All he had to do was run.

Only, as he went to lift his feet, nothing happened. They wouldn't budge. He glanced down, half-expecting to find his boots bolted to the floor. They weren't.

Raine scowled at his frozen legs, recognizing the machinations of his dragon instincts at work. His brain was in charge of his body, damn it. Not his spark-struck heart. He willed his legs to move, but they were as responsive as severed limbs.

The shiny door opened, and a man stepped through wearing a severe black robe Raine now associated with the Nine. Chieftain Pare had a short, bristly ponytail and pointed beard. Raine shuddered as he beheld the man's eyes. They were the mustardy brown of baby shit.

Something was off about the Nine. Their putrid eyes matched like a set even though they were all elected from different tribes. Raine had heard of drugs, certain powders and tonics, that had undesirable physical side effects and wondered if the chieftains indulged in a sweet smoke that yellowed their eyes the way other tobaccos yellowed teeth.

Chieftain Pare didn't glance his way, training his eyes solely on Sidian and Rosa. "Please come in. Keep the animal closely guarded."

Sidian seized his upper arm and began ushering him toward the office. Raine's feet moved free and easy, all too happy to be guided by the captain. *Unbelievable*. He was going to die because dragons had the most assbackwards survival instincts on the planet.

Sidian's chest pressed against his side as the captain steered him through the doorway. His belly flipped at the contact, at his mate's warm solidness. They entered a lavishly ornamented office, scattered with abstract sculptures and blown glass lamps. The wallpaper was solid gold with a centered band of sapphire blue.

Raine wanted to ask if that metallic sheen was real gold somehow woven into the wallpaper, but as he turned, the secretary fell away with a screech. She backed against the opposite wall and eyed him like a disease. Once Sidian had Raine fully inside the office, she dashed for the safety of the lobby, slamming the door shut on her heels.

Chieftain Pare returned to his desk, feigning a collected calm he couldn't quite pull off. Not with his clammy brow and anxious, darting eyes. And not with how he clumsily avoided any proximity to Raine, skirting his office in a manner that nearly knocked two sculptures over. A potted dwarf tree blocked that side of his desk. Its leaves rustled loudly as he shoved his way around the plant to sit.

Without looking at Raine, he pointed. "Place it in the corner over there."

Sidian led him to the corner Pare indicated. Next to the closed door, it was the space furthest from his desk. The captain's arm was steely with tension, as if he anticipated a sudden outburst.

Raine remained docile. There was nothing he could do. His damn legs refused to run, and he would cut off his own hands before harming his mate. Pulse thundering at the base of his throat, at the thought of what came next, Raine stood in the corner with his back to the wall.

Chieftain Pare snapped, "Face the wall, beast!"

Raine met Sidian's gaze. The captain was ashen, his fawn eyes stark against his wan countenance. Raine clenched his fists but turned obligingly, wondering at Sidian's discomfiture. His mate's code of honor must not have prepared him for such a clinical execution. Sidian probably thought it dishonorable to dispatch a dragon outside the field.

The most fucked up thing was, Raine felt guilty for any trauma his death might cause Sidian. He didn't want to compound the shadows in his mate's eyes. He only wanted to unveil them. Somehow, Raine knew Sidian's honor doubled as his security blanket. Raine hoped he kept it, always.

"Why am I not surprised that a Wade brother captured that thing? Absolutely brilliant, Captain Wade. Mark my words, you'll be a chieftain some day!"

Raine's veins frosted. *Over my dead body*. His vehemence surprised him, along with the deep-rooted certainty that Sidian becoming a chieftain would be a very bad thing.

"Don't fret," Pare continued. "I'm not going to kill the beast and steal your mastership from you. Why, there are hardly any dragons left. If you don't slay this one, you may not get another opportunity to promote."

Raine knew captains were promoted to masters within the guild, but he had assumed it happened after a captain showed outstanding service or put in enough years. If he was following Chieftain Pare's statement correctly, they were promoted by murdering dragons?

Bile burned his throat. *Father was a master*.

"Thank you, Commander Pare," Sidian replied, his voice quiet and husky. "My only desire is to protect Valdenia. I'm humbled by any opportunity to serve our country."

"That's a good thing, too. Your mission is far from complete. I'm afraid you won't be earning your mastership today. The animal must be taken to Obanth. Chieftain Eddic will await your arrival at headquarters. We need the extraction specialists working as soon as possible if we hope to recover the breeding beasts. It's a fucking mess. What's the matter, Captain Wade? Speak! These are arguably the most important orders you'll ever receive. If there's any confusion, it needs clearing up now."

"With all due respect, Commander Pare, what do you mean by 'recover the breeding beasts?'"

"You haven't been updated?"

"My unit encountered the dragon in Pashun. It managed to escape, but we tracked it near Campion and picked it up on Joltar Trail. We reported directly to you with the captive and will gladly transport it to Obanth. The trip will be long since horses do not abide the dragon's proximity."

"I see. You were too busy working to catch the gossip. To be brief, a herd of wild dragons infiltrated Chambrin Keep and stole the breeders. They didn't work alone, either. Arastus Chambrin betrayed guild and country. He aided the break-in. We apprehended him at the scene, before he could flee with the beasts."

Raine stopped breathing at the mention of his father.

"Arastus is already in Obanth. The extraction specialists have been pressuring him, but so far, they haven't uncovered anything useful. I'm curious to see if the arrival of his illicit pet loosens his tongue. One of them knows something and we're going to crack them like cantaloupes."

CHAPTER TWENTY-TWO

They remained sequestered in Chieftain Pare's office for *hours*. That's how it felt, anyway. With his nose tucked into the corner of the office like a recalcitrant six-year-old, Raine's sense of time was likely skewed.

Every minute in a corner felt like twenty. It had been one of his father's favorite methods of punishment, since it appeared humane on the surface but tortured Raine in reality. *So impatient*, he'd say with fond amusement, then leave Raine standing in the corner longer because he was a cruel bastard.

After an eternity of bilious hate speech for dragons and lavish praise for Sidian and Rosa, Chieftain Pare dismissed unit One-Zero-One-Three. Raine met the older man's eyes as Sidian led him out. Chieftain Pare reacted like a startled cat, with hissing, spitting eyes and a readiness to bolt.

Raine silently thanked the Divine Father and Dreaming Mother that he'd been privy to their conversation.

Not only was he not being executed (yet), but he also knew where his father was. He even had his own personal escort taking him there.

There was a spring in his step he couldn't disguise as they left Joltar's government building. Hopefully, his captors attributed his buoyancy to not being slain. They had no way of knowing how well things were working out for Raine. The thought made him smile.

Raine followed behind Sidian with Rosa at his back, their standard formation absent Tayo. Sidian walked stiffly, his fist clamped tight around Raine's tether. The captain's black mood darkened the air, sobering Raine's triumph. Sidian clearly hadn't expected to be stuck guarding the type of creature he hated most in the world for the next two weeks.

Given the captain's blatant distaste for his extended assignment, Raine assumed they would depart the city posthaste—the better to get it over with. But they were moving in the wrong direction. The city gates were the other way. Mystified, Raine focused on keeping the tether slack between himself and the silently seething captain as they progressed.

After nearly an hour of navigating the zigzagged roads, Sidian escorted them up to a tall, logged building that reminded Raine of the country cabins back home. This was not the quaint cottage-like structure he was used to, however. The cabin was colossal. With more windows than he could count at a glance, it spanned the breadth of six houses.

The interior revealed a combination pub and inn. A young brunette in a low-cut frock stood at a welcome desk in a main lobby.

Brass keys lined the wall behind her, each one tagged with a corresponding room number. Sidian reserved a suite on the ground floor.

Their room was done up in neutrals. White wallpaper plastered with splashing swans. Two beds neatly covered with reed brown quilts. A duck green chaise positioned near a hearth with a bookshelf mantle. Rosa nudged open a door off to the side, revealing a private bathroom with a marbled garden tub.

As Raine spied the bath, his palm froze on the wallpaper, where he'd been admiring its thickness and detail. He turned to Sidian, a request to bathe on the tip of his tongue.

The captain anticipated his request. He already had an arm outstretched, offering Raine his haversack. Sidian's face was a blank slate and Raine resisted the urge to paint it with the wishes of his desperate heart. *The captain doesn't care for me. He is just shrewdly observant and dislikes rooming with smelly prisoners.*

"I can watch him if you want to get us something to eat," Rosa told Sidian from her perch on one of the beds, her framed pack tossed in the center of the quilt.

A muscle ticked in Sidian's jaw. "I've got it." The captain shrugged off his rucksack and held out a handful of coins to the journeywoman. "For the food," he said.

Rosa accepted them with a coy smile. "I've seen a naked man before, Captain Wade." Her dark eyes moved down Sidian's figure meaningfully. "I can share the burden of guarding the captive, even while he's washing."

"The dragon is not a man, and I will not risk it treating you perversely. I will guard the dragon while it bathes."

Rosa needed to learn to veil her disappointment better. Her pout was its own insinuation of perversity. She offered Sidian a smile that was more than a little forced and swept from the room.

"I think you should focus on not letting her treat me perversely," Raine muttered on his way to the bathroom.

Sidian acted as though he hadn't heard him, seating himself on the white marble vanity that matched the tub. "Come here."

That husky command was a long, hot lick down Raine's spine. Sucking in a breath, he stepped between Sidian's legs, offering up his cuffed wrists. Sidian had the key in hand and unlatched him with a quick, sharp twist.

Raine kept his face averted, afraid of what the captain might detect in his features this close.

As the metal bands released, he could have wept with relief. The cuffs had tightened to tourniquets from Tayo's incessant yanking. Bees hummed in his hands as his blood circulated for the first time in ages.

As the numbness in his fingers receded, he knelt before the tub and worked the metal lever protruding next to the basin. Blissfully hot water surged from the spigot. *This inn heats its pipes.*

Raine moaned with pleasure as it splashed over his aching wrists. "I really, really miss hot baths."

Once the tub was over half full, he eagerly shed his cloak and clothing, thoughtlessly keeping his back to Sidian. As he settled against the back of the tub, stark shock was etched across the captain's features. Sidian schooled himself in an instant. It was like watching a door slam shut in his eyes.

Raine dropped his gaze. His ears burned. In his delight over the hot water, he had forgotten his ravaged back. Tayo had done a number on him with that unholy rock from hell. His flesh was grotesquely discolored, a mottled mixture of blue and yellow and green.

He closed his eyes, wracked by shame. His mate would think him weak now. Weak and pathetic and ugly.

"What happened to you?"

Preoccupied with his misery, Raine's response was delayed. He peeled his eyelids open and raised his head, reluctantly meeting the captain's stare. For a moment, Raine considered feigning ignorance. But he really didn't care to discuss it, and playing stupid would only prolong this conversation.

"Tayo," he said simply. If Sidian told him to elaborate, he would. Raine hoped he wouldn't.

The captain said nothing. His eyes were as hard and cold as frozen ponds. Raine looked away, unable to withstand the prolonged intensity of that glare. Attempting to mask his discomfiture, he reached for his haversack, only splashing a little water on the floorboards as he did so.

Plinking several droplets of oil into his bathwater, he sighed as the deliciously warm aromas of cinnamon and apples wafted on the steam. The silence in the bathroom was louder than a scream. Raine wanted to say something, anything, to alleviate the tension, but his thoughts darted like shy minnows whenever he reached for words. So instead, he fished out a cake of oatmeal soap and worked it to a milky lather.

"I apologize for the abuses inflicted upon you while under my guard."

The soap slipped from Raine's fingers at the captain's roughly spoken words. Sidian sounded like his throat had been scorched, as if he'd swallowed fire.

Raine fumbled for his soap, but it kept slipping away. Tracking it beneath his milky bathwater was nigh impossible. As he chased the soap, Raine mulled over Sidian's apology.

On the surface, it seemed almost silly that Sidian was bothered by Tayo's violence. The captain was actively escorting Raine to his own torture and execution, after all.

But Sidian took pride in a strict code of ethics that esteemed honor above all things. Torturing a dragon for information, the better to ensure national security? That was fine. Entirely aboveboard. But tormenting a captive for petty, vindictive pleasure violated his code.

Raine's heart shouldn't melt at that. He was pitiful. *Dragons* were pitiful. Where was his own pride in all of this? Sidian was upset because of his subordinate's misconduct, not because Raine had been hurt. Yet his foolish, *foolish* pulse leapt, thrilled by the idea of his mate caring.

Grasping the soap at long last, Raine muttered to his knee, "It's fine. Wasn't your fault."

He heard a sharp exhale, like a huff or a snort. But the captain didn't respond. Raine's bath rapidly cooled without a fire crackling underneath, like how his tub at home was fashioned. He debated washing his hair, but there was really no debate. Detritus littered his braid thanks to Tayo tackling him in the woods.

As he lathered his mane, creating a foamy white mound atop his crown, the captain's earlier words to Rosa replayed in his mind.

"You're wrong about me not being a man," Raine said, then instantly wished he hadn't. The silence shattered beneath his announcement like a brick tossed through a window.

A scoff sounded from the vanity. "You are male but not a man. Humanity is a prerequisite for manhood."

Raine continued to lather himself, taking an excessively long time. He stared unseeing at a shelf of complimentary toiletries above the spigot. "My species are hybrids," he said at last, focusing on a porcelain ewer shaped like a fish spewing water. "A marriage of gifts from the Divine Father and Dreaming Mother. I am as human as I am dragon. We all are."

Unable to stand it anymore, he lifted his chin to meet Sidian's dispassionate gaze. His velvet eyes were fixed on Raine. "I can see you believe that," he said evenly. "Dragons are beasts. Maneaters without conscience. Your body isn't human. It's a cheap imitation, a trick that helps your kind prey on mine."

Sidian seemed to want to say more but his soft, dusky lips formed a white line and he looked away.

A spread of roast pork, broiled potatoes and buttered beans beckoned from a small serving tray that hadn't been in their suite when they arrived. Raine eyed the feast longingly and hoped some of it was for him. There was certainly too much food for two.

Sidian wordlessly pointed to the green sofa near the hearth, which now boasted a modest fire. Raine sat on the sofa, curling his legs beneath him.

Rosa re-entered their suite, carrying a stack of plates and flatware. Sidian's back was to him, so Raine couldn't see the expression he gave Rosa.

She smirked, depositing her burden with a clatter next to the pork. "You didn't say what food to get. We deserve a hot meal. I'll stock up on trail mixes and pack rations in the morning. There's a market around the corner. It'll take no time."

Raine faced the fire as the two piled their plates. His stomach growled louder than the crackling hearth. Three plates. There were three plates. Even so, he didn't dare hope one would be offered to him. *Succulent feasts aren't appropriate fare for dragon scum*, he warned his ravenous belly.

So, he wasn't prepared for the plate that extended from behind his head. The arm holding it was fine-boned and feminine.

"Thank you," he gasped, taking it with alacrity, before the captain noticed her blunder and forced her to rescind the meal.

The room was quiet as they ate. Sidian and Rosa sat at the table, unfolding stools he hadn't noticed leaning against a wall. An uncomfortable emotion fisted his chest as he watched them from the corner of his eye. Eating on the sofa was a privilege he'd resented being denied as a child. Now, all Raine wanted was a seat at the table proper. He was only half a room away, but it felt as though an entire world yawned between him and the captain.

He finished before the Guardians but waited until they were done before bringing his plate to the table, not sure what to do with it.

Rosa's cheeks dimpled with her smile. "Just set it there, Moonbeam." She winked. "Room service will swing by and collect the dishes later."

Sidian moved to the bedside and searched his standard issue rucksack. Unfurling a large swatch of parchment over the bedspread, the captain studied a map. Not just any map, either. Raine gaped from the foot of the bed. It was his map, given to him by his father.

The captain glanced up. A taunting smirk twisted his mouth.

"Seriously," Raine burst. "That fucking chieftain couldn't shut up about how amazing a tracker you are. *A veritable bloodhound*," he mocked.

If anything, the captain's smile grew, chasing butterflies through Raine's belly even as his irritation surged.

Raine folded his arms and glowered at the map, his cheeks hot and bright at the sight of his mate's smile. As piqued as he was, his mate still affected him. It was obscene. As obscene as Sidian's mild demurs at Pare's gushing praise.

Right there, in bold, smudgy black, was the "X" he'd scratched to mark Campion. He must have forgotten it at the Sleepy Bear Inn. Frazzled, exhausted, and drunk, he and Aly had packed in a flurry. In the midst of scurrying away from psychotic dragon hunters and what-not, he'd left an unconscious Guardian captain in the same damn room as a map that would lead him straight to the Hellhole. A map that had brought the guild right to Evin and her thunder's doorstep.

Stupid, stupid, stupid.

Sidian trailed a finger over the map, tracing road lines. He skimmed East Road for a moment, then shook his head, lips pinched. Raine knew why. It would have been convenient to cut across East Road, then head south once they hit Oxlip.

But Tagetes and Oxlip would be in peak harvest for the next month or longer. Which meant East Road was currently glutted with produce wagons pulled by oxen and mules. Taking a dragon down that way was begging for disaster.

Rosa sidled next to Raine and frowned at the path Sidian appeared to favor. "No way am I roughing it in the hurly burly countryside.

I did my time as a sky watcher, squatting in those miserable hovels you call cabins, stuck in the middle of nowhere."

Sidian continued to finger the primitive trails that skirted major cities and towns. "The cabins are being retrofitted with indoor plumbing. The laborers are doing solid work. That last cabin's roof was repaired, and no animals nested in the mattress."

Rosa stomped her foot, which drew a narrow-eyed stare from her captain. "I require proper baths and beds. And society," she stressed. "I want to take the SBT."

The SBT, or Southern Border Trail, was a long, V-shaped road that connected five of the nine cities. Unlike East Road, the Southern Border Trail wouldn't be overburdened with carts and wagons. People tended to travel the SBT recreationally, usually in pursuit of the Vesper Seaboard—Valdenia's singular ocean access, thanks to a break in the Fangs.

Sidian's features grew cold. "It is not my prerogative to select the route which best satisfies your need for society."

The more they said it like that, *society*, the more Raine suspected he was missing a very crucial element to their conversation. As captain and journeywoman sniped back-and-forth, Raine studied the map.

Sidian preferred a complex route, taking intermittent dirt roads through the open countryside.

Either route had its benefits and drawbacks. While the SBT was longer, it would keep them on a single, well-maintained road for most of their journey. Sidian's path, while complicated, would cut through the center of Valdenia and shave off several days of travel time.

It would also take them back the way they'd come, putting them near the Hellhole outside Campion before they speared south. Raine hissed through his teeth. If any dragons saw him in shackles, hooked on a leash like a dog and being dragged by a team of hunters, they would kill Sidian and Rosa before Raine had a chance to stop them. It was not an option.

He looked up and found Sidian and Rosa still arguing.

"—not going to apologize for having needs. Just because you have ice for blood doesn't mean I should have to suffer," Rosa cried, chest heaving.

"Sleeping with stable hands isn't a need." Sidian sneered. "It's a weakness and a distraction."

Whoa. *Awkward*. Rosa's fingers twitching near the handle of a knife strapped to her thigh. Her dark eyes promised violence.

"I'm with Rosa," Raine chimed, before Rosa could draw her dagger and force him to protect his mate. There would be no good way to explain *that*.

Sidian slowly turned his head and raised a sardonic eyebrow as if to say, *you think your opinion counts because why, exactly*?

Raine re-crossed his arms, jangling his metal cuffs, and lifted his chin. "I'm one of the people being forced on whatever route you choose. I have a right to an opinion."

Rosa smiled warmly at him. "I agree."

Sidian looked ready to protest, his mouth thinning with displeasure at the journeywoman's support of Raine, who'd been supporting her. Raine opened his silver eyes wide, blinking into the sweetly innocent expression that had landed him later bedtimes, dessert before dinner, and an extravagant custom washtub.

Sidian's jaw ticked as he looked away. "Fine," he bit out tersely.

Rosa whooped.

A hot, insistent mouth claimed Raine's, branding him for eternity. He moaned as rough, masculine hands explored the planes of his chest and abdomen, dipping low. Seeking the needy ache between his thighs, where his cock strained his tights, close to snapping the threads of his buttons. As his shadow lover seized him through his pants, Raine woke with a ragged gasp.

His breath was loud and harsh in the pitch-dark inn suite. So loud, he didn't hear it at first. The unmistakable sultry sigh of a woman in pleasure.

At once, he understood why the lamps were extinguished. Someone should have been on guard duty, posted and alert in weak light, in case Raine tried to escape. No one stood guard now.

Raine swallowed, tasting acid as another sensual sigh escaped Rosa in the dark. His blood boiled, then iced. Whiplashing between hot and cold, he felt sick and shaken. His eyes stung. Curling his blanket tighter around his shoulders, he wished it was his father's hug.

A very real, very physical hand caressed his side.

Bolting upright with a hiss, Raine's head smacked into what felt like another's skull. There was a decidedly feminine, "*Oof.*"

"Rosa," he whispered, voice hoarse with suppressed tears.

"Shh," she whispered back. Her face was so close, he felt her breath. "Don't wake the captain."

Don't wake the captain, he thought, confused. "I thought you and the captain were ... busy," he murmured. "What are you doing?"

Instead of answering, one of her hands rooted beneath his blanket and cupped his cock through his tights, still engorged from his dream. He yelped.

Her free hand clamped around his mouth in the dark. "Shh," she hissed again.

"That is not for you," he said coldly, once her hand fell.

Rosa was as implacable as she was impertinent. "Damn, Moonbeam. I knew you would have a nice cock but this. Mm," she hummed, feeling his length. "This is a monster."

The "monster" wilted faster than an ice pop in the summer sun. Raine fought his blankets awkwardly, manacles hindering his progress. A slender finger tucked into his waistband. Raine gripped her wrist, mindful not to snap it like he had Tayo's.

He pried her off his genitals and shoved her palm into her chest. Opening his mouth, Raine wasn't sure if he was going to let her down gently or flay the skin off her hide for accosting him.

He *liked* Rosa, even knowing she was once intimate with his mate. But her incessant advances—varying somewhere between annoying and comedic—now crossed into harassment. Raine had enough.

Rosa straightened, drawing away. Her motion shifted the mattress beneath them. "You don't want me?" she whispered.

He smiled at the disbelief in her voice. His rapidly softening cock conveyed his rejection with sufficient eloquence, one would think. But if Rosa needed to hear it plainly, Raine was happy to oblige. Whatever it took to put her off permanently.

"No." Short. Blunt. Pointed. There was no way to misconstrue his stance.

The mattress dipped some more, but it was too dark to see her outline. "I'm sorry. I assumed you feared the captain's anger and hid your feelings."

Raine *was* afraid of the captain's anger and therefore *did* hide his feelings. But not the feelings Rosa referred to.

"This is so embarrassing," she continued. "I will respect your wishes from now on, I promise. I'm so sorry," she apologized again, sounding wretched.

"It's okay," Raine said, not realizing until he spoke that it was true. He had already forgiven her.

Like Rosa said, the situation had been somewhat ambiguous. Sidian bared his teeth each time Raine was within five feet of the journeywoman. With her captain playing steadfast protector against the perverted, degenerate dragon, Rosa must have thoroughly believed Raine desired her.

Silence as thick as taffy stretched the darkness. Raine shifted, wanting to go back to sleep. This time, hopefully, unmolested. Sleep would not be forthcoming, however.

He bit back a groan as Rosa said, "I'm not used to rejection. Men are such simple creatures, you know? I guess dragons are different. Or do you have someone in your life, maybe? A sweetheart or betrothed?"

Raine was half-tempted to conjure an imaginary betrothed, but his heart repudiated the deception. Dragon instincts, lodged deeper than the earth's crust, would not permit him to shame his mate by claiming affection for another, not even a fabrication.

"No," he said at length, settling on vague truths. "Dragons do not mature at the same rate as humans. I don't feel the same urges as you."

It was entirely true yet perfectly misleading. He didn't have the urge to mount lovers indiscriminately, taking his pleasure whenever and wherever it was on offer. But ever since he had encountered Sidian, Raine definitely felt *urges*.

Rosa whistled low. "I never knew that. You're so ... grown up," she muttered wryly, then sighed. "I really am sorry."

Raine didn't require a light source to guess how miserable she looked. He fell back against the feathered mattress with a soft thump. "Don't worry. I won't tell anyone you're a child molester."

She squawked as Raine buried his face into a pillow to muffle his laughter.

CHAPTER TWENTY-THREE

Over a week later, Raine was still congratulating himself on directing his mate to the SBT, far away from the Hell-hole. Had Evin's thunder discovered Raine was taken captive by a Guardian unit, they'd have struck the hunters hard and fast before Raine could call them off.

Even if he was successful in communicating, *hey, this is my mate. Yeah, I know he's human and we're both male. It's weird as fuck, but please don't kill him*, there was no chance the dragons would let Raine go to Obanth.

Rescuing his father was Raine's top priority and he couldn't risk the other dragons stopping him. It was why he'd snuck off in the first place.

The SBT was lined with quaint towns never more than a day's hike apart. They traveled all day and stayed at inns each night. After a couple days, Raine understood the true reason Rosa preferred the SBT. Sure, she liked baths and beds. She liked men, too.

Taking the backroads would have kept them from society, leaving her with slim pickings in the nighttime. The well-populated towns along the SBT offered no such social hardships.

She never brought any of her bed partners back to their room—Raine couldn't imagine Sidian's fury if she had. But she habitually disappeared after dinner and came back late at night. Usually with her hair in disarray and once with her Guardian hose on backwards.

Raine was surprised to discover he envied her carefree sensuality. Rosa could find her pleasure anywhere. She made it seem so easy and natural. Meanwhile, Raine's mate—and the sole source of his desire—was so unattainable, he'd have better luck wooing a tiger.

Although, they had made *some* progress.

Sidian was distant with Raine, but never violent or cruel. He had ceased espousing dragon hate speech every time Raine revealed an inhuman quirk. The captain had also stopped foaming at the mouth whenever Rosa came near Raine.

The timing of his attitude change made eels squirm in Raine's belly. He rather hoped Sidian hadn't been secretly awake during his excruciatingly awkward midnight exchange with Rosa.

The weather grew warmer as they trekked south. Leaves faded from the fiery reds and oranges of autumn back to verdant green. It was like watching time tick backwards, carrying them away from autumn, back into summer.

They were nearly to Vesper, according to Rosa, and the mystery of the leaves had plagued Raine since passing through Allium. He frowned at Sidian's back, noting—as always—the delicious way the captain's black hose clung to his broad, powerful build.

"Why aren't the trees turning orange here?"

Sidian barked a laugh. It was Raine's first time hearing the sound. He tripped against the flagstones, catching himself before he ate rocks and dirt.

It was pure magic, that laugh. Like the first time Raine had seen his hair sparkle in the sunlight or the first time he had taken a bath in boiling water. Utterly captivating.

"Southern Valdenia is semitropical," Sidian explained. The captain glanced over his shoulder. Raine rapidly schooled his features so he didn't look like a simpleton, still under the enchanting effects of hearing his mate's laughter.

The captain's eyes narrowed before facing forward again. "The seasons behave differently. The lower cities still experience winter, but it is mild. Snowfall is rare and melts in a day if it sticks at all."

The captain's husky tones filled the next several hours with in-depth descriptions of the flora and fauna of subtropical Valdenia. Sidian was so knowledgeable, exuding a quiet passion as he spoke of boa constrictors the size of trees and flowers that bloomed in starlight. Raine wanted to ask Sidian if he grew up in this semitropical region, but he didn't. It was like Sidian had forgotten who he was speaking to. Raine was loath to remind him.

He wanted Sidian to keep talking forever. His mate's voice was decadent caramel to his ears. It enthralled him as much, or more, than the muscles shifting beneath Sidian's skintight uniform. Raine was on a sensory high. His cock was rigid beneath his cloak, and his skin buzzed as if he'd swigged an entire barrel of mead.

They reached Vesper a couple hours before sunset. The city dazzled unlike anything Raine had ever seen. The buildings were constructed entirely out of glass. Massive, mirrored towers that reflected sun and sky, gleaming like crystalline obelisks.

The pink flagstones of the SBT transitioned to a sun-bleached boardwalk as grass yielded to white powder. He smelled the sea before he heard it, the humid air carrying undercurrents of brine and exotic scents he couldn't identify.

Vesper became another planet as the Dragon Fangs split, parting like a gaping maw. The vast, glittering sea was impossible. It was *impossible*. Eternal and alive. A mighty creature that inhaled and exhaled, it breathed a crashing, roaring surf that struck the white sand smooth over and over, the motions as endless as the sea itself.

Raine stared, mesmerized. He didn't know if the Vesper Seaboard was on their itinerary for the day, but the ocean rolled him under like a spell. Abandoning all prisoner etiquette, he stepped from the boardwalk. His boots sank into sand. Slippery and malleable beneath his feet, it was almost like walking in snow, only not. Enrapt, he forgot his captors and beelined straight for the glittering blue.

Larger waves reared back like snakes, somersaulting as they tripped across the shore. Raine's hands itched for a pen and paper, ideas springing to mind as the swirls and whorls of the ocean danced to a timeless song he could hear and feel through his skin.

The sand was so soft and powdery, too. Everything about the beach was tactile and pleasing. The smell was fresh and bright, like the wind through a mountain glen of wildflowers. The sun turned the sky and ocean pinkish purple and again, his fingers itched to capture it all onto paper.

It wasn't until a rogue wave sucked up a braided leather rope that Raine realized Sidian had released his tether.

Raine turned and scanned the boardwalk, quickly finding the two figures dressed in black bodystockings. His breath caught at the tranquil smile edging the captain's mouth, his blue-black hair feathering in the ocean breeze.

Raine's instantaneous love for the sea ... Was he somehow experiencing an echo of his mate's heart? His own heart fluttered against his ribcage as he considered it.

He rejoined them on the boardwalk, half-drenched and covered in sand, and offered Sidian the frayed end of his tether. The captain accepted it with an unreadable expression, and they continued walking.

Sandbar Inn possessed a seaside theme. Strange fish and oceanic creatures decorated the receiving rooms. Raine, wholly ignorant of marine life, released a deluge of questions as they progressed. Rosa huffed impatiently while Sidian answered him, naming and describing the creatures depicted in the tapestries and vases adorning the foyer.

"Those are orchid fish," Sidian said, as Raine stopped them for the trillionth. "They remain small. Adults are no longer than a finger."

Orchid fish. Raine inspected the beautiful purple fish more closely. They swam in a tight spiral around one of the two vases bracketing the lobby entrance. He glanced over at the other vase. That one was different, the fish adorning it a vibrant orange and banded with black stripes.

"What are these?" Raine moved to examine the second vase, pointing for Sidian's benefit. His shirt collar choked him mid-stride as someone snatched up the back of his shirt.

"No." Rosa yanked him back with a grunt. "I swear to the Divine, if I have to hear the name of one more stupid fish nobody cares about, I'm going to strangle you."

Raine cast her a sheepish smile. He hadn't meant to slow them down. The ocean's creatures were just so fascinating. More importantly, Sidian was willing to *answer*.

Sidian wasn't a talker. He issued orders and updates, and that was it. But it turned out there were a few magical subjects that unlocked the taciturn captain's husky discourse. They were all, thus far, related to Southern Valdenia's clime and creatures. Again, Raine was struck by the thought that Sidian grew up here. He imagined a solemn, fawn-eyed boy crouched by the sea, studying its life and mysteries in place of play.

As Sidian reserved the last room available at the inn, Rosa salivated at the double doors behind the check-in counter. The din of a busy restaurant sounded from within, and the lobby air was thick with the scents of roasted garlic and herbs.

Raine stared in the same direction, but his attention was snared by the translucent, floaty globs decorating the lobby walls. He flicked a glance at Sidian, waiting for the best moment to ask about the wallpaper.

"Don't you dare," Rosa whispered, catching his eye meaningfully.

Raine pouted but held his tongue. They had run out of rations that morning and been forced to skip lunch. Rosa was vicious when she was hungry.

Moving with the synchronous rhythm of three people who had been traveling together for over a week, they located their suite and entered. Raine's pout vanished the instant he spied two matching beds. Some suites only contained a single bed, and Raine would get stuck sleeping on the floor. Two beds meant Sidian and Rosa would alternate the use of one between watches, and Raine would get the other all to himself.

"I'm starving," Rosa said, tossing her pack on the bed nearest the door.

Sidian reached for the left pocket of his rucksack, where he kept his silvans.

"No," Rosa said firmly. "I'm sick of eating where I sleep. The pub smells delicious. Let's eat there."

"We are on a mission, not vacation," Sidian said. "Our priority is securing our captive, which is difficult to accomplish in a crowded restaurant."

Rosa dismissed his words with a flick of her wrist. "Raine isn't going anywhere. He's never even tried to run." Her eyes darkened as she looked at him, as if his complacence distressed her.

"And if he is simply biding his time?" Sidian asked.

He. Sidian had called Raine "he," not "it." Pure joy washed through him like liquid sunbeams. His mate was warming up to him.

"He's not," she snapped.

Raine flinched, for a one shattering moment believing Rosa's utterance was in response to his thoughts.

"All he has done," Rosa continued, "is be as sweet and docile as a fucking lamb. Raine is nothing like we were told. So much so, we should be asking *questions*. To ourselves, our leadership–"

"Enough," Sidian said quietly. Rosa's words cut off like a ribbon snipped by scissors. "Our orders are to guard and escort the dragon to Obanth. It will be done."

Ouch. Downgraded from "he" to "the dragon." *That's okay*, he told himself. *Sidian is still warming up to me*. Only, when Sidian looked at him, his gaze was bitterly accusing, as if Raine had been the one to propose a pub meal.

"It will be done," Rosa echoed, a dangerously insubordinate edge to her tone. "Fine. If you're finished rehashing orders I'm already apprised of, I'd like to go to dinner."

Raine watched Sidian take in Rosa's dark eyes, shining with challenge. Her heaving chest. The defiant tilt of her chin. Then, Sidian looked at him. Raine's stomach fluttered nervously at the captain's stone-faced stare, not sure what he was searching for.

Slowly, as if his neck muscles were as stiff and cold as his eyes, Sidian nodded.

The silence was unusually oppressive as they progressed to the pub. Rosa pointedly ignored Sidian, her head held high enough to balance a crown. A storm blew over Sidian's visage as she flagrantly walked ahead of them both, failing to rearguard Raine for the first time.

Raine didn't know what Sidian was about to do. Order Rosa back to the rear? Reprimand her? Or would he dismiss her from duty, as he had Tayo? That last one worried Raine. Sidian couldn't guard him alone. His team of three was already reduced to two and he scarcely slept, purple smudges ever-present beneath his eyes. The captain would run himself into the ground trying to fulfill his mission solo.

Even if Raine insisted he wouldn't run, Sidian wouldn't believe it. Raine couldn't blame him. It would be asinine to trust a prisoner, especially one with a rap sheet as long and severe as Raine's.

Sidian zeroed in on Rosa and opened his mouth. The glint in his eye was as punishing as a battle axe.

"What are these?" Raine asked in a rush, brushing his fingers over the lobby walls as they neared the pub's double doors.

Rosa halted with a snort and turned. Her pinched expression eased into indulgence as she beheld Raine. "I knew you weren't going to let it go. You really are a kid."

Sidian's gaze tore from Rosa with the brooding reluctance of a foxhound called to heel. Velveteen eyes pinned Raine knowingly, as if Sidian knew his captive had just deliberately hindered Rosa's discipline. Raine used his wonderment to full advantage. His silver eyes were wide and bright, his pink lips parted softly as he traced the wispy tendrils escaping one of the floaty creatures on the wallpaper. He made sure his whole demeanor screamed *innocently enchanted*.

"Those are jellyfish," Sidian answered at length, his stare no less suspicious. "They are difficult to see in the water. Their stingers can hurt or even kill a man, depending on the specimen."

Raine eyed the floaty blobs with new respect. *Jellyfish*. The name was sweet and silly. The fish was not. Well, then.

He didn't let Sidian's perceptiveness put him off his plan. Instead, Raine peppered Sidian relentlessly, inquiring after every fish and animal featured in the oceanic paintings lining the pub's entrance hall. His ruse was probably so effective because his fascination was sincere.

Raine felt almost kindred with the sea creatures, convinced some of them had come from the Dreaming Mother. They were too fantastic to be from anywhere else.

As they waited to be seated, Sidian educated him on whales, various shellfish, and a host of captivating animals that further convinced him of the Dreaming Mother's influence. He couldn't believe how ignorant he'd been. Instructor Brenk had been awful, but Raine hadn't known just how awful until now. The weedy man had neglected to educate Raine on half of the damned biosphere.

"I told Father my tutor was absolute crap from the beginning," he complained as they were seated in the inn's restaurant for dinner. "Instructor Brenk was always like, 'Valdenia became an officially recognized country two centuries ago' and 'Algebra is an essential skill for any landowner.' But do you think he ever told me that there were teensy fish that looked like horses? And that the males carried the babies? It's crazy! The next time I see him—"

Raine cut off, his face flushing. Not only did he sound a blithering idiot—his default setting if you asked his father or Aly—but Sidian and Rosa were escorting him to Obanth to be tortured and executed. He was making a fool of himself, talking about the next time he'd see anybody back home.

Silence draped their table since Raine had been monopolizing the conversation. What began as desperate, inane chatter to smooth over Sidian and Rosa's conflict had morphed into overly excited prattle inspired by their exotic surroundings.

He played with the tip of his braid, which lay over one shoulder, and looked around nervously. If only he hadn't realized his error. Then he'd still be jabbering on about his inept childhood tutor or how acutely wondrous he found oceanic life.

The restaurant's wallpaper was artfully dyed to imitate the sparkling surface of a body of water. He traced the beautiful pattern with his fingers, wondering what dye technique yielded such a unique effect. Feminine laughter startled him out of his reverie. Looking over, he saw a server waiting to take his order.

Sidian issued a long-suffering sigh. "Please excuse him. He really likes wallpaper."

The tips of Raine's ears grew hot and he focused on the server. She had brown hair, but it was streaked with caramel-colored strands. Her eyes were grayish blue. Human, but with Garganthan blood somewhere in her lineage. Her most notable feature, however, was the heartfelt smile she wore. There wasn't a drop of contention or dislike in her gaze. Quite the opposite.

"My name is Marnie," she gushed. "It is an honor to make your acquaintance."

Their acquaintance hadn't yet been made, though Raine wasn't rude enough to say so. It was a minor miracle, encountering a human so pleasant to him. Worried his delayed response would translate as standoffishness, he offered her a wide smile.

"Nice to meet you, Marnie. I'm Raine."

She beamed at him, stars dancing in her unusual eyes. He shifted on the basket-woven bench, not sure what to say in the face of such overt excitement. He'd only provided his name. Not to mention, he was a criminal of Valdenia, wanted for high treason.

The captain's thoughts must have followed a similar vein. Asperity sharpened his husky voice as he asked, "What honor is there, in meeting our captive?"

Marnie blushed but did not look away from Raine. "I've hoped to encounter a dragon all my life. My grandmother told me they are exquisitely beautiful, with hair and eyes like jewels. You're more perfect than I imagined."

Her gaze was near worshipful as she traced his features. Normally, Raine basked in admiration like a reptile in the morning sun. But there was only one person in all the world he wished to look upon him like that. He shifted in his seat again.

"Whoa, girl," Rosa said. Marnie's face turned to the journey-woman as if an invisible hand dragged her chin. "If you know so much, then you know he's not interested in any frisky business."

Marnie's blush deepened. "I couldn't help it. I wanted to see if we sparked."

Rosa tilted her head. "Sparked?"

"Yes. As a little girl, I dreamed of sparking with a dragon. When I saw Raine,"—her eyes darted to him longingly—"that dream came rushing back. Though I'm not surprised it didn't happen. That would've been too good to be true," she added ruefully.

Sidian's face was concealed by a menu and Raine wasn't sure how much the captain was paying attention. Rosa and Marnie's conversation was becoming a bit too revealing for his tastes. He cleared his throat, but they ignored him.

"So, is sparking some special thing dragons do?"

The server nodded. "Dragons mate for life. Sparking occurs when a dragon recognizes their mate. They're the most incredible, amazing partners. Fiercely devoted and passionate, with unmatched stamina." The women shared a sly smile. Raine cleared his throat more loudly.

"Not to mention they're hung like horses," Rosa purred. Raine rolled his eyes to the ceiling, painted a hazy sunglow yellow. "How do you know if a dragon sparks or not?"

His head whipped back to the two women. Marnie's lips parted, as if to answer.

"I'm starving," he blurted.

Raine's stomach somersaulted as Sidian lowered his menu, dark eyes skewering him. The captain's uncanny ability to see through Raine's bullshit bordered on disturbing. It was a talent normally reserved by his father alone.

The server, Marnie, glanced at Raine with a slightly startled smile, as if she'd forgotten he was there. Which was ridiculous, considering he was the fodder for their gossip. Marnie rattled off the daily specials, dishes he had never heard of before. It didn't help that most of his attention was on Sidian, whose gaze didn't waver from his face.

Taking in Raine's lost expression, the captain finally angled his fishhook stare away from Raine as he placed orders for them both.

As Marnie left, Rosa regarded Raine with frank interest. "You didn't tell me dragons mated for life, or that you had to spark with someone." She arched her brows, inviting him to elaborate.

Raine's heart hammered at the base of his throat. He had to answer Rosa. It was that or risk her grilling Marnie for more details. If the server revealed that a dragon's sexuality was dormant until they met their mate—or worse, said that a dragon's body could only be roused by their mate—he was fucked.

The intelligent captain would connect the dots and Raine was petrified of the fallout.

Part of him knew, down to his shimmering bones, that Sidian's rejection would be a death knell. The moment Raine first encountered the captain, his heart had reshaped its very purpose. He lived and breathed to love his mate. Without Sidian, he would die.

Raine issued a carefully calculated shrug. "I've heard it called sparking before," he said, recalling Aly's petulant whine when they hadn't sparked. "But no actual sparks occur. I think it refers to how dragons recognize their mates when they meet for the first time."

"No shit." Rosa grinned. "You mean, you don't choose your life mate? They're preselected, like fate?"

Raine nodded and tried to ignore the way Sidian's eyes narrowed. Sweat beaded down his spine at the man's suspicious glare. "Yes," he said shortly, wishing she would drop it.

"You're saving yourself for your mate," Rosa cooed. "That is so sweet, my teeth are going to rot. By the Divine, you're adorable."

"What about you?" he asked, desperate to shift the focus from himself. "Do you hope to settle down someday?"

Marnie delivered tankards of ale, coupled with dewy glasses of chilled water. Mercifully, the restaurant had grown busier. She couldn't stop to chat and flitted away. Sidian wordlessly exchanged his tankard with Raine's waterglass so that Raine had two ales and the captain, two waters. Raine cocked his head but decided not to ask. Drinking on the job was probably against Sidian's code.

No such qualm worried Rosa. She sipped her ale, swallowing appreciatively. "My parents expected me to marry and have a pile of kids by now." She laughed at his expression. "I know, right? My father was pissed when I joined the Guardians, but I was seventeen and he couldn't stop me. Maybe I'll marry someday, maybe I won't. Guess I'll have to see if I spark." She winked.

Feeling unimaginably ballsy, Raine looked at Sidian. "And you?" he murmured. His heart was a hummingbird, knocking against his throat as it sought to flee from his audacity.

Sidian's tanned face was an impenetrable mask. He lowered his eyelids, further shading his velvet eyes. "I intend to take a wife at the completion of my service. For now, my duty lies with the guild."

A wife. The words were a knife. Raine forced himself to nod. "That's good of you, to wait until you can devote all of your attention to a woman before marrying."

He didn't know how he was able to say it like that, with perfect nonchalance. The Dreaming Mother took pity on him, perhaps. It was the least she could do, considering she had bound him to a human male who scorned his very existence.

Marnie arrived with a tray of steaming bowls. With a smile, she slid an array of heavy clay dishes across the beechwood tabletop. Raine inhaled the creamy seafood stew placed before him. It smelled like the earth and sea, with exotic spices that made his mouth water.

"Is there anything else I can do for you guys?" she asked, placing two baskets of buttered biscuits in the center of the table.

"Yes," Sidian said, his voice pitched low. "The nature of our captive is sensitive information. I must ask you not to share your knowledge with anyone."

Marnie hugged the now-empty tray to her chest. "I won't." Her blue-gray eyes flickered to Raine. "But please." She bent forward, whispering. "Please be good to him. My grandma said wild dragons are being butchered by the guild." Her face pinched with distress. "They've done nothing wrong. So, whatever you're doing with him, wherever you're taking him, make sure you're doing the right thing."

Sidian's reply was pure steel. Cold, hard, and cutting. "Do not presume to question the morality of my mission. A pretty face can hide a monster better than a homely one. Until you grow up and leave your inane, girlish fantasies behind, you're nothing but a liability."

CHAPTER TWENTY-FOUR

R aine jerked awake with his heart galloping in his chest. His tights were painfully snug, constricted by his swollen cock. He squeezed his eyes shut and muffled a curse. These dreams were driving him mad. Like a spool of thread, they tugged and pulled at him nightly, unraveling his sanity.

The worst of it was, Raine had yet to find his pleasure. He awoke each night on the brink of an elusive precipice. Humans pleasured themselves, he knew. Frequently and creatively, judging by that freaky sex shop in Pashun. But he wasn't sure about dragons. So much of their sexuality was different and revolved around mates.

He was going mad wondering if release was possible. What it might feel like. But between Sidian and Rosa, he received no privacy *ever*. Sidian was too good a captain to leave his prisoner unguarded for a second, let alone enough time for an erotic self-exploration.

He sat up slowly, trying to quiet his ragged breath. From miserable experience, Raine knew he would not fall back asleep. Throat parched, he recalled the carafe of water a maid had left. It sat on a table near the window, along with a stack of crystal tumblers.

He moved cautiously through the darkness, keeping an arm outstretched to avoid crashing into furniture. Thanks to all the inns they had stayed at—a different one each night as they traced the eastern branch of the SBT to Obanth—Raine was familiar with the hazards of stubbed toes and bruised knees while navigating unfamiliar rooms.

He was two steps from the water pitcher when he registered the shadowy figure seated at the table. He didn't need to ask who it was. Raine was attuned to Sidian in a way that defied explanation.

Uncertain of his welcome, he slowly pulled the chair opposite his mate. When Sidian didn't protest, Raine sat.

"Trouble sleeping?" Sidian's husky voice curled around him like smoke.

Raine's dick ached so badly, he felt a suicidal impulse to reach down and stoke himself right there at the table, using the darkness to shield his depravity. He clenched his fists, appalled at his own perversion.

"Something like that," he whispered, though there was no need for hushed tones. If Sidian was on guard duty, it was earlier than it seemed, and Rosa was still out.

Sidian always took first watch. An arrangement which suited both the captain and his journeywoman. They had a routine now. Rosa used the early evening hours to seek and enjoy various bedfellows while Sidian oversaw Raine's nightly bath. After bathing, Raine would brush and braid his hair while Sidian tended to his supplies and gear. Rosa would assume guard duty upon her return, where-upon Sidian would shave and wash himself before retiring.

A match struck in the darkness and Sidian lit a candle. The dancing wick cast his features in equal parts light and shadow. Sidian placed the candle in the center of the small breakfast table. The soft, flickering flame enveloped them in a golden globe against the night.

The water carafe hovered halfway off the table, nearly toppling over. Raine moved the pitcher away from the edge, sliding it closer to a saucer of bright yellow wedges. He reached out and plucked one from the dish, turning it over in his hand to inspect it.

"You've never seen a lemon? It's a fruit grown near Obanth. People squeeze the juice into their water when they drink."

Lemon. It was probably a commonly traded commodity throughout Valdenia, but Raine's father limited such activity in and around Chambrin. Just one more way of keeping outsiders at bay. Always protecting his secret dragon son.

"They are particularly bright and sweet tasting," Sidian added with a sly, teasing tone that made Raine's cock twitch.

He possessed a healthy appreciation for sweets and took a hearty bite from the wedge. His face scrunched as puckering sourness ruptured across his tongue. The room flooded with the sound of Sidian's rich, deep laughter.

Raine wiped his mouth on his shirt sleeve and glowered. Sidian didn't notice. His head was thrown back, eyes screwed shut as he laughed and laughed. Raine's heart swelled at the sight, tightening his chest until it might burst. Sidian's laughter was so glorious, he could live off it.

Moisture clung to the corners of Sidian's dark eyes, and he wiped at them. Aftershocks of mirth wracked his shoulders.

Not trusting himself to speak, Raine busied himself with pouring a glass of water. The chains of his manacles clinked with his motions. He drank deeply, draining his cup in one continuous swig. Pouring another glassful, he sipped more slowly.

"What are your dreams about?" Sidian asked.

Raine sucked in a breath. Water invaded his lungs and he choked. Replacing his glass roughly, he sputtered and coughed. The candlelight flicked as he jarred the table with his spasms, until his airway cleared.

"Dreams?" Raine wheezed. His face flamed.

"Your sleep is frequently ... restless. I assume it is caused by overactive dreams."

Raine's whole body blushed, if such a thing were possible. He felt like the vermillion shellfish decorating one of the pub's paintings below. A lobster, Sidian had called it.

"Yes, my nightmares. They're about ..." His mind blanked. He was usually good at making shit up. Sitting at a candlelit table alone with Sidian made him dizzy. If all his blood would stop rushing to his prick, there'd be some leftover for his brain to work properly.

His ability to dissemble abandoned him in his flustered state, so he settled on vague truths. "They're about something I learned recently. Something that was supposed to be good news, only I'm afraid it won't end well." Raine forced a light laugh, but it sounded hollow. "I shouldn't complain. There are so many bigger issues right now, yet I continually focus on a problem that is mine alone."

Raine blew out a sigh that dragged the candlelight sideways. His fixation on his mate felt selfish. All the time he devoted to pining after Sidian could be spent attempting to solve more urgent dilemmas.

Perhaps I'd have a clue how to rescue Father or better aid Evin's thunder, he thought ruefully.

He watched the tiny wick dance in the darkly shadowed room, unsure of how much time passed before Sidian spoke. "Everyone has their own unique troubles. Thinking them over isn't selfish. Besides, if the problem is yours alone, then only you can find the solution. That makes you obligated to solve it, since no one else can."

"I guess," Raine said doubtfully. "But if there is a solution, finding it won't help anyone but me. There are better things to focus on." Like the organized genocide of his entire species for a start.

Sidian shook his head. "We are all born with intrinsic responsibilities to ourselves. Things that no one else can do for us. Physical tasks like eating and drinking are the most obvious, but there is a mental and spiritual onus, as well. And a man cannot aid others until his responsibilities to self, both mental and physical, are fulfilled. That includes seeking solutions to any problems that plague him, regardless of scale."

A reluctant grin tugged at Raine's mouth. "You sound like my father. He is big on self-care, too. He mandates mental wellness checks in his ranks and even forces his men to take a certain number of holidays. He says it's to keep his men from getting burnout, but the truth is, he's just a big softy."

Thoughts of his father stirred the anxious dread haunting him. Guilt sat like a lead weight in his gut. His father was in trouble, and it was all Raine's fault. No amount of dwelling on his father's predicament eased Raine's suffering, however. It only made him miserable and shaky, like a kicked dog.

He wasn't going to fall apart. Not now, during his first genuine conversation with his mate. Raine's mind drafted consoling images like liferafts, determined to raise his spirits. When he mentally threw Sidian and his father together, the two men most on his mind and in his heart, he snickered.

"I can see you and my father hitting it off. You two are going to meet and form a massive bond. Next thing I know, he's going to adopt you and I'll be the son who is never good enough. *Why can't you be more like Sidian?*" he mocked.

Sidian chuckled. Raine wanted to lap up the sound like fresh cream. "I'll introduce him to my parents. They'll dispel him of the notion that I am a paragon of anything after several sordid tales of my childhood delinquency."

"Is your home here, in Vesper?" Raine gave into curiosity, capitalizing on Sidian's rare, loquacious mood.

Sidian nodded, the long shadow on the wall behind him bobbing in tandem. "My father was a fisherman. He let me assist him on short voyages. We used nets to pull teeming piles of grouper and sheepshead onto his ship deck. I suspect I was more nuisance than help, but my father nicknamed me Captain, and he's called me it ever since."

"I won't tell you what my father calls me," Raine said dryly, making Sidian smirk. "Is that why you joined the guild? The 'Captain' thing," he clarified at Sidian's confusion.

Sidian's expression slammed shut. Raine suppressed a flinch, yearning to pluck his words from the air and cram them back down his throat.

He didn't expect his mate to answer, given the severity of his reaction. When he did, Sidian's voice was winter ice.

"My older brother's dream was to be a captain in the Guardians of Vale. He joined at seventeen."

It was the most common age of new recruits due to the guild's age requirement, the age his father and Nyx had been when they joined. The age Raine had thought he would join, until his father persisted in putting him off.

Sidian said, "My brother was also my best friend. I found his absence unacceptable and decided to follow in his footsteps. If I could not be near him at home, I would be near him in the guild."

Sidian's demeanor was as somber and brooding as Raine had ever seen. He wished he could reverse time, if only by a minute, and take back the question that had evoked such solemnity.

Since that wasn't an option, he tried to determine its cause. "Is there some rule about family members not being allowed to serve on the same unit, or something?"

"I never served with my brother." Sidian's voice grew raspier as he said, "He died when I was sixteen, a year before I joined."

Raine gasped his shock. "I'm so sorry," he whispered, the condolence too paltry to express his sorrow.

How much was Sidian's icy calm an effort to hide his grief? The pain Sidian assiduously concealed slipped from his ironclad control. It choked the air, as palpably thick as strath fog, and threatened to rip Raine's heart to pieces.

Sidian's stare turned inward, as if gazing at his past. "My brother visited home between missions. He shared things with me about being a Guardian. What it really entailed. I was astonished to learn wild dragons existed and could look human if they chose. I started suspecting everyone around my home of secretly being a dragon. I even got a family arrested once, but it turned out they were only humans."

Raine almost smiled at the image of a young, busy-bodied Sidian spying on his neighbors. It would have been humorous if he didn't know firsthand how devastating the consequences would have been had his neighbors truly been dragons.

"Years passed, and I got better at keeping my brother's confidences. No more families got arrested. Still, I felt isolated by my knowledge. My brother only came once or twice a year. When he was gone, I had no one to talk to about the dragons that were a big problem. Monsters that looked human and wanted to take everything from us. I couldn't wait to join my brother and start doing something about the dangers I'd known about for so long."

The seat of Raine's chair felt uncomfortably hard. He shifted his buttocks, the silken material of his tights gliding against the polished wood. Sidian was elsewhere now. He could see it by how far away his eyes were. The captain stared through the dark walls, through paper and brick and space and time.

Raine didn't know exactly where this story was going, but he experienced a sense of foreboding so powerful, he struggled not to interrupt, gnashing his teeth against his helplessness. His mate was in a stark, lonely place Raine couldn't see or touch. A place he could not wrest Sidian from. A place Sidian had to leave willingly, at his own pace.

"After my brother was promoted to captaincy, he had a strange talk with me. He said there were things about the Nine that nobody knew. That he'd had it all wrong. That dragons weren't the monsters he'd been trained to see. He swore, if he ever encountered one, he would approach in peace and speak with it."

Sidian clenched and unclenched his fists, his black eyes all pupil, as if trapped in total darkness. "A month later, our family was notified.

He died in the line of duty. A dragon killed him, burning his skin until it was black and charred. They had to use his captain's armlet to identify him."

Goosebumps prickled down Raine's arms as Sidian spoke. So, this was why his mate loathed dragons on principle. He recalled how the captain had denounced honor as a dragon trait.

It was irony at its most vicious.

Sidian's brother had believed dragons weren't monstrous. A conviction which had gotten him incinerated.

Raine had witnessed the ruthless way Guardians attacked dragons. The dragon that murdered Sidian's brother had only seen a threat. A hunter. Death. That dragon had been forced to make a snap decision. Hesitation held lethal consequences.

It had for Sidian's brother. His stomach twisted sickeningly at the needless violence.

Raine didn't know he was crying until Sidian said, "Knock it off." His tone, while gruff, was warmer. Present.

Raine blinked, surprised at the wetness on his face. He wiped his cheeks with his forearm, chains rattling.

"You didn't kill my brother." Sidian spoke with such certainty, Raine frowned. His mate read his mind, apparently, because he rolled his eyes and drawled, "It was ten years ago. I like to think my brother was taken out a beast fiercer than an infant."

"Oi, I wasn't a baby."

Sidian snorted. "What are you, twelve? You might as well have been."

"I'm nearly twenty," Raine hissed. "Are you fucking with me right now? Twelve?"

"You don't shave," Sidian mused. "So, I figured you must be some freakishly tall, brawny child. You're the one who said you're going through puberty."

"I *am* going through puberty," he said, throwing his hands up. "And thanks for bringing up the facial hair thing, really. Do you have any idea how insecure I was two years ago, barefaced while all my peers sprouted whiskers? Half of me was desperate for a beard, to prove my manhood. The other half of me dreaded it because I would look like an old man."

"Your hair does not resemble the locks of old age. It's iridescent, dumbass."

Raine felt the compliment like a warm stroke across his chest and preened. Then his eyes narrowed. "You know how old I am. My birthdate is on the wanted posters."

The grin that stole over the captain's features was heart-stopping. Sidian tucked his arms behind his head, lowering his eyelids. "Hm. Must have slipped my mind."

"You're lucky I don't push you out of your chair," Raine grumbled. They lapsed into a companionable silence, until some force compelled Raine to say, "I used to dream about joining the Guardians."

Sidian, who'd been balancing on the hindlegs of his chair, let it fall to all four and stared. Heat bloomed in Raine's cheeks, and he knew he was redder than a beet. Sidian's expression broadcasted his stunned disbelief, which only reddened Raine further.

"It's true," he confessed. "My dad is the Wolf of the Vale. The most legendary Guardian in history. My whole life, I intended on joining the guild and making him proud."

It was Raine's turn to stare at the wall, at the pulsing play of orange light and shadow. "When I submitted my application, Father pulled some strings, ensuring they'd reject it. He wanted me to stay home and command the war dragons. He left out the little tidbit that I, too, was a dragon."

If Raine had any reservations on sharing that information with Sidian, they evaporated at the comedically shocked look that crossed the typically stoic captain's features. "You didn't know?"

"Nope," Raine said cheerfully. "I mean, I knew I was different. But we didn't talk about that, you know? Father was a secretive bastard. Wouldn't give an inch. Everyone else thought I was a blanch."

Sidian arched a brow, the portrait of skepticism. "No idiot would mistake you for a blanch."

Raine shrugged, smiling ruefully. "I used to powder my hair to conceal its colorful glints, which helped the illusion. Most people avoided me, since they thought I was bad luck. Only a couple went out of their way to be cruel."

He wasn't sure if it was his imagination or not, when Sidian's eyes darkened. Raine took a drink of water, his throat suddenly dry. "Anyway." He waved a hand, jingling his metal cuffs. "One of my precious tormentors was my cousin, Olan. Who just so happened to receive an invitation to the entrance exams the same day I was denied."

Sidian dragged a palm down the front of his face and cupped his chin. "You didn't."

Why it was so hilarious in retrospect, Raine didn't know. He suppressed laughter as he said, "I did. I stole Olan's invitation and presented myself for the entrance exams in his stead."

The captain didn't share Raine's amusement. He looked grave. Horrorstruck. His hand fell from his chin, and he squared himself, staring directly into Raine's silver eyes. "How did you get out of there alive?"

"I almost didn't," Raine said, no longer laughing. His mate was too tense for him to find it humorous anymore. He explained how they'd made him wait below their fortress, the unit that had been called in to dispatch him. Then, the long journey home, crushed and angry because he'd thought the Nine wanted him dead for being a cursed blanch, like they couldn't risk his bad luck bringing hardship to Valdenia.

He shocked the captain anew when he revealed the chieftains were already waiting for him at Chambrin Keep.

"I didn't know it at the time," he cried out defensively. Sidian, whose face was morphed by incredulous outrage, appeared ready to shake Raine for his own stupidity. "Luckily, they didn't know who I was. They thought I was Olan, remember? My father reached me before they had a clue. He practically flung me out of the castle less than five minutes after dropping the dragon bomb."

Sidian was once more inscrutable. Beeswax dripped down the candle and pooled at its base, which was considerably shorter than it had been when the captain first lit it.

"That is not the story we were told," he said quietly.

Raine's gut clenched as he anticipated the man's angry denial. An accusation that Raine had made it all up.

But Sidian said nothing as another drop of wax slowly melted down the candle, which was nearly a nub.

With a start, Raine realized it was a four-hour candle. It had only an hour left, if that. "Where's Rosa?"

CHAPTER TWENTY-FIVE

Sidian's chair scraped across the salt oak floor as he stood. "I don't know." Trepidation colored the captain's words.

Raine spared a moment to throw on his boots. Sidian was still fully dressed, and they searched every public space of the inn. Alarm bells rang in Raine's ears as Rosa continued to be missing. Sidian went outside and checked the stables—Rose had a thing for horse handlers. Nothing.

They re-traced their steps, at a loss until they passed a busty inn servant exiting the restaurant. It was locked down for after hours or else it would have been the first place they searched.

"Ask her about Rosa," Raine whispered to Sidian, who frowned at him. Raine rolled his eyes. "People think I'm a degenerate traitor hellbent on destroying the country, remember? And I'm in handcuffs. She might not want to aid my stalking of her fellow woman."

At that moment, the server finished locking the doors behind her and turned. She tensed at the sight of them, pulling her keys close to her ample bosom.

"Apologies for startling you, miss," Sidian said. "I'm looking for my journeywoman, Rosa. She is dressed like me and wears her hair in a braided bun."

The woman relaxed a little, smoothing a hand down her apron. "It's a great service, what your guild does for us. I could never do what you do, guarding vile criminals like that one." She nudged her chin in Raine's direction. "There was more than one who meets your Rosa's description here tonight. A table with two such women and three men, all in Guardian hose."

Sidian asked her to describe them.

"Well, the one was really memorable. Not in a good way, either. His face looked like he had run into a shovel. Nose smashed into his head, things just not shaped right. The women were similar in appearance, so you know what they looked like. The other two men were well-muscled. One was on the shorter side, and the other had a thick beard but kept his head shaved."

Ice slid down Raine's spine when the serving woman described what must have been Tayo. He inwardly cursed himself for never telling Rosa what had happened in the woods. She'd asked once, on night watch while Sidian slept. Raine had evaded her question, not wanting to revisit the unpleasant scene or challenge her beliefs in case she held Tayo in high regard.

Sidian was tense as he asked, "Did they say where they were going?"

The serving woman shook her head. "I'm sorry. It was a busy night, and I only refilled their drinks. My friend Tam brought their food and talked to them more than I did. She works again tomorrow. If your friend doesn't show up, you can come back at the dinner hour and ask Tam your questions."

Sidian thanked her curtly and headed back toward their room. Raine struggled to match his abrupt stride and would have been amused by how much his mate was failing to guard him if he wasn't sick with worry for Rosa.

As they passed the check-in counter, the attendant—who had been absent during their initial sweep of Sandbar Inn—called out, "Captain Wade! There's a message I was supposed to give you. I tried your room but there was no answer, so I slid the envelope beneath the door. I hope that's okay?"

They bolted for their suite, throwing the door open and stumbling through. A plain, manilla envelope sat on the floor near the threshold. Sidian snatched it and tore out a letter. His fingers turned white as he read. When he finished, he smashed the paper in his fist with a curse.

"Pack your things. We need to leave."

Raine was desperate to ask what the letter said, but time was clearly of the essence. Together, they tore through their suite, hastily stuffing their scattered belongings into bags. Sidian equipped his rucksack and slung Raine's satchel over his shoulder.

There was no way he could carry Rosa's pack too. Raine stepped forward. "I've got it."

Before Sidian could protest, he strapped the unfamiliar weight of Rosa's rucksack to his back. Captives weren't supposed to have access to knives and drugs and whatever else Rosa kept in her bag, but their circumstances were extenuating enough that Sidian gave a terse, reluctant nod.

A precious seed of trust was planted in that nod. Raine's belly fluttered, and he swore to make it grow.

Sidian briskly ushered Raine through the inn's exit. Clipping to the stables, he approached a stall with a chestnut gelding, as if to secure a mount. As they neared, the gelding blew sharply through its russet snout.

"Sidian," Raine called nervously, halting.

If he came any closer, the horse would detect his predator's scent. Sidian's stride didn't slow. The tether went taut between them, and the captain gave a savage yank without turning. Raine stumbled forward.

The gelding's ears pinned back, and it brayed a warning. Sidian appeared not to notice. He tugged Raine right up to the stall door and moved to unlatch it.

The horse went feral. It reared and screamed, kicking holes in the stall wall behind it. A hay bucket went flying. Raine ducked and it sailed overhead, clamoring to the ground behind him.

"Sidian," Raine tried again. He raised his voice over the rampaging horse's din. "I can't ride. I *can't*."

His mate's eyes were wilder than a cornered beast's, blazing impotent frustration. The horse continued to kick. Clasping Sidian's bicep beneath his golden armlet, Raine dragged him from the stall. He didn't stop walking until the horse settled.

"What is going on?" Raine demanded.

"Tayo and another unit took Rosa by force," Sidian said at length. Rationality trickled back to his gaze. "They're headed to Brackshallow Lake. It's a day's journey on horseback. If we ride, we can catch up to them on the road, before they have time to set up an ambush."

Raine shook his head. "It won't work. Horses don't suffer dragons."

"Rosa is my journeywoman." Sidian's features warped with self-recrimination. "I am responsible for anything that happens to her."

As her captain, Sidian would blame himself if any harm came to Rosa. Raine wanted to tell him it wasn't his fault, but guilt sliced his heart, too. He'd never felt like such a burden. The horse's aversion was out of his control, he knew, but the knowledge offered no absolution. If only Sidian could go without him.

Wait.

"Leave me behind," Raine blurted. It was the perfect solution. He should have thought of it sooner. Sidian might reach them within the hour if he rode at full tilt.

Sidian's jaw flexed like rippling steel. "You'd like that, wouldn't you?"

"What? No. I mean, it's the only way you can stop them," Raine rushed to explain.

How the hell could Sidian think he cared about escaping? But the captain obviously did. His sneer dripped cold, bitter cynicism. It wounded Raine like a blade and he flinched.

"We travel on foot," Sidian bit out. He wound Raine's tether around his hand several times. "Move."

<hr>

Sidian made up for their lack of horseflesh by running. They sprinted halfway through the night without rest, and Raine was awed by his mate's stamina. He had been raised at Chambrin Keep, where his father's men treated their bodies like weapons, honed to be as spry and strong as possible.

Sidian put them all to shame. Hell, he could put some dragons to shame.

Not Raine, though. His handcuffs made it awkward, but he could outpace a deer at full bore, so matching the captain's speed wasn't an issue, handcuffs or no. But they'd been at it for about *five hours*. While Raine could force himself to continue, he really didn't want to. Every breath felt like shattered glass in his lungs. He was so thirsty, he could drink a river. Just open his mouth and let the whole thing flow down his throat.

By the grace of the Divine, Sidian slowed. "We can rest for a couple hours, then continue at dawn." His breath was more ragged than Raine's, though he sounded reluctant to stop.

Raine collapsed on the roadside before the captain changed his mind and decided to push forward. Before he could croak a request for water, a canteen hovered over his head. He waited until Sidian produced his own canteen before taking a swig. It was divine. Raine hollowed his cheeks until the last drop.

They had exchanged few words since leaving Vesper. Initially, because Sidian's mood hadn't been conducive to congenial conversation and Raine didn't enjoy having his head bit off. He was a dragon, not a praying mantis, thank you very much. Later, conversation had been infeasible as they sustained their grueling pace.

Raine shook the canteen, as if it might have somehow refilled itself in the seconds since he'd sucked it dry. He looked over at Sidian, who had collapsed with more poise than Raine, his back to a frondy tree.

His mate's broad shoulders were slumped, exhaustion cloaking him like a leaden blanket.

Raine's stomach growled, hunger catching up to him. Rosa was supposed to restock their rations in Vesper, but then Tayo happened. Sidian had to be famished, too. Raine sat up with a groan. He wasn't going to laze around with a hungry mate.

First, a fire. But as Raine went to seek kindling, his tether snagged. He frowned at the braided leather rope tied to his handcuffs. He'd been forgetting about the leash more and more frequently. Probably because he didn't feel like a prisoner. He was at his mate's side, the only place he belonged.

"Going somewhere?" Sidian's head leaned back against the tree, exposing the column of his throat in the moonlight.

"I'm starved. I wanted to start a fire and see if we could cook something."

The captain stood haltingly, his muscles visibly stiff from overexertion. With a long, indecipherable look at Raine, he released the tether. "I'll harvest our meal while you build the fire. If you try to run, I *will* catch you."

Raine's breath hitched as his body responded. The prospect of being hunted had never been more tantalizing. But if Raine fled, he knew Sidian wouldn't be wielding his cock for a weapon when he eventually caught him.

No, his mate would be wielding a longsword of dragon bone paired with an ocean of enmity.

That reality didn't stopper Raine's fantasies, but he managed not to drool as he acknowledged his mate's threat—for it had indeed been a threat, regardless of how desperately his libido wished otherwise.

After a final, lingering glare of warning, Sidian walked away, blending into shadows and darkness.

His Guardian hose made him all but invisible as he moved toward the looming mountains. The nearest peaks were close enough to blot the night sky, creating a formidable barrier between land and sea.

Oceanwater crept through minuscule cracks in the craggy behemoths; hair-thin rivulets that coalesced into a saltwater marsh that ebbed and flowed with the tide.

Raine watched as Sidian crept through the sodden blackness and disappeared. Whether Sidian hunted fish or fowl, he had no clue. Perhaps the captain would return with an armful of rubbery marsh plants and sea turtles for stew. Leaving his mate to his task, Raine turned to start his own.

A shadowy woodland stretched beyond the opposite side of the road, away from the mountains and marsh. As Raine collected dry sticks and twigs, tiny lizards scattered like marbles, diving into brush and underneath rocks. He watched them scurry with a smile, wondering if dragons and lizards shared a common tongue. Perhaps one day he could reassure the creatures in their own language that he meant no harm.

Raine had the fire going by the time Sidian returned from the marsh. He sported a cloth sack large enough to fit a pair of shoes. It bulged and moved, as if many things with many legs were trapped within.

"Sand crabs," he said before Raine could ask. Sidian tied the writhing sack shut, then placed it in a pot extracted from Rosa's bag. He worked fluidly around the fire, laying stripped branches over flagstones for a makeshift grill. In moments, the pot was sizzling.

Sidian stood nearby and flipped the bag occasionally until it was ready.

The meat was strange, pale and tender. Tiny morsels clung tightly to their shells, tearing reluctantly from their carapaces. Sidian split his shells and sucked the meat like an otter at a mussel bed, with the casual ease of someone who'd dined on such fare since childhood.

Raine fought for every bite, delving with his tongue and teeth. Sidian's brows arched as he observed him, amusement glimmering in the midnight depths of his gaze. Raine flushed, wishing his mate would catch him being competent, *just once*.

"We're going to Brackshallow Lodge. It's owned by the guild, named after the lake beside it." Raine must have looked as alarmed as he felt, because Sidian added, "It's vacant. A popular retreat for large-scale training sessions, but they've all been suspended due to the ongoing search for the breeding dragons."

Raine stared into the fire, cross-legged in the spiky, sand-patched grass. Sidian's stare scorched his profile, making his left cheek feel hotter than the skin facing the fire. Thanks to Pare, Sidian knew Raine had something to do with the breeding dragons' escape. The guild's priority was recovering them, which meant Sidian's priority was recovering them. And Sidian was fully aware that Raine knew their whereabouts. It sat unsaid like a weight between them.

He would die for Sidian. He would die without Sidian. But no matter how great his love for the captain was, Raine could not betray the location of those haunted, skeletal dragons he and Evin's thunder had retrieved from the Cavern.

Without meeting Sidian's penetrating stare, he said, "The unit Rosa sat with last night. They took her against her will?"

Sidian grunted an assent. "Tayo fed them a line of bullshit. They took Rosa for collateral and plan to force an exchange. My captive for my journeywoman."

The autumn night here was as warm as a summer eve at Chambrin, yet Raine shivered. He folded his arms close to his chest. "Oh."

Raine replayed every last interaction he'd had with Tayo. The vile journeyman had loathed Raine from the start. Only now, his grudge was personal.

It wouldn't surprise Raine if Tayo blamed him for his ruined face and dishonorable discharge from the guild. Raine couldn't begin to fathom the vindictive torments in store for him once handed over to his custody.

"I will not be indulging them," Sidian said. Raine swerved to face him, summoned by the steely edge in the captain's husky voice. His dark fringe fell over his brow, shading his fawn eyes from the firelight.

Raine's throat tightened. He didn't dare force words through it, fearing the emotions his speech might betray. Instead, he gave a halting nod.

A fat, wide shape hissed and skittered next to his hand. Raine strangled a scream as he fell backwards. From a respectable distance, he leaned over and inspected the creature.

"What the fuck is this thing?"

Sidian's face was as smooth as glass as he surveyed Raine on his knees, hovering above the creature. "It's a cockroach."

"Sweet Dreaming Mother, it's huge," Raine gasped. "Are you sure it's a cockroach? You could tuck that thing between two slices of bread and eat it like a sandwich."

It hissed again, very disagreeably.

"I don't like it," Raine announced.

Sidian made a strange sound, as if swallowing a chuckle. "Then stop leaning over it. I'm surprised it hasn't flown into your hair."

His stomach seized. "It has wings?"

Prophetically, the mutant cockroach selected that precise moment to take flight, flying directly at Raine's face in a buzzing whir. He screeched. Rolling to the ground as if he was on fire, his hands smacked at his head, trying desperately to fling the creature out of his treasured tresses.

Sidian's roaring laughter echoed off the distant mountains for miles.

True to Sidian's word, they hit the road running at sunrise. The marshlands crawled ever closer to the SBT as they progressed. Cattails and marigolds peeked out of the high reeds framing the trail. Dragonflies as big as birds chased buzzing insects through the air, weaving in and out of their path.

Soon, the wetlands overtook the SBT. Fortunately, the road transitioned to an upraised boardwalk, keeping their boots dry above the bog water.

Plumy swamp grasses hid the planked trail from view as it curved ahead. Raine jogged directly behind Sidian, deliberately looking over the captain's shining black hair as the tether swung between them.

Whenever his stare dipped to the broad strength of Sidian's shoulders, or worse, the delicious muscles working below his rucksack, vividly displayed by his Guardian hose, Raine's body ignited like wildfire. He had quickly learned that running with a stiff prick was as fun as his father's crushing sword drills.

As he rounded the lazily bowing boardwalk, he saw the fork, previously obscured by high, lush greenery.

The road went left or right, circuiting a wide, brackish lake. Egrets waded in the shallows, beaks intent upon the water as they sought the tell-tale glint of fish beneath the surface.

Sidian waited near the right fork, hands on his thighs as he dragged oxygen through his mouth. Sweat trickled down his brow and dampened his torso, his black hose sopping wet against his sculpted chest. Raine's gaze darted away, fixing on Sidian's boots before the sight of the captain's well-defined pectorals stirred his blood.

The scorching weather didn't affect Raine similarly. His perspiration was light and didn't condense on his skin. Sunlight blazed splendidly over his body, invigorating him. Sidian wiped the moisture from his forehead and, taking in Raine's peachy countenance, dry and unflushed, he scowled.

"What's the matter, Captain?" Raine grinned. "I thought you grew up in this heat."

"I've been primarily absent for nine years. And these uniforms are sweltering." Sidian fished a canteen from his backpack and chugged, his throat bobbing with each deep gulp.

When Sidian tried offering it to him, Raine shook his head. "You drink it. I'm not thirsty." A lie, but one he was glad he told as Sidian quaffed the remaining water.

A northward breeze, cooled by mountains and sea, swept across the marshland and tousled his braid. Sidian closed his eyes and turned into the wind, letting it card through his hair like an invisible lover's fingers.

Fuck, he's handsome.

Sidian's straight nose, high cheekbones, and wide, dusky mouth were impossibly perfect. His tanned skin hinted at his heritage, the southern tribes more sun bronzed whereas northern Valdenians were complexioned like milk tea.

Sidian pointed at a painted road sign Raine had missed. "The SBT continues left, leading to Obanth beyond the lake. Brackshallow Lodge is this way."

They walked the next mile in silence. The battered planks of the boardwalk gave way to crushed rock. Gravel crunched beneath their boots as the path carried them into a hammocked woods of oaks and palms. Sidian dumped his bags at the base of a cabbage palm. Turning toward Raine, he stretched the tether between his hands.

"Sit against the tree. I'll tie you to it while I handle the situation."

Raine's mouth fell open. "Are you kidding me?" he hissed, mindful of his volume as he spotted the lodge through thick fronds. "I'm not letting you go in there alone."

"I need to focus on extracting Rosa, something I can't do while watching you."

"You don't have to *watch* me. I can help you. Just uncuff me and give me one of your knives."

"Why would I do that when you can just bury it into my back and run?"

Sidian's words struck him like a blow. To Raine's horror, tears welled in his eyes. He threw himself into a crouch, back pressed against the jutting bark of the palm tree. His chained hands formed a visor over his forehead as he stared at the ground, ensuring Sidian couldn't see any part of his face.

The hoarseness of his voice betrayed him as he said, "Go on, then."

Raine's warm tears splashed onto a sandy anthill as he waited for Sidian to secure him to the tree trunk. For a long, agonizing moment, nothing happened. Sidian just hovered there like a solid shadow. A woodpecker's rapid, continuous knock echoed throughout the woods. Raine thought he heard a soft curse beneath it. Then, the loose end of his tether hit the ground, coiling against the scrubby grass like a serpent.

Sidian's deft footfalls faded to silence. He had left Raine behind and unsecured.

CHAPTER TWENTY-SIX

Raine lasted three minutes, if that, before he straightened. It didn't matter if Sidian wanted his help or not. No reality existed where he cowered in the forest while his mate confronted hostile forces alone. He thanked the Divine that Sidian had decided to leave him unbound at the last minute.

But why had Sidian left him loose? Was he pressed for time and decided he could just hunt Raine down again later if he ran? It sure as shit hadn't been a demonstration of trust. Not when his mate thought Raine would hurt him. *Actually hurt him.*

Raine was more likely to start a maggot farm in his bathtub than he was to ever lay a finger against Sidian.

Digging through the rucksacks, he found a short dagger wrapped in Rosa's socks. He surveyed the shimmering white blade with a grimace. But now wasn't the time to be choosy about his weapons.

Raine's passage through the woodsy hammock was far noisier than Sidian's, his lack of stealth training glaringly obvious. Using a wall of ferns and bushy palms for cover, he scrutinized the guild's lodge.

It was a large but simple structure. Rectangular and constructed from hundreds of round, red logs bleached orange from years of relentless subtropical sunlight. Curtainless windows overlooked the glassy lake, which reflected the pure blue of the sky.

He cursed at the sight of the front door, slightly ajar. It was a bold but dangerous move, waltzing through the main entrance. Sidian had sacrificed the element of surprise for a show of confidence, hoping to intimidate the other Guardians into releasing Rosa. Or perhaps counting on them to be reasonable.

All Raine had to do was picture Tayo's beady, apple seed eyes. The malice that festered in his soul like an infected animal bite. Sidian believed he was dealing with fellow Guardians, men with sound minds and honor. But any unit that teamed up with Tayo had to be equally rotten and treacherous.

He ducked back into the foliage and traced the wood line around the lodge. The back of the building had windows, as well, but these were lined with green-striped curtains.

Raine crept soundlessly below a partially cracked window. Conversation drifted through the opening, and he held his breath.

"—cut the cunt's throat if you don't tell us where the dragon is," a man said in a rough, gravelly voice.

"The Nine are already aware my unit captured Raine Chambrin. Stealing him from us will accomplish nothing except your expulsion from the guild," Sidian said evenly, without a hint of fear or doubt.

An eerie laugh erupted. It was thick and gruntled like a pig's. "Did you forget I'm part of your unit, too? Rosa told us how tame and compliant the dragon is. How the two of you *bonded* with it. I'll be telling Commander Eddic all about how you two planned on setting it free. Fortunately, we ran into Unit Two-Five-Zero-Four. I was able to tell them your plan before you could act, and they aided me in thwarting your treasonous plot."

"Not before I smashed your face in," Sidian said silkily.

A string of nasally invective was cut off by a different voice, another man. "Enough! Tell us where the dragon is. I'm done fucking around here."

"Captain, don't," Rosa cried out. "They're going to kill us anyway."

Smack. "Shut your dick trap, bitch," a feminine voice sniped.

Raine gritted his teeth, wanting nothing more than to hurl himself through the window and cut down the hunters threatening his mate and Rosa. He was fast, but he wasn't that fast. He forced himself to stay low as he moved down the row of windows.

The lodge wouldn't boast a gigantic great hall with no other rooms. There had to be a kitchen or barracks or restrooms. Something.

Raine crept to the furthest window, close to where the back and side walls met at a corner. He pushed up on the window. The glass slid an inch and his heart leapt. The curtains, a boon when eavesdropping near the hall, were devilish veils that concealed the room he was breaking into.

Praying it was empty, he lifted the window with a slow and steady force, trying to make as little noise as possible.

No daggers flung at his head. Taking this as a good sign, he hoisted himself up and over.

A desk and chair sat before the window, which he hadn't seen through the curtains. Raine's foot kicked the chair, knocking it onto its side before his upper body made it through the casing.

He threw himself the rest of the way in, not bothering to silence his clattering chains. Raine poised himself for attack, staring intently at the closed door. No one charged through. Frowning, he tiptoed near, keeping cautiously to the side of the door. His heart skipped when the floorboards creaked violently beneath his boots. He froze, waiting.

Nothing. The room was still and quiet, walls lined with a dozen neatly made bunks, all outfitted with a single pillow and thin, navy coverlet. Squatting down, Raine peered through the keyhole of the sleeping quarters.

Rosa was on the floor, her hair snatched in the thick fist of a bald journeyman with a grizzled beard. He was massive. His muscles had even more tiny, baby muscles. Rosa was pale, her dark eyes glazed with pain. Raine studied the awkward angle of her leg. It was broken. Cold fury drifted over him like snowfall.

A thin, pretty woman with her hair in a high knot stood next to Rosa and the freakishly muscled journeyman. She twisted a blade in her hands, stealing avid glances at Rosa's exposed throat.

Another man, short and nondescript but for his captain's armlet, stood in the center of the room. His hard, calculating eyes were trained on Sidian. It was the bow in his hands, drawn with an arrow nocked, that made Raine's heartbeat falter. The floor tilted beneath his legs.

Anger ripped through him like white-hot lightning, charging his blood like a summer storm. He had to calm down. Raine wasn't going to save Sidian by acting like a feral beast.

The unknown captain's drawn bow was too much for his control. Raine looked away.

His eyes immediately caught on Tayo's rearranged facial features. The man's face was concave and unrecognizable. Cheekbones shattered. Nose nonexistent. He was the stuff of nightmares.

Tayo stood closest to Sidian, a sword at his side. *Too many threats*. Raine rapidly considered multiple plans of attack, discarding all of them. He was handcuffed and had a single, small dagger. He had to make it count.

Fear coated his mouth like cotton. A faint tremor wracked his hand as he reached for the doorknob. Raine drew in a shuddering breath and channeled the bravest man he knew. With Arastus Chambrin's stubbled, cocksure smirk clenched in his palpitating heart, Raine threw the door open.

Chucking the blade with both hands—*fucking handcuffs*—it sailed true, sinking to the hilt into what was once Tayo's nose, killing him instantly.

Raine leaned against the doorframe, affecting an insouciant pose as Tayo collapsed. "Don't anyone act sorry for what I just did. How could you even eat next to that face?"

The captain trained his bow on Raine.

"Hey," Raine complained. "I don't know why you're pointing that thing at me. There are strict orders to keep me alive, you know. If you crave recognition and reward, killing me is going to get you a whole lot of neither."

The man smiled grimly and retrained the bow on Sidian.

"That's more like it. Fuck that guy. In fact, it'd be considerate of you to dispatch both of them." Raine picked imaginary lint from his ivory tunic. "The prick keeps the key to my handcuffs in his pocket. I prefer plucking it from his corpse over fighting him for it."

"I don't think you fully understand this situation, dragon. We'll be taking over custody of you once these other two are dead." The man flicked his gaze between Raine and Sidian, but kept his bow trained on Sidian.

"Well, see now. I don't really intend to play along." Raine gave an exaggerated pout. "The way I see it, you take care of those two. Then I take care of you three. I'll be out of these manacles and halfway across the country before anyone discovers your rotting carcasses stinking up this fine lodge."

Calculation gleamed behind the man's pinprick eyes and he retrained his bow on Raine, who fought his sag of relief. The scheming captain was making the decision he'd counted on for his plan to succeed. The man flicked his gaze at Sidian but kept the bulk of his attention on his new target—Raine—as he spoke.

"Now, Sidian. I know we've had our differences but right now, neither of us could end up with the dragon if we don't take him down together. Help me and Fernald get it subdued. Then we can figure out a fair way to see who takes the dragon in. Maybe do it together."

Raine widened his eyes at the captain's words and looked apprehensively at Sidian, who appeared to contemplate the short man's suggestion. "You can help me subdue the dragon, but I won't allow you to steal my captive."

The other captain nodded tersely, undoubtedly intending on double-crossing Sidian the moment Raine was dealt with. Fernald turned out to be the musclebound journeyman gripping Rosa by her hair.

The journeywoman took over guarding Rosa as Fernald lumbered over, plucking a knife from his belt. Sidian, Fernald, and the other captain faced Raine, weapons raised.

Raine charged into the room. An arrow whizzed by his head, cutting a thin red line against his cheek before he launched himself at Fernald. Dodging the journeyman's clumsy knife swings, Raine trusted Sidian to dispatch the other captain in his wake.

Fernald held his knife with a death grip; thrashing and jabbing so wildly, Raine was purely on the defensive. His damn handcuffs didn't help matters, and—with a motion he wasn't proud of—Raine crushed the journeyman's balls with his knee. Fernald yowled.

Raine seized the opportunity provided by the journeyman's pained distraction. He squeezed the man's wrist, digging his thumb into tendon and bone. Fernald dropped the knife with a rough clatter. Raine snatched the fallen dagger and swung straight for Fernald's tree trunk throat to carry out the same threat the journeyman had made to Rosa earlier.

Fernald threw out his hands, a last-ditch effort to block the blade.

The dagger slashed viciously across the man's exposed palms. He screamed, hands recoiling from the bite of the knife. Raine struck, carving a lethal gouge across the man's throat. An ugly flow of dark red pooled from the wound. Fernald flailed, gurgling as blood flooded his windpipe, then fell still in death.

Raine sat back on his knees and found Rosa unmoved from her position on the floor due to the ruined state of her leg. Her injury hadn't rendered her toothless, as the other journeywoman discovered too late.

The small woman was splayed face down on the honey oak floorboards, blood creeping from beneath her abdomen.

Rosa gave him a glossy grin, pain warring with pride in her smile. "I've wanted to do that for years. She was a disgrace to women."

Thunk.

Raine whipped around to find Sidian swaying on his feet. The sound he'd heard was his mate releasing his longsword, where it clattered to the floor. Velvet eyes, glazed and half-lidded, met his. As Sidian pitched forward, Raine speared the air faster than any arrow. He clutched his mate to his chest before Sidian hit the floor.

CHAPTER TWENTY-SEVEN

Raine woke slowly, as if floating from the bottom of a deep lake. Pushing himself upright, he groaned and fell back when his crown connected with the hardwood slats of an upper bunk. He lifted an arm to massage his aching head and froze.

The handcuffs were gone.

His heart had stopped when Sidian fell after slaying Garreth, the other unit's captain. A frantic inspection for injuries had divulged his mate was unharmed, fainting from a combination of dehydration, exhaustion, and the weakening that followed a severely violent encounter. Raine had picked up the unconscious man and tucked him into a lower bunk in the sleeping quarters, taking care to remove Sidian's sheath and boots for a more comfortable sleep.

Then Raine had set and bound Rosa's leg. It was a clean break of her tibia, and she'd fainted when he pushed the bone together. After splinting it as best he could with a fallen branch outside and bandages found in one of the deceased hunter's bags, he carried her to the barracks and made her comfortable on another lower bunk.

Bleary-eyed and desperate for sleep, Raine hadn't rested until he removed the corpses littering the lodge floor, dumping them on top of a hastily compiled pyre to be burned later. He'd then retraced the trail through the palmettos and retrieved their bags.

He had even scrubbed the blood from the floors, leaving no trace of the altercation because he was clearly turning into an overzealous housewife who wanted her husband to wake up to a clean and pleasant home. When he had started to consider laundering Sidian's unwashed hose, he went to bed, partly disgusted with himself and partly itching to do the washing and maybe start a stew so his mate could wake up to a much-needed meal.

Raine rubbed the pink skin of his wrists, half convinced he was still asleep and this was a dream. He rolled from the bed, mindful not to smack his head again, and stood, wearing only his tights. Raine had no idea how long he'd slept, but his muscles were stiff and slothful.

He shuffled to a window and pulled aside the curtain. It was dark. They'd reached the lodge around noon. Raine hadn't gone to bed until a few hours later, since he stayed awake to take care of the mess first. He must have slept the remainder of the day, though he couldn't be sure how late the hour was now.

Raine crept from the barracks so he wouldn't disturb the others, planning to wash their clothes and start a fire in the lodge's hearth. Through the windows of the great room, Raine spied the brightly dancing flames of his pyre. It was burning. He threw on his boots and stumbled outside.

Sidian stood in the shadow of the pyre, watching it burn with a blank stare. He glanced up at Raine's approach, then returned his gaze to the flames.

Raine stood next to him in companionable silence, watching the lively fire as it crackled, voraciously consuming its cadaverous fuel.

After a particularly loud *pop*, Raine said, "You removed my handcuffs." When the captain said nothing, Raine added a soft, "Why?"

Sidian faced him with a sigh. "Because I'm letting you go."

Shock and a powerful wave of tenderness washed over him at his mate's declaration. He swallowed against the lump constricting his throat. "That's not necessary," he whispered.

Sidian had a strict code of honor. Releasing Raine was treason, plain and simple. There was no gray area to hide in. Raine would die before doing anything that tarnished his mate's perception of self. Sidian's honor, self-respect, and pride in his service were things Raine would protect until his final breath.

Sidian glowered, orange firelight dancing in his eyes. "My decision is made. You're no longer my captive."

"Sidian," Raine murmured gently. For once, he made no effort to conceal his affection. "They have my father. I was always going to end up in Obanth, as your captive or otherwise. I can't leave him there."

His mate's eyes lit with understanding. Then darkened just as quickly. "The Guardians' base is impossible to infiltrate or escape. Its official name is Silvan Dredge Prison. It's a maximum-security penitentiary, where the highest profile and most dangerous criminals of Valdenia are kept. Chieftain Eddic serves as the prison warden publicly, since its nature as guild headquarters is privileged."

"He sounds like a busy guy," Raine said wryly.

Sidian's stare narrowed. "He's busy but he's smart. There won't be a way to get your father out. The guild has five thousand citizens serving terms right now. Two hundred of those units are kept at headquarters, serving as guards, jailors, and prison workers."

Raine did the math in his head. "That seems an excessive number of guards," he muttered.

"There's an excessive number of prisoners," Sidian shot back. "The building is situated against the silver mines. The guards oversee the prisoners during the day while they're forced to labor in the mines, unearthing silver ore. Within the prison, more prisoners are forced to refine the silver and press the metal into silvans."

Huh. That was one more item to add to the list of relevant things instructor Brenk had left out of his tutoring: where Valdenian currency came from.

"I don't have to worry about getting in," Raine pointed out. "If you bring me in as a captive, they'll take me past every layer of security themselves."

Sidian thrust a finger into Raine's bare chest, right over his heart, which thumped as if to meet him. "That's great. And you'll be stuck there, tortured for information and then killed when they think they've gotten everything they can from you."

Raine was stunned silent. Sidian sounded concerned. More than concerned. Scared. For Raine.

Sidian dropped his finger, though his face remained twisted in a scowl. "I'm sorry about your father, Raine. I really am. But going in there is a death sentence. If your father had the choice between both of you dying or just him, you know what he'd choose."

"You said my name," Raine whispered. Sparkling light flooded his veins like warm, bubbling cider.

Sidian pinched the bridge of his nose. "That is not what you were meant to focus on. Tell me you understood the rest."

His mate's sharp tone snapped Raine out of his stupor. In the yawning silence, he wrestled with his conscience, debating whether to ask Sidian for help. With Sidian's assistance, Raine and his father might stand a chance.

No. Raine wouldn't ask. He could never risk his mate's safety, not for any reason. But he also could not leave his father to the cruel mercies of the Nine. He had to go alone. It had been his plan all along. Nothing had changed and thanks to Sidian, he knew far more than he otherwise would have.

"You're going to try anyway." Pure bitterness laced the captain's words, making it an accusation. Raine didn't want to lie so he said nothing. The sounds of the fire grew loud in the silence. "Fine," Sidian bit out. "I will help you. But I can't guarantee success, even with my aid. Too many things can go wrong."

Raine launched himself at his mate, squeezing tightly around his waist and smashing the hard planes of their chests together. Before he could stop himself, he buried his face in the crook of Sidian's neck, inhaling the scents of smoke and sea and something else, something deep and sweet that sang to his soul.

"Thank you," he whispered into the captain's broad shoulder.

Sidian's body was warm and solid and fit perfectly against his own. Raine's lower body enlivened at the contact and he took a quick step back, before Sidian could detect his reaction.

"Don't think I'm not pissed at you," Raine suddenly exclaimed. This time, he thrust his finger into Sidian's chest. "You are not a dragon."

Sidian blinked, his only sign of surprise. "No shit. It's like you grow more intelligent daily."

"You pushed yourself too hard." *Poke*. "You didn't drink enough water." *Poke*. "And you fucking fainted." *Poke. Poke. Poke.* Raine threw his hands to his head, gripping his hair in the same frustrated way his father sometimes did. "Do you know what that did to me? I thought you were hurt. I thought you were—" He cut off.

Sidian didn't say a word. Just stared, his eyes mirroring the fire. Raine huffed. "After I explained our hasty journey here, Rosa said you were probably sun sick and dehydrated. That will not happen again." He glared hard at Sidian, who still didn't speak. "I'm making you soup. You need salt and protein and water. We aren't going anywhere until you've recovered."

His tone dared the captain to argue. Sidian merely arched a brow. "I prefer seafood stews scented with saffron, but a hearty bowl of venison and vegetables is also acceptable."

❧❧❧❧❧❧ ❧❧❧❧❧❧

Rosa's leg injury put her out of commission for the mission ahead. And so, the following day, after a seam-splitting lunch of venison stew, Raine and Sidian assembled Rosa a week's worth of shelf-stable rations—nuts and citrus foraged from the woodland and some heartier fare that had been squirreled away in Garreth's pack.

"I'll alert Master Kollus of your location when I arrive at headquarters," Sidian told Rosa, hovering next to her bunk. "They'll send a unit to retrieve you."

Rosa gripped the cloth of Sidian's arm, glaring intently. "What you're doing isn't right. Don't take Raine to Silvan Dredge. You know what they'll do to him, Captain. He doesn't deserve it."

Raine and Sidian had agreed not to inform Rosa of their plan. It wasn't from a lack of trust. More like, the knowledge would endanger her. Better for Rosa to remain entirely ignorant. If the hammer fell, she would escape unscathed.

"I have a duty," Sidian said coolly, jerking his arm sleeve from her fingers.

Rosa's face crumpled, just for an instant, before her features tightened with righteous fury. That instant tore Raine's insides out like a cleaned trout.

"To hell with your duty," she spat, the words hoarse with her turmoil as she battled tears. "Raine." Her voice was deathly urgent as she leaned forward, peering out of her bunk to lock eyes with him. "Don't let him take you. You're stronger than the captain. He doesn't have me or Tayo to help control you. Please run for your life. If you go to Silvan Dredge, they're going to torture and kill you."

Raine blinked away his own sheen of stinging moisture. She sounded so heartfelt, so caring. He'd grown used to one-sided affection in his short time as Sidian's captive. It had been a while since anyone evinced more than a passing desire for him to continue breathing—and that, not out of fondness, but only because Raine's corpse wasn't what was on order.

In the short span of a day, both Sidian and Rosa had come all the way around. Not only did neither of them wish him harm, but they appeared to value and respect him. It was a miracle, considering what they were to each other. Hunters and quarry. Guards and captive. Humans and dragon.

That last one didn't ring right. It wasn't true, he realized. Humans and dragons weren't inherently enemies. They could be on the same side. The only thing stopping them was the guild.

No, the Nine. The Nine directed the guild's actions. Everything stemmed from them, like a poisoned well.

Raine crouched low, surveying Rosa with her sleep-mussed top-knot and splinted leg, which was propped on a mound of pillows.

Her head shook at whatever she saw in his face. "Raine, no." She started rocking forward as if she was going to somehow stand and stop him.

He restrained her by pressing a palm to her shoulder, pinning her against the pillows piled between her back and the wall. "Rosa, listen. When you guys arrested me, I was on my way to go find my father." Her frown cleared as her eyes widened. "Exactly," Raine said, seeing that she got it. "Sidian is committed to his oath to the guild. He will finish escorting me to Silvan Dredge. But even if he listened to you and released me—"

"You'd go there anyway," Rosa finished. "Oh, Raine." Her arms stretched out. His knees sank into the mattress so she could embrace him. "Be careful," she murmured in a hot whisper against his cheek.

His arms squeezed her back. "I promise to try very hard not to die." He drew back and smirked. "I'm sure I'll do better than you, at any rate. How weak are you, that Tayo managed to kidnap you?"

She scoffed, but her lips curled. "Tayo didn't manage anything. It was that freak of nature Fernald who got the better of me. When he grabbed me, I tried stabbing him with a fork and it bounced off his skin like rubber."

"Don't worry. His dagger didn't bounce." Raine wanted to withdraw those words the second they came out. He'd been going for levity when he teased Rosa about Tayo getting the better of her. His reference to Fernald's bloody death had the opposite effect of a joke. Rosa's eyes were grave once again, this time shadowed with traumatic memory as well as concern.

"Good riddance to all of them," Sidian said evenly. "They were a disgrace to the guild, unworthy of their uniforms."

"I'm not sure our uniforms are anything to be worthy of," Rosa muttered, almost too soft for Raine to hear.

"What was that?" Sidian asked, eyes narrowing.

"Nothing," Raine chirped brightly. He stepped left, blocking Rosa from Sidian's hawk-like scrutiny. "Rosa was just admiring your uniform. She's right. You definitely rock it. Has the Nine ever mentioned putting your image on recruitment posters? The whole country would sign up."

Sidian was unmoved, his narrowed gaze no less suspicious. He must have caught the gist of Rosa's utterance, even if he hadn't heard it all.

"You sound like you'd be the first in line," Rosa teased.

He yelped as she pinched his ass cheek. Massaging the abused flesh, he turned to give her a mock glare. Before Raine could threaten to pinch something of hers in retaliation, Sidian snorted behind him.

"That's because he would be."

Rosa laughed, stretching forward to steady her propped leg as she shook with mirth. "Your face," she gasped. "It's as pink as pomegranate juice."

Raine shrank away from the bunk. He didn't know what pomegranate juice was, but his cheeks felt like hot coals at Sidian's matter-of-fact assertion. There had been something in his voice, a smoky hint of knowledge that made Raine's breaths come shorter.

How much did Sidian know? Had he somehow figured out Raine's attraction? He couldn't have. Raine had deliberately concealed it from him all this time, essentially pretending all nineteen-year-old dragons were walking erections.

"Get your things," Sidian said, glancing through the parted curtains. "We should reach Obanth by nightfall if we leave now."

"I didn't realize we were so close." Raine gathered his dirty clothes and hairbrush from the bunk he'd used, then took his time packing them into his haversack so his blush could fade. Once his face felt the same temperature as the rest of him, he faced Sidian, who beckoned him with a wave. His other arm cradled a strappy bundle of dark fabric.

"Rushing to the lodge expedited our progress. We were originally on target to reach Obanth two days from now. Turn around."

Raine eyed the lumpy roll of fabric and metal sticks Sidian held, then presented his back to the captain. "What is that?"

"A tent, courtesy of Garreth's unit," Sidian said, fastening it to Raine's back. "I clipped two bedrolls to my rucksack, but you need to carry this."

"I thought you said we'll reach Obanth tonight." Once Sidian stopped messing with the buckles, Raine faced him, his head cocked in confusion. Why would they need a tent?

Sidian flicked a glance at Rosa. "We're leaving now. A rescue unit should be here in no more than three days."

For a man burdened with a pack as large as Sidian's, the captain moved with remarkable swiftness. His black boots made no sound as they crossed Brackshallow Lodge's great room and exited the door.

"Take care," Raine called to Rosa, hastening to catch up.

"No, *you* take care—"

Rosa's anxious tone was cut off by the door closing. Raine frowned at Sidian, who arched a brow. "What? You want me to leave the door open, so any passing ruffians or vagabonds can waltz inside?"

Raine adjusted the tent pack's straps so they wouldn't bite into his shoulders. "Why do we need a tent?" he repeated in lieu of a reply.

Sidian took several steps away from the door, heading down the lodge's stone walkway. "We've scarcely slept in two days, going on three." He glanced over his shoulder, as if making sure Raine followed. Satisfied, he faced forward. "Freeing your father won't be easy. Worst case scenario, we'll have to fight our way out. We have to be well-rested and in peak performance, if there's any hope of success."

Raine nodded, then realized Sidian couldn't see since he was walking behind the captain. "Makes sense. You want us to make camp before we get there so we can rest up before facing them."

It should have been a daunting prospect, and Raine might have actually been daunted if he wasn't on his way to rescue his father. To save Arastus Chambrin, he'd face the entire guild and then some.

They traced the stone path as it curved around the lake, directing them back to the SBT.

The lake was gorgeous, even up close; a placid mirror framed by reedy grasses and wading egrets. Fat, green leaves floated like bowls near the water's edge. Upon each one rested a blooming flower, each as large as Raine's fist. His eyes traced the glint of darting fish as they rounded the lake. They hadn't been able to take this route to the lodge yesterday; stealth had been paramount to saving Rosa, and the lake path was situated in direct view of the lodge's front windows.

Dusty pink and white flagstones glittered in the sun as they reached the SBT. They walked in companionable silence. Raine's mind drifted, lulled by the delicious contrasts of hot sun and cool, ocean breeze. He kept picturing his father's face. His broad, stubbled grin and short, peppery hair. His coffee-brown eyes that crinkled with his smile. He hoped his father wouldn't be too upset when he saw Raine. The man undoubtedly wished his son would remain safely sequestered in a dark hole somewhere, damn whatever Raine felt about it.

Too bad. Raine couldn't leave his father to his fate any more than Arastus Chambrin could leave his son to suffer. They were family. It was as simple as that.

The hours passed swiftly and with minimal conversation. Raine left Sidian alone, knowing his mate wanted to come up with a plan. Finally, over a walking supper, Sidian started talking. He described the layout of Silvan Dredge Prison in detail, first explaining its three levels aboveground: temporary holding cells, administration offices and conference rooms, and finally, records and storage.

"Everything that involves the guild is kept to the lower floors. There are four basement levels. Your father will be in the fourth and lowest level, where the maximum-security cells are located."

Raine swallowed his mouthful of pecans. There were pieces stuck in his teeth, so he swigged his canteen to clear them away. "Is there a way out of the prison from the fourth level, or do we have to find a way to reach the surface first?"

"No doors on the third or fourth floors lead outside. The closest way out is an emergency exit on the second floor."

"You don't always need a door to exit a place," Raine pointed out. "Are there no chimneys that far down?"

"No. There are no hearths or chimneys on the fourth level. Nobody cares if a prisoner catches a chill. Anything else that requires a fire is taken care of elsewhere—"

Sidian halted so suddenly, Raine nearly plowed him over. "Oof."

Raine threw up his palms to catch himself against Sidian's rucksack, accidentally spilling his last fistful of pecans. He pouted as his pecans tumbled across the road and sunk into the sandy cracks between stones. He had really wanted to eat those.

"What's wrong?" he asked Sidian, peering around to see for himself the disturbance that had cost him his nuts.

Earlier, they had to avoid a yellow spotted taipan snake, which had curled up in the center of the sun-warmed stones of the border trail, flicking its tongue more rapidly as they neared. But there was no snake this time. The SBT unfurled like an endless tongue, its pinkish stones now appearing a ruddy red in the waning daylight.

"There might be a way out," Sidian murmured, almost to himself. "Maybe ... What day is it?"

"Oh, um." Raine's nose scrunched in thought. "Saturday?"

"That's what I thought," Sidian said. He sounded curiously satisfied. Raine opened his mouth to ask what was so special about Saturday, but Sidian continued. "The sun is starting to set. We should make camp now. Obanth is on the other side of that curve."

The Southern Border Trial came closer to the Dragon Fangs than any other road. Elsewhere in Valdenia, sprawling foothills and forests buffered major roadways from the Fangs. There were no such barriers where they stood. On either side of them, sweeping mountains jutted straight out of the earth's flat, craggy crust and towered over them like ancient gods.

Raine traced the mountain ridges, readily spotting the curve Sidian referred to. The Fangs sat like a mouthful of teeth, barring the strip of road where the SBT bowed around a mountain's base and disappeared from view.

Narrow swaths of grass and talus field were all that separated the mountains from the roadside. Raine shrugged the tent carrier off his back. Sidian picked a private spot to pitch their tent, where fragmented boulders the size of small houses would block the sight of them from passersby. By the time everything was set up, twilight quickened around them. The sunset stacked the sky like a layered cake. Yellow, orange, pink, blue.

"You can lay down," Sidian said, climbing out of the tent where he had set up their bedrolls. "I want to do a quick perimeter check before retiring."

Raine admired the gleaming halo of Sidian's hair, shining in the last rays of sunlight. When Sidian disappeared around the boulders, Raine's gaze dropped to their tent. His stomach fluttered, sending sparks of awareness through him as he spied the bedrolls through the flap. They were squished together so closely, they overlapped a little. It was going to be him and Sidian. In that teensy tiny tent. Alone.

He swallowed, his mouth bone dry as explicit images from his most recent dream danced through his mind. They were hazy and half-remembered, but the bits he could recall made his pulse leap.

How had he gone from being a frigid prude to a raging pervert? The Raine of two months ago would be aghast at his thoughts. For a moment, he tried harnessing the old Raine's aloof indifference to sex. It was no use. His body was a furnace throwing off pure lust. His blood heated to a feverish degree the longer he stared at their overlapping bedrolls.

Him and Sidian. In that teensy tiny tent. Alone.

He climbed into the tent before Sidian could complete his perimeter check and find Raine standing there, dumbstruck with a hard-on. The tent cloth was dark green and satiny. Its material was so thin, he was surprised at how well it blocked the light and wind. He claimed one of the bedrolls and laid down on his back, tucking his knees slightly when his boots brushed the tent wall.

In the quiet hush of oncoming night, he waited for Sidian. His heart knocked steadily at the base of his throat. *No big deal. This is no big deal.* That's what he told himself, over and over. And it was true. This wasn't a big deal. He just needed to chill out, play it cool, and not do anything that might freak Sidian out and decide Raine was the scummy kind of dragon, after all.

Several moments passed, then Sidian entered. Raine stiffened and relaxed by turns, frantically trying to act natural. His efforts were wasted, as Sidian immediately faced the tent flap and sealed it. It was like someone blew out a candle—the inside of their tent now as dark as midnight.

Sidian's rustling motions jostled Raine as the captain laid down beside him.

That's all it took. Heat speared Raine's cock. A needy, presumptuous appendage, it regarded their sleeping arrangements like a salivating lecher. Raine squeezed his eyes shut and tried to pretend it was Nyx or his father sharing his tent.

Sidian's warm, solid shoulder pressed against his own.

It was impossible. Raine's entire universe narrowed to the small point of contact at their shoulders. His cock hardened so painfully, he could have staked their tent with it. Sidian's scent filled the cramped space, perfusing Raine's every breath; smoky like his voice, salty like the sea, and a crisp, divine aroma that made his balls tighten painfully.

Raine laid awake for a very long time.

CHAPTER TWENTY-EIGHT

Sidian was already awake and had breakfast ready when Raine emerged from their tent the following morning. Scrubbing sleep from his eyes, he surveyed the captain blearily. There were large, mossy boulders to perch upon, ever-present this close to the Dragon Fangs. Raine sat on a low flat rock that jutted from beneath the taller one Sidian had claimed.

He took the cheese and oranges handed to him before putting his back against the granite. They sat facing the mountain range. Sweeping, sharp peaks, like the teeth of the world. Raine was reminded of his boyhood fantasies.

"I used to think Valdenia was a mouth," he confided.

Above and behind him, Sidian's response was delayed. Likely from chewing. "Come again?"

Raine grinned to himself, recalling his childish terror of the mountains. "The mountains encircling Valdenia. When I was little,

I was convinced they were real teeth. I lived in constant dread of the monster swallowing one day."

A husky laugh pebbled him with goosebumps. "When did you stop believing our country was a giant mouth?"

Raine was glad his mate couldn't see his blush, which was hot enough he knew his head resembled a cherry. "I didn't." A snort sounded above and Raine smiled despite his embarrassment. "My father was a total prick and encouraged it. Told me to pray to the Divine Father that we never had too long a dry spell. He said that the rain was what kept the monster from swallowing, but if its throat ever got too dry, it would swallow to moisten it."

He crammed the last bite of crumbling cheese into his mouth and stood. Sidian was shaking in silent mirth above, his own cheese half-eaten. "I like your father," he said once he sobered, then did as Raine had and popped the remaining cheese into his mouth in a single, large bite.

Raine rested his elbows against the mossy green carpeting Sidian's perch and smirked. "Yeah, well it bit him in the ass, big time. I was too afraid to sleep alone for years. And too young to understand why my father would ever want privacy in his bedchamber."

Sidian's lips curved as he peeled his orange, listening.

"When I was, I don't know, nine or ten? My father had enough. He sat me down and explained that my name was Raine. And therefore, so long as I lived and breathed, Valdenia would always have Raine and never swallow."

"You bought that?"

Raine glared at his incredulity. "I was a little kid."

"Yeah, a really stupid one."

"I will push you off this rock."

Sidian snorted. "We don't have time to play."

An image of him and Sidian playing—wresting—came unbidden. Raine was grateful for the boulder he leaned upon as his blood surged south, leaving him lightheaded. His neck bent down as he breathed through the headrush.

When he straightened, Sidian's velveteen gaze was fixed on him. "I will pin you later," he murmured.

Raine's head fell forward once more. He bit his lip on a whimper. *That's not what he means*, he told his prick furiously. It was no use. Raine's cock was in fantasyland—one where a hot-eyed captain covered his body, pinning his arms.

He couldn't meet Sidian's gaze. Not with these wildly perverse thoughts and images rampaging through his mind. Raine lowered himself to his seat and forced himself to concentrate as he peeled his oranges. His prick, once roused, could remain as hard as an iron bar for hours. Fortunately—or unfortunately—that meant Raine was used to functioning through arousal. He just needed to erase Sidian's stirring words from his conscious mind and he'd be fine.

"We have to leave the tent and your belongings behind," Sidian announced from overhead.

Raine choked on a section of orange. "What?"

"Permitting you the comforts of your own possessions will make me appear sympathetic. I must remain above suspicion for my plan to work."

Raine didn't know what that plan was, precisely. Sidian refused to elaborate. Something about Raine's reaction needing to be absolutely genuine. And for some reason, it wouldn't be if he anticipated whatever Sidian had in store.

He stuffed the remaining fruit into his mouth and jogged to the tent, extracting his haversack by its tightly woven strap.

Raine returned to the flat rock and sat with his satchel upon his lap. His hands moved over the oil vials, gently clinking them. Feeling bereft already, he dabbed his current favorite scent—cinnamon—onto the teeth of his hairbrush, then combed his opalescent mane until it glittered.

He was dexterously weaving the locks into a fishtail braid when Sidian hopped down from his perch. His shadow blotted the morning light. "I don't know how callous I'll appear when I am forced to produce such an immaculately groomed captive," Sidian mused, his lips curling with irony.

Raine turned up his nose. "Dragons prioritize cleanliness and take pride in our appearance." He gave a slow, deliberate perusal of Sidian's deliciously proportioned figure. Every ounce of his derision was utterly feigned. "Unlike some people."

Sidian smoothed away the black locks that fell over his face, staring down at Raine as he finished tying back his hair. "You find my appearance lackluster?"

The pleasantly husky timbre of his voice prickled Raine like an intimate caress, and he shivered. "There's room for improvement." He struggled to disguise his sudden breathlessness.

Sidian's fawn eyes were pure velvet and richly intent on him. Raine's pulse surged as his mate knelt before him, bringing their gazes level. His breath held as Sidian leaned forward, pressing his soft mouth to Raine's ear. "You talk in your sleep," he whispered.

Fuck.

Sidian reaffixed Raine's handcuffs before they left their campsite. During their hour-long walk to Obanth, Raine stewed in panic.

The captain had said he *talked*. In his *sleep*. Raine's dreams were primarily hazy, erotic episodes of him and Sidian in explicitly compromising positions. He didn't recall ever speaking in them and wracked his mind for what he could have said while unconscious.

Whatever it was had put a wicked gleam in Sidian's dark eyes. The man practically smirked whenever Raine accidentally made eye contact. Each time, his face caught fire and he looked away quickly. Once, Sidian outright laughed at his blatant embarrassment. By the time Obanth's white walls loomed ahead, Raine still hadn't asked Sidian what he'd heard, though it was evident the captain was waiting for him to pluck his courage.

As they drew closer, Obanth's walls shocked Raine to his core. Pale white stone that glinted creamy blues and pinks and greens. He'd never seen anything like it, except for the hair on his head.

Inlaid on the walls of either side of the main gate was an oversized insignia of the guild: on a lush green field, three silhouettes posed defensively, protecting nine majestic mountains in the distance. The symbol was intended to represent a Guardian unit defending Valdenia. Raine saw pawns protecting nine corrupt men with ugly, yellow-brown eyes.

Raine was forced to walk in front of Sidian, who followed closely, his chest brushing against Raine's back with each step.

His queasiness at upcoming imprisonment and probable torture didn't stifle the healthy flow of blood to his prick at their proximity.

He was so immersed in the feel of Sidian's breath at his neck—a warm tickling sensation that stoked the fire in his blood ever hotter—he scarcely registered the details of the city as they progressed.

It felt like no time had passed from the moment they entered Obanth until he was being led to the prison. Even without Sidian's in-depth description of the guild's prison-slash-covert headquarters, Raine would have recognized the structure immediately for what it was: a fortress.

The windows were caged with thick, black metal bars that glittered with crushed diamonds. Even the upper story windows. A hulking curtain towered higher than the outer walls of the city. It was tipped with dragon bone barbs that would shred the flesh of anyone, human or dragon, who thought to climb over. An intricately scrolled gate stretched between stone, Silvan Dredge Prison dead ahead.

As they approached the gate, Raine spoke without moving his lips. "What do I say in my sleep?"

Sidian slid his hands to Raine's upper wrists, cupping the flesh above his manacles as if to keep a firm hold on his captive. Raine hoped the captain couldn't detect the rapid thrum of his pulse through his skin.

"You'll have to succeed in this endeavor to earn that information," Sidian said, his voice the barest whisper.

Gooseflesh erupted along Raine's arms and neck while cool, blessed relief eased a knot of tension in his stomach.

Sidian was messing around with him. That meant whatever Raine muttered in his sleep wasn't as incriminating as he'd feared.

Challenge accepted.

Two black-robed figures descended the wide, stone steps of the prison and met them in the curtilage. Eddic and another chieftain, one Raine hadn't met, were flanked by no less than four Guardian units. A dozen hunters clad in tight, black hose identical to Sidian's surrounded them.

"Outstanding work, Captain Wade." Eddic halted a cautious distance from them. His eyes were sallower than ever and Raine wondered anew what noxious drug the Nine partook that yellowed eyes instead of teeth or skin. "Has it been venomed?"

"Yes, Commander Eddic. I also dosed it with a poppied tincture to keep it docile."

Raine played his part well, the only role Sidian had assigned him. His eyes were heavily lidded, and he did his best to seem zoned out and insensate to the conversation around him.

"Excellent work," the other chieftain said.

He was ancient, his wrinkled skin so paper-thin, it looked pasted on. His sallow eyes were hungrily assessing, roving over Raine in a manner eerily reminiscent of someone else. Throughout Raine's entrance exams, Chieftain Tyrus had eyed Raine like a doll. Or a sumptuous rug. A thing he wished to keep. This chieftain wanted to keep him, too. Why or what for, Raine didn't know. But all the fine hairs of his body stood on end and he knew it was nothing good.

"Thank you, Commander Brandor," Sidian said with a slight bow.

Brandor. So this was Rokeshin's chieftain. The northeastern city where Valdenia's army was concentrated. It was odd to think of this frail man, who appeared one stiff breeze removed from death, as the leading ruler of Rokeshin's mighty citadel.

Brandor's beady yellow eyes were more reptilian than a snake's. They remained fixed on Raine. It was like the man was entranced. And not in a nice way. "You'll do," he whispered, almost to himself. "You'll do."

"Captain Dewan," Eddic barked. Brandor shook his head, as if clearing it. One of the captains separated from the pack of hunters and stood at attention. "Show Captain Wade to Chambrin's cell." To Sidian, Eddic said, "You may deposit the dragon with the traitor. A touching reunion might loosen their tongues."

Raine's pulse raced, but he didn't allow his eyes to brighten at Eddic's words. He kept his face dull and movements slow as Sidian ushered him from behind, trailing Captain Dewan's wake. The hunter led them to a discreet door painted the same hue of speckled beige as the prison. There was no doorknob, but it swung inward at Dewan's command.

A journeyman held the door open, granting them access. Dewan nodded to the journeyman, but his stride didn't falter as he continued down a dreary flint hallway. An archway revealed a stairwell. They descended, passing several levels until they reached the very bottom.

"They put Chambrin in cell thirty-eight," Dewan told Sidian, picking a key ring off a wall hook. They moved down a corridor of prison cells. "He hasn't said a word since his arrival. Commander Eddic is eager to see if the arrival of his pet breaks his silence."

"Let us pray it does," Sidian said. "It is past time for Valdenia to be put to rights."

Raine clung to the familiar husky voice of his mate, which soothed the jagged edges of his mounting anxiety. He loathed being belowground and of course, they had to put the damn prison in the basement. Black spots danced on the edges of his vision as he scented the moldering decay of deep, dank earth. *Hang in there*, he ordered himself. *Father needs you.*

Dewan paused before a cell, ticking keys on the ring until he located the one meant for cell thirty-eight. There were no lights in the cell, but the lamps lining the aisle filtered through the bars. Raine's father was shackled to the stone wall of his cell, arms and legs in chains as he huddled in a dark corner.

The cell's metal bars opened sideways. Raine's stomach lurched as a violent shove sprawled him forward. He landed rough on his chest and chin, his arms secured behind his back making it impossible to catch himself. The metallic *snick* of the cell latching sounded before he could right himself.

"It was clever of him, passing that thing off as a blanched born," Dewan remarked as the two captains strolled away.

"If they would instate mandatory evaluations at birth, things like this wouldn't slip through the cracks," Sidian said, sounding irritated.

"Tell me about it. After this, you can bet your bottom silvan they'll be inspecting every citizen of Valdenia. Man, woman, and child."

Raine waited until their voices faded entirely, then stood. The lantern outside the cell illuminated him from behind and he heard a ragged gasp.

"Son," his father croaked, that one utterance cracking his throat like brittle porcelain.

Raine barreled into his father's arms. A razor sharp shoulder blade shook against his cheek, Arastus Chambrin sobbing as he rocked his son.

Titans of joy and sorrow clashed in Raine's chest, emptying from his battlefield body one tremulous tear at a time. Soon, his body was drained and sore like a wrung-out sponge. He slumped against his father and closed his eyes, wishing more than ever that his handcuffs were off, if only so he could return his father's embrace.

A rancid odor smacked him out of his emotional cocoon. Rearing back, he made out his father's features in the dimness.

"You stink," he said, voice thick from crying.

A dry cough wracked his father. It took a moment to recognize the sound as a laugh. "You smell like cinnamon and sunshine. Even captured by the enemy, you manage to be a priss."

Raine didn't offer a sally in return. He was too busy noticing how painfully thin his father was. The Wolf of the Vale had shrunk to little more than a fleshy skeleton with an overgrowth of unkempt beard. Raine counted his father's ribs beneath his filthy, tattered shirt. "Have they not fed you anything?"

Another rumbling cough. The sound sent a lick of ice down Raine's spine. "They ... gave us a bad batch of clams over a week ago," his father rasped. Thin, cold fingers combed back Raine's hair and smoothed down his braid. "Every prisoner who ate them has contracted a wasting disease." His father voiced it like an apology. "I'm dying."

CHAPTER TWENTY-NINE

It happened. After all this time, it happened. The sky blackened to nothing as mountains met and cinched in a perfectly serrated line. The mouth of Valdenia snapped shut and swallowed the world.

Raine was trapped in that dark, wet throat as the monster worked him down to oblivion. Then lights beamed the darkness away, wresting him from the jaws of death.

"Slab the dragon in the question room." That was Eddic speaking, he thought distantly.

Hands grasped his arms harshly, bruisingly. Raine resisted, stretching toward his father. His manacled wrists made true resistance impossible. With a mighty heave, the hands yanked Raine several feet backwards. He stumbled, but the hunters gripping him—one on each side—held him firmly upright.

"Stop," his father demanded. The full power and authority of Arastus Chambrin, elite military commander and Guardian master, boomed like thunder as he roared. "Let my son go. Take me instead."

"He speaks," Eddic crowed mockingly. "One visit with your little pet and your iron is reduced to putty. Pathetic."

A hunter slammed the cell shut on his father's howling grief and rage. Raine's sanity snagged on the sound. The hunters dragged him through a riveted metal door, then strapped him to the surface of a low slab table. They left him there, alone in the damp earth and inky darkness. The monster's throat working him down.

A bolt slid, echoing like a coffin latch.

Raine understood where he was. A torture chamber. They'd secured his arms and legs with leather stays, priming him for a violent interrogation. He tried to care. Tried to summon fear or dread. But all Raine felt was soul-crushing anguish.

A wasting disease. His father had a *wasting disease*.

Wasting diseases were always fatal. A hellish, irreversible process where a body consumed itself. No amount of food or rest or medicine cured it.

He would not cry. *He would not cry.* Fucking extraction specialists were probably on their way, scalpels at the ready. Raine would be damned if he shed a single tear. These pieces of shit weren't going to get their kicks by witnessing his grief.

Raine began counting. With his eyes closed against the oppressive darkness, he counted to one hundred. Then two. Then three. He was over a thousand before the door re-opened, admitting two journeymen. They hung glowing lanterns at either side of the stale room.

Behind them trailed Eddic and Sidian, followed by two guildmembers in pristine white hose. They were a peculiar sight, their uniforms a stark foil to their black-clad brethren. One wore thick lenses on his face. His short, dark hair was salted with age and slicked back on his head. The other white-garbed hunter was younger, wearing his hair in the high topknot that so many of the guild preferred.

"How nice to see you again, *Olan*. Or should I say, Raine Chambrin?"

Raine held his tongue, mindful of Sidian's description of one under the influence of the guild's poppied tincture. He could not be both articulately sassy and drugged to the gills. Silence was his best guise.

Eddic tutted and leaned forward, a hard edge in his smile. "I'm sure you know why you're here but for the sake of official record, I'll tell you anyway. You, Raine Chambrin, are an illegal dragon who has perpetuated innumerable crimes upon Valdenia and its citizens. I have brought our best extraction specialists to obtain the illicit knowledge you possess. I know you assisted in the theft of Valdenia's prized assets contained in Chambrin's Cavern. You will tell us their location."

Sidian stood past Eddic's shoulder, his features cast in shadow. Raine forced himself to ignore his mate, had to trust that the man who owned him heart, body, and soul could somehow forestall his pending torture session.

The younger extraction specialist moved to the corner of the room. Raine tracked his progress, noticing a wheeled tray for the first time. The tray clattered noisily as the man rolled it to the room's center. It was lined with sparkling silver instruments similar to Jaska's jewelry making utensils. Thin and sharp.

The older, bespectacled man gave Raine a kind smile that chilled his blood. No longer was he trapped in a grief-induced haze of indifference. The monster had spat him out.

Tearing his gaze away, he found Eddic's smug, saggy face leering down at him. "I will tell you nothing," Raine said. To his shame, it was not a pretense of being drugged that slurred his words. His fear was so intense, it swelled his tongue, making words difficult to form.

Eddic beamed, as if he had agreed to cooperate. "I think you will. You see, we didn't set this room up for you."

As if on cue, the chamber door pushed open and something cumbrous wheeled inside. The extraction specialists reached below the surface of Raine's table. A hinge released, and they repositioned the table so that Raine, still strapped tight to its surface, faced the room in an upright position. His stomach bottomed out as he saw a table identical to the one he was strapped to, the figure of Arastus Chambrin belted flush to its surface.

His father was bound and gagged, but conscious. Raine made out more details than he had in the cell, taking in the gaunt cheeks beneath his father's tangled beard, his gray flesh and drooping eyes. His father's expression was stricken as he stared at Raine.

The younger extraction specialist lifted a sharp instrument resembling a letter opener.

"I'll begin with the most pressing question, shall I?" Eddic's thin lips warped into a poor facsimile of a smile. "Where are the dragons?"

The man in white approached his father, idly twirling the silver blade.

His father's sunken gaze remained fixed on Raine. He received the message in his father's earnest coffee eyes as surely as if he spoke it aloud. *Don't tell them anything.*

These might be the final moments of Raine's life. He would not spend them disappointing the man who held him more precious than anything in this world. His innards twisted with terror, but he made sure none of his trepidation appeared on his face as he beamed at Eddic. "Have you searched your mouth? Judging by the stench of your breath, one or two dragons could be hiding in there."

Eddic waved a hand without looking away from Raine. The man with the penknife gripped his father's hand and sunk it into his index finger, shoving it straight beneath his fingernail. His father garbled a shout through his gag, bony chest heaving beneath his ratty shirt.

Raine squeezed his eyes shut, gritting his teeth so hard, they were in danger of breaking. Already, answers formed behind his lips. Treacherous truths that would condemn every last free dragon to death. But he couldn't breathe a word of it. No matter what they did to his father. Or to him.

Eddic tutted with false sympathy. "That looked painful. And to think, your father needn't endure any more suffering. All you must do is tell me where the dragons are."

Fawn. Fawn. Fawn. In through his nose, out through his mouth. Raine used the rhythmic, calming breaths Savere had taught him in the Hellhole to settle his fraying mind. Opening his eyes, he smirked at the vile cretin whose face was so close to his own, he could count the fine wrinkles creasing his mustardy eyes.

"I've been accused of having a dragon in my pants, but I'm not sure that's what you mean."

Eddic smiled, as if he appreciated Raine's bawdy joke. "Take his father's hand."

Raine's eyes widened as his breathing exercises faltered. Frantically, futilely, he struggled against his bindings, staring helplessly at his father.

General Arastus Chambrin was the picture of serene indifference. The harsh lines of his frame were so still and relaxed, he seemed more apparition than man. His eyes held nothing but love and reassurance as they beheld his son.

The bespectacled man lifted a razor-sharp saw, so thin the blade wobbled like a swai fish through the air. Raine shuddered, his heart and limbs encased in ice as it neared his father's vulnerable flesh. He opened his mouth, the damnation of his entire species on his tongue.

A distant explosion shook the room. Grit and dust loosened from the stone ceiling, powdering Raine's face and hair. The slab at his back reverberated. Distant, panicked shouts were muffled but audible through the door.

"Investigate," Eddic snapped, addressing the two journeymen who'd borne lanterns into the chamber. As they filed out, Eddic faced the bespectacled tormentor. "His hand," he repeated, more urgently.

Another explosion rocked the chamber, this one closer. The tray of surgical instruments clattered.

"Continue without me. I'll return shortly." Eddic's black robes billowed as he swept from the room.

The instant the door clanged shut, a light glinted. The younger extraction specialist cried out, clutching at his chest. A black handle jutted where a man's heart was kept. He crumpled to the floor at Raine's father's feet.

Sidian flung a second knife. The bespectacled man danced agilely out of the way, and the blade smacked harmlessly against the wall behind him. The extraction specialist's spry reflexes belied his age as he dodged another dagger with an acrobatic spin. He whipped his serrated saw at Sidian mid-twirl, who dodged it with an economical sidestep.

Sidian and his opponent went motionless, their eyes locking across the tray of gleaming torture tools. The extraction specialist rushed the tray, spilling a dozen silver instruments as he snatched a weapon. Sidian calmly grasped the jutting hilt over his shoulder and withdrew a pale longsword of glittering dragon bone. The same sword he'd skewered Raine with the night they first met.

The extraction specialist brandished a short, needlepoint knife with a gleeful expression. A wide, maniacal grin that showed top and bottom teeth. He wore the look of a man who had already won. An infinitesimal tightening around Sidian's eyes relayed his confusion.

"You're trying to save them," the extractor crooned, his voice high and uneven.

The white clad hunter turned, as if dismissing Sidian. His lenses flashed like mirrors against the lanterns as his stare settled on Raine's father. Stark terror liquefied Raine's viscera. No sooner than he comprehended the extraction specialist's intent, a blur of white hurtled toward his father.

Sidian shot after him like a streak of living shadow, shoving the instrument tray out of his path without slowing. The wheeled tray tumbled over stone, crashing riotously against the door.

A vicious scalpel, razor thin and surgically sharp, plunged through his father's concave abdomen.

Raine screamed, piercing and hoarse, as the scalpel slid upward, sluicing deeply into his father's vital organs. Sidian seized the man's wrist and ripped it away from his father. The needlepoint blade came out blood red.

The scalpel wasn't inside his father for the duration of a whole heartbeat. But that fraction of a second was all the extraction specialist had needed to ensure a violent, agonized death.

Raine didn't look away from his father, whose face was screwed in pain, his features a stark pallor beneath prison grime.

Not as Sidian savaged the man in white, until he became the man in blood red. Not as Sidian embedded the scalpel, wet with the blood of his father's organs, into the man's right eye to finish him. Not as a third explosion rocked the room like an earthquake, shaking more dust onto his head than if he'd powdered his hair on purpose. Not as Sidian unlatched the leather straps binding him with quick, too clever fingers.

Raine could hardly stand. The room was shaking so terribly from all the explosions. He fell once, twice. The third time, he looked up and saw Sidian standing still and grave and without a single tremor. His mate wordlessly offered a hand to assist him.

And Raine realized.

There weren't any more explosions. The shaking was all him.

There wasn't time for this. He grasped Sidian's outstretched hand and clung as Sidian pulled him to his feet. His legs held, and Raine's gaze flung to his father. Arastus Chambrin's features were drawn tight enough to split open. Excruciating pain coated his eyes like glass.

Raine flew across the chamber, stepping over corpses without a thought. His father was all that mattered.

Reaching his father's side, he clawed at the leather belts cinching him to the torture slab. He dimly registered Sidian's assistance. They unbuckled the remaining stays together and Raine ungagged his father.

Arastus Chambrin slid to the floor, resting his back against the vertical table. Raine dropped to his knees and gently clasped his father's hand. It was chilled, as if his father had been shoveling snow for hours instead of sitting trapped in a musty, subtropical dungeon.

"Can you walk? If you can't, I'll carry you," Raine told him. "It's going to be okay. We just need to get you to a doctor—"

"Son." Raine snapped his jaw shut at his father's tone. "I'm going to be dead in a matter of minutes." His voice was thin but strong. Too strong for final words.

"Father, no. I can get you out of here. I can—"

"Listen to me." The harsh command startled Raine like a sudden clap of thunder. His father swallowed and gasped. "Please," he said, more gently. "If you are to live, you must hear me."

The tough, callused hand of a lifelong warrior cupped his son's face. Raine laid his palm over his father's hand, holding it there as he nodded. Tears poured from his quicksilver eyes in swift, unending rivulets but he was silent.

"The Nine have a secret. I do not know it. But I know they are desperately afraid of dragons. I suspect their secret is tied to their fear."

Raine's father paused, breath labored. He removed his palm from Raine's cheek to clutch his bleeding abdomen.

"Father, please," Raine choked. "There may still be hope for you."

"You have been the light of my life." His father's other hand slipped from Raine's grip. Reaching up, he combed his fingers through his son's hair as he had done a hundred thousand times. "I could not love you more than if you were my own flesh and blood. I'm so fucking proud of you."

"Stop." Raine's voice cracked.

Sidian knelt behind Raine. A hand squeezed his shoulder.

"You're ... a Wade boy," his father said, his words growing more effortful. His face was sickly white. The hand on Raine's shoulder clenched in shock at his father's statement.

"I am Sidian Wade," he said solemnly.

Raine's father smiled weakly over his shoulder. "Your brother is ... a good man." He looked at Raine. "Go to the fifth spine. Do not be followed. I'm so sorry ... I always meant to take you."

His father's eyes closed. His entire body sagged, waxen and still. A scarlet bead pooled at the corner of his mouth. Raine's tears flowed like rivers as he smoothed his father's brow, imitating the affectionate gesture his father had reserved for him so many times.

A disturbance sounded beyond the door, muffled shouts and a loud bang.

"We need to leave." Sidian tugged his shoulder. Raine didn't move. His body might as well have been encased in concrete. He'd come to save his father. How could he leave him in this dark, hateful place?

"Raine." The urgency in Sidian's voice batted him like raven's wings. "Your father is gone. His spirit rests with the Divine Father. We will soon join him if we don't go *now*."

Raine was frozen. He couldn't move. Couldn't talk. Couldn't think. His heart had shattered, breaking everything else with it. Raine wasn't a person or a dragon or anything anymore.

He was just an aching mass of meat and bone and nothingness. The guild could carve out his skeleton and make all the fancy weapons they wanted. Raine didn't care. He wouldn't even feel it.

Powerful arms swept him from behind. Sidian cradled Raine to his chest and began to run. A faint, faraway part of Raine understood he was being carried. But it was the vaguest impression of reality possible. As if it was happening to someone else. He stared unseeing as Sidian ran through a maze of dark passages.

A fetid stench of rancid decay permeated Raine's insensate daze. He gagged on the smell as Sidian carried him into a cloud of swarming flies. Sidian dropped Raine to his feet without ceremony. Then, using both hands, he spun the valve of a heavy, iron access door. It was circular and mounted several feet off the floor.

Death blossomed ripely in Raine's mouth as the hatch swerved open, revealing a cylindrical tunnel. He choked back another gag, his mouth watering with nausea.

"What the fuck is that?"

"A trash chute." Sidian slapped the flies away impatiently, then gestured for Raine to climb inside.

"Sidian, I have very specific rules regarding garbage and my person. Specifically, that *my person is not to be submerged in garbage.*"

"Burning day is tomorrow, so the trash pit is at its most disgusting right now. Meaning it is being avoided by everyone. Eddic doesn't like the smell or the bugs, so the chute empties outside the prison walls."

"We're already underground. Where the fuck does this thing go?"

Sidian growled his frustration. "The prison was built on high ground. The chute carries the garbage beneath the prison and dumps it at the backside of the hill."

The distant clamor of chaos and shouts sounded in the direction they came from. Sidian became a wildly gesticulating shape in the buzzing corridor. "They are going to reach us soon. If we jump now, before we're seen, they won't know where we are. They'll spend hours searching the prison before they figure out we're gone."

Raine grit his teeth but stepped forward, feeding his frame into the massive, circular hole in the wall. The metal of the waste duct was slick with slime, and he shuddered as it coated his fingers and seeped into his tights.

Sidian climbed in behind him and shut the door to the chute, submerging them in reeking darkness.

Raine reached behind him and clamped Sidian's legs around his waist before allowing the angle of the chute to pitch them forward. The ooze coating the duct accelerated them down the noxious tunnel, its grade angled to carry garbage down and away.

Not only garbage, he realized a minute later, as bright light appeared ahead and they were ejected from the chute. Momentum carried them on invisible wings, arcing them high before they fell, sinking into a week's worth of prison refuse.

Raine scrambled upright.

Gazing down, he saw that he'd been deposited in a mound of beetles and maggots. The insects writhed and devoured a bloated, rotting corpse.

He stared dumbly at the wriggling mass where eyes should be. A fat centipede curled from the corpse's ruined mouth like a hellish tongue.

Raine abruptly turned and projectile vomited into Sidian's chest.

CHAPTER THIRTY

R aine was a wraith that breathed and moved. He trailed after Sidian ghost-like as they hiked the woods carpeting the rolling foothills of the Dragon Fangs. He waded through the forest as though deep underwater. When Sidian tried talking to him about what his father had said, his words were muffled and disjointed to Raine's grief-logged ears.

For days, nothing penetrated his fugue, wherein he relived each precious moment he had shared with his father, reverently polishing each memory like Jaska tending to his jewels. Below the grim line of reality, Raine was content with his recollections. He was afraid to resurface, refused to return to the place where new memories with his father could never be made.

The woodlands glutted with deciduous trees, the forest floor littered with a fiery carpet of fallen leaves. Raine was insensate to the change in their surroundings until a week after their escape.

"Your hair has been falling out in clumps. There's an enormous bald spot on the back of your head."

Sidian's words fell like stones, splashing slow and deep through the lake of Raine's grief. As they settled around him, their garbled meaning became clear.

He flashed back to awareness with a strangled gasp and clutched at his precious mane. "No." His fingers felt frantically around his scalp, but he could not detect where hair was missing. "Where? Where?"

He whirled and found Sidian as still as a statue, gaping. His black hair was matted with filth, plastered flat to his head. Purple crescents lined the delicate skin under his eyes like bruises. His typically smooth-shaven face was shadowed with stubble.

"Raine," he said softly, raising a hand in a soothing motion, as if Raine was a skittish colt eager to bolt.

"Where am I bald?" Raine glared, panic tripping his pulse as he continued feeling gingerly around his crown.

"You're not bald." Sidian took a cautious step forward. "But you've been unresponsive for days. I was beginning to think your mind was damaged. Nothing I said penetrated your fog."

Relief coursed through him, as cool and swift as the wind whispering through the fire-bright sweetgums and silver maples. He was so glad not to be bald, he forgot to be angry at Sidian for his cruel lie.

Lowering his hands from his head, he frowned. The last thing he remembered was falling into a sea of insect larvae. And the corpse. He shuddered, rubbing his hands against his cloak to wipe away phantom maggots and ick.

His cloak? Sure enough, Raine sported a woolen cloak, dyed a rich burgundy and lined with ermine. Sidian sported a deep blue coat with a stitched diamond pattern.

He answered Raine's unasked question. "I took advantage of the occasional country houses we passed." Sidian turned, revealing a pack strapped to his back. He faced Raine once more, dark brows angled down. "You really don't remember any of this?"

Two russet squirrels chased each other through the underbrush, stirring the leaves between Raine and Sidian. They scampered up a black walnut tree and turned, chittering angrily at Raine. Warning him away from their territory. He smiled faintly, then looked back at Sidian.

"I'm sorry," he said, and meant it. "I didn't mean to disappear into myself like that. I'm back now, I promise."

Sidian closed the gap between them, lining their stares. "I will accept your apology on the condition that you remain lucid," he said seriously.

An immediate consequence of Raine's regained cognizance became apparent as the wind shifted. His nostrils were assaulted with the sour, putrid stench of their sludge-sodden clothing and unwashed bodies. "We smell vile," he moaned. "I have to bathe. Now."

His mate rolled his eyes heavenward. "I took some bathing supplies from a cottage yesterday, but the creek is cold—"

"I don't care," Raine said flatly.

Sidian wanted to argue. Raine could see it in the tight lines bracketing his eyes and mouth, but the man veered left, spearing off from the game trail they'd been following. Raine followed him through a dense thicket of underbrush. Branches snapped like candy sticks beneath his boots.

He spied Sidian's dark form below, where the ground gently sloped to a fast-moving creek. Sidian sat cross-legged on the dry, loamy bank, tucked out of reach of the passing stream.

"You're going to freeze your balls off," he warned as Raine reached the creek. Sidian made no move to disrobe or touch the water.

Raine had no such reservations. He shed his boots, cloak and filth-crusted clothing with alacrity. The creek was almost a river. Water, fresh from snowy mountain peaks, rose to his belly button as he waded to its icy center.

As a creature who reveled in boiling water, he was bitterly cold. But he would have scrubbed himself with snow and exfoliated against a glacier to remove the fetid slime from his body.

Raine scrubbed himself thoroughly while Sidian brooded at the creek's edge. He kept finding dried maggots and other unmentionables in his hair and shuddered. *Rinse, repeat. Rinse, repeat.* Gelid water numbed his limbs, making his task more difficult.

"Here," Sidian called. Raine looked up in time to catch a crudely formed cake of lye soap.

He thanked Sidian effusively before lathering his body and hair. After a brisk final rinse, he waded to the bank. "If you want to wash, I'll clean our clothes," he offered.

Water sluiced down his bare chest and legs as he exited the creek, and Raine resisted the shy urge to cup himself. His mate had seen every naked inch of him, in multiple states of arousal at that. The horse was well out of the barn, as the saying went.

To his surprise, Sidian stood and stripped in quick, efficient movements. He had expected Sidian to demur his offer.

Raine faltered as Sidian shoved his Guardian hose down his thighs—immediately reminded that, while his mate had gotten regular eyefuls of his unclad body, he had not seen Sidian in any state of undress.

His face flamed as he took the crusted bundle Sidian handed him. The breath squeezed from his lungs as he glimpsed a broad, strong back curving into perfectly round, muscled buttocks.

By the sheer mercy of the Divine, Raine managed to wrench his eyes from the display. It took multiple clumsy scrapes of his hand to pluck his own discarded clothes off the ground. Moving several paces downstream, he concentrated on washing their clothes. He did *not* ogle the fantastic display of rippling muscle and manhood that beckoned like a feast.

It made no difference. Raine's cock was fully engorged and cloud-gazing within minutes, despite fixing his stare determinedly on the laundry. If picking dried vomit chunks off his mate's Guardian hose couldn't diminish his ardor, nothing would. He dunked the sodden black garment into the stream and grimly accepted it was just another humiliating day of being naked and aroused around Sidian.

Raine wrung out their clothes and searched for sunny branches to hang them dry. He climbed the gentle slope leading back to the trail and discovered a pocket of warm, buttery light as the ground leveled. A leaning maple's lower branches propped their wet garments like splayed fingers. Laying on his back near the tree, he closed his eyes and soaked golden sun rays through his damp, chilled skin.

A shadow fell over his face. Raine opened his eyes to find Sidian looming overhead.

Raven black hair clung wetly over his brow and eyes. Water droplets shone like crystals on his tanned skin. One bead of water slipped down Sidian's abdomen, which was so deliciously taut with muscle, Raine could have used it as a washboard when he'd cleaned their clothes earlier. As Raine's gaze mapped the droplet's progress, his cock twitched like a curious puppy.

"Dragon puberty's a real bitch," Sidian observed wryly. "You're hogging the sunlight."

Raine shuffled over, making room for Sidian to stretch beside him. They listened to the sounds of the forest in silence, shoulders touching. The creek babbled rhythmically as squirrels scampered about, burying treasured nuts for winter fare.

Raine's eyes closed against the direct brightness of the sky. "I really am sorry I've been so ... absent. I shouldn't have made you handle everything yourself, especially not for as long as I did."

"I wasn't under the impression it was voluntary," Sidian murmured.

Raine hesitated. There was such a difference between exposing skin and exposing self. One was much harder than the other.

"I don't think that it was," he whispered. "Even now, it feels like there's this force building inside of me, trapped between my heart and throat."

It was powerful and frightening and indescribable. Could a heart physically rupture from grief? If the answer was yes, Raine knew he was dying.

Sidian nudged his shoulder. "Tell me about him. Your father."

It was the easiest, most natural thing in the world. Raine talked. Sidian listened. Their hair and clothes dried completely and still Sidian listened.

Sharing his most cherished memories with his mate was more cathartic than any amount of time hiding in his own head. Sidian was no stranger to grief. Raine soon realized Sidian had demanded he speak of his father because he understood the healing power it would bring.

Their conversation shifted as Sidian shared the details of his own struggle with loss. Raine pictured a fawn-eyed boy, too serious for his years, throwing himself into the life his brother had left behind, struggling to live and breathe for them both.

"Your father," Sidian said slowly, after they had lapsed into silence. "He made a comment about my brother before he passed." His tone was careful but questioning.

"I heard," Raine said, recalling his father's final words with a pang. "He must not have known of your brother's passing." And now, he never would.

"Arastus Chambrin retired from the Guardians of Vale years before my brother joined. I don't know how they would have become acquainted."

"My dad used to take apprentices. Guild prospects who showed special promise. He stopped when I was little, so I didn't meet most of them." Two orange, star-shaped leaves drifted downward, joining the plush mound surrounding them. "I never understood why he quit apprenticing. By all accounts, he loved it. Now I realize it was because of me. He distanced himself from the Guardians to keep the Nine from discovering what I was."

Raine's chest spasmed painfully as he recalled his father's adamant refusal for him to join the guild. The ferocity of their arguments. All because of secrets. Secrets and love.

"My brother ... The last time I saw him, he almost sounded like your father. He was mistrustful of the Nine and seemed sympathetic to the dragons they hunted."

Ice slid down Raine's spine. If Sidian decided his brother's death was ultimately caused by Raine's father, for planting ideas in his head, it would be another wedge driven between them. The first wedge, Raine's species, had already ensured Sidian would never mate with him. After what had happened to his brother, Sidian could never love a dragon. Not like that.

But they might yet be friends. Great friends. The true, lifelong kind. That was, if Raine's father wasn't somehow connected to Sidian's brother's demise.

"He must have been one of your father's apprentices," Sidian continued, spreading tingles of alarm down Raine's neck and stomach.

"I've only met a few of them," Raine hedged, inwardly cursing. He didn't want to lose Sidian's esteem for any reason. Not for being a dragon. Not for being his mate. And definitely not for something his father may-or-may-not have said to Sidian's brother once upon a time. He didn't think he could bear it. He stared into the sun's glare, his pulse pounding like a war drum as he asked, "What was your brother's name?"

"Nyx. Nyx Wade."

Raine leapt off the ground, as if the earth spat him out like a bad taste. He blinked down at Sidian, his train of thought unraveling at the sheer virility and size of his mate. The man looked like a fallen god, too perfect to be real. Raine's excitable pulse directed his blood south.

Hurriedly, he spun to conceal his reaction, moving to pluck their nearby clothes from the branches. He tossed Sidian's black hose somewhere near the man's chest where he still laid upon the ground. Raine couldn't aim too carefully without revealing his body's response, and now truly wasn't the time.

"Ten years ago," Raine murmured, his mind spinning like a top as he stuffed one leg into his slightly damp tights, then the other. "Sidian, your brother was the last apprentice my father took."

Raine tugged his socks and boots on before facing his mate. Sidian had dressed as well and stood clad like a shadow, features pinched in confusion and a little anger.

"I find your reaction to a man who's been deceased for a decade a little too theatrical," he said, his voice punishing in its severity.

Raine winced and rushed on. "Nyx was my babysitter. He became like family." Sidian's stare sharpened. Raine raked his hands through his hair, still spiraling at the intricacies of fate. "I didn't know his family name, so I didn't connect him with you. And you haven't told me his name until just now."

They possessed a strong family resemblance that had him kicking himself. *How did I miss it?* Raine's veins flooded with warm, honeyed joy. He beamed at Sidian, more radiant than the sun.

"The last time I saw Nyx was near the end of this summer."

Sidian's expression hardened to granite. "I don't find you amusing." His smoky tone hinted at a brutal fire.

Raine flapped his arms, imagining he looked like a crazed turkey. He *felt* like a crazed turkey. "*Listen to me.* Your brother is alive, Sidian. My lying, asshole father told me Nyx is on some long-term, super-secret guild mission and I wasn't allowed to tell anybody if I saw him."

Sidian remained implacably shuttered. Raine groaned aloud in frustration.

"They both made it sound so deadly serious, I never told a soul. Nyx visits Chambrin once a year or so, but he keeps his hood up and doesn't talk to anyone except me and my father. I just saw him. Weeks ago. I would not lie to you about this," he implored.

Sidian was unmoved, white-lipped with fury by the end of Raine's clumsy explanation. He looked away, towards the river. "No offense to you, but I'll believe it when I see it."

Raine saw it then. The frailty of Sidian's hope. How crippling it would be for him to lose his brother twice, should Raine be wrong.

"You're going to see it sooner than you think. The last thing my father said was go to the fifth spine."

Sidian looked back at him. "I heard, but I don't know what that is."

"My father used to make up bedtime stories about the Dragon Fangs for me." Raine's throat knotted with painful memories. He swallowed against it, determined to explain. To make Sidian understand. "We came up with our own names for different sections of the mountain range. A stretch near Pashun always looked like the back of a dragon in flight so we numbered the peaks as spines on its back. We're already enroute. If we keep moving north, we should reach the fifth spine within the next moon cycle."

Sidian absorbed this, then snorted. "So, what, you think I'll find my brother there?"

Raine smiled softly. "Once, when Nyx had to leave, I couldn't stop crying. I missed him and didn't want him to go." His gaze turned inward as he recalled that particular evening. Raine had been young, maybe eleven summers. "Nyx pointed at Moontop. He said if I was ever lonely or missed him, to look right at the peak of that mountain. My father said to go to the fifth spine. Sidian, the fifth spine is our name for Moontop."

TO BE CONTINUED

Thank you so much for giving a new author a chance! I'm an avid reader, and I know exactly how difficult the decision can be, to pick up a book from somebody unknown. I sincerely hope that your decision paid off and this read was enjoyable!

Raine Chambrin's journey will continue in *Snared*, the second and final book of the duology, *When Nightmares Reign*.

Keep reading for a brief excerpt of *Snared*.

EXCERPT OF SNARED

CHAPTER ONE

From his perch on a half-rotted log, Raine leaned forward and fetched another spiral into the dirt. The ground was moist yet firm and yielded nice, clean lines to the stick in his hand. A shadow fell over him, and he paused. Tilting his head slowly upward, Raine expected to see a swath of steel-gray clouds.

It felt as though they were being chased by a perpetual storm—a side effect of the substantial weather system brewing along Valdenia's western flank. It was a foreboding sight that spurred him and Sidian each morning. Eventually, it would catch up with them, but each day they evaded the pending downpour was a win.

The sight that met him wasn't a sea of ominous clouds, however. It was Sidian. His bronze cheeks were flushed a ruddy hue from the chill. In one fist, he clutched two rabbits by their hindquarters. The creatures were limp, dead.

Raine's stomach woke at the sight. It stretched and yawned a low, painful growl.

"Snails in sun hats, huh?" Sidian's head cocked as he surveyed Raine's most recent wallpaper design. He snorted. "You should have put them in scarves and winter caps."

Raine flushed, resisting the urge to scrape out his drawing. He hadn't told Sidian what they were, these images he carved whenever they stopped to make camp for the evening.

How could he? It was too embarrassing. While his mate was out hunting their meals, for their very *survival*, he was dithering on a stump with a stick, creating fanciful patterns on the ground that he hoped would one day decorate sitting rooms and bedchambers.

Oh, Raine did more than that. He helped build their shelters and fires. And he was superior at cooking since the flames couldn't singe his fingers.

But still. He wasn't providing for his mate, and it *galled*.

He'd tried. Many times over the last fortnight. As it turned out, he was a lousy hunter. His mind wandered without permission, spinning mushrooms and winterberries into whimsical wallpaper patterns. Meanwhile, their supper would wander right by without him realizing.

Swallowing his pride was easier when it meant Raine could also swallow the hot, scorched meat of Sidian's hunts.

"Here. Let me." Raine took the limp carcasses from Sidian and began to skin them near the fire.

Sidian settled on the log Raine abandoned, his boots careful not to scuff Raine's snails. The fire crackled and whipped against a bitter wind as Raine worked. Blood and viscera painted his hands. It felt deliciously warm, his fingers half-numb.

The days grew ever colder with the earth's unfailing tilt from the sun. Their northward trek only compounded the season's change; so much so, Raine felt as if they'd been slingshotted from one extreme into the other.

Weeks ago, they had been in the balmy subtropics, scrambling through palmettos and frondy foliage to put as much distance between themselves and Obanth as possible.

Then, green had yielded to amber and gold. Palmettos, to deciduous birch and maples. Darting lizards and whizzy hummingbirds all disappeared. Now, they were firmly in continental territory, camping in a coniferous section of the Fangwilds, where autumn's breath held a promising bite of winter to come.

Another icy gust slurped Raine's body heat like the greedy mouths of frost giants. He shivered. Skewering the rabbits with a stripped branch, he held it over the flames. *What good is a mountain range if it can't be bothered to block the fucking wind?*

"We have to get more supplies before we go any further." Sidian's husky voice was stilted, as if he suppressed chattering teeth.

Raine frowned against the twilight, wishing for the hundredth time that his mate would let them swap coats. Sidian had pilfered their outer layers, along with other basic supplies, while Raine had been insensate from losing his father. Submerged in a grief-logged lake, he'd been too incognizant to realize Sidian gave him the best of everything.

While Raine sported a red cloak, lined with winter ermine, Sidian wore a medium-weight jacket that wouldn't keep anyone warm once darkness fell. Not in this climate. Every time Raine tried swapping coats, Sidian refused. He stubbornly insisted Raine required a hood to conceal his identity should they pass humans.

There were no humans in these woods. They were in true wilderness, a place where rocky earth rejected agriculture. A place where white-capped mountains birthed clear, rushing rivers. But this close to their source, those rivers were mere creeks and streams. They hadn't glimpsed so much as a hunting cabin or hermitage in days.

"How are we g-going to get supplies, exactly?" Raine wasn't as adept at controlling his shivers.

Another heat-slurping gust swept their campsite. Wood clattered and fell, leaving a gap in the slanted wall behind Sidian, where their makeshift shelter stood.

Sidian's frame shuddered. He dug his fingers under his arms, bracing himself against the chill. "We're coming up to Drakkus Valley. Several villages sit near the Fangwilds."

Villages meant humans. And Guardians.

Raine rotated the skewer to cook the backsides of the rabbits. The smoky scent of seared meat wafted enticingly. Almost as enticing as the heat licking his fingers.

"Are you s-sure that's wise?" Raine asked carefully.

"We're well beyond Oxlip," Sidian said, correctly interpreting the reason for Raine's reluctance. "This area is significantly less populated. We'll go someplace quiet to get what we need."

Raine chewed his bottom lip, thinking there *wasn't* any quiet place near Drakkus Valley. Not right now. Winter might be hovering like an eager specter, but it was still peak harvest.

The Drakkus Valley was the tip of a massive swath of fertile land that stretched all the way to Allium. The Pash-Ox Trading Route would be glutted with merchants until the last of this season's grains and hardy vegetables were distributed.

Raine pressed along the rabbits with his forefinger and thumb to test their doneness. Satisfied by the meat's consistency, he snapped the fire-blackened branch in half and passed a skewered rabbit to Sidian. His mate ate delicately, tearing at the outermost meat to release the steam before biting down. Raine scarfed his portion as only a dragon could. The heat didn't blister his mouth, and he fought a moan as he chewed a bulging mouthful.

All too soon, he was down to gristle and bone. He tossed his skewer into the fire and watched Sidian pick apart his own rabbit.

As always, a crushing wave of tenderness enveloped Raine as he surveyed his mate. The most precious being in all the world. It was strange—and frightening—to feel his heart beating inside his chest and know that it was all an illusion. That his heart wholly and completely resided in this man. And that he would never get it back.

Sidian's velvet eyes met his, and Raine's stomach swooped like a flock of starlings.

"I don't know," Raine said softly. "We've m-made it this far without issue only because we've stuck to the Fangwilds. Going into town, any town, f-feels risky."

"All this hunting and foraging slows us down." Sidian paused to take another bite. "Once we have proper supplies and rations, we'll cover ground more quickly. We can reach Moontop inside a week."

Moontop. Raine's blood buzzed at the thought. Sidian still didn't believe Nyx was there. It was one of those things they didn't discuss. Along with Arastus Chambrin's demise, the location of the breeding dragons, and Sidian's defection from the guild.

Those topics weren't off-limits, per se. But they were tricky, like navigating a field of gopher holes in the dark.

Could they really reach Moontop so soon? Raine knew their progress had been hindered by a lack of food, but he hadn't realized just how much. Sidian's idea of grabbing supplies grew more attractive as he considered it.

He couldn't fucking *wait* to see the look on Sidian's face when he was reunited with his long-presumed dead brother. Sidian wore his grief like a mantle. It made him cold and closed off. Wary and distrustful and wounded. Raine longed to rip it off him, to see what Sidian might be like without its weight.

But going into town …

Raine was eager to get to Moontop. More so than Sidian, considering he was the only one who believed in what—or, rather, *who* awaited them. But Sidian had aided Raine's escape from the guild and was currently on the run with him. Which meant any encounter with Guardians would not only endanger Raine's life … but Sidian's, as well.

Unacceptable. "We can't. Sidian, the guild will be after you, too. If anything happens to you—"

He broke off as another flush swept his face. Then immediately scolded himself. He was allowed to worry. His concern for Sidian didn't have to mean anything *salacious*. They were friends. It was perfectly normal for him to want to keep Sidian safe.

But he knew it wasn't just friendship that compelled him.

Flustered, he turned and busied himself with smothering the fire. Darkness would be upon them soon, and given their criminal status, they only ever kept a fire long enough to cook.

Thanks to a combination of them sticking to the deeper parts of the Fangwilds and a healthy dose of luck, their smoke had yet to draw any unwanted visitors. But as much as Raine yearned to keep the fire going—last night's cold had damn near frozen his marrow—it was better not to tempt fate.

"I've received considerable training with both stealth and swords," Sidian murmured at his back. There was a wryness to his tone, a gentle amusement. His mate still didn't know how keenly Raine felt for him. That the thought of Sidian in danger made Raine into an animal.

Raine was desperate to keep it that way. The very last thing he wanted was to watch their friendship disintegrate like sun-brittled sand because he couldn't be a friend—and *only* a friend—to the man who housed his heart and shared his soul.

"You are shadow and death," Raine drawled, attempting to ease the intensity of his aborted declaration from earlier. "A m-mighty captain, indeed. But still just a man, and Guardian swords are rather sharp."

Raine's eyes darted to the hilt jutting behind Sidian's shoulder. The Guardians of Vale all possessed glimmering white blades hewn from dragon bone. A macabre necessity, since the only thing that could pierce dragon skin was their bone. And the Guardians of Vale—for all their varying good deeds—were secretly dragon hunters at their core.

And what pierced dragon flesh with the ease of traditional steel also cut through humans like a hot knife through butter. If Raine accidentally touched the wrong side of Sidian's longsword, he'd nick a thumb. But Sidian would lose his.

It was one of the reasons the guild was so well-trained. They had to be, in order to wield their blades effectively while matching dragon-fast reflexes.

"I could take you, couldn't I?" Sidian purred, a gleam in his dark eyes. His lips curled in a manner Raine knew was meant to taunt him. And it did, but not in the way his mate imagined.

Oh, yes. Sidian could take him. *Right here, right now, please.*

Raine grit his teeth against a surge of lust. For the thousand-millionth time, he was grateful for the length and thickness of his coat. He burned for Sidian constantly. A fierce need that never relented.

Somehow, miracle of miracles, he'd grown used to it; being enflamed for his mate. And no matter how great Raine's ardor was, his cock had its limits. His erection would eventually abate, like a kicked puppy that finally understood his master did not want to play.

"I'm man enough to admit when my sword skills are inferior," Raine said primly. And by the Divine, did that sound filthy. He was glad for the cold. His red ears probably just seemed wind-bitten. "But if your ex-comrades are anywhere n-near as good as you" —and they were, regrettably— "then your ability to defeat me won't guarantee your victory against other Guardians."

"How little you think of me." Sidian stood, his rabbit picked clean to the bone. His shoulder brushed against Raine's as he tossed his skewer into the smoldering embers. "I can handle a sword better than any unit we might encounter."

Raine's mind plunged into the gutter. That husky voice, so close to his ear, practically whispering about his sword prowess ... *Fuck.*

He stood there like a tongue-tied simpleton, miming a fish out of water and wishing Sidian would stop looking quite so closely at his countenance, which surely revealed every depraved fantasy he'd ever had about his mate.

A drop of ice struck his nose. Then another. In seconds, a merciless deluge drenched the world. Thousands of heavy raindrops pummeled him. The fire was sodden ash, the ground already gone to mud.

Sidian's face twisted in an echo of Raine's misery as he reached for his hand and tugged. Raine savored the contact as they ran into their shelter. A scruffy lean-to of branches and brush, it was *not* watertight. Frigid drips worked their way through the slanted roof and splashed on his head every few seconds.

"F-Fucking hell," he moaned, yanking his hood overhead.

Dried leaves and pine needles insulated them from the freezing ground, and the branches held back the wind. But their shelter was by no means intended to withstand a torrential downfall.

Raine glanced sideways at Sidian and bit back another curse. His cloak insulated him from the steady trickle above, but Sidian wasn't as fortunate. His black hair was plastered to his head, and water seeped through the thick fabric of his coat.

"No," Sidian said, reaching a hand to stop Raine as he fumbled for the buttons of his cloak.

"You're getting soaked," Raine protested. "Water doesn't get through my c-coat. We can use it as a blanket."

Sidian shook his head. "You'll get too cold if you remove it. My coat's made of wool. It'll be fine."

But for how long? The air only *felt* freezing. As the rain was proving, it wasn't actually cold enough for snow.

Yet.

Raine put his back to one of the tree trunks bracing their shelter and closed his eyes. Defeat welled inside him as he considered their situation.

His mate was *cold*. His mate was cold and wet and exhausted from working so hard to provide.

Vicious claws raked inside Raine's chest, brutal and punishing. He had to do better. His mate deserved more than this. Squatting in the rain, drenched and shivering without enough food. *I will not fail him.*

"Sidian, please take my coat. I don't need it."

Raine reached for the top button of his cloak. Sidian stopped him again. His fingers dug forcefully into Raine's hand. A warning.

"Leave it."

There was a darkness to his mate's command, a note of finality. Raine gnashed his teeth but didn't argue. Truth be told, he was powerless when it came to Sidian. The man could ask him for anything, *anything*, and Raine would give it to him.

If only Sidian would request something selfish for a change. *Give me your rabbit skewer. Switch me coats. Lay in the mud so I may step on your back as I cross this puddle.*

Any one of those would be preferable to Sidian demanding they share food equally. That Raine keep his coat. That whatever they suffered, they suffered together.

It was untenable. *Let me suffer*, he wanted to scream. *Let me bear every burden. Let me* love *you.*

Sidian scooched closer, until their bodies pressed together. Raine's pulse leapt, as it always did when they had to share warmth. But as he glimpsed the blue tinge of Sidian's lips and the bleached white of his damp skin, his burgeoning arousal sank like a stone.

Raine's dragon blood meant he ran hotter than a human. It was a heat Sidian seemed to perpetually crave. His subtropical roots withered in the frost, though he always tried to conceal how affected he was. Probably so that Raine wouldn't rip his cloak off, scattering every button in a great rush to swaddle him with it.

Raine had been proud—so foolishly proud—to be able to provide warmth for his mate. To *be* that warmth, even. He could see now that it wasn't enough. Their conditions were worsening along with the weather.

Sidian was right. Their current gear was too meager to sustain them this far north. The threat of the guild was immaterial to his mate freezing to death.

"We'll f-find better gear tomorrow," Raine said, uncertain of who he was trying to reassure more. "In one of the smaller villages, like you m-mentioned."

Sidian grunted his assent, likely forgoing speech because his teeth really would chatter.

Any supplies scavenging scheme was risky. But it was that, or die out here, exposed to the elements. Something his mate had already realized.

The storm howled and battered their shelter. They huddled together more snugly, their heads and limbs overlapping like littermates seeking warmth and comfort. Raine felt every shudder and breath of his mate, and concentrated on covering as much of Sidian's exposed skin as he could.

That Sidian didn't try to deter him said more than anything just how chilled he was.

In the pattering darkness, they slept.

About the Author

Misu Loy published her first novel in April of 2023. With dozens of characters inside her head—all clamoring for the spotlight—it's safe to say, many more books are forthcoming.

Romance is the genre she lives and breathes. Readers should anticipate lots of slow burn stories with enemies-to-lovers dynamics. Those are Misu's favorite kinds of stories—and thus, her passion.

When Misu isn't working her day job or writing love stories, she's usually walking her doggos, reading fiction, or pestering her spouse and family to go to the park or play Scrabble with her.

Visit www.MisuLoy.com to connect with Misu or see what she's up to.